FALLING IN

LUCINDA BRANT BOOKS

— Falling Series —
FALLING IN
FALLING UP
FALLING OUT

— Roxton Foundation Series —
NOBLE SATYR
HIS DUCHESS
HER DUKE
THEIR GRACES

— Roxton Family Saga —
NOBLE SATYR
MIDNIGHT MARRIAGE
AUTUMN DUCHESS
DAIR DEVIL
PROUD MARY
SATYR'S SON
ETERNALLY YOURS
FOREVER REMAIN

— Alec Halsey Mysteries —
DEADLY ENGAGEMENT
DEADLY AFFAIR
DEADLY PERIL
DEADLY KIN
DEADLY DESIRE

— Salt Hendon Books —
SALT BRIDE
SALT REDUX

'Quizzing glass and quill, into my sedan chair and away —— the 1700s rock!'

A *New York Times*, *USA Today*, *Amazon*, and *Audible* bestselling author of award-winning Georgian historical romances and mysteries, Lucinda's books are renowned for their wit, heart-felt drama and a happily ever-after. She has degrees in history and political science from the Australian National University and a postgraduate degree in education from Bond University, where she was awarded the Frank Surman Medal. *Noble Satyr*, Lucinda's first novel, was awarded the $10,000 *Random House/Woman's Day* Romantic Fiction Prize, and she has twice been a finalist for the Romance Writers' of Australia Romantic Book of the Year. Her novels have garnered multiple awards and become worldwide genre bestsellers. Lucinda lives a stone's throw from the beach, in a writing hut with wall-to-wall books on all aspects of the Eighteenth Century, collected over 40 years—Heaven. She loves to hear from readers (and she'll write back!).

FALLING IN

An Enchanting Georgian Fairytale Romance...
of sorts...Regarding a Dashing Adventurer
and a Wallflower with a Penchant for Pineapples

Lucinda Brant

A Sprigleaf Book
Published by Sprigleaf Pty. Ltd.

This is a work of fiction; names, characters, places, and incidents
are the product of the author's imagination or are used fictitiously.
Resemblance to persons, businesses, companies, events,
or locales, past or present, is entirely coincidental.

*Falling IN: An Enchanting Georgian Fairytale Romance...of sorts...
Regarding a Dashing Adventurer and a Wallflower with a Penchant for Pineapples.*

A YA retelling of *Dair Devil: A Georgian Historical Romance,*
available as Book 3 in the Roxton Family Saga.
*Back cover reviews are for the *Dair Devil* edition of this book.

Typeset in EB Garamond.

ISBN 978-1-922985-30-9

10 9 8 7 6 5 4 3 2 1
Perfect Bound Paperback Edition. (i) I.

for my darling daughter

Cinda Ann

ONE

CAVENDISH SQUARE, LONDON
THE FIRST WEEK OF MAY

ALISDAIR 'DAIR' FITZSTUART pulled the white linen shirt up over his shoulders, scrunched it into a ball and tossed it to his batman. Bill Farrier caught this crumpled article with his one hand and shoved it inside a large canvas haversack, atop His Lordship's midnight blue silk waistcoat and matching frock coat. His master's black leather jockey boots he had set beside a high stone wall, out of the way of passers-by. Pedestrians, however, were unlikely given the location and the hour.

Red Lyon Lane was at the rear of a row of elegant townhouses that fronted Cavendish Square. Tradesmen and their ilk used it. It was not an address frequented by young gentlemen, unless engaged in mischief.

The three inebriated young men taking hearty swigs from a wine bottle being passed amongst them were most decidedly up to no good. Bill Farrier knew this for fact. The phlegmatic ex-soldier also knew no good would come of their antics.

It was dusk and there was a new moon. It meant the night would be as black as soot. This was just as well. His master and two friends might have a chance of escaping into the night without being caught or recognized. He had every confidence in Major Lord Fitzstuart. Five years as His Lordship's batman had given Farrier a measure of the young man. He would follow him to the ends of the earth and fall off the edge if required. He did not have the same confidence in his master's civilian companions. They looked to have as much courage under fire between them as His Lordship had in his pinky. But as they had been the Major's boon companions since his school days at Harrow, it was not his place to pass comment unless asked. Farrier had not been asked.

He remained silent and patiently waited for His Lordship to divest himself of the remainder of his clothing: Stockings, buckskin breeches, and linen drawers. He then flicked a finger at a linkboy to step forward, as if illumination by a flaming taper would shed light on the discussion taking place, or, at the very least, provide a spark of warmth for the bare-chested Major.

DAIR WAS OBLIVIOUS to the cool spring air, toes curling in the cold earth beneath his feet as he asked his batman, "Carriage up the laneway, Mr. Farrier?"

"Yes, m'lord."

"And the beadles paid off?"

"To be deaf as a plank of wood? Yes, m'lord. We won't hear a cry for assistance from that lot."

"Good. Once Lord Grasby and I slip through the garden door, you hare off with the kit and we'll see you at the carriage in the Square. Not outside Romney's house. Position it across the street. We'll make a dash for it." In the orange glow of the flickering taper, he caught Farrier's glance of skepticism at his drunken blond school friend and said confidently, "Don't worry. I'll sling him over a shoulder if necessary."

"Very good, m'lord." Farrier said no more about it. "Breechcloth?"

"Breechcloth."

When Bill Farrier handed him a thin braided leather belt, Dair draped it low on his narrow hips, fastened the leather ties into a knot and gave it a tug to ensure it was secure. He then slid the knot to sit just below his right hip so that the two rectangular flaps of soft calf-skin sewn to the belt were positioned front and back, providing the only modesty covering between his legs. Looking up, he saw his blond school friend Grasby frowning at him in puzzlement.

"Farrier has one for you, too."

Lord Grasby stared at his best friend, naked but for a strip of cloth between his muscular thighs, and his self-confidence plummeted into his stomach. He gawped.

"Is that *all* an American Indian wears?"

"In summertime—Yes."

Lord Grasby gave a snort of panic. "You're hoodwinking me!"

"No. It's this or nothing at all," Dair responded, comfortable in his own skin. "You'll feel more the warrior once the war paint is applied. Every man can hide behind war paint. Now, do get a move on, before the ladybirds flit away into the night."

Lord Grasby liked the idea of hiding behind war paint. He whipped off his drawers, snatched the belt with breechcloths attached from the ever-patient Farrier, who had been standing at his side for some little while, and threw it around his waist. Being acutely self-conscious, he secured the belt ends in a rush, and breathed a sigh of relief to have completed the task in record time. Unbeknownst to him, the two breechcloths were not front and back as he thought, but left and right, against his bare flanks.

Cedric Pleasant could not contain himself. The laughter burst from him; the look of relief on Grasby's face the final straw. Dair turned away to hide his grin, and Cedric staggered about, hunched over with uncontrollable mirth. Hands on hips, Grasby glared at them, wondering what was amiss. Finally, Cedric turned and, unable to speak because he was laughing so hard, waggled a finger in Gras-by's direction. His lordship glanced down, saw the source of his friends' mirth, and was swift to try and set matters to rights, face ablaze.

"Blast it! It's all caught up now!"

"May I be of assistance, my lord?" Farrier asked at his most bland, as his master and Mr. Pleasant continued to fall about, unable or unwilling to control their laughter.

"Yes. Yes. All right! And be quick about it!"

Grasby suffered the ministrations of the batman to adjust the sit of the breechcloths with chin in the air, and with all the dignity of a man in his dressing room and not naked in a laneway.

"If you would just check to see that the knot you tied is still secure, m'lord, then all will be well."

"Can't you do that for me, too, damn you?" Lord Grasby demanded through clenched teeth.

When the batman remained silent with his left arm raised, Grasby finally looked at him. Where the man's hand should have been, there was only air. Curiosity got the better of him, and he peered into the void of Farrier's coat sleeve. In response, Farrier thrust his arm up through his sleeve and out popped a stump. It was capped with a small, polished silver hook, the fitted silver cap secured by a leather strap buckled about his forearm.

Grasby leapt into the air.

Dair and Cedric Pleasant, who had just mastered control of their features, spluttered once more into wild laughter, and this time so hard they fell back, shaking shoulders against the high stone wall surrounding the garden of George Romney's townhouse, as if needing its support to remain upright.

"For king and country, m'lord," was Farrier's bland response to Lord Grasby's reaction to his amputated hand.

"You scared me half to death! Damn you!"

The batman bowed, and with a flourish wriggled his arm so that the stump was again hidden, with only the tip of his hook visible within his coat sleeve.

"Thank you, Mr. Farrier," Dair said, taking his bare shoulders off the stone wall. "You've had your amusement for the evening; ours is yet to begin. Time to fetch paint pot and ash."

The batman bowed and retreated, leaving behind him a heavy silence.

"Nine years in the army and you come out of it with a few knocks and dents, but poor Farrier has the rotten luck to lose a hand," Cedric Pleasant said into that silence. "Still, you both managed to keep a head on your shoulders, and that's the main thing, isn't it?"

"You could've damn-well told me!" Grasby threw at Dair. "I'll have nightmares for weeks." He gave a shudder of revulsion. "Damned unpleasant..."

Dair's face tightened. He was on the verge of reminding his friend that there were thousands of Farriers out there who had lost limbs, not to mention those who had made the ultimate sacrifice, all in the service of their king and country. And all so gentlemen such as Grasby were at liberty to go about their daily lives undisturbed and unfettered. Instead, he pushed the unspoken diatribe back down his throat and turned away to take the paint pot from his batman.

"Watch and learn, Grasby," he said, beckoning his best friend closer.

In the soft orange glow of the linkboy's lantern, Dair painted his face with white stripes cheek to cheek across his beak of a nose. Satisfied, he exchanged the paint pot for a cloth dusted in charcoal. This he rubbed into his closed eyelids, extending the blackness out across his temples into his hairline. The whites of his eyes were now stark and menacing, and his large white teeth brighter and sharper.

Dair turned this macabre grin on his friends, who opened wide their eyes and smiled their appreciation of his transformation. And when he threw back his head and howled at the moon Grasby joined in, infected with his friend's enthusiasm.

Farrier and the linkboy gathered up the gentlemen's belongings, while Dair went over the mission plan to raid the painter's studio one last time, particularly the timing of Cedric Pleasant's dramatic entrance with sword drawn. When his friends nodded their understanding of how events would unfold, he added,

"When Cedric threatens to stick me with his sword, that's our signal to get the hell out of there—"

"—looking suitably terrified," Cedric Pleasant added.

"We'll be scared stiff, dear chap," Grasby confirmed.

Dair smiled. "Cedric saves the day, and the divine Consulata Baccelli has eyes only for her newfound champion. Couldn't be easier."

The friends shook hands.

"Gentlemen, let the adventure begin!"

AT THE VERY moment the three friends masquerading as American Indians were tiptoeing into the garden of George Romney's townhouse via the back gate, Lord Grasby's wife, his sister, and his brother-in-law, were being welcomed at the front door by Mr. Romney's butler.

TWO

M R. WILLIAM WATKINS noted the late hour under the light cast by a flambeau, then slipped his engraved timepiece back into his waistcoat pocket. He paused at the base of three shallow stone steps to allow his sister Lady Grasby and Miss Talbot to enter Mr. George Romney's residence before him.

"Tell me again why you insist we view your unfinished portrait now?" he asked Lady Grasby in a voice of resignation, waving away a footman who had stepped forward to take his cloak, a sure sign the visit was to be of a short duration. "We do not have an appointment and Mr. Romney is possibly away from the house, or perhaps he is with a client...?"

"It will take but a moment, William," Lady Grasby replied, removing her gloved hands from an oversized mink muff. She shoved this at the butler. "As we had dinner two houses from this door, it would be foolish of me not to call. Mr. Romney is unlikely to refuse me. I have had nine sittings to date. Yet...there is something...something not quite right with the portrait. I am so distracted by it that I cannot remember any of the dishes at Her Highness's table. Only that there was a centerpiece, an elaborate sugar confection of sheep grazing—"

"Cows."

"Cows? Were they?" Lady Grasby frowned, momentarily diverted. "Are you certain those sugar lumps were cows, Aurora?"

Rory (no one but her sister-in-law called her by her birth name) nodded, and pretended to cough, a gloved hand to her mouth to hide a smile at the pained look of tolerance on Mr. Watkins' long face.

"A delightful pastoral scene of bovines," Mr. Watkins confirmed. "And there was a dairy maid—or were there two, Miss Talbot?"

"I cannot recall, sir. But it was delightful," agreed Rory, allowing a footman to take her red wool cloak. "Lady Cavendish says Her Highness has the most talented confectioner in all England, and I believe her."

Lady Grasby shrugged. "I am sure it was delightful, and I would have found it so, were I not worried over my portrait. I heard only one word in five of the conversation, though that prattlepate Lady Cavendish had a great deal to say."

"As did her corpulent husband." Mr. Watkins gave a loud sniff of derision. "Which was surprising, given he rarely pauses between mouthfuls to breathe, least of all speak. One day I fear Lord Cavendish will—*pop*."

"Oh dear, I hope I am not the unfortunate sitting beside him when he does," Rory quipped, amusement in her clear blue eyes. "One trusts Lord Cavendish will have the good manners to *pop* in privacy..."

"It is of no interest to me if Lord Cavendish bursts all over the dining room!" Lady Grasby announced, exasperated, moving further into the hall. "Did you catch Lady Cavendish's prattle over the trifle, Aurora? Did a merchant's daughter *reject* an offer of marriage from Major Lord Fitzstuart?"

"That is what Lady Cavendish reported," Rory replied. She paused in thought. "Though... I am more surprised that an offer was *made*, rather than one was rejected."

"Why say you, Miss Talbot?" Mr. Watkins asked curiously.

"From my observation of him, Major Lord Fitzstuart does not seem the sort of gentleman given to flippant marriage proposals."

Lady Grasby turned from addressing the butler and frowned in puzzlement at her sister-in-law.

"The girl is worth twenty thousand pounds or more. Her fortune has merchant roots to be sure, but William says the Major cannot afford to be selective in his choice of bride—"

"—because the ancestral home is a crumbling pile of ruins," added her brother with a sniff. "And the Fitzstuart fortune all but dwindled to dust by the absent earl."

When Rory turned inquiring eyes of surprise on Mr. Watkins—that he would know such intimate details regarding the Fitzstuart finances—he smiled his embarrassment.

"Not precisely ruins," he corrected diffidently. "The estate in Buckinghamshire isn't what it could be. The house is eighty years old and yet it stands incomplete. And there isn't much the Major can do about it while his father remains an absentee landlord. Yet, I doubt he would, if he could. His peccadilloes mirror those of his father and require what meager resources he has at his disposal."

Rory cocked her head in thought. "Perhaps he was rejected because it is rumored he keeps a mistress and has children by her? Regardless that he comes with the guarantee of a title one day, some females are not persuaded that is enough to accept a proposal of marriage."

Mr. Watkins inclined his bewigged head to Rory. "I agree with you, Miss Talbot. His lordship is a reprobate and a womanizing scoundrel. No female in her right mind would accept such a man for a husband."

Rory managed to suppress a smile. Leaning lightly on her ivory-handled walking stick, she said steadily, "Perhaps he was rejected because she was not sufficiently in love with him?"

Lady Grasby shooed quiet the butler, who was giving her the good news Mr. Romney was free to receive her, and said dismissively, "Rot, Aurora! Love has nothing to do with marriage. The children of merchants are raised to believe first and foremost in the value of a *thing*. Love is an ideal, an emotion of the highest order. As such it cannot be measured, so can hold little or no value for such practical people."

Rory wondered if her sister-in-law was speaking from the experience of having a grandfather whose vast wealth had been accumulated over a lifetime as a Billingsgate fishmonger. But as she had used the third person, Rory could only hope, for her brother's sake, that her sister-in-law had quite forgotten her own family's fishy beginnings.

"Now let me hear not another word about Lord Fitzstuart," Lady Grasby continued. She covered her sister-in-law's gloved hand with her own and said quietly, "Truth be told, it is your brother's slavish friendship with Major Lord Fitzstuart that keeps me awake at night. Sometimes, I think... Sometimes I wonder if Grasby cares more for that man than he does me! I wish—"

"Grasby is devoted to you," Rory interrupted.

"—the Major had never survived the war in the Colonies!"

Rory gasped. "You do not mean it, Silla!"

"Unfortunately, he is possessed of the devil's own luck," Mr. Watkins said on a sigh of annoyance, offering his tearful sister his perfectly pressed and folded white linen handkerchief. "The more dangerous the mission, the more daring the cause, the more Fitzstuart is eager to play the hero. It is a marvel indeed then that he came out of the army with all four limbs and his head intact!"

Rory looked from sister to brother, stunned.

"I cannot believe my ears. Mr. Watkins, you may decry the man for being a reprobate and a womanizer, and you, Silla, may dislike him heartily and be jealous of the time Grasby spends in his company... Indeed, there is not much Major Lord Fitzstuart can say in his own defense for his want of conduct, but neither of you have the-the *right* to wish him *dead*. How-how uncharitable, and His Lordship a war hero!"

William Watkins smiled thinly and looked secretive.

"My dear Miss Talbot, the Major is considered *reckless* in the extreme. So much so that I am not the only one who has wondered aloud if he has made a pact with—" He paused, looked over his shoulder at the butler, who quickly looked away, and pointed a gloved finger to the floor, and whispered, "*You-know-who.*"

Rory blinked at the man's outrageous suggestion that Major Lord Fitzstuart had managed to undertake and survive perilous and often life-threatening missions while in the army only because he had sold his soul to the Devil.

"No one mentioned wanting Fitzstuart *dead*," Lady Grasby argued with a pout. "If you are not careful, Aurora, such a spirited defense of a gentleman you do not know in the least, and who would not know you from Eve, will be construed as the unhealthy interest of a delusional and plain spinster for a handsome rake!"

Rory's face ripened. Spinster she may be. Delusional she was not. Nor was she plain. Her hair might best be described as damp straw-blonde. Her eyes were blue, but so pale as to be thought cold. But her face was heart-shaped, and her skin unblemished, so on balance, she was considered sweet and pretty, if not beautiful. If she was plain, it was only when in the orbit of the dark-haired beauties with cheeks flushed from flitting about the dance floor. With not enough beauty to overcome a passable dowry, Rory had no expectations of marrying for love or anything else, and was resigned to living her days as she had begun them, as her grandfather's dependent relative.

Thus, for her beautiful sister-in-law—a remarkably pretty brunette with damp brown eyes—to underscore the reality of her situation, in such a blunt manner, *and* in public, was a piece of spite that bruised Rory to the core. She knew her sister-in-law was not cruel by nature, but having been indulged from an early age, Silla did not often think of others before herself, and thus could be unconsciously unfeeling.

Rory was surprised yet grateful her sister-in-law had not stated the glaringly obvious. That was left to William Watkins, who shared his sister's unwitting lack of tact. He made Rory mentally wince and wish she were a mouse so she could scurry through a hole in the kicking boards when he replied to his sister's unfeeling remark with one of his own, and with a sickly-sweet smile.

"I am certain Miss Talbot's interest in the Major goes no deeper than an appreciation of his exceptional athleticism. That is often the way, is it not, that what is lacking in ourselves we greatly admire in others. You, my dear Miss Talbot, cannot help being a cripple, just as I cannot be blamed for my poor eyesight. It is God's will, and thus we abide it with good grace and forbearance."

"If you will follow me to the upstairs drawing room, Mr. Romney will be with you presently," the butler intoned in the silence which followed Mr. Watkins' homily.

"You do have your eyeglasses, William?" Lady Grasby asked, bunching up her apricot silk petticoats to ascend the staircase as rapidly as possible in high-heeled mules. "I so want you to examine the portrait, to tell me what it is about it that is vexing me." She paused on a sudden thought and looked over her shoulder, a gloved hand to the polished balustrade. "Don't trouble yourself to come up, Aurora. We will not be above half an hour."

"That would be for the best," Rory responded with false cheeriness from the base of a staircase that would take her twice the time to ascend than anyone else but a small child taking its first steps. "I know so little about art that I would be of no help to you whatsoever." Her gaze swept the hall for a settee or a wingchair. "Mr. Romney must have a suitable vestibule for visitors on this level..."

She was talking to herself. The butler and Lady Grasby, with her brother a step behind, had disappeared up the staircase.

ONE OF THE painter's assistants stepped into the hall from the studio at the back of the house, his artist's smock covered in colored paint daubs, in time to overhear the conversation between the three late-night guests. He offered Rory to follow him to a small viewing room off Mr. Romney's painting studio. There was a fire in the grate and a comfortable chair to sit upon to wait.

The fire was welcoming, but Rory's interest was not in the many painted canvases stacked against two walls, or in those propped on easels ready for inspection, but in the sounds of commotion coming from the other side of a door left ajar by the assistant. Interest piqued, Rory entered the large well-lit room uninvited and found it brimming with activity and laughter.

THREE

Rory was halfway across the room and standing by an artist's easel, where was propped a painting in the first stages of composition, before her trespass was noticed. She took only a cursory glance at the painting, more interested in the group of scantily dressed females on the wooden dais in front of her, their modesty saved by strategically draped diaphanous silks. While these draperies covered their torsos and flowed to their stockinged feet, the sheerness of the fabric did little to hide their limbs. All possessed the long shapely legs of the opera dancer. This was confirmed when three of their number broke from the group and danced out across the stage, holding hands and twirling this way and that on the balls of their stockinged feet, slim graceful arms offering an elegant counterpoint to their footwork.

They appeared as Greek statues of glistening white marble come to life with their sculptured white limbs and powdered faces. Rory delighted in their exuberance and agility, so much so that it was several moments before she realized she was being addressed, and by the principal ballerina fanning herself by the chaise longue.

"I beg your pardon," Rory apologized. "I was so taken with your companions I did not hear your question."

Consulata Baccelli did not immediately respond, taking her time to appraise Rory's gown of striped mint green taffeta with underskirts of embroidered lilac silk, the outer petticoat ruched and bunched behind to affect the fashionable polonaise.

Here was a lady of style, if not of the first society, and she wondered where the young woman's male chaperone could be—a personal maid at the very least—particularly at this late hour. A lady of quality did not venture out on her own, and never into the homes of men, painters in particular; all sorts of riffraff could be present.

But Consulata did not have to wonder why the young woman used a walking stick. When Rory had silently crossed the room, it was evident in her awkward gait that she needed it to move about. The short hem of her polonaise, which was some three inches off the ground, exposed her trim ankles in their white clocked stockings. Also revealed was her inwardly twisted right foot in a built-up heeled silk shoe, which answered the question as to why the young woman had an uneven gait.

Consulata thought it a great shame the young woman would never dance or be graceful in her movements, which surely meant she could never show herself to advantage. But the girl's spontaneous delight at watching the ballerinas playfully spin out across the stage decided Consulata that here was a young woman without malice, and she immediately decided to befriend her.

"Signora—"

"Signorina. Signorina Talbot," Rory corrected with a smile, gaze turning to Consulata Baccelli, because the dancers were being ushered back into formation by a weary assistant, another hurriedly coming to his colleague's aid to help adjust drapery and flowered headpieces. "They dance delightfully. I'm sure you all do."

"*Sì.* We do. But me, Consulata Baccelli, I am the most delightful dancer of them all." The principal ballerina laughed behind her fluttering fan at her own conceit. "I would show you but for these outrageous robes Signore Romney, he has made us wear." She indicated the blue damask chaise. "Come, sit here with me."

When Rory looked about her, as if a chair closer at hand would be more suitable, Consulata smiled and patted the damask cushion.

"Come. Amuse me until the excitement, it begins."

Rory reluctantly mounted the dais, climbing the three wooden steps, and sat where requested, walking stick kept close to her side, a gloved hand about its mahogany stick.

"You must be thrilled to have a painter of Mr. Romney's skill and reputation to immortalize you and your beautiful dancers," she said conversationally.

"Signore Romney he paints us not as dancers but as part of a Greek allegory. Me? I prefer to be painted as I am, a ballerina most famous. But this—" Consulata waved a plump wrist covered in pearls at the large canvas propped on the easel. "this painting that has us all dressed in these ridiculous sheets of annoyance, it is painted for the Duke of Dorset. He will hang it in the gallery at Knole. And because Dorset he is my lover, he will have me painted, dancing. And *that* painting he will hang in his private apartments, for his eyes only."

Without wishing it, Rory blushed. Her grandfather would be horrified to learn his only granddaughter was conversing with the notorious mistress of the Duke of Dorset. He would expect her to excuse herself at once and return to the small waiting room. But she was not the least offended or prudish, and replied with a smile she hoped oozed a worldliness she did not in the least possess.

"The Duke is sure to treasure such a painting. A graceful figure as you possess is to be admired and deserves to be immortalized."

Consulata was pleased with this response and beamed.

"I think we will be good friends, Signorina Talbot. I will have Dorset invite you to dinner. Then you and me, we can laugh and reminisce together about the little escapade Major Fitzstuart he arranges for his pleasant friend."

Rory tried to keep the interest from her voice and the surprise from her features.

"Major? Major Lord Fitzstuart?"

The dancer nodded and her dark eyes crinkled with amused mischief.

"Promise me, Signorina Talbot, not to tell Signore Romney's servants. It is most important to keep the surprise so the Major's pleasant friend, who is naturally infatuated with me, believes I am terrified, and he has saved me from a fate worse than death."

Rory was so intrigued she could only nod. She shuffled down the chaise longue in anticipation of receiving Consulata's confidence regarding Major Lord Fitzstuart. But no sooner had she done so than the dancers at her back began jumping up and down and squealing their delight. This had Consulata Baccelli on her feet. At the same time, one of Romney's assistants threw paints and brushes into the air as if in panic and fled the room, while two of the dancers swept up the trailing folds of their drapery, skipped lightly down the three steps of the stage and ran across the studio towards the three sash windows.

Such was the instantaneous outburst of excitement from the dancers that Rory instinctively swiveled to look over her shoulder—at them, not out across the studio to see what had caused their agitation. By the time she reoriented herself to look at the open windows, an intruder had dropped silently into the studio and was chasing the two dancers across the room.

Rory was shocked into speechlessness by such outlandish behavior, and while she blinked several times in response, as if convincing herself the scene presented before her was indeed unfolding, she did not sense any immediate danger. This surprised her, because the intruder was male, and naked but for a belt around his waist that positioned a modesty cloth between his legs. Watching him chase after the giggling dancers, who were showing no resistance to being caught, the cloth proved no covering at all, and Rory's face flooded with the heat of outrageous embarrassment.

And then, within the blink of an eye, her acute embarrassment turned to profound shock, and from shock panic sprang, not for herself but for the intruder.

When he came running up the room towards the stage and caught the two squealing dancers about the waist and held fast, Rory saw that his hair was powdered gray, his eyes blackened, and his laughing face covered with thick stripes of white paint. But it was a thin disguise that would fool no one who knew him. Rory knew him better than anyone else. The naked intruder was Harvel—Harvel Edward Talbot, Lord Grasby—her only brother.

FOUR

RECOGNIZING HER brother, Rory was up off the chaise longue and leaning on her stick. When a hand caught at her gloved wrist, she tore her gaze from Lord Grasby cavorting with two giggling dancers and stared unseeing at Consulata Baccelli.

"Do not be alarmed," the ballerina reassured her. "There is no danger. The Major and his friend, they are merely playing a game—"

"I must get down from here at once!"

Consulata's grip tightened but her smile remained.

"That is not possible, not until the performance it is over. Please sit and maintain calm."

A second male intruder had now dropped into the studio via the sash window. It was Major Lord Fitzstuart. Her gaze reluctantly returned to Consulata.

"You do not understand. I cannot be seen here. I must go, without delay!"

"Why are you such a wet goose about a trifle of a thing?" the ballerina demanded indignantly, voice rising as she tried to be heard over the excitement. She was furious with this young woman to whom she had given a front row seat to the handsome Major's outrageous display. "You are tiresome in the extreme!" she declared, up off the chaise. "I do not apologize to one who goes frigid with fright at the sight of a man uncovered! Eh? The male body 'tis beautiful, powerful, *stupendo*. If one is to faint, it is in appreciation! You want to run away over a thing that is most natural, but Consulata, she will not allow you to do this!"

She grabbed Rory's shoulders, swiveled her to face into the studio, and gave a snort of satisfaction.

"Now take a good look at what is before your eyes, because me, I have a vast experience of men, and none is more impressive in its handsome masculinity than the figure possessed by Major Fitzstuart. *Ecco*!"

Rory did not struggle to be free of Consulata's hold, neither did she do as requested and search out the Major. She kept her gaze on the middle distance, where strewn across the floor were the paints, artist's brushes and paraphernalia that had been tossed into the air and left scattered and spilled by a retreating assistant. She wondered how she could possibly forestall her sister-in-law and Mr. Watkins from entering the studio. They were just one floor above, and the disturbance was so deafening and constant that had they been three floors higher, they could not fail to hear the high-pitched squeals of the dancers being chased. It was only a matter of time before every person within the Romney household came rushing to find out what all the commotion was about. And if Lady Grasby discovered one of the intruders was in fact her husband of three years, Rory was certain her brother's married life would not be worth living thereafter.

To save her brother's marriage from ruin, the family from scandal, and for the sake of domestic harmony, Rory knew it was her duty to make every effort to cross the studio and lock the door on the outside world. Her sister-in-law and Mr. Watkins must be prevented from entering at all costs.

And then the little voice within her, the voice that came to her when she was alone with her thoughts in her bedchamber, or out in her hothouse nurturing her precious pineapples, uttered the two tiny words she knew so well.

What if?

What if she remained on the stage as Consulata Baccelli demanded? It would be the height of bad manners for her to disrupt the Major's performance. What harm could there be in her presence? She smiled to herself, smoothed out her petticoats and resumed her seat on the chaise longue. With back straight, one gloved hand about the carved ivory handle of her walking stick, she slowly lifted her gaze and allowed her light blue eyes to calmly look out across the dance floor.

Oh my... In all her daydreams, he had never looked like *that*.

Stripped to his breeches and white shirt was as undressed as her imagination could take her. Never, in all her conjured fantasies, would she have believed she would see her brother's best friend naked but for a cloth between his thighs.

When he stopped and threw back his head with laughter to find her brother gleefully writhing about the floorboards with two dancers collapsed on top of him, she was given further opportunity to appraise him. And just as the dancers appeared to her fashioned from an ethereal marble, so, too, did the Major. His broad back and shoulders were smoothly polished, the muscle contours to his arms and legs as chiseled as a classical statue of Apollo.

And when he turned and ran towards the stage where she sat, and she saw that his face was painted, with two long braids either side of his handsome face, she gasped, breath coming short and quick, as if needing air to stave off light-headedness. Her throat burned dry, the Major's masculinity far exceeding the expectations of her naïve daydreams. Small wonder the dancers were applauding and jumping up and down in admiration! Mentally, she was engaged in doing the same.

Recovered from the shock of revelation, she allowed herself to be caught up in his display of male bravado and athletic prowess.

One of Romney's assistants, who was brave enough to stand his ground, put up his fists. The Major laughed and welcomed the challenge. With hands to his hips he confronted the assistant, challenging him to make the first strike. When the assistant did just that, the Major nonchalantly ducked this way and that, avoiding contact with the run of jabs punched into the air. Seemingly tired of the game, he finally went in for the attack. His fist connected with the assistant's jaw on the first punch and the man reeled back in shock.

Rory half rose from the chaise.

The dancers at her back cheered.

The Major followed up his punch with a series of strategically placed short sharp blows to the man's body. The assistant collapsed, crumpled onto the floor, winded.

Rory applauded.

The dancers cheered louder than ever.

The Major turned to the stage in recognition of the acclaim, but the dancers, Rory included, gasped, smiles replaced by agitation as a second assistant made a run at the Major from behind, a chair raised above his head, ready to bring it down upon the Major. Instantly, the Major swiveled on the balls of his feet, saw the chair in the air, dropped to a crouch and put his shoulder forward. The assistant ran straight into the Major's shoulder whereupon he was lifted off his feet, lost his balance and his hold on the chair, and was flipped into the air.

As the Major straightened, the chair and the assistant crashed to the ground. The chair bounced and splintered. The assistant landed on his back, winded, self-esteem shattered. When he could breathe, the assistant scurried from the room on all fours to the accompaniment of the Major's hearty laugh and the taunts of the dancers.

All resistance at an end, Major Lord Fitzstuart turned to the stage and bowed with a flourish.

FIVE

S PELLBOUND, Rory watched, fascinated, as the Major continued to play-act for his appreciative female audience: Crouching at intervals, as if taking cover behind a thicket; peering around the side of the canvas balanced on an easel, as if it were a rock, his face split into a grin. Then he became serious, lost the grin, and with a hand to his brow, pretended to scout for the enemy. The dancers jumped up and down more than ever, applauding his charades, some even dared to shout out, demanding he notice them specifically. But he remained in character, and skillfully traversed the battlefield of strewn artifacts to be found in a painter's studio: Paint brushes scattered like broken sticks, a palette dropped like a soldier's shield, and paints of all colors spilled out of their mixing pots and splashed across the floorboards like the blood of the wounded vanquished.

Cheers and squeals of delight from the stage accompanied this successful crossing of such a perilous battlefield, and in celebration, the Major howled at the moon, fists raised in victory. The dancers continued to applaud, and all hoped they would be the one the Major captured when he invaded the stage.

Consulata Baccelli leaned forward on the chaise longue, the diaphanous silk slipping off her shoulder invitingly as she called for him to join her. And when the Major looked her way, she beckoned him with a sultry smile and one crooked finger.

It was all the encouragement he needed to take a flying leap for the chaise longue.

WHAT MAJOR Lord Fitzstuart could not see and thus did not know, and what the dancers saw but promptly ignored, was the sudden activity at his back. A raiding party had invaded the studio; the door had been flung wide open and banged against the wood paneling. The smack of wood hitting wood was lost in the din of the dancers screaming for the Major's attention.

Rory not only saw the door burst open but was also witness to Mr. Cedric Pleasant striding purposefully into the center of the floor space before dramatically drawing his sword and holding it aloft, like a valiant knight of old on a quest to smite the enemy. He followed his theatrical entrance with the bellowed pronouncement that *He, Cedric Pleasant Esq., had come to save the day.*

Disappointingly for Mr. Pleasant, no one but those at his back heard this brave declaration.

Mr. George Romney, Mr. William Watkins, and Lady Grasby, and a gentleman unknown to Rory following on their heels, burst through the doorway, almost at one and the same time, and once inside, fanned out across the room in search of the source of the wild commotion, which was directly before their eyes.

Rory instantly shot to her feet.

Someone—*she*—had to warn her brother.

At the edge of the stage, her gaze shifted from the intruders to her brother, who was now sprawled on the floor and content to stay there. Two dancers were running their fingers over their captive in search of his most sensitive ticklish spots. And by her brother's giggling fit, with his long thin legs kicking out wildly, he was enduring their chosen method of torture as best he could.

It said much for her sisterly devotion that despite the shocking nature of her brother's circumstance, watching Grasby laughing and enjoying himself had her smiling with loving indulgence. It had been years since he had been so at ease. She had almost forgotten he could laugh heartily.

Rory's indulgent smile sealed her fate. Had she not paused in contemplation to watch her brother with loving affection, she might have had sufficient time to avoid disaster by flinging herself out of harm's way. By the time she looked away from her brother and returned her gaze to the doorway she was met with a terrifying sight.

Every fiber of her being conspired against her, and she could not move a muscle.

Major Lord Fitzstuart had taken a mighty leap and was in full flight of reaching the chaise longue. He was hurtling straight towards her and there was nothing she could do to save herself. She closed her eyes tight and took a deep breath. Braced for disaster, she hoped for the best.

SIX

D AIR MADE A flying leap for the dais.

The cheering, squeals and clapping were deafening.

And then the unexpected happened.

It was so unexpected that time slowed to allow the moment to be etched in the collective memory of those present. There was such disbelief that no one spoke, and no one moved for a matter of moments, wondering if it was all part of the Major's display of outrageous bravado. He had not received the moniker *Dair Devil* by sitting about White's playing at cards.

Dair was in full flight of his leap when into his path stepped the female in mint green and lavender silk petticoats. Where in the name of Jupiter had she sprung from? Her timing could not have been more disastrous. Did she have a brain the size of a pea not to comprehend what would happen to her by such an idiotic move? It was impossible for him to stop mid-leap.

His soldier's instinct told him that if he did not take immediate evasive action, his large beefy carcass would slam full force into this simpleton. Bones would be broken. Hers. She looked to be a quarter of his weight, was wafer-thin in fact, and with a walking stick in her gloved hand, must be as frail as eggshell. There was no time and no possibility of being heard, even if he did shout out a warning. The bevy of beauties, who only moments before had been jiggling and giggling and calling out encouragingly, now saw the disaster about to befall him, and they scattered, screaming, to get out of the way.

Dair took the only action left to him to avoid catastrophic consequences. He tucked in his arms, twisted his body and braced, hoping this would be enough to alter his trajectory and throw him wide of the idiotic creature. His quick thinking would have worked had the female remained where she was and not turned. It was as if she sensed an ominous presence, and in trying to escape it she again stepped into his path.

There was no option left to him.

He landed heavily on the stage, momentum carrying him forward, and he scooped up the female simpleton, pulling her hard against his torso as he kept running. He held her fast against him as his bare feet scrambled to resist inertia. His thigh slammed into the corner of the chaise, startling its occupant, who flopped forward before sprawling backwards across the cushions with an involuntary screech when the tipped chaise landed back on all four of its spindle legs with a thud.

Dair judged the edge of the platform to be a few feet in front of him, that there was then a drop and a gap of some five feet before the plastered wall at the back of the studio. The last thing he wanted was to fall into the gap with his captive; she might land under him and be crushed. And even if he did leap the gap, there was nowhere to go. They would slam into the wall. While he might suffer a few bruises and abrasions, there was no guarantee he could prevent his captive from breaking bones, possibly ribs.

He needed to do something, fast. Out of the corner of his eye, he caught sight of the linen drapery, used as the painter's backdrop. It was billowing in the breeze from the open sash window. He calculated it was within reach.

With his captive held fast in one arm, he stuck out the other, grabbed a handful of this material and prayed the curtain rod remained rigid. The material needed to remain stitched to its rings long enough for them to become entangled, which should stop them from falling off the edge of the stage.

His strategy worked.

Speed coupled with motion spun them into the folds of linen. The curtain swung wide. Dair's shoulder hit the wall with a thump, and then the curtain and its two occupants swung back to the stage and came to a halt. The couple were rolled up in the material but remained upright and unharmed.

Pleased with his efforts at averting a disaster, he let out an involuntary chuckle. For several seconds, all he could hear was his own heavy breathing, and all he could feel was his heart thudding against his ribs. Far off, at the other end of the studio, there was a great deal of commotion, but here, wrapped in this linen cocoon, there was only silence...

His captive was breathing heavily, too. Her breath blew on his bare chest, where her forehead was pressed, and she was trembling, no doubt from fright. But she was not screaming or moaning, which told him she was unhurt. No broken bones then. Good. He possibly had a nasty bruise to his thigh and another to his shoulder, but that was as nothing compared to the bruise to his ego, courtesy of this idiotically unaware female wrapped safely in his arms.

Who the devil was she, anyway? Where had she come from? Why was she on the stage surrounded by dancers dressed as Grecian nymphs when she herself was dressed from head to foot? His wine-befuddled brain searched for answers. She must be a friend of Consulata, invited to witness his charade. Perhaps she was a singer, or an actress who catered to the needs of men of his social class? Mistress of one of Dorset's cronies, perhaps? That made sense.

She was certainly not one of those delicately nurtured females, like his sister and cousins, and his mother, who wouldn't dare dip an expensively shod toe into a painter's studio without a male chaperone, and for fear of encountering the very women for whom he and Grasby had been performing. A drawing room miss would have fainted or be screaming her lungs out by now. The severe shock of being swept off her feet by a near-naked man would surely bring on a fit of hysterics. Yet she was not hysterical. Perhaps his captive was too frigid with fright to put up a struggle?

He wondered if she was not idiotic after all, but rather a cunning little minx. Idiotic in the execution of her gambit—no one in her right mind threw herself in front of a dragoon whose chest was the width of a sedan chair—but cunning in that if she had been wanting to get his attention, she now had it, undividedly. And she was not backward in coming forward in letting him know what she wanted from him, either. Vixen.

What was that saying Cedric repeated *ad nauseam* after one too many bottles of claret? *Carpe* something? *Carpe... Carpe diem...* Seize the day! That was it. He grinned. He wasn't above seizing the moment. Be damned what was going on beyond their cocoon.

He closed his eyes and snuffled at her neck, expecting one of the sweeter headier scents concocted by Floris, and was pleasantly surprised. This scent was much more subtle, and alluring. It was an indefinable, barely-there mingling of scents, of vanilla, and of lavender, but mostly of her. It triggered within him a deep longing that he could neither describe nor wished to acknowledge and his hand convulsed in her thin chemise, scrunching up the linen between his long fingers as he drank her in.

And when she lifted her head off his chest and he tilted away from her, but just enough for him to see her face, to see if she was just as caught up in the moment as he, big blue eyes, limpid under heavy lids, blinked up at him. And when she went on tiptoe to invitingly press her mouth to his he needed no further invitation. He gave himself up to the moment...

IT WAS THE wooden pegs in the plasterwork that gave way first. They held the metal brackets to the wall. One metal bracket came away and fell with a clang to the stage, just as the wooden curtain rod, bowing under the weight of its two entangled occupants, snapped in two. There was a great whoosh and clatter of wooden curtain rings as they slid off the splintered ends of the broken rod.

Dair and his female captive found themselves drowning in drapery.

It was over within seconds.

Caught unawares and no longer supported by the curtain pulled taut by their weight, the cocooned kissing couple struggled to stay upright. With lightning reflexes, Dair's arms enveloped and tightened about his captive. And as they were knocked to the ground, he stuck out his elbows and took the brunt of the fall. Trapped in the drapery, they rolled over and over, fell off the stage and into the narrow gap between it and the plastered wall.

Dair landed on his back, his captive on top of him, clinging to him as if he were the only piece of flotsam in a raging sea. Both were shaken but unhurt. Both lay still, taking deep breaths, to recover their equilibrium, if not their dignity. Then suddenly both realized their latest predicament. As they had rolled off the stage, the linen unraveled, setting them free as they dropped into the gap. They were now a tangle of arms and legs, with breechcloth askew, panniers twisted and broken, layers of carefully constructed silk petticoats crushed and disheveled, and all of it on display.

Dair thought it a great lark.

Grinning, he put an arm behind his head and settled in, not at all perturbed. His grin turned to genuine good humor watching his captive struggle to disentangle her limbs and her garments from his brawny form. And without his help, with not much success. He could see by her mulish expression his lack of assistance annoyed her, but when she managed to sit upright and rake her mussed blonde hair from her flushed face, he caught at her wrist. He had every intention of pulling her back down on top of him to continue where they had left off wrapped in the curtain, everyone else be dammed.

Then a voice boomed out across the studio, above the commotion. Dair stayed his hand around his captive's wrist, a finger to his lips lest she speak, and rose up on an elbow to listen. It was not Cedric Pleasant declaring he had come to save the day. He did not recognize the voice, but he recognized the bark of command. It was accompanied by footfall. And that, too, was familiar. It was men in boots marching in synchrony. At best guess, he would say a dozen men, maybe more.

Soldiers.

SEVEN

R ORY HAD NOT meant to kiss him. On the contrary, she was one breath away from vocalizing her affront that it was the height of rudeness to sniff at her neck, at anyone's neck! She should have been terrified, distressed, even hysterical, to be pressed up against him with nothing between them but a flap of doeskin. So that's what a naked male body looked like. She'd never seen one before, or knew what to expect, except what she had gleaned from studying the tapestries in a folly temple on her godparents' Hampshire estate.

Almost twenty years old and a complete ignoramus about matters of the heart, more precisely, matters of lust. *Twenty*. She could hardly believe her own ignorance!

Pressed against a naked male body she, as a spinster, had a duty to faint. At the very least she should do everything in her power to fight him off and thrash her way out of the cocoon. Scream. Anything to get herself as far away as possible from such potent masculinity. Her unsullied reputation demanded it. Her family would expect it. Polite Society would condemn her for not doing so.

But Major Lord Fitzstuart had shaken her well-ordered world as if it were a mesmerizing show globe. Afloat in a sea of colored liquid possibilities, she came to the realization that this impromptu visit to

George Romney's studio was turning out to be the most exciting night of her staid life. Nothing ever happened in her day-to-day existence that was not sanctioned by convention, considered acceptable, peaceable and *safe* for the unmarried granddaughter of a peer.

And now here she was in the arms of the handsomest, most wicked war hero of the age. What should she do? She knew what she wanted to do, but it was contrary to everything she had ever been told or taught. What was that saying her brother's friend Cedric Pleasant used at every opportunity... *Carpe... Carpe—Diem*. That was it! Well, she would seize it, and the consequences could go hang!

What was the harm in a single simple kiss? One kiss and she would know one way or the other if kissing was overrated. She had never been kissed, and certainly never in the way females wished to be kissed by handsome men, ardently and without restraint. While alone in her Pinery one day, she had allowed herself to daydream about kissing, the mechanics of a kiss, and how it must make a person feel. She concluded that if two people thought about it before committing to the act, they would not do it. Her daydreaming had led her to completely cover a maturing pineapple plant with tanner's bark, until the gardener alerted her to her abstraction.

Two people with their lips pressed together. What was so special about that...?

He was so warm and so—so *male*. He smelled of pepper and musk, and freshly squeezed limes... Fascinating how the skin on his face appeared smooth and yet his chin was rough, like the sharp punched points of her grandfather's silver nutmeg grater... His nose really was large and beak-like. She'd noticed that about him before... And his eyelashes... They were quite long and dark... She was sure her lips were swollen... He tasted salty and delicious... Had the windows been closed on the night air and a fire started in a grate...?

Oh my!

It had never occurred to her that to truly enjoy a passionate kiss, their mouths must open. It was so—*decadent*. And he was so—*delicious*. She pressed herself against him, not wanting him to stop. She wanted everything about the moment to be burned into her consciousness: The feel of him pressed up against her; his fingers

entwined in the hair at her nape and the lavender satin bow that held
it in place; and the wondrous way he kissed, as if he truly, fervently
desired nothing and no one more than he did her.

Oh, how easy it was to spiral into erroneous belief. And all it
took was one kiss…

RORY WAS BROUGHT back to the immediate present when Dair
gently squeezed her upper arm and, with a wink and a finger to his
lips, signaled for her to remain silent. No explanation was necessary.
The loud regular clatter of boots on floorboards, accompanied by the
squeals of alarm from the dancers, had her scrambling off him and
kneeling at the edge of the raised platform to see what was
happening.

Just inside the doorway was the celebrated painter Mr. George
Romney, arms folded, shoulders hunched, and looking troubled.
Beside him was his brother Peter, grinning from ear to ear. They
shuffled out of the way of a contingent of uniformed militia who
were marched in by a ruddy-faced captain of the guard. The soldiers
came to an abrupt halt halfway up the length of the studio, where
stood the stout young gentleman Mr. Cedric Pleasant, looking
resplendent in an eggshell blue frock coat with metallic thread and
spangles. His legs were splayed, displaying his strong calf muscles to
great effect. He was holding aloft a sword before an audience of
crying and panicked dancers and declaiming that he had "come to
save the day".

What lessened the impact of this manly stance and declaration
was that Cedric Pleasant had strode into the middle of a large splotch
of spilled paint, and now had splatters all over his buckled shoes. The
rest of his rehearsed speech was abruptly terminated by the captain of
the guard barking out orders to his soldiers.

What worried Rory most was the whereabouts of her brother.
She prayed he had managed to dive under the table draped in cloth
that had upon it all the paraphernalia needed by a painter of
portraits. Better still if he had managed to climb back out the

window he had climbed in through. He was not amongst those now gathered in the studio, so when there was a tug on the lace at her elbow, she readily turned away from the melodrama.

She was surprised the Major remained nonchalantly propped on an elbow out of sight.

"Report, fair scout! What's happening out there?"

"You don't want to see for yourself?"

"Let me guess," he said. "Twelve—maybe fifteen—militia, not including their captain...?"

Rory looked out into the studio, counted, then nodded, impressed.

"Couldn't ask for better odds! I would be insulted if there were fewer than a dozen. Six, and the wagtails would mistake them for customers. Eight, and our canary birds think they're for the round house for soliciting. Now with a *dozen* of our city's finest invading the premises, they suspect something far more serious is on the boil."

Rory frowned.

"Wagtails and canary birds? On the boil? I have no idea what you're talking about but it's nothing to do with aviaries. And, I would hazard a guess, contrived for your own amusement?"

Surprised, Dair stared hard at Rory for the first time since crashing into her. While he liked what he saw—she was a shapely little thing with big blue eyes and glowing hair—her self-possession and the intelligence in her expression unsettled him. He wasn't sure if she was laughing *at* him or *with* him. Instinct said the latter, so he took a leap of faith and confided in her, saying at his most nonchalant,

"You aren't particularly perturbed that Mr. Romney's studio is overrun with uniformed ruffians?"

"Why should I be?" she said with a shrug, adding with a cheeky smile, "I have a war hero to protect me."

"Ha! That's true!" he replied, and felt his face grow hot. *God! Was he blushing?* He felt sick to his stomach at such weakness. Plenty of women had used that one-line gambit on him, fluttering their eyelids and pouting their reddened lips, and to bed the most beautiful of them he let them think it had worked. But he had never blushed at the remark.

"A war hero masquerading as an American Indian," Rory teased.

"For a wager—all of it," he blurted out, as if a confession was required of him.

"Yes, I thought that might be the case. But those poor—*wagtails and canaries*—the dancing girls? —they don't know that do they? And the militia... I hope you aren't out of pocket for their invasion. Or will your winnings cover expenses, too?"

"Clever." His mouth twitched. "I'll wager my breechcloth you know what *perturbed* means, too."

Rory turned away to look out over the stage again; anything to stop him staring at her so fixedly. She was feeling quite faint. She told him what was happening, adding, "The captain has two of his men guarding the door, which is now closed. You won't escape that way, if that was your intent?"

He tugged again on her lace and gestured with his thumb over his bare shoulder. "Door behind us. And it's unlocked. What's the gentleman with the sword doing now?"

"He's put away his sword and is talking with the captain."

"Mr. Pleasant will be as grumpy as a kicked toadstool to have his performance upstaged. Wise of him to sheath his sword and not play the hero. He's no coward but it would be idiotic to challenge men in uniform, particularly with such odds stacked against him."

"A war hero would. *You* would. Nothing frightens *you*."

For the second time in as many minutes, Dair was startled by such ready conviction. But he quickly recovered his sangfroid and inclined his head in acknowledgement, saying with a grin, "I'll frighten them into submission. I doubt any of those boys have seen a Colonial least of all a native of that continent."

Rory's gaze flickered over his painted face, with its two long braids dangling either side of his ears, and then across his wide bare shoulders, but dared not let her eyes drop any further, and quickly brought her gaze back to his face with its blackened eye sockets and painted stripes across his nose. That he was watching her intently was evident in his fixed stare.

"Yes, you will," she said calmly. "But it wouldn't require you to wear such an absurd disguise. You don't look like an American Indian in the least."

"*Absurd*? And how many American Indians have you—"

"I've seen etchings!"

An involuntary burst of laughter was quickly muffled when he clapped a hand over his mouth. He leaned into her with a raise of his eyebrows.

"I'll show you my etchings if you show me yours..." But when she frowned, not understanding the inference, he sat back, suddenly uncomfortable and said with unusual brusqueness, "Next time I need to appear ridiculous, I'll seek your advice!"

"You don't need my advice. You do quite splendidly on your own! Oh! Oh! Now that was rude of me! Forgive me!"

He grinned, watching her fluster and flounder her apology, cheeks apple red with embarrassment. He chucked her under the chin.

"You, my sweet-mouthed delight, are nothing like Consulata's usual coterie of female friends... I'm glad you threw yourself in my way."

"Threw myself?" Rory gasped loudly. "*Threw myself*?" She did not know what else to say to such a startling accusation. She was saved further embarrassment and explanation when Dair put a finger to her lips to quiet her and jerked his head at the stage.

"Listen! Sounds like an argument. Female tearing strips off some poor fellow. It's not Consulata. When she fires up it's all Genovese and gestures! Who did you say was out there?"

"I didn't."

Rory peeked over the ledge, but she knew who owned the agitated voice without needing to do so.

Into the startling diorama of soldiers standing to attention, dancers huddled together, and a painter's studio in disarray, swept the Lady Grasby, followed by William Watkins a stride behind. Both rushed up to Mr. Romney demanding answers.

Rory had no idea what was being said, there was too much competing noise. She could well imagine the painter was being accused of the world's ills by her sister-in-law, who was gesticulating widely with her folded fan.

Dissatisfied with the laconic painter's responses, when he pointed out the captain, her sister-in-law readily turned on this uniformed officer and proceeded to flay him with no regard for his rank, his mission or their audience. Drusilla's weapons of choice never wavered: The Talbot family pedigree that stretched back to Edward the Third; her grandfather-in-law's earldom, which her husband would one day inherit; and the Earl's noble connections to every Privy Councilor, which would see the captain shipped off to St. George's Island in the Southern Ocean, if he did not do as she commanded.

Rory sighed and turned to Dair to say somewhat apologetically, "Lady Grasby is threatening the captain, and he is looking most decidedly intimidated."

"Grasby? *Lady* Grasby?" Dair's ears burned. He sat up. "Tell me, Delight, do you see a wide-eyed ginger-haired fellow, thin as a whipping post—a scribbler with a blotter and pencil? Is he making copious notes?"

She nodded. "He is. And he cannot write quickly enough for the conversation. He's just broken the tip from his pencil, and it's jumped out of his hand. Oh no! The poor fellow went to ground trying to recapture it and has had his hand trodden on by Mr. Watkins—"

"Mr. *William* Watkins? *Weasel* Watkins is there too? Hallelujah! It is a happy day indeed!"

Rory looked over her shoulder in time to witness Dair punch the air with joy.

"Weasel? *Weasel* Watkins? Is that what you call him?"

She tried to stifle a smile, but Dair saw it and pointed a finger at her.

"Admit it, Delight! The moniker fits him like a glove. Those squinty eyes! Those bushy brows! Those thin, disapproving nostrils!"

"I will admit to nothing. And shame on you. Not everyone can be an Adonis. Certainly not Mr. Watkins. But he does dress his faults well."

"But he does dress his faults well," Dair mimicked, pulling a face of disgust.

Rory couldn't help herself—she giggled.

"Never in my wildest imaginings would I have believed Major Lord Fitzstuart capable of envying another. You could wear a sack, and females would swoon at your feet. Poor Mr. Watkins must use all his sartorial skill to fashion himself into something worthy of a female's attention. You enter a room in a sack and poor Mr. Watkins' efforts would be for naught."

"Come here, Delight," he commanded gently, and pulled her down beside him, a firm grip on her gloved hand. There was no roguish smile when he looked into her eyes. "It's time for me to end this charade," he said quietly, and without artifice. "But before I make my grand exit, I want your name. You're not a dancer, and you are not an actress. Your conversation—*everything about you*—tells me you've been well cared for, or were in the past. No. Don't struggle. I don't want to cause you distress. I want to offer you—" He huffed, glanced away, then looked back at her in exasperation. "The Devil! What am I offering you...?"

Rory swallowed hard, throat dried with expectation, gaze riveted to his handsome face. By the deep lines between his black brows, she knew his mind was in a turmoil of indecision.

"How am I to know if you don't?" she asked in a small voice.

His gaze dropped at that, but not away—down, down to her mouth. Then down further still, to the square low-cut décolletage, and just peeping out around its silken edge, the pretty lace border of her chemise. He caressed a fold of the delicate lace between the tips of thumb and forefinger, itching to caress much more... Finally, he lifted her chin with his forefinger and brought his gaze back up to her face.

"You know what I want, Delight. You don't kiss a man the way you kissed me without expectation of a result. Well, this is your lucky day. I'm going to give you what you want."

Rory blinked. It was her turn to experience turmoil. Her mind throbbed with the competing emotions of joy and dread. Joy because she saw that he desired her. She might be ignorant, but she was no simpleton. The handsomest man in London found *her* desirable. No one had looked at her like that, *ever*. He certainly had never known of her existence before today, despite both of them being in attendance at the Roxton Easter Ball less than a month ago. But joy was quickly swallowed by dread, the dread of what he was about to propose. One kiss and he presumed to know what she wanted. Men were such immediate creatures!

She did not want to hear what he had to offer and shifted away, to brush down her petticoats, to get her gown and herself in some sort of order before she was discovered, as was inevitable. Her sister-in-law had stopped verbally abusing the captain, and he was now addressing his men. The dancers had quieted, too. A thump close by made her jump. There was footfall on the stage. The chaise longue was set upright. For the first time since they had landed in the ditch, Consulata Baccelli was heard complaining in her own tongue.

Yet, before Rory could take a peek to see what was going on, Dair pulled her into his arms.

EIGHT

"WHAT IS IT about you that compels me?" Dair wondered aloud. "I must be mad! No matter. It is done. Whatever you want. House. Carriage. Clothes. Give me a week to arrange it. 'Till then go to Banks house in Chelsea. It shares a wall with the Physic Garden. Lil—Lily Banks. She'll take you in until I come for you, no questions asked. Just mention my name. Repeat the directions so I know you won't forget. Say them!"

"Banks House in Chelsea. The house shares a wall with the Physic Garden. Lily Banks will look after me, no questions asked. Who's Lily?"

"A friend—a very good friend." He grinned. "Mother of my son."

All the blood drained from Rory's face in shock. Though why this was so, she had no idea. It was not as if she were unaware the Major kept a mistress and had illegitimate offspring. The habits of noblemen and their mistresses were readily talked about in every drawing room. She had even been present at a discussion between two long-suffering wives of peers conferring on the care and nurturing of their husbands' children by various mistresses. Her sister-in-law had whisked her away before she could hear more.

Yet, to her, such conversations were just that, conversations like any other. She had never really given much consideration to what was, for many wives of peers, a fact of life. But to have it baldly stated to her face, and by the man himself! She was not sure what was the greater upset: His Lordship in nothing but a breechcloth or having him tell her he had an illegitimate son by a woman named Lily Banks.

For several seconds she could neither feel nor hear. She watched without seeing as Dair peered over the stage, then ducked down again and said something to her. But she did not hear him. All she could think about was a house in Chelsea, his mistress and their son. What had he offered her? A house? Clothes? A carriage? But what about Lily Banks and the boy? Was Lily Banks being cast aside for her, or was she an addition to his harem? How many other women were there? And children? What would her brother think? *Her brother*? Why had Grasby intruded into her troubled thoughts about the Major and his nefarious lifestyle?

Grasby! She could hear him. She mentally shook her mind clear and discovered Dair had disappeared.

"DAIR! Dair. For pity's sake! Don't leave me here to rot!"

It was Grasby, pleading. But from where? His voice was muffled, as if he was down a deep well. Soldiers were now scrambling over the studio. Rory knew she would be discovered! Oh, where was the Major?

No sooner had Rory wondered this than he appeared, out from under the platform. He slithered on his stomach far enough out so he could raise his shoulders then twisted his body around onto his buttocks. He was covered in cobwebs and dust.

"Coy little thing, aren't you?" he stated without criticism when Rory quickly averted her gaze, adding by way of explanation for his disappearance. "Went to reconnoiter. My friend's got himself stuck under the stage, so if you'll excuse me, I must go to his aid. Oh! A word of warning: Stay low when the fighting—"

"*Fighting*—?"

"—starts." He crouched and called out under the platform,

"Never would abandon you, Grasby! Just do as I say! You can't come forward. The gap is too narrow, even for your skinny carcass! You have to back out, rump first!"

"*Oh God! No! Not that way!*" whined Lord Grasby in despair. "Dair! Dair! You've got to *save* me!"

"Will do, dear fellow! But must create a diversion first. When you hear a roar of noise and the girls screaming, that's when you scuttle backwards the way you came in, and as fast as you can. Got it?"

"Got it! A great noise and screaming and I back out."

"As fast as you can!"

"As fast as I can!"

"That's the spirit!"

"Dair! Dair? Where do I go? Do I make for the window?"

"No! Not the window! Across the platform. On the other side there's a door—"

"A door? On the other side of the platform? Oi!? What's that racket? Sounds like a damned rhino stomping above me!"

"Soldiers looking for—"

"She's sent *soldiers* to look for me? I'm done for!"

"Not you! Nothing for you to worry about!"

"Worry about? I don't care about the militia! It's *the wife*—Silla —she's out there, Dair! She's going to *kill* me! Dair! Dair..." Grasby adding in a small voice, "I've lost my breechcloth... Dair?"

Dair swiveled on his toes, hunched over, shoulders shaking and a hand clapped to his mouth to stifle an outburst of laughter. Tears of glee filled his eyes. He turned back to face the black void under the platform but before he could speak, Grasby hissed.

"Dair? Dair, did you hear me...? You're laughing! I know it! This isn't amusing! This is *my* head on the block!"

Despite controlling his laughter, Dair could not hide his grin, and it sounded in his voice. He wiped tears from his eyes, smudging the soot.

"No. Not amusing at all! But it's not your head that's the concern."

"Damn you to hell for getting me in this fix!"

"Yes. Yes. I'll be there soon enough. Just put your hands over your gadso and get across the stage and through that door as fast as you can! Make for the carriage. Grasby? Grasby!"

"Yes! Yes! Door! Carriage! Have a care with Silla. Be gentle. Her nerves. The shock... Are you listening to me, Dair? Dair? Dair! Devil take you! Stupid prank! Stupid..."

The rest of Lord Grasby's tirade was swallowed by the noise of the dancers being herded under protest back onto the stage.

Dair popped his head up and took a look across the stage to ascertain the position of the soldiers. Most were still in formation awaiting orders. The civilians were by the door, as was Lady Grasby and the Weasel, and two soldiers guarded the exit.

Strange they were positioned there; that was not part of the agreement with the captain. The dancers were all huddled on the stage and blocked his view of the right side of the studio. He presumed it was Consulata prone on the chaise longue; all he could see of her was a fan fluttering to and fro in agitation above the back of the chaise. And there, standing in the center of the room beside Mr. Cedric Pleasant, was the newssheet reporter, pencil and blotter in hand, looking wide-eyed and interested, as if he had hit on the story of the Season! Dair smiled. He would give him his story all right, and more.

Finally, he decided it was time to make his move. In farewell, he tugged on a long lock of Rory's hair, come loose from her mussed coiffure, then stood up and stretched his legs. When she went to do likewise, he signaled for her to remain seated, out of sight.

"Stay here. There's bound to be blood spilled. Nothing serious, but I don't want you getting mixed up in the fracas—"

"*Blood?* You will be careful, won't you?"

He instantly thought of his nine years in the army since a youth of fourteen, and the bloody carnage he and his comrades had survived. No one had ever asked him to be careful then or cared. He laughed harshly, a look over his shoulder to see if he had yet been noticed and brushed away Rory's apprehension.

"Not mine! That lot out there. Well, maybe a little drop of mine," he conceded at her frown of concern. In an impulsive move, he leaned down, whispering near her ear, "I'll be careful, just for you..."

Then with his teeth, he tugged free the lavender satin ribbon tied in her disordered hair, chuckling at her sudden intake of breath.

"Every warrior gets his share of the spoils of war," he explained with a grin as he hastily tied her satin ribbon to the end of the braid hanging in front of his right ear. "Now wish me luck!"

Rory was not given the opportunity to wish him anything at all.

Dair was up out of the gap and onto the stage, standing tall with arms akimbo, before she could utter a syllable. Then he bellowed into the room with all the enthusiasm of a man relishing the result of his invitation.

"Well, lads! Who wants to come at me first?"

And at that invitation, all hell broke loose.

NINE

Rory's grandfather Lord Shrewsbury was in his seventieth year, but today he felt a hundred and seventy. It was on days such as this that he contemplated resigning his post as England's Spymaster General. He would retire and live out the rest of his days here, at his Dutch house at Chiswick, with his beloved granddaughter for company. Together they would watch watercraft sailing up and down the Thames—all the ills of the world, all the vileness and intrigue consigned to the pages of his secret history.

But he was determined to remain Spymaster General until he had caught the traitor within the bureaucratic ranks of his own spy network. And how did he know there was a traitor? He had recently received intelligence that an agent of France based in Lisbon who was, for the right price, willing to not only betray his countrymen, but divulge the name of this traitor.

So, it was vital to make contact with this French double agent. Shrewsbury would send his best man to Lisbon, a man who possessed the skills to disappear into the local setting, could speak whatever language was required of him, was expert in handling all types of weaponry and, if caught, would be able to withstand the torture meted out to foreign spies. It was a dangerous and challenging assignment requiring great courage and cunning, but he was confident Major Lord Fitzstuart was up to the task.

The Major was licking his wounds after a particularly riotous evening the night before at a painter's studio. Shrewsbury had not read the finer particulars of a report into what had occurred, but he knew dancers, drink and fists were involved, as it always was with the Major. Half a dozen souls and an aggrieved painter were seeking reparation and revenge. None of this bothered Shrewsbury in the least. Young men, particularly young men who risked their lives, needed distraction. And such men would be naughty boys given enticement and opportunity.

Shrewsbury's mouth twitched on a memory as he beckoned the Major out from the shadows and further into the room.

"Come take a seat, Major," Shrewsbury said with genuine warmth. "Do the honors with the teapot, Watkins."

When his secretary half rose out of his chair, pulling a face in the process, Dair waved a hand at him to resume his seat.

"Don't put yourself to the bother, Watkins. I'll fend for myself. You might need to consult your notes on the off chance I don't get my facts straight. Was I pummeled by ten, or was it twelve, soldiers?"

"I—I can't—I don't—" William Watkins blustered and pretended to look through his notes by shuffling paper.

Dair smiled crookedly, but even this small action made him grimace. He instinctively touched the corner of his mouth where his lip was split, and an ugly blue-black bruise was getting uglier by the hour. Above his left eye his brow was also black and swollen, and there were abrasions and bruises to his knuckles. Every part of him felt raw. But for all that, he could still stand upright.

"It was ten," Dair stated, dropping a sugar lump into his teacup and stirring. He sipped gingerly at the black brew. "Not the best odds, but I came out of the lacing better than some of those leatherheads."

William Watkins wondered how the Major knew he'd written up an extensive report of the drama played out at Romney's painting studio the night before. He'd witnessed the entire inexcusable episode, and it reinforced what he thought of Major Lord Fitzstuart:

The man was an animal. He couldn't wait for Lord Shrewsbury to read his report, and he was in gleeful expectation that this arrogant luggard would get his comeuppance.

"So, it's a spell in the Tower for me, is it, sir?" Dair asked Shrewsbury with a deadpan expression as he nonchalantly sprawled out in a chair beside the secretary.

"What?" William Watkins blurted out. "*The Tower?*"

Dair lifted his black brows with mock surprise; and even this made him twinge. He had no idea eyebrows had so much feeling in them.

"Isn't that where fellows of noble birth are thrown who disturb the peace?"

"Is it?" William Watkins asked hopefully, looking expectantly at his employer.

"Don't be idiotic, Watkins!" Shrewsbury said dismissively, which instantly had the secretary's shoulders slumping. "Can't you see when you're being baited? A fearless, trained soldier like Fitzstuart, who's willing to risk life and limb for king and country, clapped up for a minor skirmish? What a complete waste of talent and energy! What we are going to do is put it about the Major is cooling his heels for a few weeks at His Majesty's pleasure. No questions will then be asked as to his whereabouts."

"And where will I be *about*, sir?" Dair asked.

"I have particular use for your—*skills*—on the Continent. Lisbon to be precise. But before we discuss what it is I want you to do while you're in Portugal, there is something I need you to do—*for me*—" He looked at his secretary, "—and for Mr. Watkins."

Dair met the old man's bespectacled eyes without a look at the secretary.

"Whatever it is, if it's for you, sir, consider it done."

"Good. I want you to forget the incident at George Romney's studio ever happened."

"Pardon, sir? Incident?"

"Yes. Very good," replied Shrewsbury with a grin. "That's precisely how you will react and respond if anyone asks you."

Dair glanced suspiciously at William Watkins. "At Romney's studio?"

The old man nodded.

"You know it was just a piece of tomfoolery with some pretty dancers, and a bit of a beat-up with the militia." Dair shrugged a shoulder. "Nothing to write home about, sir, and tame into the bargain."

"*Tomfoolery*? A bit of a—of a—*beat-up* with the-the militia? *Tame*?" William Watkins shrieked. "The damage alone to Mr. Romney's studio, I calculate to be in the hundreds of guineas! As for the great distress to—"

"Thank you, Watkins," Shrewsbury interrupted. "I understand your concerns, and I have your report—all twenty-five pages of it."

Dair pulled a face. "Only twenty-five pages. No embellishment then?"

"When His Lordship has had time to digest what I've written, he will see that your preposterous posturing—"

"Say that five times, Watkins. I'll wager you can't."

"—has caused immeasurable damage to the—"

"Yes. Yes. Hundreds of guineas' damage," Dair stated flatly, with an exaggerated sigh. "Send me the account. Romney should be thanking me. The write-up in the newssheets alone will increase his trade in portraits tenfold. Not to mention those just calling on him for a gawp at where the action took place; he might persuade them to buy something in oils, too."

"There will be no write-up in the newssheets," Shrewsbury said smoothly. "The reporter's notes were—confiscated."

"Burned, my lord," Watkins primly assured him. "I saw to it personally. And the editor was informed spirits were detected on the reporter's breath, so his verbal account cannot be relied upon either."

"Well, aren't you a treasure," Dair drawled sarcastically. "What did you offer of yourself to keep those dancers quiet?"

While Watkins was genuinely shocked, Shrewsbury chuckled.

"A secretary's loyalty only stretches so far—"

"—and his gadso not far enough."

Mr. Watkins had no idea what a gadso was, but when the old

man laughed with genuine good humor, he was convinced he was being slandered; with Shrewsbury's next comment he knew it was so, and his face flushed purple with embarrassment.

"That's not fair on Watkins, is it? There's no point in comparing a Billy goat to a prizewinning bull, is there? If you must know," the old man continued seriously, "your cadre of female admirers have been threatened with Newgate if they so much as squeak a word about last night. And Signora Baccelli will keep her pretty mouth shut, if she wishes Dorset's continued devotion. Romney will be compensated; several lucrative commissions sent his way to sweeten his silence; his wastrel brother's debts paid into the bargain. Mr. Cedric Pleasant has given his word never to speak of the incident, as has my grandson. There only remains for you to give me your word of honor to do the same. In fact, I want you to do more than that. I want you to claim to have been so drunk you have no recollection of the evening whatsoever."

Dair was annoyed by Shrewsbury's high-handedness for what he considered nothing more than three friends having an evening of fun and games. That it ended in a riot was not strictly his fault. That was the fault of the militia, and the Spymaster's orchestrated means of having him arrested. He had willingly fallen in with Shrewsbury's plans, was prepared to be thrown in the Tower, if necessary, or sent off on some God-forsaken mission abroad, all for the cause of furthering British war efforts against the Colonial rebels.

But what he was not prepared to do was be reprimanded for a harmless prank that had seen his friend Grasby the happiest he had been in years, and all because Weasel Watkins and Grasby's stiff-necked wife had taken offence.

He felt the sort of discomfort he had experienced on the numerous occasions he was brought before the headmaster at Harrow to be thrashed for some minor infraction. One glance at the secretary, and he knew that was precisely how Watkins wanted him to feel. He was sorely tempted to put a fist into Watkins' self-righteous smile. Instead, he lifted his heavy chin and his tone became belligerent.

"That could be difficult, sir. I mightn't be too bright, but I do have an exceptional memory... And I haven't yet been drunk enough not to remember the night before. Now Grasby, on the other hand, he was drunk, and shouldn't be held accountable, because I was the one who got him drunk. I'll take the blame for his actions, readily. But I'll not cower in a corner all because your lily-livered secretary and his nose-in-the-air sister took offence about something they should not have witnessed in the first place!"

Shrewsbury removed his eyeglasses, closed his eyes and pressed the bridge of his nose between thumb and forefinger. He sighed and said tiredly, "Watkins...be so good as to take yourself off."

"*Off*? But—My lord! I understand that as your secretary I should do as you request—But as Lady Grasby's *brother*, it is my duty as her representative to be present while you discuss the inexcusable infractions that occurred at Mr. Romney's house."

Shrewsbury opened his eyes and focused on his secretary, who stubbornly remained seated behind his desk.

"You may have such feelings, Mr. Watkins, but they are irrelevant. The day your sister married my grandson she became a Talbot and part of my family, and thus no longer your responsibility, whatever your strong brotherly feelings. But I have no objection to you seeking out Lady Grasby at this hour of the day. She may well be up and in need of your brotherly shoulder to cry on. No doubt there are plenty more tears to come," he murmured to himself as Watkins quietly closed the door to the book room.

"Aside from almost ruining my grandson's marriage," Shrewsbury continued, addressing Dair, as he leant back in his chair and crossed his hands over his round belly in its silken waistcoat. "And that it could take an immaculate conception for my granddaughter-in-law to conceive, as she won't have her husband within twenty feet of her person, what happened last night I couldn't care less about, but for one important fact. It is this fact that compels me to seek your word of honor as a gentleman that you will, from this day forward, not reveal to anyone, by word or gesture, that you remember a single detail of what occurred within the walls of George Romney's studio."

Dair sat up, all attention.

"Sir, if it means that much to you, then yes, I readily give you my word as an officer and a gentleman. If you wish me to say I was drunk beyond cognition, then so be it. But may I know why? Why the secrecy and the need for me to forget? If Lady Grasby wishes to blame someone, then that someone should be me—"

"Oh, she blames you, all right! And I do not blame *her* for that! You made a mockery of her husband, and in turn her marriage, and before witnesses. She is a prideful, vain creature and may never recover from the humiliation. She certainly will never forgive you. That does not bother me in the slightest. That you have forgotten the details of the entire evening will go a long way in appeasing her self-esteem. She may yet be able to look you in the eye with her head held high upon your return from Lisbon. An absence of some four or five weeks should also soothe Grasby's anger with you."

"For getting him drunk?"

Shrewsbury waved a dismissive hand.

"I wish I'd been there to see your play-acting for myself. I have no doubts Grasby enjoyed himself immensely, until he realized his wife and her brother had become part of the audience. A most unfortunate happenstance. But that's not what angered Grasby, or why I extracted your promise. Lady Grasby and Mr. Watkins were accompanied to the studio by my granddaughter, Grasby's younger sister. As to what she witnessed, and how much, I have yet to find out..."

TEN

DAIR'S EXPRESSION of polite interest told Shrewsbury everything he needed to know. Somewhere in the deep recesses of the Major's mind there was possibly a dim awareness that his best friend had a sister. Given time, he might even be able to recall in his mind's eye a picture of her as a child, when he had occasionally come to stay between school terms. That he had no idea as to her age and would not be able to point her out if ten young ladies of good family were lined up for his inspection, did not surprise Shrewsbury. In the Major's world, Aurora Christina Talbot did not exist. And why should she?

They would have been introduced at some stage when Rory left the schoolroom. They came from the same wider social circle, and their more intimate circle of friends and relations would have intersected from time to time when attending polite society engagements. This social interaction would have increased over the past six months since the Major resigned his army commission.

The most recent of these was the Easter weekend spent at the Duke of Roxton's Hampshire estate. He was grateful Rory had been invited to join the small parties made up of people her own age when they played at charades, picnicked by the lake, attended evening music recitals, and danced at the gala ball. And it was on the dance floor where a more intimate social interaction between eligible young men and women occurred; a chance to look each other over without a chaperone breathing down the back of a girl's neck.

But Rory could not dance. So the Duchess of Roxton gave her an excellent vantage point to watch the dancing, and by association, the guests saw that his granddaughter was a favored guest. And those doyens of Polite Society, who put great value on such things, were politely reminded of Rory's place within it, that she was the grand-daughter of the Earl of Shrewsbury.

There were occasions when unsuspecting guests wondered aloud why such a pretty little thing was not married, and needed no answer when Rory rose to her feet with the aid of her stick. The look of abject embarrassment, often pity, that crossed these same puzzled powdered faces when his granddaughter limped off—she trans-forming in their eyes into a wholly different and undesirable being because of her uneven gait—made him want to pummel to dust each and every one of them.

But what broke his heart, and never failed to bring tears to his eyes, was the never-ending sparkle in her blue eyes, blue eyes just like his, of wonder and excitement for the world around her. This was never more evident while she watched the country dancing, cheeks flushed with the joy of living. It was as if she were taking every step with the dancing couples. He would have given anything and every-thing to be able to make that happen for her...

"Sir...? My lord? Lord Shrewsbury?"

It was Dair, on his feet, at Shrewsbury's desk. The old man looked to have taken ill, such was the paleness to his cheeks and the glassiness to his eyes. But just as quickly, he snapped to his old self and waved Dair away.

"I want my granddaughter to forget last night ever happened," Shrewsbury snapped without preamble. His inability to offer Rory a cure for her physical infirmity always made him feel frustratingly inadequate. "I pray that in time it will become nothing more than a distant nightmare. And it must have been a nightmare for a carefully nurtured female who has never stepped outside this house without a chaperone and never been left alone in the company of a man who is not her brother or her grandfather, *ever*. She is unmarried and likely to stay that way after witnessing your disgusting and unsavory behavior!"

"I beg your pardon, sir?" Dair asked with civility, racking his brain to make sense of the old man's emotionally charged rant, when not ten minutes earlier he had been having a chuckle about the whole episode. "Aside from Lady Grasby, who was an unintended witness to our—um—shenanigans, there was no other female that—"

"Goddammit Fitzstuart! My granddaughter was witness to the whole sordid episode! And from what Lady Grasby has been weeping into her pillow, it sounds as if she and my granddaughter were subjected to a scene ripped straight from the pages of a bacchanalian orgy!"

In frustration, the old man shoved aside the papers in front of him, as if wanting to distance himself from the event and the Major.

"Fooling about for the admiration of sylph-like dancers and their ilk, I couldn't care less about. How many you bed and how often is your business, and I say good luck to you! You play a dangerous game for your country, and the stakes are impossibly high, so you deserve to play equally as hard. But... There are times—*this time*—when such behavior goes beyond the pale. My granddaughter, Grasby's little sister, is an innocent, and she was there, damn you!"

"I understand, sir. You don't have to tell me twice," Dair said in a rush, feeling uncomfortably warm under his stock. "You can't think I would have carried on the way I did, would have allowed Grasby to compromise himself, if I'd had an inkling that she—that my best friend's sister—would be a witness? My word on it, sir!"

Shrewsbury nodded, calmer, hearing the sincerity in the young man's voice.

"I suppose not... You were not to know... It's just that her presence, it alters the entire episode, doesn't it?" He cocked an eyebrow. "I wonder if you would have acted any differently knowing Lady Grasby and Mr. Watkins were part of your audience?"

Dair could not hide his grin.

"I did know, sir."

This elicited a reluctant laugh from the old man.

"Almost makes me wish I'd been a flea in Watkins' wig, just to see Her Ladyship's face. Now *that* is between you and me and no other." He pushed back his chair. "So, when next you see my granddaughter, you will act as if last night never occurred; feign complete ignorance. She will be comfortable then—we all will." He came around the desk. "And that goes for Grasby and anyone else who mentions Romney's studio or asks a question. You were too drunk and have no recollection of events. You're a good actor. If anyone can convince my grandchildren, you can."

"And Watkins? What about him?"

"Mr. Watkins will do as he is told. And he knows what's at stake. He wants his sister to give the earldom of Shrewsbury an heir as much as I do. It will cement his place in the family. Better to be thought of as uncle to an earl than remembered as the grandson of a Billingsgate fishmonger." When Dair snorted his skepticism, Shrewsbury smiled. "All very well for you not to care, you've got royal Stuart blood in your veins, not estuary water like the Watkins. Now put on a good show and you'll be believed. My granddaughter, for all her youth and inexperience, has a keen mind and an even keener eye; comes from all that sitting about observing people. She'll see through the façade if you don't make yourself believe it, too." He put out his hand to Dair. "I'm relying on you, my boy."

"You can, sir," Dair replied, taking the old man's hand in a firm grip. He was still trying to put a face and a name together for Grasby's sister and coming up blank. Ultimately, that was unimportant. He had given his word, and to Shrewsbury, the last man in this world he would ever want to disappoint. "I won't let you down. My word on it."

Shrewsbury smiled, mind at ease. "You haven't yet... Now let me have a pitcher of ale fetched, and we'll drink it on the terrace and take a walk in the garden. Fresh air helps clear the mind, and to focus it. There's still much I need to tell you before you set sail for Lisbon—"

"Grand! Grand? The most wonderful thing has happened! Crawford was the first to make the discovery! It's just like the one in the book. Oh, you must come to the Pinery and see it for yourself!

Oh! Do-do forgive me. I thought you were alone. Crawford said your guests had gone..."

"Rory. Come in! Come in, my dear!" Shrewsbury coaxed as his granddaughter took a step backward, to retreat from the room. "I know you've been introduced before today, but I shall do the honors again, because introductions at a function, where there is always a crush of persons filling up a drawing room, is no introduction at all, really, is it? This is Major Lord Fitzstuart, your godmother's cousin; Grasby's friend Dair from his Harrow days. Major, this is my grand-daughter, Aurora Talbot."

The only sound in the room was the thud of Rory's book hitting the floor.

ELEVEN

SPEECHLESS, Rory watched Dair slowly retrieve her book. Her eyes did not leave him for a moment. He went to his haunches to collect *A General Treatise of Husbandry and Gardening* by Richard Bradley, then straightened to his full height, leaving her eyes level with the engraved silver buttons on his black linen frock coat. For some inexplicable reason, fully clothed he looked taller and much wider. He completely blocked her view of her grandfather's desk.

He made her a slight bow of acquaintance, murmured a platitude that the pleasure was all his, and held out the book; and all this without making eye contact. She was so happy to see him again that the coldness in his manner and tone did not immediately register. She was also too preoccupied with wondering if he would notice she was not wearing panniers with her petticoats, something she avoided when at home, and if there was dirt smudged on her cheek.

She had remembered to remove her gardening gloves, so her hands were clean, but her flimsy white apron over her white muslin gown (not the most practical of colors to go trowelling in amongst the compost) was also smudged with dirt. She had not meant to go to the Pinery after nuncheon, because she had to ready herself for the excursion to the theater. But the gardener had sent word of the most marvelous news, of an emerging pineapple flower, and so she just had to see it for herself there and then.

When her grandfather gently reminded her to take her book, that the Major was still holding it, she was suddenly shy at forgetting her manners. She realized, too, that she was rudely staring at the front of his broad chest and had not looked up at his face. Yet, when she went to take her book, she noticed the state of his thumb. The skin was ragged and bloody at the knuckle.

Her concern for his well-being far outweighed her embarrassment and uncertainty. Without permission, she gently turned over his right hand and saw that the rest of his knuckles were similarly raw, and there was bruising, too. She was sure his fingers were swollen. What she failed to notice was that the moment she touched his bruised flesh, he reacted, his grip on Bradley's treatise tightening, so much so that she could not have pried the book out from between his fingers had she used both hands and all her force to do so.

"You took a dreadful beating," she whispered. "I'm afraid I wasn't brave at all. I fainted with your first blow..."

With her fingers still resting on the back of his hand, she lifted her gaze from his injuries to his chin and then to his mouth. Here she paused, blue eyes widening with concern at the split in his lip. She then looked up into his eyes. The bruising to his face caused an involuntary intake of breath.

"I hope—I hope you took something to ease the pain. You really ought to apply a raw steak to that eye, to bring out the bruising, and so your lip doesn't scar, there is a remedy—"

"Thank you, my dear," Lord Shrewsbury interrupted gently and removed the book from between Dair's fingers. "I'm sure the Major has done all he can for the time being."

"Of course. Of course," Rory murmured with a nod, again embarrassed to have forgotten her manners, and for speaking so frankly.

Coming to a sense of her surroundings, she discovered the Major no longer had her book and that she was holding his hand. She instantly let go and whipped her fingers to the middle of her back to clutch at the bow that tied on her gossamer apron. Her right hand tightened about the carved ivory handle of her walking stick because she had the sensation of swaying, as if aboard a ship in rough seas.

"Please excuse me, Miss Talbot," Dair said dully. "I know the way to the terrace, sir. I'll see you there at your convenience."

He gave a small nod, stepped past Rory, and left the room.

She watched him go, a strange lump forming in her throat. She was all at sea. She had no idea what had just happened, but it left her desolate.

Why did he not know her? Neither of them needed to speak of the particulars of the previous evening, but there was no need for him to pretend nothing at all had occurred. He had given her an address in Chelsea. They had kissed! Perhaps it was the presence of her grandfather that made him stilted and cold? But he could have winked down at her, to let her know he was well aware of her existence. She would never have betrayed him.

And then she had a sudden awful thought that could account for his behavior. It was not coldness, it was embarrassment, and an awkward embarrassment she had encountered many times before but which she ignored because she could not alter herself.

Last night he had not seen her walk. Now he had. And now he knew her for a cripple. She could not blame him for being surprised by such a discovery. But did he now disdain her because she had such an imperfection? His features had not changed. He had not shown a disgust of her or worn an expression of pity. In fact, he could have been a brick wall such was his lack of emotion. Something, call it intuition, but something deep within her told her his coldness in manner, more correctly a lack of any reaction whatsoever, was not because he was being judgmental. Whatever his foibles, she did not think intolerance one of them. Then why was he like stone?

Her grandfather gave her the answer, and his explanation left her more forlorn than she thought possible. Had the Major looked upon her with disgust, that was at least a show of some emotion, and she could then have dismissed him as unworthy of her.

With her book pressed to his chest, Lord Shrewsbury put an arm about Rory's shoulders and kissed her temple.

"There. That was not so difficult, now was it, my darling? Did I not tell you and Drusilla the Major was so drunk last night he was unlikely to remember a single detail of what happened? And I was right. He doesn't. No recollection of events past the point of trespassing into Romney's studio. It seems he and your brother and Mr. Pleasant polished off a goodly number of bottles of claret before the start of their mischief-making. Blind drunk, the three of them. We ought to forgive them their disgrace, don't you think? Particularly the Major. Any man, particularly a young man, who fights as bravely for his country as he has deserves to play just as hard. The horrors of combat can greatly affect a man. Even a strong-minded man like the Major must have his dark moments. A bit of drunken tomfoolery allows such men to forget those moments, however briefly."

He kissed her again and hugged her to his side, adding with real regret, "What a piece of rotten luck for the three of them that your small party happened to pay a visit on Romney at the same time. All three are, when not drunk to dissipation, true gentlemen and are abjectly apologetic to have caused you and Drusilla the slightest distress. If it is acceptable to you, I will not have them apologize in person, it will only further distress your sister-in-law. The sooner the entire episode is behind us, the better. Don't you agree, my dear?"

Rory nodded, not entirely convinced that her brother and his friends were so drunk as to have lost all memory of their behavior, particularly Mr. Cedric Pleasant, who was perfectly lucid and clothed the entire time. Her brother was drunk, that was true, but the Major? If she detected spirits on his breath, it was not so marked as for her to think him drunk, and she had not tasted alcohol on his tongue...

Instantly, heat flooded her face at the remembrance of his deep kiss. If he went about kissing females unknown to him in a way that made them melt against him, what must his kisses be like for females he truly cared about?

"Are you perfectly well, Rory?" Lord Shrewsbury asked, arm still about her shoulders. He had felt her sway and shiver. "You told me at breakfast you did not suffer any nightmares, and you would tell me if there were anything else troubling you...?"

She forced a smile and took back her book. "Yes. Of course, Grand. I slept well indeed."

"Shall I come to the Pinery to see your great surprise?"

"No. No, Grand. The Major—Lord Fitzstuart is waiting for you on the terrace. The surprise can wait. Besides, I must change into my outfit for the theater…"

"We have been looking forward to this afternoon for some time, have we not? And I have an added surprise for you. Your godmother has invited us to visit her box."

"Oh? How-how lovely. I shall enjoy discussing the play with Mme la Duchesse."

Shrewsbury walked Rory from the book room and through the anteroom to the long gallery, his conversation all about the upcoming visit to Drury Lane to see Sheridan's *School for Scandal*. They stopped before a small closet with a half door, inside which was a bench with a velvet cushion upon it. Running vertically through the closet was a silken rope that threaded through a system of pulleys attached top and bottom. This allowed the closet, which was in fact a lifting chair, to be raised and lowered with ease by its occupant.

Shrewsbury had the lifting chair installed fifteen years ago, patterned on the one in the French king's private apartments at Fontainebleau. As a child she had been required to call on a footman to carry her up and down the broad staircase, with its many steps twisting up through the center of the Dutch house. Seated on the velvet cushion, Rory could pull herself up and down with ease to the first floor where her rooms were located. Shrewsbury could still recall the look of absolute delight on her little face when she took her first ride in the lifting chair, her brother racing up the staircase to try and beat her to the first floor. It was a game they never tired of, even now.

Two footmen stood sentry either side of the lifting chair, and one opened the half door for Rory, but before she could step inside, Shrewsbury put his hand over hers.

"Rory. My dear. I do not want you to have to recall particulars of last night that might distress you, but Mr. Watkins told me he found you crumpled in a gap at the back of the stage—that you had fainted…"

"Yes. Yes, he did. I did."

"Do you remember how you got there, or why you fainted?"

"I cannot—I cannot recall the precise moment, no..."

"Mr. Watkins has written up a report of the evening—"

"A-a report? Why?"

"Please. Do not alarm yourself. None shall read it but me. And if in the meantime if you do recall any particulars... I hope you will confide in me..."

Rory hesitated, then slowly met her grandfather's blue eyes. She smiled weakly.

"Of course, Grand."

LORD SHREWSBURY watched the chair ascend, Rory waving to him, he smiling and waving back. His granddaughter's hesitation to respond to his questions, the way she avoided his gaze, her smile that was not a genuine smile, were all signs of concealment. He had not been a spy for His Majesty for as long as he had without knowing she was hiding something from him. Knowing Rory as he did, she would only withhold the truth to protect another. He suspected that other was her brother, Harvel, Lord Grasby.

He was fond of Grasby, who was his heir, but it was Rory he loved. From him she had inherited the Talbot blue eyes and quiet determination, and from her mother a sweet nature and delicate Nordic features. Shrewsbury had despised the children's mother, his daughter-in-law Christina, with every fiber of his noble being. She had brought out the worst in him in every conceivable way. And she had abandoned her family in their hour of most need.

Unable to come to grips with her baby's deformity, she threw herself off a balcony. The world was told Christina had died in childbed. Her husband—Rory's father—was inconsolable at losing his wife and drowned himself. Thus leaving the care of a little boy of five and a newborn to their grandfather.

One day he had made an impromptu visit to the nursery, to discover his little grandson huddled in a dusty corner, being beaten with rushes. With his thin body, he was doing his best to shield his year-old baby sister, who was screaming uncontrollably. An iron shoe was clamped about her twisted little foot and secured with iron rods and bolts just below her chubby knee, forcing it into the correct alignment. Her brother had been attempting to remove this device of correction, and for his compassion had got a beating that broke the skin on his back.

That very day, Shrewsbury took control of every aspect of the children's lives. New servants, new tutors, new, bright surroundings. No more beatings, no more iron shoes or clamps and talk of "curing the cripple" was forbidden. He had agents scour the Continent for a physician able to treat his baby granddaughter's deformity and found one in Professor Petrus Camper in Amsterdam.

An expert in many fields, Camper was also an expert on feet. And while unable to cure Rory's club foot, he gave Shrewsbury the necessary assurances Rory was normal in every other way. From that day forward, brother and sister grew up inseparable. Grasby was his sister's champion, and Rory her brother's greatest supporter and confidant.

So, it was easy for Shrewsbury to believe the siblings would protect each other, even lie for one another; that Rory would keep from him certain particulars of events at Romney's studio all to shield Grasby. He would not press her for information. He would find out in other ways. Watkins' report would be a start. Having those who were present questioned would provide a more complete picture. Writing out his instructions to trusted agents could be postponed until tomorrow morning. The Major was waiting for him. Tonight, he meant to set aside the troubles of the kingdom, and more importantly, within his own family, and spend a leisurely evening in the company of his granddaughter. Yet, he could not shake the belief that Rory had not been honest with him—that she had felt the need to lie, and that troubled him more than he cared to admit.

TWELVE

RORY HAD LIED. And she had never lied to her grandfather before. It made her heavy of heart. She had lied, not to protect her brother, but to protect Major Lord Fitzstuart. If the Major had no recollection of the night before, more precisely his encounter with her, then what was the sense in her recalling the incident, and to her shame? What purpose would it serve for her grandfather to know the truth? It would only cause him great distress. And for the Major to be prompted to remember an episode he clearly couldn't care less about and, had he been sober, would not have engaged with her, was a humiliation she could not endure.

She did not blame the Major for his lack of memory. For him the encounter was just one of many; *she* just a number in a long line of countless females with whom he had trifled with over the years. *Trifled with...* What an inane expression! In her case, it was apt. But she was certain Major Lord Fitzstuart had done a great deal more than *trifle with* other females.

All she had done was engage in a brief kiss. A kiss that was not worth his remembrance. But to her, not only was that kiss a moment to treasure, but the entire evening had also been so exciting she had committed it to memory. Such an encounter was never likely to happen again, which simply underscored her sheltered existence. She looked down at the book in her hand. In her day-to-day life she was a crippled spinster whose prime interest was the nurturing and cultivation of the pineapple.

Distracted with her thoughts, she handed her walking stick to her maid without seeing her and climbed up on the window seat with its view of the formal gardens. Bradley's treatise on gardening she dropped on the rug, all the joy of her discovery overridden by her malaise. Her head ached and she felt hot, and yet strangely cold. Perhaps she was coming down with a fever? The studio had been without heat and she without her cloak... But in his arms, she had not felt cold at all; quite the opposite...

She found her woolen shawl at her feet and went to put it about her shoulders, when her maid, Edith, did this for her.

"You look worn to threads! Too much time spent in the heat of that Pinery," the older woman castigated her lovingly, fussing with the shawl. "And after the upset last night, I dare say it's all added to the extra color in your cheeks. Now you sit there nice and quiet, and I'll have a cup of tea fetched. You have time for a cup before you change for the theater. But first let me remove your shoes..."

Rory nodded, hugging one of the tapestry cushions to her as she snuggled deeper into the pillows at her back. As she always did, Edith removed the shoe from Rory's right foot first.

Just like the pretty shoes worn by countless young ladies, Rory's were often covered in material that matched her gowns. But unlike most shoes, which had identical lasts, Rory's were made to fit her left and her right foot individually. A master cordwainer, recommended by Professor Camper, had been making her shoes since she was a little girl. He took casts in plaster of Paris and made shoes that conformed to the twisted shape of her right foot; except for mules, she wore the latest fashionable footwear.

The shoes Edith held, as she covered Rory's stockinged feet with her white muslin petticoats, were purple satin slippers with low heels of white leather. Rory stared at the shoes and swallowed back tears. She barely heard Edith tell her to have a little doze while she fetched the tea, and turned her face to the window as the heavy curtains were drawn across the window seat. Snug in her little corner, it was only then that she realized tears were sliding down her flushed cheeks.

Foolish! Stupid! Ridiculous creature! she castigated herself. *Stop feeling sorry for yourself this instant! Crying for no good reason. If you must shed tears, then do so for not telling Grand the truth. So last night was the most exciting night of your uneventful life? Be thankful it happened at all. You now have a memory to keep, and it is yours alone to cherish...*

"Rory? Rory? Are you there? May I come in?"

Rory dashed both hands over her damp cheeks just as the curtains parted and Grasby stuck his head between the hanging velvet. He looked sheepish, and was in undress, having shrugged a silk banyan over white shirt and brown velvet breeches; a matching silk turban covered his short cropped blond hair.

Rory nodded and gathered up her white muslin petticoats, sitting up against the cushions to give her brother space on the window seat's tapestry cushion. He needed no further invitation and eagerly scrambled to join her, quickly closing the curtains again, as if hiding them away from the rest of the world. For Grasby, he couldn't think of a more comforting place to lick his wounds.

"Remember when we'd hide in Grand's book room?" he said with genuine affection, back up against the wooden paneling. Following his sister's lead, he wrapped his arms about a tapestry cushion and hugged it to his chest. He was already starting to feel better. "We would giggle and whisper to each other to be quiet. Grand never said a word. He pretended he didn't know we were there behind the curtains! Even when he had meetings with those long-nosed fellows from the Foreign Department who came and went with all those papers. I don't think we ever fooled him, do you?"

Rory shook her head. "No. Not once." She smiled at a memory. "There was that time you tumbled off the seat and onto the carpet in full view of Grand and his visitors. They did not break sentence and continued on with their meeting as if nothing was untoward. Even when I had to show myself to help haul you back up behind the curtain, not one of them said *boo*."

Grasby smiled crookedly. "I didn't fall, Rory. You pushed me out."

Rory widened her blue eyes. "Did I?"

"Yes, you did! Don't think you can pretend innocence. I know you better than that!"

They both laughed and then immediately fell into an awkward silence. Rory returned to gazing out the window, oblivious to the view of blue sky, green velvet lawns and a topiary garden that stretched to the river. Grasby anxiously watched her. He saw her flushed cheeks were wet and knew she was upset. It wasn't difficult to figure out why. Despite his own sad and sorry state of affairs pressing down upon him, it said much for his brotherly devotion that he pushed those aside, concern for his sister's well-being overriding all else. Still, he avoided the topic uppermost in their minds for a little longer, enjoying just sitting with her, the world shut out.

"I thought I'd be turned away at your door; that you'd be dressing for the theater," he said in a rallying tone. "Whenever Silla makes ready for an outing, particularly if she knows important people will be in attendance—whoever they are, but Silla knows 'em! —her dressing begins straight after nuncheon. I dare not interrupt. Not that I would. After nuncheon I prefer a nap. I still manage to dress in half the time. I daresay that's because I don't have to be laced and buckled into panniers..."

"Edith is fetching tea... Then I'll dress..."

"Yes. I asked her to fetch me a cup, too. Have you decided on a gown? Didn't I hear you tell Silla you were wearing the purple silk brocade worked with multi-colored flowers—"

"I know I've been boring you and Grand to frustration with my enthusiasm for Sheridan's new play, and what I'd wear on the night."

"You never bore us, Rory, and Silla's been just as enthusiastic. Though... I suspect it was for the spectacle rather than the play itself. She still hadn't made up her mind on what gown to wear as late as yesterday..." He looked suddenly embarrassed. "But that's no longer a dilemma for her. She says she is too humiliated to attend Drury Lane; and never again in my company... Rory? Rory, did you hear me? Silla's staying home..."

Rory reluctantly looked away from the view. She had just caught sight of her grandfather and Major Lord Fitzstuart. They had strolled out of the shadows into the sunshine on the terrace, drinking ale from silver tumblers. Ale consumed, a footman took away the tumblers and the two men stepped off the terrace onto the gravel path. They were side-by-side, but the Major being so much taller than her grandfather had respectfully dipped his right shoulder, hands clasped lightly behind his back, an ear to the old man's conversation.

"What is it? What's the matter, Harvel? You look so tired. Did you not sleep at all last night?"

"Not a wink," he confessed. "The chaise in my dressing room is lumpy, and the fire was left to die, so I froze." He shrugged. "Not the servants' fault. How were they to know I'd be in there all night? Still... Any lackey with half a brain could see how matters stood. I only had to poke my head into Silla's dressing room, and she threw a Meissen dog at my head. Can you believe that? She assaulted me, *her husband*, with porcelain!"

"Did it strike you?"

"No. Missed. Nice figurine, too. Gift for her birthday... She's got a good arm on her, Silla. Comes from being a keen archer. Thank God she didn't have her bow and quiver handy."

"Oh, Harvel! You poor lamb. Silla *will* forgive you... But best not to show yourself at her rooms for the next little while... She's had an upset."

"*She's* had an upset?" Grasby puffed out his cheeks, indignant. "Tell me one person who hasn't! I don't mind saying that my self-esteem is in shreds. Never more embarrassed in all my days as I was last night, being pounced on by the militia as if I were a common criminal! Damned cheek."

Despite her brother looking miserable, Rory couldn't help giggling. She put out her hand to him in sympathy. "But what were the soldiers to think when you ran across the studio without your clothes?"

"I was supposed to make for a door, but with Dair taking on the entire militia, and blows being exchanged left and right, I was disorientated. Turned in the wrong direction. An easy mistake to make—"

"Oh, yes. I agree."

"—so, there was nothing for it but to high-tail it to the open window," Grasby continued.

His relief at being able to finally tell his side of the story, and to such a sympathetic ear, outweighed his consideration for the fact his conversation was wholly unacceptable for the ears of his younger sister.

"I had almost made it to freedom, too, when the constabulary was alerted to my escape, and two of 'em threw me to the ground! Bones could have been broken! Mine! As if it wasn't galling enough to try and hide my-my *vulnerabilities* with one hand while making a dash across open space, a big brute sits on m'chest, leaving me no opportunity to cover anything at all! I tell you, Rory, if not for that brute, and me making a turnip of myself, Silla wouldn't have recognized me at all!"

"Oh?" Rory was all ears and wide-eyed attention. "But surely wives can distinguish their husbands without their clothes?"

"Much you know! Wives don't *look*. But I have this blasted birthmark, and when she saw *it*, she fainted dead to the floor! I—"

Suddenly, Grasby swallowed his words, realizing he had not only contradicted himself but also that they were discussing a topic grossly unsuitable for the fairer sex, and his audience was his little sister. He was so used to confiding in her, and she had always listened to his troubles, that no topic, until that moment, had been off-limits between them.

THIRTEEN

Grasby had come to her rooms to apologize for his gauche conduct, and instead had merely confirmed that he was no gentleman. He was in every sense what Silla had branded him: An unmitigated, unfeeling ass! Yet, before he could construct a sentence of apology that would convey how deeply remorseful he was for his behavior, Rory further tied his tongue in knots with an acute observation that also set his ears aflame.

"Do you mean wives don't look because they choose not to and wish to be kept in ignorance? Or do you mean a wife merely *pretends* not to look at her husband unclothed because it is considered ill-mannered of her to do so? Because I cannot believe a wife would choose to be kept in ignorance, but as it is ill-mannered to stare in any social situation, I can readily believe the latter."

She wrinkled her nose in thought.

"That would explain why, when this topic is raised in conversation by wives at social gatherings, the gentlemen present are well out of earshot. There is a good deal of giggling behind open fans, about dimensions and estimates. And Lady Hibbert-Baker keeps a little betting book."

Grasby sat bolt upright. His face reflected his feelings. He was appalled and flabbergasted in equal measure. His voice pitched higher than usual.

"Estimates? Dimensions? A *betting* book? I don't believe you! You're fibbing!"

"What reason have I to fib?" Rory argued, indignant. "Besides, I don't understand the half of what they are giggling about."

"No. No, you wouldn't," Grasby readily agreed with a grumble.

"I thought gentlemen were constantly making wagers about females?"

"But not about one's *wife*. Never about one's wife, or sister, or mother, for that fact. A man is not a gentleman if he did. It's bad form and not tolerated at the club to mention—"

"—but perfectly acceptable to mention one's mistress?"

"That's a different matter entirely!"

"How so? They are females, too. And whatever Society cares to brand them, they remain females with hearts and minds, desires and dreams..."

Grasby was unable to construct an intelligent rebuttal to his sister's acute observation, so burst out with frustration, "One visit to Romney's studio and you're suddenly an expert on fallen women!"

Rory smiled, blue eyes full of mischief. "Oh? But I thought they were Opera dancers..."

"They are Opera dancers but—"

"Silly. Of course they are not only dancers. Particularly Signora Baccelli. Everyone knows she is the Duke of Dorset's mistress, even gilded caged birds such as me. I just never thought I would meet a nobleman's mistress. It was such an enlivening experience... By the bye, when males refer to females as *wagtails and canary birds*, are such ornithological terms euphemisms for *whore*?"

"Stap m'vitals, Rory! Silla is right. I'm not only the most damnably bad husband, but I am also a wretchedly poor brother. You shouldn't know about such things as wagtails and canary birds or be listening to those hen-witted wives and their-their—*trumpery*."

"Easier said than done when they loudly discuss a particular wager as if I am not there at all."

"Here was I, thinking you were safe at these tea parties. Silla has the gall to accuse me of being the worse sort of brother, and she's taking my sister to dens of iniquity. I'll have a word with her—"

"You can't. She isn't talking to you, remember? Besides, I don't believe she has any idea what these wives twitter on about behind their fans. She's just not curious."

"Curious? That's one word for it. Eavesdropper is another." Rory pouted.

"How can I not be when I am practically the only one at these tea parties who is unmarried? I am too old to be herded about with girls enjoying their first season, and far too young to sit with the pompous spinsters sporting ear-trumpets. And because Silla is kind enough to take me with her when she goes calling, her friends and acquaintances forget I am unmarried." She glanced at her brother and said with a shrug as she pulled the woolen shawl closer about her, "And once I am seated, it is not a straightforward thing for me to remove myself from the hearing of such conversations. I don't like to cause a fuss, and my stick—" She forced a smile. "Why is it that some people think that if you have a limp, you must also be deaf? It is all so terribly embarrassing for the person shouting at me to be told by our hostess that just because I walk crookedly, doesn't mean I don't have two perfectly working ears!"

"Rory—forgive me. I didn't think..."

"Oh, don't upset yourself on my account. They don't mean to be rude, and I have grown accustomed to such assumptions."

"That's magnanimous of you. Still, to be forced to listen to such distasteful conversations goes beyond the pale. And those wives call themselves respectable. Ha!"

"Oh, but they are. It's a harmless piece of funning, in its own way." She smiled cheekily. "As harmless, perhaps, as pretending to be an American Indian for a troupe of dancing girls." When her brother covered his face with his hands, shame-faced, she added seriously, "I am unharmed and uncorrupted by the incident, so no hurt was done. And it helped clear up one matter that had been puzzling me..."

"Puzzling you?"

"Yes. The silly wagers written up in Lady Hibbert-Baker's betting book... I had an exceptionally limited knowledge of what a gentleman looked like without his clothes, all guesswork. But after last night I no longer—"

"*Good Lord.* I've corrupted my own sister." Grasby groaned, a hand to his brow, as if shielding his eyes and himself from any further frank confessions. "Hang me now!"

"To tell a truth," she said quietly, leaning into him and ignoring his melodramatic outburst, "I was more shocked to discover men have hair here." She placed a hand to her décolletage. "I was not prepared for that at all."

"Please, Rory! No more," Grasby begged, and dropped his head into the tapestry cushion. After a few seconds, he sat up again. Setting his turban to rights, he let out a great sigh. "It is times such as these that I do sincerely wish we had not been orphaned. Only a mother is equipped to answer her daughter's questions."

"Silla confided that Mrs. Watkins told her absolutely *nothing* about *anything*."

"Well, that's at least *something*." He peered keenly at his sister. "Is that all Silla told you?"

"Most decidedly. Silla confided in me in a moment of weakness. I think she did so to warn me off, should I try to take her into my confidence, to seek answers to intimate questions she was not prepared to answer."

He sighed his relief. But no sooner did he allow his shoulders to ease than he had a sudden thought.

"I don't—Rory... I don't have a hairy chest..."

"No. No, you do not..."

Grasby took a moment to digest this. And in that moment, Rory blushed scarlet. He knew instantly whom she had been describing. It turned his frown of puzzlement into one of suppressed anger, and he gritted his teeth.

"Watkins said he found you unconscious behind the stage!" he said flatly, fighting to master his emotions. "He intimated you were back there with Fitzstuart for some time—*alone*. I threatened to knock his teeth out if he ever mentioned that circumstance again.

Tell me the truth, Aurora. Were you alone backstage with Dair Fitzstuart?"

Her brother had only ever called her by her full name once, many years ago, and she could not recall there and then why he had done so, only that he had been furious with her—as furious as he was now.

Oh dear, she was about to lie for a second time in as many hours, and she felt tears behind her eyes. But she would not give up the memory of the kiss exchanged with the Major. If she did, the kiss would be construed by others as something sordid and undignified, something of which to be ashamed. She was not ashamed, and regardless of how the Major and others viewed that brief intimate moment, she was intent on preserving the whimsy that he had enjoyed their kiss just as much as she.

"There is nothing to tell, Harvel. I said the same to Grand. I fainted at the first drop of blood. I have no stomach for men hitting each other. I am grateful to Mr. Watkins for carrying me to safety. It was truly frightening."

"Frightening? I don't doubt it! You should never have been subjected to such an appalling ordeal. Never." Still furious, Grasby hit the painted sill with the side of his fist. "A curse on Dair, always playing the hero! Always getting himself into some scrape that has him beaten up at best, and almost killed at worse! Sometimes I wonder why I tolerate his damned heroics. *Bloody idiot...* Rory, he's my best friend, but you are my sister, and if I thought he had taken advantage of you—touched as much as a hair on your head—that would be an end to our friendship. I'd defend your honor; the consequences be damned."

"I know that, Harvel," Rory replied quietly. "I also know the consequences of such an encounter would be one-sided. He is a soldier; you are not. He has been trained to kill; you could not. And he would kill you..."

As if to underscore the truth of her statement, there was a burst of harsh laughter from the garden. Rory pressed her forehead to the windowpane and saw the subject of their discussion.

The Major had a firm buttock propped on a low stone wall, long booted leg swinging as he leaned into a lighted taper, held out to him by a footman, to bring his cheroot to life. Her grandfather was standing next to him holding a small porcelain basket. She knew the container. It held crumbs for the school of carp that lived in the pond surrounding a central fountain of leaping dolphins. The water to the fountain had been turned off to allow for routine cleaning, which was why their conversation, if not their words, was audible. The Major exhaled a stream of smoke into the blue sky and said something which made her grandfather laugh and shake his head.

Brother and sister observed the two men in silence, Grasby sitting back once his grandfather handed off the porcelain basket to a lackey to resume his stroll with Dair amongst the topiary.

"Forgive me, sugarplum," he said quietly, calling Rory by an old nursery nickname. "I have shamed myself doubly. Last night I acted the complete lunatic and today I'm swearing my head off. I am a disgrace and have no excuse."

Rory slid down the window seat to embrace him.

"You are the best brother in the whole known world, and I would not trade you for anyone. Yesterday I would not have thought you capable of swearing, least of all of running about an artist's studio naked, and you surprised me by doing both! Of course, such behavior behooves me to remove your halo and replace it with little horns and a forked tail. But I shan't love you any the less."

He shook his head with a smile, realizing she was trying to make light of his gross transgressions for his benefit, but he saw no humor in his ungentlemanly conduct. He pulled back to look in her blue eyes.

"Thank you. I deserve to have my halo confiscated. My brother-in-law now thinks me a lascivious freak. My grandfather shakes his head with disappointment, and my wife...? Silla is so disgusted by my behavior she wants nothing more to do with me. She blames Dair and demands I cut the connection. That's her stipulation for a reconciliation between us."

"But... Surely, she can see that the three of you were merely funning. There was no real harm done. And if we—Silla, Mr. Watkins, and I—had not happened upon your mischief-making, then she would have been none the wiser to it."

Grasby huffed and rolled his eyes.

"She's not as charitable with her forgiveness as you. She has never approved of Dair, though she cannot give me a reasonable explanation for her dislike. I had no idea just how much, until his return from the fighting in the Americas. This last six months she has taken every opportunity to revile him, and now her attitude has become something of an embarrassment. You're right. It was just a piece of giddiness. And there was never any danger of me being unfaithful. So I told Silla. But will she listen to reason? No. She merely becomes hysterical and throws things at me! I told her she must accept my friends as they are. I will not give them up. Dair Fitzstuart is my best friend."

"But Silla is your wife, Harvel."

"So you see my dilemma. She must be made to understand. I will not be swayed. Until she does, we will remain estranged."

"Then we had best put our heads together to find a resolution acceptable to you both," Rory replied, glad the focus of their conversation had shifted away from her involvement in the Romney studio raid, yet disturbed that her brother's marriage was in such strife.

"And what better way to do so, than over a cup of tea?" she added in a much brighter tone, for the benefit of her maid who had made her presence felt with a slight clearing of her throat. "I'll pour, Edith. Thank you."

Edith had gently parted the curtains, and was flanked by two upstairs maids, one with the tray of tea things, the other with the silver teapot and its warming stand.

Grasby continued to brood, staring out the window while his sister fussed with the tea things. He watched his grandfather and his best friend stop at an intersection of paths. Here the old man counted off using his forefinger and fingertips, Dair nodding in response as he drew on his cheroot. He remembered Dair telling him once that a soldier smoked; an officer took snuff. He knew Dair was not partial to powdered tobacco and had little time for those of his fellow officers who stayed well out of the line of fire, taking snuff in a striped marquee, while soldiers were being blown to bits on the battlefield. Thus he smoked in their company to annoy them. And he could annoy them. He, heir to an earldom, socially outranked most of his fellow officers, who were the second and younger sons of noblemen and had no title to look forward to, other than the rank bought on commission.

But what annoyed these officers more than Dair's disregard for social rank, and his care-for-nobody attitude, was that the ordinary foot soldier venerated Major Lord Fitzstuart, and would follow him headlong into battle, no questions asked. No wonder his fellow officers called him arrogant and foolhardy and had no time for him or his heroics because it showed them up for what they truly were—painted papier-mâché fighters. One spark from Dair's cheroot and up in flames they would go.

Grasby smiled and found himself sipping hot milky tea before he realized he was holding a porcelain cup and saucer. He pulled himself out of his abstraction to make a confession.

"Truth is, I have no right to curse Dair for his reckless antics. He is the bravest man I know. With his family—his father in particular—holding him in little regard, is it small wonder he has no regard for his own safety? No, Rory. I will not abandon him. I cannot. It is Silla who must see why I cannot, or she will be miserable, and make me miserable into the bargain."

Rory had to ask the question. "Why, Harvel? Why risk your marriage?"

"If not for Dair Fitzstuart, you would not have a brother, Silla would not have a husband, and Grand would not have an heir to his title and estates. I'd be dead and buried!"

FOURTEEN

WITH SUCH A willing and sympathetic ear, Grasby was soon confiding in Rory details and anecdotes about his best friend that, had Dair Fitzstuart been consulted, would have remained buried in the past, not to be repeated, and certainly not to the granddaughter of his mentor.

"Second year at Harrow was when Dair first came to my defense. I was being pummeled to a pulp by Bully Biscoe, a great big ape of a boy one year above us. Can't recall what for. I don't think he liked the straw color of my hair. Or was it my blue eyes? Whatever it was, it was not something I could alter about myself, even had I wanted to. Cedric did his best to pull the ape off me, but his chums got hold of Cedric, who had a pretty good fist on him, and held him down while Bully got to work on me. That's when Dair stepped in. In those days, he wasn't much bigger than me. But he could fight! Had Bully knocked cold before he knew who had hit him!"

"Which is why you became fast friends... You, Mr. Pleasant and Lord Fitzstuart," Rory stated to move the conversation along when her brother paused and shook his turbaned head at a memory. "When was the second time he defended you?"

"Second time?"

"You said Lord Fitzstuart came to your defense for the first time when you were at Harrow... So there must have been a second time."

"Clever! But it wouldn't be right of me to tell you the particulars. Suffice it for me to say I was staring down the long length of a blade, point held to my chest by a man who believed I had taken liberties with a—um—*female* under his protection."

"His sister? Wife? Not his daughter?"

"No! No! No! Not that sort of female or that sort of protection."

Rory's eyes widened, but she was matter of fact. "A wagtail. Please continue. Unless I am in the wrong and you need to correct me...?"

"No. No correction necessary. It was just before Dair headed off to join his regiment and Cedric and I were off to Oxford. We were celebrating the birth of his—well, that doesn't matter. We were out celebrating and ended up at a particular direction that welcomed young gentlemen. The man with the sword fancied himself in love with my—friend. I was not in a position to defend myself. He had every intention of spilling my blood. Dair got himself involved and to bring the story to its conclusion, he mortally wounded the man. It was a fair fight, with seconds, and a fair outcome. The man knew how to wield a blade, and if not for Dair, I would've been the one bleeding to death all over the floor."

"Then you do indeed owe him your life. Strange he did not go on to Oxford with you both, but instead went into the army. Not the usual route for the eldest son of an earl, is it? More tea...?"

Grasby held out his teacup.

"There's nothing usual about it! And nothing usual about Dair's family. Father deserted his Countess and three children when Dair was about ten years old. Went off to the West Indies and never came home. Dair said it was as if his father had died, but that there was no body to bury." Grasby dropped a sugar lump into his tea and replaced the silver tongs in the bowl being held out to him. "We may have been orphaned, Rory, but we had Grand to take care of us. Dair and his sister and brother were left to their own devices. The Countess shut herself away. Heartbreak sent her mad for a time—"

"The Countess of Strathsay? *Heartbroken*? Perhaps that explains why she is not a nice person."

"It don't explain why she's as cold as a frozen lake to everyone, including her own children! No motherly instincts, as far as anyone can tell. But she's Dair's mamma, so I won't hear a word said against her."

"Nor should you. But just because *she* is cold-blooded doesn't mean he is. His father must be warm-blooded, and Lord Fitzstuart takes after him... Perhaps that's why the Earl sailed off to the Caribbean?"

Grasby shrugged. "Possibly. Never asked. All I do know is that while the Earl lives on his sugar plantation, his English estate falls into ruin. He won't spend a penny on its upkeep. Nor give his heir power of attorney to act on his behalf. So Dair plays a waiting game. Waiting for his father to die. Waiting to inherit. Waiting to be able to do something other than wait." He frowned. "It worries me that while he waits, his luck could turn. You can't be forever risking your life and not expect death to catch up with you in the end."

"Death catches up with all of us eventually," Rory said quietly. "But I don't understand why he tempts death. He seems to me..." she began, then instantly corrected herself before her brother realized her slip, "What I've heard said about him is that he has a zest for life. That he enjoys every moment of it."

"Well, you would, wouldn't you, if your next breath might be your last! What Dair should be doing is getting married and producing an heir. Then the Earl might consider giving him control of the estate. That's Grand's opinion. But since Dair went into the army against his wishes, Strathsay has refused to release a penny of his funds or give him any responsibility."

"But if his father has not been in England for over a decade, who looks after his estates, if not his heir?"

Grasby sighed and looked blank for a moment. "Cousin, I think. Yes. Dair's principled second cousin, the Duke of Roxton. Holds the purse strings, and if any of the Fitzstuart siblings need funds, they have to go cap-in-hand to him."

Rory peered out the window. Her grandfather and the Major

were nowhere to be seen. Only the gardeners remained, clipping hedges and raking gravel. She sighed and settled again amongst the cushions.

"He would hate going cap-in-hand to anyone... He would find it humiliating."

"Yes. Yes, he does. But it's not an unusual circumstance in itself. Plenty of sons live by handouts and IOUs until they inherit. I would be, if Grand hadn't given over the management of the estates to me when I married Silla. Now I have occupation, and still much to learn, but when I do inherit the title, Grand knows the estates will be well looked after. But few men are like Grand..."

"The Earl of Strathsay should be ashamed of himself! Not just for leaving his family, which is inexcusable, but for treating his children, particularly his eldest son and heir, with such contempt!" Rory said hotly. "Making them beg to a relative for their inheritance. Making his heir do likewise, when he should be head of the family in his father's absence... I take back what I said. The Earl is not warm-blooded at all. He is as cold and unpleasant as his countess. I'd say they were a perfect match. The wonder of it is that ice doesn't run in their son's veins, too!"

"Rory, there is no reason for you to upset yourself," Grasby said quietly, wondering why she was suddenly so passionate, though he knew her to possess great empathy. "This state of affairs has been going on for over a decade. It's nothing new."

"Then I am not in the least surprised he has a reckless disregard for his heritage, his position in society, and his life! He is still being treated like a little boy of ten. He has no reason to grow up, has he? He might as well stay ten, for all the good it would do him to try and take responsibility for his family and his inheritance. While his father lives, and while he remains obdurate, Lord Fitzstuart can do nothing but wait. And everyone knows that boys who are without occupation and purpose will create mischief one way or another."

Grasby blinked. "By Jove, Rory," he whispered, adding in a much louder voice as her explanation took hold, "you've hit the proverbial nail! I've never thought about Dair's situation in that light. But you just might be right. In fact, it makes perfect sense. How clever you are!"

"Thank you. But I am not so clever," she smiled, yet dimpling at such praise. "His situation is not so different to that of females waiting to be married. Until we marry, we have little purpose in life. We are just burdens on others, in every way. But once married, we have a position in society, a house to run, and God willing, children to raise and worry over. It must be the same for eldest sons, particularly those who are shunned by their fathers. They wait, too. At least unmarried females have fathers and brothers to look after them, and who they can look after in their own small ways. Although that too diminishes when brothers find wives..."

"You will never be a burden, Rory. I mean to look after you, always."

"I know that, dearest. I wasn't thinking of me but speaking in generalities. I shall make an excellent aunt one day, and Silla will be pleased to have me. She will love your children, but I do not see her spending many hours in the nursery, do you?"

Grasby was about to say that the way matters were presently between him and his wife, it would take almost a miracle if the nursery received any occupants in the future. He was saved commenting when Rory continued, and he again found himself surprised by her naïve insight.

"I dare say army life was good for His Lordship. Aside from the very real possibility of being killed or maimed in battle, the day-to-day discipline of a regiment does give men purpose. It may even keep them out of mischief until they are granted leave, and then perhaps they go a little wild...?"

"I can only agree with you," Grasby smiled. "Though I wonder how many officers you've engaged in conversation?"

"It is all observation and conjecture, dearest brother. I've seen soldiers on parade, not Lord Fitzstuart's 17th. It must take an inordinate amount of time and effort to shine all those buttons on their scarlet coats and polish their jockey boots until they reflect the sun! As for keeping their white breeches whiter than white—whose idea was it to put soldiers in such an impossible color?"

"But it does make them look the part—all that scarlet and white."

"It does. And we have not touched on the hours that must go into taking care of their mounts. All that brass tack and leather, and the shine to their beautiful coats. To see the dragoons mounted is a sight to behold, is it not?"

"It most certainly is. Astonishing what a bit of spit and polish and a scarlet coat can do for a man," Grasby teased his sister, and then peered at her closely. "You've not fallen for a uniform, have you, Rory?"

"Certainly not!" she retorted, and to hide the heat in her cheeks threw her cushion at him, which he caught and threw back at her, laughingly.

"Good. Because I don't want you marrying a uniform. I found it difficult enough having my best friend go off and fight. I couldn't bear for you to worry yourself over a husband doing the same."

Rory giggled. "I do love you for thinking I might marry at all!"

"Why shouldn't you? I mean, you're pretty enough, and some men find blue eyes attractive."

"I'll take that as a compliment." Adding seriously, hoping her tone sounded offhand enough not to arouse suspicion, "So why did Lord Fitzstuart buy a commission?"

"I shouldn't confide this in you. But I know if I don't tell you, you'll just go and ask Grand the same question... And it possibly won't come as a surprise. It's been whispered about enough times that you may have heard it spoken of at one of those tea parties Silla took you to. Besides, Dair makes no secret of the fact he has a natural son, never has."

"Lily Banks' son?"

Grasby nodded. "So you have heard. Yes. Reason Dair was shipped off to the army. He was barely fourteen but was always a brute of a lad even then, and she, well she was old enough to know better! Old enough to get herself pregnant in the hopes the heir to an earldom would marry her!"

"But how could she manage to get herself pregnant? Isn't a child a blessing from God?"

"Not this sort of child, Rory," her brother said darkly.

Rory frowned and was instantly uncomfortable, not liking her brother's words or tone. She left the window seat to fuss with the tea things, hoping occupation would soothe her emotions. She lifted the silver teapot and realized there was only enough tea for one more cup, so snuffed the candle warmer and replaced the teapot on its stand. She then stacked the teacups and came back to the window seat where her brother still sat, watching her.

With her thoughts collected into coherent sentences her brother would understand without becoming emotive, she said quietly, "Harvel, it upsets me to hear you speak of a child in such a meanspirited way. A child is a child, and that's all he is. He comes into the world blameless, and yet he is immediately branded by others because of his parentage, or his characteristics, or his-his deformities, as being worth less than nothing—"

"Rory, I didn't mean you."

"I know that, dearest. But it doesn't lessen the pain I feel when I hear a child shaped into another's making. I've come to terms with my shortcomings. I have a privileged life that shields me from the ugliness in the world. But for you and others to condemn a child because its parents are not married... How easily you forget that our own mother was illegitimate."

"I had not forgotten. Though I wish I could."

"Why? Because our mother was a seamstress and our father the son of an earl? Our parents' marriage was an unequal one, but even Grand admits their union was happy. For you to wish otherwise, is to wish away their happiness. It also condemns my existence, for in the eyes of many, I am God's punishment for my father marrying far beneath him."

"Anyone who says so isn't fit for dog meat!"

"So are those who condemn Lily Banks' son because he is illegitimate."

Grasby did not argue the point with her. He had never won a debate with his sister. Instead, he said flatly, "His name is Jamie— James Alisdair Banks."

"Oh! I do like that name. And he gave the boy his Christian name, too..."

"Dair would have given him his legal name, if he'd been permitted. That was not going to happen, neither was a marriage. The old Duke of Roxton saw to that and had it all sorted. Lily Banks kept the baby and Dair went into the army. That was almost ten years ago, and a lot of water has flowed under that bridge since then!"

Rory scowled. "Meaning?"

Grasby could have bitten off his own tongue for his want of propriety. Still he answered her.

"Meaning, Lily Banks was married off and has birthed four more children since she had Jamie."

"Is she Lord Fitzstuart's mistress? Are those four children his too?"

"Mistress? *His children*? Good God! No! She was a pretty little thing who caught Dair's eye. Five children later, do you think Dair would be interested in such a woman?"

Knowing Lily Banks was married and not Lord Fitzstuart's mistress cheered Rory more than she cared to admit, but it did not stop her saying, tongue firmly in cheek, "Dear me, she must be old enough to have a toe in her grave! I can't imagine His Lordship being attracted to such an old crone."

"Haha, sister dear! To own to a truth, I've no idea what Lily Banks looks like, only that her son by Dair is the spit of his papa. By all accounts, her husband is a fine fellow. He's a botanist, or is he a plant collector for a botanist? Whatever, he's an adventurer who travels the world in search of exotic plants."

"Then that explains why they occupy a house next to the Chelsea Physic Garden... I wonder if Mr. Banks knows anything about pineapples... Harvel, I must dress now, or I shall be late. And Grand hates to be kept waiting..."

Grasby hopped off the window seat and shoved his hands in the pockets of his silk banyan. "I dare say Banks might know something about pineapples..."

Rory hooked her arm about her brother's and walked with him

to the door of her sitting room. "Are you sure you won't accompany Grand and me to the theater?"

Grasby stopped on the threshold, the door opened for him by one of Rory's maids.

"And give Silla more powder for her cannon? Besides," he added with a guilty grin, "the theater is more your thing than mine. Silla's anger has just given me a good excuse not to attend... Oi! Hold on a moment! I never told you Lily Banks lived next door to the Chelsea Physic Garden. So how do you—"

But Rory had closed the door on her brother before he could quiz her further, already making plans to visit the Chelsea Physic Garden to learn what the gardeners could tell her about the cultivation of the pineapple. She might even be able to offer an exchange of information. She would take along her gardener, and perhaps she could coax Silla to accompany her and make a picnic of the day. And if she happened to wander close to the stone wall and peer over at the house occupied by Lily Banks and her family... It would be serendipity if she caught a glimpse of Mrs. Banks and her children, and most particularly the boy who was the image of his father. After all, had not the Major invited her to Lily Banks' house, no questions asked?

Rory would have been greatly surprised to discover that while she was thinking of Lily Banks and Jamie, Dair Fitzstuart was thinking about her and his promise to her grandfather, and what he could do about it.

FIFTEEN

The morning after his visit with the Earl of Shrewsbury, Dair arrived at the Hanover Square residence of his cousin just before midday and found the house in the midst of a family celebration. He had no wish to disturb the gathering and so told the butler he would wait on the steps of the main staircase. He stripped off his tan leather riding gloves and dropped them into the crown of his hat, permitted a footman to shrug him out of his gray woolen greatcoat, and gave up his sword and sash to the butler. Declining any sort of beverage, he asked for a taper to light a cheroot, then took up a position on the stairs that allowed him to stretch his long booted legs in their thigh-tight buff breeches as comfortably as possible. Here he lounged, smoking, both elbows resting on a step across the broad of his back and staring at the full-length life-size portrait of a titian-haired beauty, his grandmother, Augusta, the first Countess of Strathsay.

But it was not his grandmother he saw in his mind's eye as he stared at the imposing canvas, but a young woman of twenty, with pale blue eyes that held a twinkle of candor. She was not beautiful, but she was very pretty. She was not plump as was the fashion, but delicate, like a fine Meissen figurine. Her hair was an indeterminate pale blonde, and while her mouth was perfectly formed, her lips were the palest of pinks. She was a female who, until the raid on Romney's studio, he would have passed in the street, or in a crowded drawing room, and not given a second glance. He certainly would not have sought her out for conversation or, for that matter, anything else. That was because his two-days-ago-self had always equated paleness with triteness.

But now he could not stop thinking about this pale beauty. After the raid on Romney's studio, while his battered and bruised body was being patched up, he was so consumed with going over in his mind every detail of their encounter that he failed to react to the blistering sting when Farrier applied linen bandages soaked in an antiseptic preparation of turpentine, alcohol, and aloe to his abrasions. This caused the batman to wonder aloud if his master had suffered an internal rupture that had left him numb to pain. To which Dair had ordered Farrier to stop fussing like an old maiden aunt and just get on with it.

While he toyed with the purple silken hair ribbon he had taken from her as a war trophy, he decided her pale prettiness was a subterfuge, just as snow blanketing a multitude of terrains left the landscape featureless. But he was not deceived. He caught the sparkle of mischief in her smile, and the humor in her eyes, at the outrageous situation in which she found herself, bound up with him in a curtain and then on the floor at the back of the stage.

His *Delight* was no simpering miss, no fainting couch habitué. She confidently and playfully answered him back without artifice. Nor did she try to flirt with him. She was, quite simply, herself, and he found that fascinating. He was not good with words, but to him, for want of a better analogy, she was a star amongst a thousand twinkling in the night sky, unnoticed and unappreciated, until the fates had intervened. It was only then that she caught his attention, not unlike a shooting star streaking the black night sky, and in the most bizarre of circumstances. How could he ignore her after that?

God, he must be going soft in the head, waxing lyrical about blanketing snow and night skies filled with stars! What the bloody hell was wrong with him? One too many knocks about the ears on his last tour of duty could account for it. Or it could be that nick from a rebel bullet that had grazed his scalp. He knew of some men forced into restraining jackets, no longer able to cope with the endless bloody scenes that played over and over in their heads: Of limbs hacked off and heads blown to a meaty pulp; screaming death, and crying orphaned children; and rebel civilians who had no place on a battlefield, taking up arms only to be slaughtered in their thousands... Yes, all that could give a soldier a straw bed in Bedlam.

But had he truly survived nine years in the army, with all its attendant horrors, to lose his head over a female whom he now realized was so out of his reach that she might as well be living in Vladivostok?

When she had walked into Shrewsbury's study and dropped a book at his feet, the blood had drained from his face. Seeing her—no, hearing her voice, with that note of eager expectation—had him smiling before he even knew what she was saying or what she looked like. And then it hit him all at once, like a hard fist to his gut. Here was his shooting star and she was *Shrewsbury's granddaughter*.

Worse, two minutes before she showed up, he had given his word to forget all about the previous evening—to forget all about *her*. He felt he had been tricked out of something precious. Yet, he knew Shrewsbury was doing nothing less than he aught: Protecting his granddaughter's unblemished reputation.

He had remained on his haunches, taking an inordinate amount of time to pick up her book before rising to his full height, hoping he had mastered his shock enough not to alert Shrewsbury. Trying his best to remain passive and in control—numb was a better word—he had held out the book, looking not at her but over her fair hair. He just wanted her to take it so he could get out of there as quickly as possible. Instead of doing so, she surprised him, not only by showing concern for his wounds, but more so because she spoke to him as if they were old friends. And what did he do in response? The only thing he could: Remain mute and exhibit all the emotional depth of a log of wood. Callous idiot!

But it was when she touched him that he was forced to muster all his skills as a performer. She held his hand as if it were the most natural thing in the world for her to do so. Every fine hair, every square inch of skin on the back of his hand smarted, the sensation far more intense than the wounds already inflicted. He forced his mind elsewhere, as he had been trained to do in the event of capture and torture. And this was torture. Worse than thumb screws and flame.

One short sharp sentence and he escaped to the terrace. He was staring at clipped yew trees and boxed hedge rows set out in geometric patterns before he realized a footman had followed him out-of-doors. The servant offered him a tumbler of ale—he downed it in one and demanded another.

He had suffered a monumental shock. No. Two shocks. The pretty pale female he had playfully tried to seduce at Romney's studio was not a harlot, nor was her reputation remotely tinged with immorality. She was the Earl of Shrewsbury's granddaughter, and he was mortified. Had he known, he would not have acted towards her as he had. He certainly would not have said the things he did. But, to his abiding shame, he knew himself for a liar. He did not wish to apologize for his behavior towards her. He had enjoyed their banter, more so because it was honest and unstudied. Most of all, his over-whelming desire upon hearing her voice again was to take her in his arms and kiss her as he had kissed her when they were cocooned in a linen curtain.

Leading his first cavalry charge had been fraught with less terror than what he had experienced in Shrewsbury's study. He couldn't wait to set sail for Portugal.

With thoughts of Portugal and his imminent mission came the realization he had been sitting on the stairs of his cousin's Hanover Square mansion for at least twenty minutes. He was supposed to be on his way to Portsmouth, before anyone saw him out and about in London. After all, for all concerned, he was presently locked up, cooling his heels for his behavior. He'd sent Farrier in his place, much to his batman's disgust. Farrier would be spending the next month as a guest of His Majesty. Dair had told him to think of it as a holiday. Farrier had told His Lordship he could think of a few things to call his involuntary incarceration, but the word "holiday" was not one of them.

Dair was about to send a footman to the drawing room to

disturb his cousin when the door opened and she came out into the passageway in a whirlwind of ivory satin petticoats with metallic thread embroidery, golden hair threaded with matching ivory satin ribbons, face flushed and radiant. Dair could not help smiling to see her so happy; a far cry from the widow who had mourned the loss of her beloved husband for three sorrowful years. The reason for her happiness followed her out of the room. Jonathon Strang Leven, newly elevated Duke of Kinross, was just as splendidly attired in dark velvet, his India waistcoat of gold and silver metallic threads dazzling against his brown complexion.

Dair realized then that the family celebration was a wedding, and he slowly rose to his boot heels to greet the noble couple and to offer up his congratulations.

DAIR HEARTILY SHOOK the hand of the Duke of Kinross and bowed formally over his cousin Antonia's outstretched fingers. And when she pulled him closer and presented her cheek, he kissed her diffidently, awkwardly shy in her presence, despite knowing her all his life. If Antonia noticed, she did not react, nor did she acknowledge the grazes to Dair's knuckles, the cut healing in his lip or the dark bruising to his left eye.

A short exchange of platitudes and it was obvious Dair wished to have a private word with his French cousin. So the Duke of Kinross made his excuses and returned to the drawing room, leaving the cousins alone at the bottom of the staircase. Antonia spread out her petticoats and sat on the stairs. Invited, Dair did likewise.

"I like your new duke," Dair stated, once again stretching out his long legs across several steps. "He's a good man." He smiled. "You wouldn't have married him otherwise. And he has made you happy."

"Yes. I am very happy—again."

"Not many are blessed with one good marriage, but to have two..."

"One day I hope you will be as happy as I am, Alisdair."

"But—Cousin Duchess—you don't even like me."

Antonia lost her smile, and she lost her English tongue, saying in a rush of French, "That is a great piece of nonsense and it offends me!"

Dair politely inclined his head in acknowledgment of her status to say and do as she pleased, but as her first cousin he rudely shrugged a shoulder as he drew back on his cheroot. He answered her in her own tongue. "You would be the first to chide me if I were not truthful with you."

"But you are *not* being truthful, you are making an ill-informed judgment about my feelings."

"Then forgive me. I am neither good with words, nor with feelings..." He returned his gaze to the full-length portrait of Augusta, Countess of Strathsay. "I can't blame anyone for my lack of brains. But I hold responsible that woman's son—my father—for my lack of feeling."

"If you wish to cast blame, then blame her—our grandmother," Antonia stated, also regarding the portrait. She reverted to her heavily accented English, "She turned your mother against your father. Your father he took a ship across the sea to be rid of her. But you cannot run away from yourself. Augusta she was a beautiful heartless woman, as cold as a serpent." Antonia gave a little shiver of revulsion. "Please. Let us not talk of her on this of all days."

"Why, if she was such a serpent, do you keep our grandmother's portrait on your wall? If I owned her, she'd be wrapped in a sheet and stuck in an attic or consigned to a dusty corner of some picture gallery."

"I keep her there as a reminder—a reminder that a beautiful visage does not always bring with it a beautiful heart. Beauty is a gift from God and should not be abused or taken for granted. Those blessed with physical beauty cannot assume the appearance of goodness, they must *be* good and that requires *doing* good."

"On second thought, don't ship her off. What you need are some candles, incense and an altar. A papist shrine, if you will, to your archangel of beauty. Which, when you think on it, is fitting, given our grandfather was a papist general for the Old Pretender."

"It is important, is it not, that those blessed with great physical beauty have a duty not to abuse their gift?" Antonia continued, ignoring his quip. "To be a self-destructive care-for-nobody intent on self-harm is a great waste; it is also arrogant in the extreme."

Dair removed his gaze from their grandmother's portrait and slowly turned to look at Antonia, face devoid of his thoughts. He took the cheroot from his mouth.

"Is that how you see me, Cousin? Don't spare my feelings now. If I am to be served up a lecture for dinner, I want all twelve courses with lashings of humiliation!"

Antonia was silent a moment, and then she told him her thoughts, honestly and without artifice.

"This man you pretend to be, this conceited Adonis who abuses his body in fights and scrapes with lesser beings, he is not a gentleman. He pretends not to care for anyone or anything. He does everything to excess. He never refuses a wager and so carries out ridiculous dares for his friends to make them laugh, or rich, or for no good purpose at all. This man, I do not know him in the least. And I do not care to know him. But that does not stop me caring about him and worrying. I worry he will start believing in the façade he hides behind so that one day these two beings, they will merge, and then he will be lost to us, and to himself."

"I am what I am."

"No! You *pretend*. You act. But you have inhabited the role for so many years now, you cannot tell the difference between the two. But sometimes the real Alisdair Fitzstuart emerges, and when he does, I know there is hope for him—for you. So, you will please promise me to stop trying to kill yourself in as many interesting ways as possible. This last, in a painter's studio, of all places."

"Cousin Duchess, I can promise you that if I do get killed it will not be because I wished to die."

"You think putting yourself in harm's way, it is a laughing matter? Have you not been listening? You have an obligation, if not to yourself, then to others, to live up to your potential."

This drew from Dair a reluctant laugh, and he found himself apologizing for his behavior rather than defending it, which had been his intention. Such an unexpected turn-around also surprised him and made it all the more difficult to put his request to her, particularly when it meant disclosing that he was again about to put his life in danger, and in a far more perilous way than a scrape at an artist's studio. So it was with an accompanying bashful smile that he withdrew a sealed packet and a small leather purse of guineas from an inner frock coat pocket.

"Do I have your permission to speak now, Your Grace?" he asked quietly. When she nodded, he placed the sealed packet and small leather purse between them on the step. "Thank you for believing in me... But it makes my request that much more difficult to ask. This," he said holding up the sealed packet, "I want you to keep in a safe place. You may never have to break the seal, but in the event of my death—"

Antonia sat up tall. "Your death? Alisdair, what—"

"Please, Your Grace, I need to get through this without interruption. The packet contains my last will and testament, which is self-explanatory. Once my demise is made generally known, I want you to give it to your son. Roxton will know what to do." He put the packet back on the step and held up the leather purse. "For the boy's birthday. It's in a month, but I might not make it back—back in time. There should be sufficient guineas for a fine family feast and his gift." He smiled self-consciously. "No idea what he wants. Last time he wrote, it was a musket or a microscope. A soldier or a physician. He can't decide. But at ten years of age, what boy truly knows what he wants to do with his future? At that age I wanted to be a pirate. Ha! At least he doesn't have the weight of birth on his thin shoulders. He can tread a path of his own choosing." He glanced at Antonia then said, "If it were my choice, I wouldn't have him follow me. His mother says he has a fine head on his shoulders, so I am hoping he chooses the microscope. But in the event you think the only place for him is the army. So be it."

Antonia blinked. "You are giving Jamie to me?"

"If anything were to happen to me, yes. Guardianship until his twenty-fifth birthday, when he will get the bulk of his inheritance, such as it is at the present. If I were already in my father's shoes, and earl, I'd have considerably more say in the distribution of the largesse... If you and your new duke would keep an eye on him as he grows, I'd be eternally grateful." Dair gave a lopsided grin. "You're the only two people I know who won't look down on him because of his birth."

"Alisdair... Roxton would never look down on your child, any child, and perhaps he is a more fitting guardian, yes?"

"No. We are barely on speaking terms. And who can blame him for that after what happened at the regatta? His son almost drowned and I was distracted with the finish line at any cost... Jesu! What must he—you—think of me...?" He drew back on his cheroot and blew smoke across his shoulder, away from Antonia. When she remained silent his mouth twitched into a crooked smile. "Thank you for not asking... Perhaps I'll tell you one day..." He rallied and added, "Even if we were on the best of terms, he and Deborah have enough of a brood, and another on the way. Besides, after all those years on the sub-continent as a merchant, your new duke is far more open-minded to possibilities and potential. I watched him around Roxton's boys; Frederick idolizes him." Dair frowned on a sudden thought. "But if you would prefer that I not—"

"No! No! Of course we will do as you ask," Antonia replied, holding back tears. She laid her fingers over her cousin's large hand. "Jonathon, he will agree with me. It will be an honor. Truly." She sniffed and smiled when Dair drew up her hand and kissed it. "But it will not come to that because you will return to us from wherever it is you are going, and Jamie he will be able to thank his papa for the microscope in person when next he sees you."

"I hope that you are proved right, Cousin Duchess. And thank you. My mind can rest easy now."

He stubbed the smoldering end of the cheroot on the sole of his boot, and dropped the butt onto a silver tray a quick-thinking footman held out to him. After helping Antonia to her feet, he gave her the sealed packet and the purse. She slipped these under the first layer of her satin gown, into one of two embroidered long pockets, tied about her waist between the layers of her petticoats.

"As far as the rest of London is concerned, I'm spending the next month in the Tower. You and Kinross may know it's Portugal for me.

You'll be pleased that it's not a country we are presently at war with —a nice change. Shrewsbury tells me we have a trade agreement with the Portuguese and import barrels and barrels of port..."

"But you are not going for the port."

"No. And that's all I can tell you," he apologized. "I'll bring your new Duke and Roxton back a dozen bottles or a crate, whatever I can manage."

"Be safe, *mon cher*."

Dair bowed over her hand, and because she was looking up at him with such worry he impetuously kissed her cheek. "I will do my absolute best to remain alive, *ma chère cousine*. Promise."

SIXTEEN

R ORY SPENT A fortnight campaigning her sister-in-law to accompany her to the Chelsea Physic Garden. She even co-opted her grandfather and Mr. Watkins to her cause. Both agreed fresh air, a picnic and different surroundings would lift Lady Grasby's spirits. Rory even tried to bore her witless, in the hope that incessant talk of pineapple propagation and the need for Crawford to consult with the gardeners at the Physic Garden would be enough to force Silla to say *yes* to the excursion. Lady Grasby remained implacable.

Rory's last line of attack was guilt. The visit to the Physic Garden had to be within the next three weeks. Rory and her grandfather were then off on their annual holiday to Hampshire, to the Duke of Roxton's estate, Treat. They would be away for a month. How could she leave her precious pineapple plants solely in Crawford's care if he had not been to visit the physic gardeners to know how to properly tend them?

Perhaps her grandfather would have to go to Treat without her this year?

Lady Grasby would not be drawn out of her self-absorption, nor could she be made to have the slightest twinge of guilt. She took to having supper in her rooms, so as to avoid not only Rory's enthusiastic conversations, but also the conversations of the males of the household. Everyone seemed to have forgotten not only the incident in question, but also the utter humiliation she had suffered at Romney's studio—humiliation so great she could never again venture beyond Talbot House for fear of being ridiculed. As for returning to the studio for the final sittings of her full-length portrait, that was now out of the question.

Lord Shrewsbury, who had little time for his grandson's wife as an individual but valued her importance in the dynastic preservation of the Talbot line and the Shrewsbury earldom, took it upon himself to lecture her. He told her that exhibiting moral outrage because her husband cavorted with dancing girls was mundane in the extreme. It reeked of the behavior of the worst sort of Billingsgate fishwife. As the wife of a nobleman, she needed to get on with her only purpose in life: Producing an heir. Married almost three years and there was still no sign of a pregnancy, so what was wrong with her? His lordship's lecture was interrupted with the news his carriage awaited to take him to St. James's Palace. Which was just as well. Lord Shrewsbury fled his own book room to the sound of Lady Grasby's howling sobs.

The only member of the household who seemed unaffected by Lady Grasby's behavior was her husband. Aside from his altered sleeping arrangements, Grasby carried on with life as if the Romney Studio incident had never occurred. He spent time at White's. He dined out with Mr. Cedric Pleasant. He had meetings with his man of business, with his steward, and he was fitted for a new suit by his tailor.

He knew his wife was being shamelessly self-centered and childish and it gave him pause to remember why he had married her in the first place: Not because he fell in love with her but because his grandfather said that with a dowry of fifty thousand pounds, she was the one he should marry. That she was beautiful certainly helped make up his mind. Part of him was flattered she was distraught by his behavior, it showed she cared. But he was as determined as ever not to give in to her demands to end his friendship with Major Lord Fitzstuart.

That his best friend was languishing in the Tower was of far more concern than his marital troubles. So was the fact his wife refused to accompany his sister to the Physic Garden, even though she knew Rory could not go without a female companion to an invitation-only all-male place of work and study.

But Grasby knew how to get his wife to bend to his will. Three years of marriage had taught him that much.

One night, while taking her supper alone, Grasby sauntered into his wife's presence and told her flatly that she was not to worry herself about being imposed upon to go anywhere. He would be taking his sister to the Physic Garden on the morrow, and her presence was neither required nor wanted, because the lovely Maria Hibbert-Baker had kindly agreed to be Rory's chaperone. If she wished for the carriage, it was hers for the day, because he and his little party would be traveling by barge, an added treat for Rory and Maria.

His ruse worked. Silla instantly took exception to Maria Hibbert-Baker taking her place, as he knew she would. Had Grasby not married Drusilla Watkins, Maria was next in line to be asked.

Later that same evening, Lady Grasby told Rory a leisurely sail down the Thames would be just the tonic she needed to clear her head. Perhaps while they were at the Physic Garden one of the apothecaries would be good enough to offer up the latest in herbal remedies for megrim.

Rory was thrilled the excursion was finally going ahead as planned. And because she was happy, so, too, was Grasby, William Watkins, and Lord Shrewsbury.

For the time being at least, the Talbot household was at peace. And then it rained. There were unusual summer thunderstorms, and it continued to rain heavily all week. When next the sun shone brightly, ten days had elapsed and it was the day before Rory and her grandfather were due to set out for Hampshire.

Still time enough to visit the Physic Garden, in Lord Grasby's opinion.

So off they went, in the Earl's private shallop, powered by eight beefy rowers in the Shrewsbury green and salmon-pink livery. The barge, with prow, stern and rail carved and gilded with fanciful sea creatures, was equipped with a carpeted indoor room with painted ceiling and gilded furnishings. A carpet was draped over this tilt, and there was even an awning of Plunkett blue cloth, providing shade from a summer sun that beat down fiercely for the first time in weeks, if one wanted to enjoy the cooling breeze off the river.

RORY HAD THE most marvelous time strolling the Physic Garden, her party dutifully trailing behind her wherever she went. She could hardly contain her excitement and wonder at all she saw. She inspected various herb beds, listened attentively to the young apothecary-in-training who was their guide, and stared in awe at the only olive tree in England that had managed to thrive in the English climate. Though, she was not surprised that on such a hot day a native of the Mediterranean region was growing so well. For this comment she received such an enthusiastic response from the student apothecary, that when he took her and her party into the magnificent orangery, with all its glass panels and tubs and tubs of oranges, lemons and limes, he spoke almost exclusively with Rory. By the time they had moved on to the distillery and plant preparation areas, where medicinals were manufactured, he had lost his shyness and forgotten all about the fact that Rory was a pretty young woman.

Rory could not have been happier, particularly when the head gardener informed her he knew just the gentleman to discuss pineapple cultivation with her. He had taken the liberty to send word up to Banks House some twenty minutes earlier. Mr. Humphrey was an expert in bromeliads, and he lodged at Banks House, where he was presently enjoying his afternoon repast. He would send Mr. Humphrey to the barge, if Miss Talbot did not mind the inconvenience of having her nuncheon interrupted...?

It took mention of her grandfather's shallop for Rory to remember she was hungry, and that Grasby had come to fetch her ten minutes ago. He was patiently waiting by the imposing statue of Sir

Hans Sloane, benefactor of the gardens. With mittened hand firmly about the ivory handle of her walking stick, she took her brother's crooked arm with the other, leaning on him a little heavier than usual. He scolded her lovingly for not taking the time to rest on one of the many benches dotted about the gardens, and said a straw hat was unlikely to provide her with enough shade on such a hot day as this. Where was her parasol?

"I gave it to Silla, who did not bring hers. You're right of course. I had quite forgot how ferocious the sun can be... Only now do I feel the ache in my ankle and hip."

"Let's get you out of this heat... I sent Crawford off to eat his nuncheon with the rowers and the others who tagged along with us. We're all down at the south wall embankment."

"South wall...?"

"Where the shallop is docked."

"Oh! So *that* is the south wall." Rory tried to sound offhand. "Silly me! Always confusing my compass points."

"I decided the picnic was best had indoors or under the awning. It's far too hot out here in the open of the gardens. Besides," he added with a crooked smile, "Silla returned on board two hours after we set foot on dry land, citing the sun's rays as her enemy. So giving her your parasol was for naught." He sulked. "At least something else has upset her other than me!"

"Yes, at least," Rory murmured, distracted, "So the house—the one with the Jacobean chimney stacks on the other side of the wall—that must be Banks House...?"

Grasby wished he could see his sister's face, but it was hidden under the wide brim of her straw hat. Her innocently delivered question, however, did not fool him and he suspected it was accompanied by a blush.

"I wish we'd never had that conversation about Lily Banks. You're curious and you want to see her for yourself. And if I didn't know you better, and know that you do indeed have a keen interest in pineapples, I'd say this entire excursion is an excuse for you to go on tiptoe and peer over that wall to see what—"

"I don't need to go on tiptoe. And why shouldn't I be curious after what you told me about her?"

"Dair doesn't talk about her, or his son, to anyone. But he just happened to confide in me the once. And now I've told you—"

"I have no intention of breaking your confidence, Harvel."

"But it hasn't stopped your curiosity, has it? There's really nothing more mysterious about her than what I told you. She's married and has had four more brats. What more could you possibly want to know?"

A great deal, in Rory's opinion. What did she look like? What was her nature? Did Dair Fitzstuart still care for Lily Banks, and she for him? Perhaps her marriage was a sham, to cover her immoral relationship with the Major? Did their son truly look like his father? Was he worthy of his father, or was he spoiled beyond permission? Was it a happy household? Who lived at the house? Did they live in comfort? Was Mr. Banks accepting of his wife's child to another man? Did he love his wife? Was he a willing cuckold for His Lordship? Was Mr. Humphrey just a lodger...? The list went on and on...

And until she saw Lily Banks and Jamie for herself, she was sure she would go on wondering and dreaming about them. Just as she dreamed about Major Lord Fitzstuart and that kiss, and why, in her grandfather's book room, he had acted as if he did not know her from a lump of sugar!

Her heart raced and she felt as giddy as a summer gnat trapped in an upended drinking glass, to think Banks House was within reach. All that separated the Physic Garden from this house was a low stone wall, built as a deterrent to four-legged beasts, not man, to stop them entering the Physic Garden and trampling and eating all the carefully laid out and tended specimens. There was even a closed, but unlocked, latched gate between the two properties, and a well-worn path that wended its way through the trees.

She was staring at the gate and wishing she could go through it, up to the house, on the pretext of introducing herself to the lodger, Mr. Humphrey, when, to her great surprise, a man appeared out from between the trees. He strode down the gravel path, then veered off it, crossed the small patch of grass covered in wildflowers wilting in the heat, and came straight up to them. Leaning a bronzed forearm across the top of the low stone wall, he lifted his cap and smiled in greeting.

"Beggin' an interruption, kind lady and sir, but would you be the quality wishin' a word with Mr. Humphrey who lodges at Banks House?"

Grasby recoiled to be spoken to without giving the man permission to address him. Where was the servant's manners? One look at the rolled-up shirtsleeves and sunbaked forearms, the neckerchief tied about the red throat, and the gap-toothed smile in a sweaty face, and it was obvious that not only was the man an outdoor menial, but he was also at the base of that servile pecking order as well.

Rory stepped forward and lifted her chin so the servant could see her face under the brim of her hat.

"Yes, I am Miss Talbot who wishes a word with Mr. Humphrey about his expertise in pineapples."

"I don't know anythin' about them there pine-whatsees, but the mistress sent me to apprehend if you would care to come up to the house, to have your word with Mr. Humphrey. The mistress also asked if you would care to join her in a cold cordial. It's fair wicked in this heat and there's shade in the garden—"

"Thank your mistress for her offer of hospitality," Lord Grasby enunciated coldly. "We have shade and refreshment enough on our barge."

"Where Drusilla and Mr. Watkins would rather we did not disturb them," Rory said behind her fluttering fan. "Besides, it would be rude to refuse the invitation—"

"—from someone we have never met? No, it would not be rude, it would be saving the embarrassment of having us foisted upon them," Grasby replied, not caring the man could hear every word. "Who sends a stable hand? Should be an indoor footman. Besides, it's not proper for my sister to make the introduction of such— *people*."

"Perhaps they do not possess an indoor footman? Perhaps the indoor footman is engaged elsewhere? Isn't it enough the offer was made, not how it was made?"

"It matters to me, and to any persons with manners," Grasby enunciated, nose in the air, the epitome of the arrogant nobleman. "There is a correct way of doing things, or better not to do them at all. And if persons don't know how to be correct, then they are mere knight and barrow pigs who aren't worth our condescension!"

"I never took you for a prig, Harvel. You are being petty-minded and obstinate to stop me going through that gate."

"What if I am? I am only thinking of your welfare. Best we remain on this side with our dignity intact, than on that side with who knows what kind of persons—spongers, smellfeasts and malaperts, for all I know!"

"That's just it. You don't know, do you?"

"I know more than you, and that's enough!"

Rory blinked. Perhaps her brother had been affected by too much sun and was not himself? She had never encountered him so rudely implacable, and, as far as she was concerned, without cause to be so.

"You call the Major your *friend*," she whispered fiercely, "yet you refuse to acknowledge *his* friends?"

"Ah, that's different, and he would agree with me. You're a female and my sister. You are a lady and shall remain one. I won't have your reputation—*or you*—corrupted by an association with persons of unknown lineage and dubious reputation. We already know one of their number has no reputation to speak of—"

"Reputation shredded by her *association* with *your* best friend! So that is hardly *her* fault, is it?"

"Ha! I told you. She was old enough to know better."

"I won't have you apportion *all* the blame on her. It takes two to make a baby. And I—"

"Steady on! Steady on!" Grasby demanded, taking a step away, shocked. "You've had a bit too much sunshine, sister dear—"

"—have done the math," she enunciated. "He had not turned fifteen years old when his son was born, and she must have been around the same age or slightly older. Children themselves."

"You can't go declaiming loudly about the birds and bees,"

Grasby hissed, a significant sidelong glance at the servant, who continued to patiently lean on the stone wall. "Not before—"

"But according to you, Harvel, it doesn't matter what *we* say in front of our inferiors."

Grasby could offer no further argument, so he gave up and said on a sigh, "Come on, sugarplum, let's get you to the barge and some shade..."

"Harvel, we cannot refuse the invitation," she whispered. "We cannot. Mr. Humphrey has kindly offered to talk to me. When will I have another opportunity? Not for months. And the hostess of Banks House has offered us refreshment. These people are the friends of *your* best friend."

"Rory, to be honest, I don't know what these people mean to Dair. I certainly have not the least notion what Lily Banks means to him now. But one thing I do know, they are not of our social circle, and as such we should stay well away."

"I do not agree with you, and I will not abuse hospitality freely given, from whatever quarter." When her brother threw up a hand and looked awkward, she added conciliatorily, "Tell me this: Will sharing a cooling cordial with the occupants of Banks House and having a word with the Physic Garden's bromeliad specialist be any more of a corrupting influence on your sister than her sharing the chaise longue with the notorious mistress of the Duke of Dorset and her dancer friends at Romney's studio?"

"Oh, not you, too!" Grasby moaned with a roll of his eyes. He straightened, wiped a hand over his mouth, and let out a long breath of frustration. "I'm never going to hear the end of that piddling episode, am I?"

Rory smiled sweetly.

"No. Not unless you start treating people as you find them, not as your rank dictates you should." And before her brother could add anything further to the argument, she turned to the servant and accepted his mistress's kind offer with a smile. "We'll follow along shortly. I use a stick, so it will take me a little while to make my way along the path."

"Right you are, miss! I'll let Mrs. Banks and Mr. Humphrey know y'comin'," the man replied with a grin, and with another doff of his hat, turned and strolled back the way he had come, whistling as he went.

"I had a nice wedge of pheasant pie, a hunk of the best Cheshire, and a bottle of Bordeaux awaiting me at the barge," Grasby grumbled, opening the gate, then closing it again once Rory and he had passed through. "I hope you're pleased with yourself. And don't blame me when you get the shock of your life to find these people don't know the first thing about how to behave as they ought before the granddaughter of an earl!"

Rory let him see her cheeky smile of triumph. "Thank you, Harvel. But as *I* know how to behave as *I* ought, that's all that would matter to Grand."

He gave a grunt, offered his arm, and did not speak again until they were through the trees and at the edge of a clearing.

Lawn swept left, down to a clump of willows along the riverbank, and right, up to the house, a compact red brick Jacobean manor with ornate chimneys. A row of French doors that opened out onto a wide terrace were flung wide and secured against the outer brickwork by hooks, allowing ease of access into the house, and any breeze off the river to flow inside.

As the servant who had issued the invitation was nowhere to be seen, Grasby and Rory made for the terrace and the French windows. Here, in the shadow of the house, a carpet covered the tiles and set upon it was a dining table laden with a feast—a side of beef with all the trimmings, a leg of lamb, bowls heaped with vegetables, gravy boats and dishes of condiments, two large crusty loaves of bread, wine glasses and carafes. Dinner plates on either side of the feast held half-eaten meals, bone-handled knife and fork left atop the food. A child's frock coat was suspended from a chair back, and in another place, where the dinner plate should be, several wrapped packages were stacked and as yet unopened. Everything indicated a meal in progress. Yet, it was the chairs, pushed out and at every angle to the table, that told the story. It was as if the diners had left the feast in a great hurry. But why? What would cause more than half a dozen people to suddenly down knife and fork and flee?

Brother and sister looked at one another, mute, unable to provide a single plausible reason.

SEVENTEEN

LORD GRASBY was about to suggest to Rory they leave. It was beyond his comprehension why people would just up and abandon a splendid meal. He saw no reason to wait it out and have his suspicions confirmed that the family were far beneath their touch. And staring at all that food just made him hungrier. If he didn't get back to the barge post-haste, to his pheasant pie and Cheshire cheese, he feared he would lose his mind to starvation and help himself.

And then he instantly dismissed the idea of returning to the shallop. Rory's mittened hand was gripping his coat sleeve so tightly he knew it was only sheer force of will keeping her upright. The walk up to the house was twice the distance, and thus more than twice the effort, it would have taken for her to reach the barge. She needed to rest and elevate her foot upon a stool. He would not have been at all surprised if there were blisters. And she needed refreshment.

Without asking, he scooped her up and carried her to the closest chair, kicking it out wide from the table so he could sit her upon it. He then looked about for an empty tumbler amongst the dining table clutter. He found one at the far end of the table, where the child's coat and packages were, and also a jug of cordial.

He filled the tumbler then stuck his nose into it and sniffed, before taking a sip of the cloudy bittersweet liquid to taste if it was acceptable. Only then did he give it to his sister. When he told her to drink the lemon water because it was, in his opinion, perfectly acceptable refreshment, she did so without fuss. His precautions on her behalf to satisfy himself the cordial was suitable made her smile. He then went in search of a footstool, and crossed into the house, leaving her alone on the terrace.

RORY KNEW HER right foot was blistered and taking a peek at her stockinged ankle, she saw that it was swollen. She itched to slip off her specially constructed shoe and wriggle her toes. But she was not at home. With only herself to blame for wanting to visit Banks House, she was not complaining. She would not have missed this opportunity for anything. She cheerfully drank the rest of the lemon water and felt better. Sitting in the shade also helped, as did removing her straw hat, which she dropped into her lap. She prodded her coiffure with her fingertips then took up her gouache-painted fan that dangled from her wrist, unfurled it with a flick, and stirred the warm air across her flushed face.

When her brother did not reappear after five minutes, Rory became apprehensive. She hoped he wasn't giving its occupants a lecture on manners, or how to treat their social superiors. She was beginning to wonder if some of Silla's misguided ideas about her elevated station had rubbed off on him.

Grasby had never cared for penurious points of etiquette, claiming only dear old dowagers in their dotage were intent on enforcing rules that everyone in their circle knew practically from the cradle.

But where were the occupants? Why had they left the table in a hurry? Where was Mr. Humphrey? What was so urgent everyone was required to be someplace else? What now had happened to her brother?

No sooner had she posed these questions than she was greeted by a great wall of noise. It made her jump. She was glad she had finished all the cordial in her tumbler for she certainly would have spilled it across the front of her glazed cotton petticoats. She turned from her view of the lawn and looked over her right shoulder to the French windows.

A crowd of people spilled onto the terrace. Men and women, both young and old, scampering boys, a crying baby in a basket, several loping dogs, and three youths deep in conversation and in no hurry at all. All were in high spirits, and all resumed their places at the table, scraping in their chairs. Three little boys ignored Rory in their bid to satisfy their hunger, scrambling up onto their designated chairs with the help of the adults, and immediately taking up their forks to continue eating what food had earlier been put on their plates. The adults resumed their seats but did not eat, a smile of acknowledgement at Rory's presence, but seemingly too diffident to do anything more than nod mutely when she smiled in return.

Several maids followed the family onto the terrace, carrying even more dishes, and bottles of wine which they placed at intervals in amongst the clutter. Next came a male servant carrying a footstool, and this was placed in front of Rory. The servant positioned it to her satisfaction and then took himself off, leaving Rory at a table of diners who knew she was there but treated her as if she was more specter than flesh. She breathed a sigh of relief when her brother reappeared, the sigh turning to a gasp when her gaze alighted on the dark-haired beauty at his side. She was grateful when a maid offered her a glass of wine. It gave her something not only to drink but to look at rather than stare at the woman who must be Lily Banks.

This was confirmed when they were introduced, Grasby coming to stand by her chair as Mrs. Banks proceeded to introduce the rest of her family seated about the table: Her grandmother Mrs. Clare Banks, her parents Mr. and Mrs. Harold Banks, her brothers Charlie and Eddie, and a cousin, Arnie, and four of her five sons. Clive, eight years old, wanted to be a soldier like his Uncle Fitz. Bernard, six, was going to sea to be a pirate. Oliver was three years of age and until two months ago had been the baby of the family, that is, until baby Stephen's arrival.

Rory had no way of knowing if the adult relatives were Lily's relations or her husband's, but it did not matter, nor could she hope to remember everyone's names, though she did her best to commit to memory the children's. The only family members not at the table were Lily's husband, who had departed on a voyage to the South Seas just two weeks ago, but who was home long enough to be at the birth of his fourth son, interrupted Grandmother Banks, which he had not been for the births of Bernard or Oliver.

"My eldest, Jamie, is in the study setting up his microscope with the help of Mr. Humphrey, who knows about these things," Lily Banks said with a smile. "Both should be joining us soon, unless they get so caught up in some scientific investigation that they forget the passage of time—"

"Which happens more often than not around here!" stuck in Father Banks with a grunt of laughter. "When he's preoccupied with somethin' or other, Jamie would forget to eat if we didn't put food in front of him!"

"Lord Grasby, won't you sit?" Lily Banks asked. "There is plenty of food for an army, though all my boys but Jamie eat as if they are about to go into battle! Please," she insisted, and smiled when Grasby finally flicked out the skirts of his blue linen frock coat and put his bony knees under the table. "We said grace earlier, so if you don't mind, we shall continue with our birthday feast. Pass up your plates to Father Banks and he will cut you a few slices of beef and lamb."

Once Lily Banks was assured everyone at the table had what they needed, and were busy eating and drinking, the boys under the careful eye of their grandparents, she turned to Rory and Grasby and addressed them matter-of-factly.

"You must have wondered why the terrace was deserted, and so soon after I sent Old Bert with the invitation to speak with Mr. Humphrey here at the house. Please forgive me if I have separated you from your party. No sooner had Old Bert gone off to the gate than Mr. Humphrey tells me he saw you arrive by barge with a large group—"

"Don't concern yourself, Mrs. Banks," Grasby told her with a smile between mouthfuls, tucking in to the heaped plate of meat and vegetables put before him. "They were fatigued by the sun and are enjoying an afternoon nap, with little reason to think we are not amongst them. Isn't that so, Rory?"

Rory was amazed at how quickly her brother had adapted to his new surroundings, and how a kind smile and the attentions of a beautiful woman had done wonders to soothe any misgivings he may have had at sitting down to a meal with a woman he had earlier intimated had the manners and morals so far removed from their own as to be considered unworthy of their notice.

Regarding Mrs. Banks now, in her plain green linen gown and fitted jacket, black hair swept up and held by unadorned pins and one green ribbon, and no jewelry, she presented as any wife and mother of modest means and manners. It was her beauty that set her apart from her kinswomen, and from what Rory could deduce in all of five minutes of meeting her, she was modest about that, too.

She set down her wine glass, as if this had taken all her attention, and smiled at her hostess.

"As my brother says, it is of no consequence. Lady Grasby will be resting and completely oblivious to our truancy, though perhaps Mr. Watkins may be fretting as to our whereabouts. Perhaps we should send word...?"

"That won't be necessary—yet," Grasby stated, and, ignoring eye contact with his sister, said with a bright smile directed at Mrs. Banks, "You were about to tell us why the terrace was deserted..."

"Yes! We all went out to the front of the house to see the most magnificent carriage—"

"—pulled by six black high-steppers, with two outriders, and four footmen," stuck in Father Banks, slicing more beef for his grandsons' plates. "*All* in livery."

"We had to see the carriage for ourselves," Grandmother Banks continued. "It's not every day—not *any* day—when a carriage pulls up in front of our house, all black lacquer and gold paint."

"I only wish its noble occupant had stepped down from the carriage rather than have Jamie step up inside for a private word.

Then we all could have seen her fine clothes," Mother Banks said on a wistful sigh. "Makes the gift-giving all the more special, don't it? To think our Jamie's the only one of us to have been inside a conveyance sat in by nobility. The inside would be lined with fine silks and brocades I imagine..."

"I doubt Jamie was thinkin' about the noble posteriors who've sat on those silk cushions!" Eddie Banks snorted.

He received a cuffing from Father Banks for his impertinence; Charlie laughing loudly at his brother's discomfort and thankful he wasn't the one to embarrass himself before strangers.

"Poor Jamie was reluctant at first," Lily Banks confided to Rory and Lord Grasby, ignoring the activity at the far end of the table. "I couldn't blame him. To be summoned inside such a magnificent carriage all alone, and by a duchess! Any ten-year-old would be nervous."

"And not only a ten-year-old, Mrs. Banks," Grasby agreed. "I'd be shaking in my stockings to go it alone."

The young adult Banks brothers exchanged a wide-eyed stare before raising their glasses as one.

"Hear! Hear! That's what we said," offered Charlie and clinked glasses with his brother Eddie, both back in accord with each other.

Grasby put down his knife and fork, a glance at his sister. "If you don't mind me asking, who came calling?"

"The liveried footman who delivered the summons said a name I'm not familiar with," Mrs. Banks apologized. "Kin-something—"

"Kin*ross*. Her Grace the Duchess of Roxton and Kinross," Charlie announced with a superior smile. "May I mention the connection out loud, Pa? That footman did, so if the Duchess of Roxton and Kinross owns to the connection..."

Father Banks gave a shrug of a shoulder and stuck out his bottom lip.

"It's up to your sister to say it or not. It hasn't bothered you 'til now, Lily, and it's not like we hide it. And Jamie has always known who his father is and what he is. His Lordship acknowledges him as his own. But we got quality at the table today. Your past and his and the boy's parentage might not sit well with them..."

A small smile played about Lily Banks' mouth, and Rory held her breath, wondering if this was the moment for revelation, and if so, would she be able to detect if the lovely Lily was still in love with Major Lord Fitzstuart. Indeed, if they still had a connection, other than being the parents of an illegitimate son.

But when Lily Banks went to speak, Grasby intervened, and Rory could have kicked him.

"Not our business why Her Grace was here. If it's all the same to you, we'll just take it as read she came to speak to your son Jamie."

"If that is your wish," Lily Banks replied placidly and returned to eating the rest of the vegetables on her plate.

"Pardon my female curiosity," Rory said into the heavy silence, Lily Banks' unquestioning submission to her brother's proclamation giving her voice an unintended edge, "but I have a great desire to know why the Duchess of Roxton and Kinross came all the way from Westminster in a magnificent carriage to give Jamie a gift. I presume today must be your son's birthday, Mrs. Banks?"

Lily nodded. "Yes. It is. He is ten years old today."

Rory glanced about the table, ignored her brother's significant look, and said as she cut her slice of beef into small chewable bites, "What a pity His Lordship couldn't be here to share the day with his son."

"Rory!" Grasby hissed under his breath. "You're playin' with fire, and I don't care for it."

"That's why the Duchess of Roxton and Kinross came," Mother Banks volunteered, when no one else would reply after Lord Grasby's audible hiss. "She brought Jamie's gift because his father couldn't, and because Her Grace is Lord Fitzstuart's first cousin."

"Now, mother, you've gone and said it, and Lord Grasby here didn't want it to be said," Father Banks said with a shake of his head, though he didn't sound upset with her. "He possibly knows Lord Fitzstuart in his society. Still, I'm glad it's out in the open where it should be. Jamie is my grandson and it matters not a drop to me he was born on the wrong side of the blanket. I don't care who hears it or knows it! Not in this house. No offence, m'lord."

"None taken," Rory answered for her brother and rather too

buoyantly for Grasby's liking. She looked about the table at the Banks family and saw that their attention was focused on her brother, who was cutting into this third slice of beef as if he needed to exert full force to ensure his meal was indeed dead. "Please. Won't one of you tell the rest of the story of the Duchess's visit...?"

All were willing to comply, and it was Grandmother Banks who took up the story.

"A footman pulled down the steps for Jamie to climb up inside the carriage, and another footman stood to attention at the open door, nose in the air as if he himself was a duke! Poor Jamie. He stood at the bottom of those steps peering up into the darkness as if it was a scaffold he was about to climb! But then Her Grace appeared in the doorway. What a sight she was! A real beauty. And wearing such heavenly silks and sparkling jewels befitting her rank. Though she needed none of it to improve what God has blessed her with."

"She was everything and more what you imagine in your dreams a duchess would look like," Mother Banks interrupted, eyes wide and voice full of awe. "Her petticoats were a lovely shade of soft pink, all covered in silver embroidery and spangles. And there was so much yardage that her petticoats filled the opening of the carriage! And I saw her shoe, too. A pointed toe and matching pink satin and silver thread. She was so lovely! She put out a gloved hand to coax Jamie up inside—"

"And we got to admire her heavenly bosom—"

"Welcoming smile," Mother Banks interrupted her husband, giving him a swift nudge in the ribs with her elbow and a dark look before again addressing Rory. "*Such* a beautiful lady. Of course my Lily is just as sweet-faced."

"Oh, Mother!" Lily Banks laughed. "No one is as beautiful as the Duchess of Roxton and Kinross. I'm sure Lord Grasby and Miss Talbot would agree heartily."

"Yes. Yes. Her Grace is said to be quite breathtakingly lovely for a woman of her age," Grasby muttered.

"And got the most admirable bosom I've yet set eyes on, too," Father Banks stated with satisfaction, a wink at Charlie, Eddie and

Arnie, all of whom grinned from ear to ear. But what he said next turned their smiles into looks of abject disgust. He nudged his wife and said with a chuckle, "Not quite up to your sizable magnificence when you were at the height of your wet nursing powers, m'dear, but mighty close! What? Am I to beg everyone's pardon for sayin' what was before m'eyes?" he complained when not only his wife scowled at him, but so did his mother and his daughter.

He threw up his hands, got to his feet on a grunt, and made a bow before resuming his seat. "Beggin' Your Lordship and Miss Talbot's pardon for being so blunt. But I ain't used to speakin' before refined company. What I should have said, to put it in words my female family members would approve of, is this," He then mimicked the awed wonder in his wife and mother's voice when speaking of their noble visitor, "The Duchess was wearing the prettiest embroidered bodice. Covered in tiny bows it was. So low-cut it was, too. Showed off her ample bosom to perfection—Well, mother, is that better?"

The entire table erupted into laughter at his mimicry that it took several seconds for everyone to calm down. Father Banks looked to his guests who were not laughing, but politely smiling.

"No offence but we do like a good laugh over our beef..."

"Please, Mr. Banks. You are not required to apologize at your own table," Rory replied, a heightened color in her cheeks. "We are *your* guests. Besides," she added, unable to suppress a smile, "I am all for plain speaking, and so is my godmother, Her Grace of Roxton and Kinross. She will tell you so herself."

There was a collective sense of revelation and awe that the pretty young lady with the pale hair and fine features was the goddaughter of such a divine personage. It was as if the Duchess herself had come amongst them and all had slack jaws of wonderment. The only person not impressed was Grasby, whose ears had turned bright red at Mr. Banks' speech. They grew hotter at his sister's confidence, though he was not at all surprised by her naïve truthfulness.

"Why his father saw fit to gift a ten-year-old boy a microscope is beyond me," Grandmother Banks stated to no one in particular, lifting a shoulder in dismay. "I thought His Lordship might give him a pony of his own, or a cricket bat. That's more in keeping with what a ten-year-old boy should have."

"Granny, you know it is the perfect gift for Jamie," Lily Banks said mildly. "You saw his delight when he came out of the carriage, carrying that mahogany box as if it contained the most precious object in the world! He couldn't wait to go to the study, and he is still there with Mr. Humphrey. Both have forgotten that we are all here celebrating his birthday without him. But I do not wish to discourage his curiosity. Jamie wants to be a physician when he is grown," she confided to Grasby and Rory, and scooped up her crying baby out of its basket and cuddled him.

"Well, that's what he says today," stuck in Mother Banks.

"How splendid!" Rory enthused. "Then a microscope is the perfect gift. No doubt he and Mr. Humphrey are at this precise minute peering down the lens at a magnified beetle's wing, or at a flower petal. I'm sure he'll soon move on to more interesting matter such as a flea's leg and blood from a rat—oh! Excuse me. That was not polite of me, was it?"

"My sister also has a keen interest in all things scientific," Grasby explained, hoping to turn the conversation to a general topic more in keeping with the dinner conversation he was used to. "Her principal interest is in plants—pineapples to be specific. Which is why we are here to see Mr. Humphrey... Do you—do any of you know anything about the pineapple...?"

"No, my lord. We don't. But our lodger Mr. Humphrey I am sure will offer up an evening's worth of discourse on the subject! And there's nothin' to forgive, Miss Talbot," Father Banks stated as he scraped back his chair and stood. He pulled the napkin from the front of his waistcoat and dropped it on his plate. "The conversations that go on at this table between my son, when he returns from one of his expeditions, and Mr. Humphrey, would turn your fair hair black, Miss Talbot. Full of rats, pestilence and pygmies! Still, got to be more civilized than hearin' about amputations and savages runnin' amok, which is what we get when Jamie's father and his batman put in a rare appearance. Now, my three monkeys," he said, rubbing his hands together as he addressed his grandsons, "if you have demolished all that is on your plates, I'd say it's time for that game of cricket I promised. Eddie. Charlie. Arnie. Which of you three is batting first?" he asked, as his sons and nephew scrambled to their feet. "Perhaps His Lordship would care to join us in the game?"

Lily Banks' two eldest boys ran up to Grasby and stood by his chair. "Would you? Would you play cricket with us, sir? Would you? *Please.*"

"How can you refuse such eager little faces, Harvel?" Rory laughed at the resignation on her brother's face and said confidentially to the two little boys, "My brother is very good with the bat. But don't let him bowl. Put him in the outfield where he can take a catch."

"Thank you very much!" Grasby declared, reluctantly putting aside his napkin. "I have been known to take a wicket or two."

"Two. That's all you've taken!"

"So much for a lazy day on the river," Grasby grumbled with false resignation, but with a smile at the two little grubby faces eagerly peering up at him.

He shrugged out of his frock coat, Arnie Banks coming to his aid and laying the article over the back of Grasby's vacated chair, but not before covetously eyeing the cut of the cloth, the worked metal buttons and the delicate silver thread embroidery on the upturned cuffs and pockets.

Grasby removed the lace ruffles at his wrists and proceeded to roll up his billowing sleeves to just below his elbows. "Thank you for a most splendid repast, Mrs. Banks," he added with a short bow to Lily.

But when he straightened, Rory saw he was pale and she quickly grabbed her stick to stand, a natural response, but one that was not warranted when he turned and strode off in pursuit of Father Banks and his three sons. She soon realized the reason for her brother's lack of color when she accepted a cup of tea from Mother Banks.

Lily Banks had untied the front of her linen jacket and had put her son to her breast, the baby suckling contentedly. It was on the tip of her tongue to enquire about the baby when the cascade of lace at her left elbow was unceremoniously given a tug. She put her teacup on its saucer and turned to find six-year-old Bernard standing by her chair. He had not followed his brothers Clive and Oliver down to the lawn with the men but stood staring at her. When Rory smiled, he pointed to the footstool.

"Your foot's crooked. What's wrong with it?"

EIGHTEEN

"**B**ERNARD! Hush! That's not a question to ask our visitor."

It was his mother, and she was mortified.

"But her foot is all wrong, Mamma. Look!"

"Her name is Miss Talbot, and you are being discourteous. Please forgive him, Miss Talbot. He has always been the blunt one in the family, and if not the most inquisitive. He has to know about everything, just like his big brother Jamie."

"It's perfectly all right, Mrs. Banks. When I was your age, Bernard, I would ask my grandfather so many questions he looked as if he was about to burst and his wig pop off his head." She smiled when the little boy giggled. "I will answer your questions, if I am able."

"Can you walk with your foot like that?"

"I walked here. In fact, I walked around those gardens on the other side of the wall, and then I walked up the path through the trees to your house," she answered calmly as she brushed her petticoats over her ankles. "I use a walking stick. Here. Would you like to take a closer look?" She held out her stick to Bernard. "Do you see the pineapple carved into the handle?"

Bernard readily took the stick and peered at it as if it were the most fascinating object he had ever seen, from the intricately carved ivory handle that resembled a pineapple fruit, down the length of its polished mahogany stem, to the worn end.

"Do you need this to walk always?" he asked curiously.

"Not always, but it is better to have it as not, so I don't trip and fall."

"Can you hop?"

"On my left foot, yes."

"Skip?"

"With great difficulty."

"Jump?"

"Up and down? Yes. But only if I am *very* excited."

Bernard smiled, then asked, "What about run? Can you do that?"

"No."

"Not even if a great big bear were chasing you?"

"No. Not even then. I would try, of course. But I'm afraid if a bear were chasing me, it would catch me. Do you think if I asked it, it would dance with me?"

"Silly! Bears don't dance; not unless they're on a chain and been trained."

"You're right, of course."

"A bear would eat you as soon as look at you!"

"Bernard! How awful of you to say so," Lily Banks chastised.

"But true." Rory smiled at the little boy. "Don't worry. I will make certain to stay indoors if I hear there are any bears loose from Brookes' Menagerie—"

"The one on the Tottenham Court Road?" Bernard interrupted.

"Yes, that one."

"I would like to visit there one day."

"Perhaps one day you will," Rory replied encouragingly.

"Can you ride?"

"Yes. Riding makes it easier for me to get from place to place."

"You have boots?"

"Yes. Special ones."

Bernard frowned and asked in a whisper, "Can you get your foot fixed?"

Rory shook her head. "Sadly, no. This foot is with me forever, just as you will always have curly hair, except when it is wet. Then it is straight, isn't it? But my foot is the same, wet or dry."

Bernard had a thought, and his eyes opened wide.

"Swim! Can you swim? Can you swim like a—like a— *mermaid*?"

It was his mother who laughed.

"Bernard! You do have silly notions. Miss Talbot needs her stick to walk; she can hardly use it in the river to swim."

"I beg your pardon, Mrs. Banks, but Bernard's notion is an excellent one," Rory countered, gaze remaining on the little boy who had flushed to be admonished before a stranger. She smiled and took hold of his hand and drew him closer. "I think you are very clever to ask if I can swim. I don't need my stick in the water, do I? The water keeps me afloat."

"Do you—Do you swim like a mermaid?"

"I have never seen a mermaid, so I do not know how they swim. Perhaps my grandfather has seen one, because he was the one who taught me to swim, and I can swim very well indeed."

"With your arms; not your legs."

"Oh, you *are* clever! I do use my arms more than my legs, though I can kick with my legs, which helps me along." Rory took a sip of her milky tea. "Any more questions?"

Bernard shrugged. "No. If I think of more can I ask you?"

"Of course."

"Thank Miss Talbot for answering your questions—"

"Thank you."

"—and now leave Miss Talbot to sip her tea in peace," Lily Banks said firmly. "Off you go and play with your brothers."

Bernard handed Rory her stick with a shy smile then raced across the terrace, down the steps and out onto the lawn to join in the game of cricket. When he looked over his shoulder, Rory waved to him. He gave a wave in return and did a tumble on the grass for good measure.

Turning to Lily Banks, Rory was about to say how much she was enjoying the afternoon and to thank her for sending Old Bert to invite them up to the house; she hoped she would see Mr.

Humphrey and meet her son Jamie before it was time for her and Grasby to return to the barge. But instead of this calm speech of thanks, she said nothing at all. She was speechless.

In shock, she lost the grip on the handle of her teacup. It clattered to the saucer and toppled. The drop of tea left in the cup splashed over the lip of the saucer and stained the blue satin riband nestled in the crown of her straw hat still resting on her lap. She was just grateful the tea had not found its way to her flowered petticoats. Still, she made a fuss with the hat, if only to regain her equilibrium and hope the heat in her face had faded enough for her to look at the new arrival.

First her book, and now this teacup! He would surely think her the clumsiest female in existence!

Out onto the terrace had stepped Major Lord Fitzstuart.

NINETEEN

A MUD -SPATTERED great coat concealed a dark plum riding frock and buff breeches, and with his jockey boots similarly caked in mud, the Major looked to have been astride a horse all day, and in varying degrees of inclement weather. He still wore kid riding gloves, but had removed his black felt hat, revealing unruly shoulder-length black hair, damp from exertion or rain, or both. Gone was the bruising to his eye and the deep cut to his lip had healed, leaving a small purple scar. His skin had a healthy glow, as if he had seen many days of sun, and the dark, close-cropped beard gave him a piratical appearance. But it was at his eyes Rory stared without blinking. He was tired, as if he hadn't slept in a week, and he was staring at her in a way that suggested he wanted her to read his thoughts. Those thoughts were most discomforting, because she received the strongest impression he was not pleased to discover her at Banks House.

She was the first to look away, and fussed with the teacup and saucer, placing it on the table. She then inspected the stained silk ribbon as if it required all of her attention.

In her forced preoccupation, the Major stepped forward and made his presence known to Lily Banks.

Rory pretended not to notice, but out of the corner of her eye she saw him remove his gloves and place a bare hand lightly on Lily's shoulder. The grazes to his knuckles had also healed, and his hand, like his face, was sun-bronzed. He stooped, said something at Lily Banks' ear, kissed her cheek, then stood tall. That kiss, light and perfunctory as it was, had the power to make Rory blush, and with abject despondency. And when Lily Banks half-turned in her chair with an exclamation of delightful surprise, the baby still at her breast and a hand out to Dair in greeting, Rory's blush ripened into one of unwanted interloper.

Here was a couple pleased to see each other; a couple used to intimacy; a couple who shared a child...

For the first time since arriving at Banks House, Rory wished she had taken her brother's advice and returned to the barge. For a reason only known to her heart, she felt a great pressure in her chest. It was pain, the aching pain of affection not reciprocated or wanted. She was such a fool! He had never singled her out in the past, why, after a drunken kiss he did not remember, would he single her out now?

As if in answer to her question, he made her a small bow when Lily Banks mentioned her by name, though she was so preoccupied with her thoughts she had no idea what was said. But it did not matter, the acknowledgment had been made and that was all that was required of him. He did not look at her again, nor did he include her in his conversation.

The oppressive feeling pressed down even further watching the interaction between the parents of Jamie Banks. Yet she could not dislike Lily Banks or feel any jealousy toward her just because the Major was at ease in her company. Lily Banks did not flirt with him, or act in any way that indicated they were anything but friends of long-standing. Why was it, she wondered, that females who had children out of wedlock were instantly branded the lowest forms of life, incapable of constancy, honesty and decent behavior? And yet, their male counterparts were thought anything but immoral. She had always scowled at such uneven standards. Of course, Harvel branded her bookish and said she would be locked up as mad if she ever dared voice such thoughts in decent company. Silla had called her ruminations wicked and never to be repeated, certainly not in front of the vicar.

The general flurry of activity sparked by the Major's arrival allowed Rory to retreat into the background, to her usual place as observer at gatherings. In many ways, it was a relief not to have his eyes upon her; it helped quiet her heart and permitted her to drink a second cup of tea without spilling a drop.

Servants scurried back and forth from the house. Great coat, gloves and hat were taken away. Dirty plates and empty bowls were removed from the table. A space was cleared for the new arrival. Clean plate and cutlery, fresh bread, a tumbler and a jug of ale were all placed before him. And the Major did not hesitate to fill his plate with the remnants of the birthday feast, answering Lily Banks' question, after a hard swallow.

"You'd be famished too if you'd not eaten a good English meal in over a month!" He pulled a chunk of crusty bread from a fresh loaf and sopped up gravy. When he could speak again, he said with a grin, "Two slices of beef and I'm already feeling human again. No! Don't say it. I know. It will take a shave and a bath before I can present as human, but I wanted to get here as soon as possible." He looked out at the cricket game in progress. "I don't see Jamie. Where is my birthday boy?"

Lily Banks told him about the visit of the Duchess of Roxton and Kinross and the presentation of the microscope, adding after she had tied and adjusted her jacket, baby put to her shoulder to gently rub his back to settle his stomach, "He's in the study with Mr. Humphrey, peering at all sorts of queer objects through a lens. Poor Miss Talbot has come to see Mr. Humphrey specifically, and Jamie has taken all his time, so has yet to show himself."

"Then get them out of there, Lil. I didn't gift him a microscope so he could monopolize your lodger's time and attention. Not when Humphrey is wanted elsewhere. And I don't want Jamie neglecting his food and his obligations. Did his brothers eat their dinner at the table with the rest of the family?"

"Yes, of course."

"Then why not Jamie?"

"He did. We all started our meal, then were interrupted by the Duchess's carriage. But poor Mr. Humphrey did not have the opportunity to finish what was on his plate once Jamie saw what was in the mahogany box."

"Lil, he should have come back to the table. He's the eldest. He needs to set the example. And don't say because it's his birthday he can be shown leniency. He does it every time he can get away with it. He should not've had access to the microscope until after he'd finished his meal with the family. And he should've been made to wait until Humphrey had eaten his fill. That's just good manners. The poor chap's stomach must be growling!"

"Yes. Yes, of course. You're right," Lily Banks murmured and scrambled to her feet. "You know how he is when he gets distracted... He's so terribly clever. Much cleverer than the rest of us."

Dair poured himself another tumbler of ale.

"Being clever is not enough. He needs to know how to use his cleverness in the right way, to be mindful of others. And he needs to spend time out of doors, enjoying fresh air, sunshine and cricket, like every other boy his age."

"He prefers the study..." When Dair made no reply and drank down his ale, Lily added quietly, "I'll have him fetched at once..."

When she went to put the baby back in his basket and he began to fuss, she just stood there, flustered, wondering what to do with him.

Without a second thought, Dair took the grizzling infant and held him up to his chest, a large hand spanning the tiny back to keep him firm and upright, the baby's wet chin resting on his shoulder. Sensing Lily was still there, he said quietly,

"Don't take it to heart, Lil. I'm tired... I'll stay the night, if it's not too much of an inconvenience—"

"Never. Your room is always made ready."

When he smiled and nodded, Lily Banks disappeared inside the house, leaving a heavy silence at the table. Rory wished the two older Banks women—who were seated at the furthest end of the terrace, heads together talking—would turn and notice the new arrival. She hoped Jamie and Mr. Humphrey were not long in coming. She put her teacup on its saucer and lifted her gaze to the sight of the small bundle cuddled against the Major's shoulder, while he continued to eat ravenously, using his fork as best he could, with only one hand free, to cut as well as scoop up the vegetables on his plate. He held the infant unselfconsciously, as one adept at doing so, and as if his embrace were the most natural and most comforting place to be.

There was something wonderful about a big handsome man holding such a tiny, vulnerable little being with one large protective hand. It brought inexplicable tears, tears Rory quickly blinked away. She mentally admonished herself for being sentimental, that even this small domestic scene involving the Major had the power to provoke such an emotional response in her.

She turned her gaze to the lawn and watched the cricket match in progress. Her brother, in the outfield, sleeves rolled to the elbow, had a hand up, shielding his eyes from the sun. One of the Banks brothers was batting. Another was bowling. The three boys were doing tumbles on the lawn with only a halfhearted interest in the game. Rory suspected the adults were completely dominating the match, so the children had lost interest. She looked away, to see if the Banks women still had their heads together. They did.

She returned her attention to the table and was startled to find the Major regarding her steadily. He must have had his eyes on her profile for some time, such was the intensity in his gaze, but she did not look away.

"Before you dare to ask, Miss Talbot," Dair said flatly. "The answer to your burning question is no, this brat is not mine. Nor are his three elder brothers. They have a father, and their mother is a devoted wife. Only Jamie belongs to me."

"Thank you for being frank, my lord," Rory replied levelly. Despite a heaviness of heart, she was affronted by his presumption. "But I do not thank you for thinking you can read my mind. It will surprise you to know that what I was truly thinking about was the wonderful job Mrs. Banks has done in raising her sons, mostly on her own; what with her husband the intrepid explorer, and you, an offi-cer, leaving her alone for extended absences. I was also thinking how lovely it must be to have other family members around at such times. Not having uncles or aunts or parents, and only one grandparent, it was such a pleasure for Harvel and me to sit at a table with a large happy family group. It reminded me of the few times we visited my godparents at Treat—"

"Miss Talbot, I apologize if I offended—"

"My lord, you should wait until I have finished my diatribe before you decide if you owe me an apology or not," Rory inter-rupted, the sparkle back in her blue eyes when he promptly closed his mouth and glanced away. "As we are being frank, then let me be also. Even though it is none of my concern, if Jamie has a gift for science, and his natural inclination is to spend his time peering into lenses and classifying insects and plants, and whatever else catches his inter-est, then his mother is wise to let him do as he pleases, rather than force him to do what pleases *you*. I have never met your son—"

"—and yet you presume to know him?"

Rory smiled crookedly. She wanted to say that though she did not know the son, she was confident she understood the father's proclivities. Instead, she answered, a little less stridently than before.

"No. Not him. But if you cast your mind back to your tenth birthday, as I have done mine, can you remember what you were eating? I surely cannot. But I am confident you remember what you were doing..."

Dair did not hesitate. He shifted the baby to his other shoulder, again holding him there with a splayed hand, and said bluntly, "I was outdoors skimming stones on the lake. I preferred—*I prefer*—to be outdoors. Anywhere but a book room. Such stuffy rooms give me the headache. Charlie and I were waiting for our father to join us. He was in his study; a place he rarely left. He'd been watching Charlie and me from his study window... When he finally joined us, he gave me a birthday gift I will never forget. The next day he departed for London. We never saw him again. And before you make comment," he added with a thin smile, "I am not forcing Jamie out-of-doors because that is what I did at his age, or what I think he should be doing. He needs to be reminded he is one of five brothers, and on this of all days. Between you and me, his mother, his grandparents— even Lily's husband—all indulge him because of who he is, rather than because he is clever. My great-grandfather was Charles the Second, so he has royal blood in his veins, however polluted, and one day I will be the Earl of Strathsay. That's a heady mix for his mother's family, whose antecedents never rose beyond their position of servant these past three hundred years. But it does not remove the stain of his illegitimacy."

Rory cocked her head and said pensively, "Perhaps that bothers you more than it does them..."

This forced from him a reluctant laugh. "Yes, perhaps it does..." He glanced over at the two older Banks women. "Lil's mother was the family wet nurse, then nursery maid; her father was a gardener on the estate... That is, until the unthinkable happened—"

"You fell in love with Lily Banks."

Dair put down his fork, pushed his plate away and took up his tumbler. He drained the cup. She sensed he was about to confide something in her, but the sudden commotion at his back forestalled him and the moment was lost. He scraped back his chair, Lily Banks scooped up her baby, and a tall thin boy ran up to be crushed in his father's embrace.

There wasn't a dry eye on the terrace at this loving reunion between father and son; even Rory was quick to dab tears away before anyone noticed.

The hubbub brought the older Banks women bustling to the table. They embraced Jamie's father. Mother Banks took Dair's handsome face between her hands and heartily kissed his forehead before enveloping him in a crushing embrace.

Dair laughed when she scolded him for not alerting them to his presence, nodded obediently when she enquired if he had enough to eat, and grinned when she said it was just as well because she did not want him dying of hunger after surviving all those years as a soldier. She had a vested interest in his welfare. After all, she had been his principal source of nourishment from birth until two years. Where-upon Lily Banks told her mother to hush, and that she made the same observation every time Al (for that was what Lily called the Major) came to visit after one of his long spells away. And this last spell had been all of five weeks.

Dair took the attention in his stride, laughing and grinning and shaking his head at the women, before resuming his seat and drawing his son to him to tell him all about his birthday.

"I do always say it, too," Mother Banks confided to Rory as she eased herself onto a chair as a pinch-faced maid put a fresh cup of tea before her. "But I ask you, Miss Talbot, why shouldn't I say it? I'm proud His Lordship has grown into a mountain of a man. What wet nurse wouldn't be? He was not a big baby. There was a time, just after he was born, when his father worried he wouldn't survive. But I told His Lordship I'd get his heir through his first year, and I did. Truth told," she added in a confidential undertone, pulling her shawl closer about her round shoulders and leaning into Rory's chair, "I'm not surprised he was such a scrawny baby. Starved, of nourishment and affection. The Countess is a cold woman *in every sense*. Loathed the begetting, the birthing, *and* the feeding of children. That's God's honest truth!"

"*Mother*! Miss Talbot is unused to such conversation. She is a *lady*," Lily Banks whispered fiercely, an eye to the Major, who was listening attentively to the boy's wide-eyed recounting of his visit with the Duchess of Roxton and Kinross in the opulent interior of her carriage. "I dare say she is not only embarrassed, but offended, too. Poor Miss Talbot came here to speak to Mr. Humphrey about pineapples, not hear your stories about Al as a baby. Forgive my mother, Miss Talbot. Mr. Humphrey should be here directly. I don't know what is still keeping him..."

Rory smiled and swallowed and hoped her face wasn't as red as it was hot. Mother Banks' eye-opening revelations would have knocked her brother off his seat with shocked mortification. He certainly would have used them as a prime example of why he had not wished his sister exposed to the crude sensibilities of the Banks family. But watching the Major and his son interact, the obvious love they had for each other, indeed the entire Banks clan's great affection for Lord Fitzstuart, and his affection of them, was a balm to her finer feelings.

For how could she truly be offended by Mother Banks' truthfulness when couched with the warmth of feeling she had for the Major? Besides, her own behavior was wanting, for if she had stared at Lily Banks' beauty when she first saw her, she stared twice as hard now at the beautiful boy with the mop of dark red curls who had his father's dark eyes. Oh, Jamie Banks would break hearts just like his father when he was old enough...

"Miss Talbot...?" It was the Major. He brought her out of her abstraction, an arm about his son's shoulders. "Jamie, this is Grasby's sister, Miss Talbot. You remember Lord Grasby—he accompanied us to Mr. Pleasant's shooting box..."

"Grasby? Yes, I remember Grasby." The boy made Rory a quaint little bow and said solemnly, "How do you do, Miss Talbot?"

"I am very well, Jamie. May I call you Jamie?"

The boy smiled. "Everyone does."

"I should like to see your microscope one day, if you will allow me."

The boy's eyes lit up. "Would you? Mr. George Adams of Fleet Street made it," he said with awe. "He makes the best microscopes. It's brass and has *three* Lieberkuhn objectives, so I have both a compound body and a simple magnifier. And it all comes apart and fits into this big wooden case..." He looked up at his father. "May I show her, Papa? May I?"

"You may. But not today. Miss Talbot must leave us now, and you need to eat the rest of what you left on your plate. But before you finish off your nuncheon," he added, handing his son Grasby's frock coat, "please take this to Lord Grasby and tell him not to wait. I'll bring Miss Talbot to him."

Rory was about to enquire why His Lordship was terminating not only her visit but her brother's involvement in the game of cricket, when the Major turned away to speak with a rotund gentleman in bagwig and spectacles who had just stepped onto the terrace from the house. Their conversation was brief and then the gentleman followed Jamie down the terrace steps to the lawn. Rory watched his progress and sat up when three figures on the edge of the lawn came into view. Jamie was still holding her brother's frock coat;

Grasby had his back to the cricket game, hands on his hips, while the third figure was slightly bent forward with his hands clasped, as if in supplication, yet he was the one doing all the talking. It was one of the footmen from the shallop, and by his stance, and her brother's arms akimbo, she was certain the servant was giving Grasby an earful of complaints, courtesy of Lady Grasby.

TWENTY

DAIR EXTENDED his hand to Rory. "Come. Let me help you up."

She removed her feet from the footstool, and he kicked it out of the way with the toe of his boot. Helping her to her feet, he held her hand until she was steady and leaning on her stick.

"Did you come by carriage?"

"No. My grandfather's shallop."

"By river? How pleasant for you. The return journey should give you ample time to have a full and frank discussion with Mr. Humphrey about your pineapple flower—your first, I believe?"

"You remembered the flower?"

"You were so excited; you dropped a treatise on gardening at my feet! I gather the plant does not flower often?"

"Crawford and I have waited two years to see one. A flower means a pineapple fruit is not far away."

"Then it is rare and something to be animated about. I hope Mr. Humphrey's advice is useful. Now please give your stick to Mrs. Banks." When she hesitated, he smiled. "You'll get it back." Done as requested, he took a step away, still holding her hand, and looked her up and down, gaze pausing at the point of her beribboned bodice that highlighted her small waist. "If I'm not mistaken, under those fetching flowered petticoats are a set of light-weight panniers?"

"Yes. But—"

"No buts, Miss Talbot. I am now going to pick you up. As I do so, please bunch up your petticoats to collapse the panniers. It will make my task that much easier. Mrs. Banks will then return your stick, which you will hold without accosting me, and I shall then carry you to your barge. Understood?"

"Yes. But—"

He didn't wait to hear her excuses. He effortlessly lifted her and she quickly did as he asked, Lily Banks coming to her aid to brush down the layers of light cotton over Rory's stockinged shins. She was then handed her stick. Hurried farewells and thank-yous exchanged, Dair strode off across the terrace towards the trees that provided privacy between the south wall and the Physic Garden. But he had not gone more than fifty paces when he stopped under the shade of a spreading oak.

"Miss Talbot, if I am to deliver you to your barge without incident, you need to be supple in my arms. Not a plank of wood, for that is what I am carrying at the moment."

"I can walk!"

"You can. But not in your present state. Mrs. Banks mentioned you have blistered your feet. I'd wager you're stubborn enough to still walk, just to spite me. But don't think of yourself, think of your brother. In the time it would take you to walk back to the barge, I fear Grasby may have jumped overboard and be lost to the tangle of Thames reeds. I gather Her Ladyship is aboard your vessel?"

"Yes. And most reluctantly, too. Harvel and I left her and Mr. Watkins alone for quite some time..."

"Thank you."

Rory tilted her head to look at him. His face was so close she could see the individual hairs of the beard covering his cheeks and jaw. It was black, like the hair that fell across his brow... Like the hairs on his chest... With the light browning to his skin, he did indeed look the pirate.

"Thank me? For what, pray?"

"For not bringing Her Ladyship and Weasel up to Banks House."

"Oh, they'd not have come within a hundred feet of the place! Oh! That was—"

"—the truth. I'm surprised Grasby gave you permission to do so."

"He didn't. But he could not stop me."

He chuckled.

She smiled, liking the sound.

"Of that I have no doubt. You're a determined little thing, aren't you?"

"I was invited—invited to Banks House..."

He did not hesitate in his response and sounded surprised.

"Were you?"

"Yes. But... But I won't tell you who invited me because you would be more than surprised. You would be shocked."

"Would I? I am not a man easily shocked, Miss Talbot."

"That I believe. You must have had some horrifying experiences while in the army."

"Yes."

"And you must've been not much more than a boy when you joined up."

"Fourteen..."

He set off again and had only gone a few yards when she said quietly, "I hope I'm not too much of a burden."

"None at all. I've carried wounded soldiers from a battlefield. Believe me, when men are dead or dying, they are twice their weight. You, Miss Talbot, are as light as a fairy's gossamer wings."

As he carried her along the path, Dair tried to see her face, but it was hidden behind a quantity of hair having escaped from an enameled hair clasp and falling across her brow. He had no way of knowing her mood. What he did know was that he liked having her in his arms again, very much. Yet, the sensation was also oddly disconcerting, as if he had no right and no reason to hold her. Why did she befuddle him so? Why, when he had stepped onto the terrace, and discovered her sitting there in her pretty flowered petticoats, was he overwhelmed with the desire to scoop her up and kiss her?

God he hoped she wasn't going to mention the night at Romney's studio. If she did, he would have to lie to her again and plead complete drunken ignorance, as he had promised her grandfather he would. And that was another thing that bewildered him. He was uncomfortable with the thought of lying to her, of keeping up the subterfuge of indifferent dolt. For the first time in many years, he had no wish to play-act. He just wanted to be himself; to be himself *with her*.

When she shifted slightly in his arms, interrupting his thoughts, he caught the faint perfume of lavender in her hair mingled with the scent of vanilla from her warm skin. It was such an evocative scent that a quiver of need shot straight through him. He desperately wanted to kiss Aurora Talbot again. And he needed to kiss her again, to satisfy himself that the kiss they had shared at Romney's studio was nothing special. He did not want it to be special; it could not be anything but ordinary. There was no room in his life for sentiment. Sentiment carried with it the expectation of marriage, an institution he reviled.

After witnessing years of his parents' hate-filled union, he had sworn never to succumb to the oxymoron that was "wedded bliss." He had witnessed the violence and vitriol that comes when two people are trapped in a marriage neither can escape. His parents' marriage had been hell on earth, for them, and for him and his brother and sister.

One kiss shared with Aurora Talbot and he would be satisfied that he was no more or no less attracted to her than he was to any pretty female who caught his wandering eye. One kiss, and his life would return to its previous untroubled state before the incident at Romney's studio, where he was able to fall into bed with a certain sort of female, make love with mutual abandon and satisfaction, then move on to the next beautiful nymph who gave him a come-hither smile—no questions asked, and no expectations of anything other than what it was, for either party. So the sooner he kissed Aurora Talbot, the sooner his equilibrium would be restored.

Taking a moment to collect his thoughts, he cleared his throat as well as his mind and said with mild disinterest, not having heard what she said, only that she had spoken through her tangle of hair, "I beg your pardon, Miss Talbot, but talking of fairies had me away with them!"

"I said that there isn't a thing either of us can do to change the past. But just because we cannot change events, does not mean I cannot change my opinion. And it cannot stop me feeling the way I do, now that my opinion has altered. Does that make sense?"

"Perhaps you need to explain it to me more fully?"

"May I?"

"By all means," he replied blandly, thinking that if he allowed her to babble on it might help him ignore how she made him feel.

"Thank you... You see until you mentioned just now about carrying the dead and dying from a battlefield, I had not thought too deeply about what you and your brother soldiers endure in the army. Oh, I knew it must be wretched and too horrible for words, but I could never imagine what horrors you faced on the battlefield... But what you said just now, it was in such a matter-of-fact way that it instantly made me feel as if I was amongst the carnage—"

"Forgive me. It was not my intention to upset you."

"Oh, there is nothing to forgive. I am not upset. I just want you to know I would like—*like* isn't the right word—I would be *honored* if you ever wanted to tell me about your time in the army. Any of it. Grand tells me I am a good listener in that I do not interrupt or pry."

"I shall keep your offer in mind."

At that Rory gave a tinkle of laughter. "By which you mean you have no intention of telling me anything at all! No matter. My offer stands."

When he remained silent and continued down the path and out into the clearing, she allowed herself to put her head on his shoulder and snuggle into the softness of his plum velvet frock coat. Unbeknownst to her, she breathed in deeply and sighed her contentment, enjoying the masculine salty scent of him mingled with traces of bergamot and woody tobacco leaf.

"I've been traveling since first light," he muttered self-consciously. "I must be disagreeable to you."

"No! No, not at all. I like it—I mean—*you*—I mean your frock coat—Your *frock coat* is most agreeable."

He remained tight-lipped, square chin and dark eyes straight, but her panic of correction made him mentally smile.

They had come to the low stone wall that divided the Physic Garden from Banks House. Instead of opening the gate and passing through it, Dair carefully set Rory on top of the stonework.

"It saddens me you were forbidden to marry Lily Banks," Rory said conversationally as she set her walking stick by the wall. "I like her. She is quite lovely, and not just in her appearance. She has a good heart and a gentle soul. I like her family, too. They are all well-meaning personable people. They certainly consider you part of their family. And Jamie—it is obvious you love him dearly. All that truly matters is the deep affection you, Jamie and Mrs. Banks have for one another. In such circumstances, Society's good opinion is about as meaningful as a bowl of cold oats, is it not? Jamie has a great look of you..." When he grunted, she added steadily, "It was not my intention to offend you, my lord."

"You did not, Miss Talbot."

With a short bow, he excused himself and walked a little way through the field of wildflowers, shrugging his shoulders and stretching his arms, as if to rid a stiffness in his muscles. He then walked on; hands shoved deep into the pockets of his frock coat.

TWENTY-ONE

Major Lord Fitzstuart might say she had not offended him, but Rory thought otherwise. She was always too honest for her own good. Her thoughts came tumbling out without the circumspection her grandfather cautioned she needed. Her muddled speech was meant to reassure the Major that she was not judgmental about the Banks family, or offended he shared a son with Lily Banks, or even that he had a continuing relationship with Mrs. Banks, whatever that was—she was not precisely sure. Though, having now spent a few hours in her company, she was convinced she and the Major were not lovers, and had not been since her marriage.

She watched him closely as he came back to her, a hand through his mussed hair, and that's when it struck her. Why had he been in the saddle all day? And if he had, then it was no wonder he needed to stretch his limbs. He was tired and aching, and yet he had put himself to the bother of carrying her back to the jetty. And why were his face and hands lightly bronzed, as if he had spent days in a climate where the sun shone so brightly it could turn a man's skin caramel. Surely there was no place this side of the Channel where it had not rained in the past month, that would give rise to such a complexion. She concluded he must have been absent from England for at least four weeks. Was that why he had allowed a black beard to grow upon his face, as if he had not the time or inclination to shave in days? Or was it part of something more mysterious, a disguise perhaps?

The sun's brightness made her squint and place a hand to her brow, as he rejoined her at the wall. He moved into the path of the sun's rays, to block the glare from her eyes, leaving her in his shadow.

She smiled up at him, removing her hand, and said blithely, "I had always assumed an inmate of the Tower spent most of his day locked up. It just goes to show that we on the outside know little about what occurs on the inside of His Majesty's premier prison..."

For one moment he had no idea what she was talking about. He'd forgotten he was supposed to have spent the past month locked up; though he had not forgotten his batman was still languishing under lock and key masquerading as him. He did not want to lie to her, but he wasn't going to give the game away, either.

"Why do you say so, Miss Talbot?"

"No doubt my grandfather could tell me. He knows the history of the Tower and its guests as well as he does the veins on the back of his hands. Perhaps inmates of the Tower are not permitted the implements to shave their beards for fear they might do themselves or others an injury. But I am certain inmates rarely go free with such a healthy glow to their skin as you have."

Dair put up a thick black eyebrow with studied surprise. "Is that so? Perhaps I was permitted more exercise time in the courtyard. I hate being cooped up, particularly in small spaces."

Rory's blue eyes narrowed and her voice held a note of triumph.

"Even were that the case, my lord, more time in the courtyard would have meant more time soaked through to your skin, and a possible cold caught for all your need of the outdoors. It has been raining on and off this past month—and at the Tower, too. Black clouds do not part even if for the innocent, and the charges brought against them a ruse for some higher purpose..."

For a moment he said nothing, and she wondered if he would refute her claims. But then he showed her a white smile and shook his head.

"Bravo, Miss Talbot. Naturally, I cannot tell you where I've been or what I've been doing."

"Oh, I don't care about that! Oh! That is not strictly true. I care *you* are home safe, but as to what you've been doing and where you've been..." She pretended a moment to think on the matter, twirling a long lock of her fair hair between her fingers. "Not Paris. Not warm enough. And you have only been away for a little over a month... So you didn't sail off to the Caribbean and back... I would hazard you were somewhere down the Channel, towards the Mediterranean... The south of France? Spain, perhaps...?"

"With this beard, I would not blame you for thinking I had taken up piracy on the high seas or smuggling in the coves of Cornwall."

Rory's gaze locked on his fingertips lightly stroking his bearded jaw and she longed to reach out and do the same. She wondered what he would be like to kiss with a beard. Would it be just as delicious as that first time? Were the hairs on his face as soft as those on his chest? Would they tickle or annoy her?

Stop it, Aurora Christina Talbot! Your thoughts about this man are no longer delightfully wicked—they have turned ridiculously obsessive. He kissed you once and now you think there is some sort of connection between the two of you? There is not. Whatever you felt, it could not possibly be reciprocated. Stop being naïve, you little idiot!

So said the voice of reason. But she could not help herself, particularly with the man standing in front of her in all his piratical handsomeness. She so wanted to know what it would be like to kiss him with that beard. She swallowed and pressed her dry lips together and said with a nervous laugh and a shrug, in her best manner of appearing off-hand,

"Pirate. American Indian. Officer in His Majesty's Army. Smuggler, perhaps... I wonder what other disguises you wear when you are absent from Society's drawing rooms...?"

"Your grandfather should consider employing you. Your observational and reasoning skills are second to none."

Rory beamed with pride at such praise. But she noted his voice was flat and he had skillfully avoided a direct response. Also, he showed not a flicker of recognition when she mentioned American Indian. He was either an exceptional actor, or he had indeed been blind drunk the night at Romney's studio. Either way, her voice of reason dared to smugly confirm that such a lack of a reaction in him was proof she meant less than nothing to him.

"Not from want of effort, but learned over time," she said with a small unconscious sigh of defeat in response to her little voice of reason. "And from boredom. There simply isn't much to do at balls and the like when one is confined to a chair."

"You cannot dance—at all?"

She heard the note of concern in his voice, and it snapped her out of her preoccupation. That would serve her to rights for listening to the doubts expressed by her inner voice instead of concentrating on the here and now! The last thing on this earth she wanted from him was sympathy; the second last, to appear maudlin. She was rarely, if ever, self-pitying, and she never used her malformed foot as an excuse, or as a way of appearing interesting to others, or to elicit sympathy.

She had been taught from a young age that to draw attention to herself in any way was the height of bad manners. Upon leaving the nursery and going out into Society, her grandfather had warned that it was her responsibility to put others at ease and to ensure they were not made uncomfortable in her presence. To do this she must be aware of her limitations. He said she was the most beautiful girl in the world and everyone else would soon see this too, if she was simply herself.

She believed her grandfather and did as he counseled. But what had never occurred to her, until she had set eyes on the very man who now stood before her, was to ask the question she now asked: Would she ever be desired for herself?

"You are right. Grand should employ me," she replied, ignoring his question as he had earlier ignored hers. "The tittle-tattle I could recount to him after hours of observing others over the rim of my teacup! But I don't need to tell you, do I? I suspect in your chosen occupation you need to be a master of observation. Though—in your particular case—you are accomplished at concealing your skills."

"Concealing my skills?" The corner of his mouth twitched. "I have more than one?"

She ignored his flippancy, breathing a mental sigh of relief that he did not pursue whether or not she could dance, and excited to have unmasked him. The more she thought about it, the more she knew her supposition to be correct. She recalled her unsettling impression of him the times she had watched him at balls and Society gatherings from the comfort of a chair and behind her fluttering fan: There was something about the way he played the big-headed Merry-Andrew a little too well. And it perplexed her that her grandfather quietly defended him whenever dinner guests dared to suggest Major Lord Fitzstuart was nothing more than an arrogant buffoon and a self-serving dullard, a disgrace not only to his royal heritage, but also to his august kin, the Duke of Roxton and his family.

She had always wondered what the connection could be between her grandfather and her brother's school friend. She assumed it was simply her grandfather keeping a fatherly eye on the Major, since his own father had deserted his family and his country. Possibly this was true, but she now believed there was nothing simple about their association. She could have kicked her own shin for not suspecting earlier that the Major was the Spymaster General's protégé. It made perfect sense, and the Major played the game very well indeed.

"Every spy hides behind a façade, or he would not be good at spying, would he?" she said matter-of-factly, and when his smile died she pretended not to notice, adding cheerfully, "Observation is an important skill. Not too many persons can do two things at once well, least of all observe a room full of people while pretending disinterest in his surroundings. And you are particularly skilled, because you are usually the center of attention, so it must be doubly difficult for you." She cocked her head and screwed up her little nose in thought. "You have perfected the practice of blustering arrogance so well that you may call it your own, thus most people take you at face value—"

"Face value? You give me a great deal more credit than others who own to knowing me better."

She shrugged. "Why should your family, friends and acquaintances think you anything but what you present? Major Lord Fitzstuart can be dared to take on any wager, must win at all costs, and plays the big handsome buffoon so convincingly no one questions his performance. Society rarely looks beyond the superficial. It prefers to believe the most salacious answer is the correct one and does not change its opinion once formed. That is how a sweet-natured female of good character can be branded a whore for all eternity, when, as a mere girl, she made the mistake of falling in love with a handsome boy out of her marital reach and had his babe out of wedlock as a consequence."

He was surprised by her keen and succinct summation. He knew she was referring to Lily, and agreed with her, but all he said was, "Thank you, Miss Talbot. You have made your point."

"I meant no malice in my reckoning, my lord."

He held her gaze, and she stared back at him openly and without guile.

"Perhaps I missed my true calling?" He said flippantly. "Perhaps I should be treading the boards...?"

"Oh, but you have the stage every time you step into a room," she countered with a superior smile. "There isn't a head—male, female or powdered—that doesn't turn in your direction when your name is announced. And then your performance begins!"

He grinned. "Aren't you the clever one!" He made her a sweeping bow. "If one is to perform, then an audience is a must, and there is none better than an adoring female audience."

She glanced down at the flowered cotton mittens that matched her dress, and smoothed out an imaginary crease, thinking of the enthusiastic reception he had received from the dancing girls at Romney's studio. Taking a deep breath, she schooled her features into a smile, with a twinkle in her eye and a dimple in her cheek.

"You need not go to so much bother. You could stand in the middle of a room, say and do nothing, and your adoring female audience would still be more than satisfied. Much like a statue fashioned of marble, or a full-length painting by Sir Joshua or Mr. Romney. I pity the verbiage of the gentleman poet who attempts to compete with your visual feast."

At that he threw back his head and laughed heartily. When he could speak he moved to close the gap between them. Hands flat on the stone wall either side of her petticoats, he leaned into her, eyes level with hers and only inches away.

"My dear Miss Talbot," he purred, "I'll wager you a guinea that every time I strode into a drawing room, you itched to use your walking stick to trip me up."

"Why would you think me so mean-spirited?" she asked softly, gaze riveted to his unblinking obsidian stare.

"That's just it. I think you are the least mean-spirited person of my acquaintance." He gave a lopsided smile. "Having me fall flat on my face would at least allow some other arrogant blusterer the chance to take center stage."

"But to trip you up would deprive your adoring female audience. I could not be *that* mean-spirited to *them*."

"Touché, Miss Talbot."

"Though... I have a confession," she added hesitantly, and a little breathlessly because he continued to hold her gaze. "There was more than one occasion when I wanted to trip you, but my impulse was a purely selfish one, and I refrained from doing so."

He leaned in even closer. She unconsciously mimicked his action and inched forward. A hair's breadth was all that separated them.

"You should have been selfish a long time ago, Miss Talbot..."

TWENTY-TWO

Rory could barely breathe. The pressure was back in her chest, as if her heart was too big to be contained in her ribs, and the tingling sensation had returned to her limbs. Did he have any idea how close his mouth was to hers? And then she felt his lower torso press gently against her legs. To her astonishment her knees parted of their own volition, allowing him to step right up to the wall.

She blinked and drew in a sharp breath, shocked. For the sake of her reputation, and for propriety, she should shove him away as hard as she could and bring her knees instantly and firmly back together. But as she had been in a far more compromising position with him when wrapped in a curtain, to show outrage now would not only appear ridiculous but rather disingenuous.

So she allowed her response to be instinctive, rather than do what she ought. Her legs closed around him, stockinged knees finding anchorage, hugging either side of his slim hips. And once fastened, her feet curled about the back of his thighs and locked and would not let go. Her legs might be concealed beneath the yardage of her flow-ered petticoats, but there was no hiding the intimate proximity of their bodies. It mattered not that his hands remained flat to the stone wall and hers were clasped in her lap, or that they were fully clothed. Rory knew of no other place she wished to be.

And now he would kiss her. That's what they both wanted, surely? She desperately wanted to kiss him, and if he did not take the initiative soon, she was sure she would faint with the anxiety of anticipation. She had kissed him first at Romney's studio, but that was when he had thought her one of the dancers, and thus had not known her identity. But gently-bred females did not take the initiative. They waited to be kissed. They waited to be noticed. They could spend their whole life waiting but wait they must.

But her *what if* voice dared to suggest that perhaps he was waiting for her to kiss him? There she went again, with her *what ifs*! *Dolt*! Men such as the Major waited for no one and nothing. If he had any inclination to kiss her he would do so in the next minute or not at all. Perhaps he was merely trifling with her? It was possible he had orchestrated this intimate scene for the purpose of teaching her a lesson for calling him a big handsome buffoon and an arrogant blusterer. But surely he knew she had meant it as a compliment to his acting abilities? So she continued to wait and ruminate, unaware that her breathing had become shallow and her face flushed with longing.

WHILE HE MIGHT not be privy to her doubts and wishes, Dair was aware of her in every other sense. He wanted to kiss this delightfully pretty creature all over, starting with her exceptionally kissable mouth. He would then remove the gossamer modesty fichu covering the low square neckline of her bodice, to drink in the scent of her: A heady mix of soft vanilla and sweet lavender, but mostly the scent was uniquely her—tender, honest, and adorable.

He was alert to the fact she had trapped him between her legs, and he smiled to himself. All that was between them were the cotton layers of her floral petticoats. Yet, contrary to popular opinion, he was not a conscienceless lothario with no thought to the consequences. The truth was that since receiving the life-altering news that he was to become a father at the tender age of fourteen, the possible consequences of satisfying his lust were never far from his thoughts.

He had no intention of defiling the lovely Miss Aurora Talbot. A simple kiss would suffice. Of course, he realized that even a simple kiss shared with an unmarried spinster of good family and unblemished character would be frowned upon by his peers as thoroughly ungentlemanly. But he convinced himself that Miss Talbot was a sensible, clever female who would see their kiss for what it was: A fleeting springtime flirtation. Just as she had behaved sensibly after their encounter at Romney's Studio, she would keep this kiss to herself, for which he would be eternally grateful.

He smiled into her eyes, anticipating their kiss, and when she smiled back, it was all the encouragement he needed. But unlike his behavior at Romney's studio, when he had mistaken her for a pretty dancer in need of a new benefactor, and treated her accordingly, he was determined to show her he could be gentle and considerate and treat her with the respect that was her due as his social equal. Above all, he wanted her to enjoy the kiss as much as he did and take away a pleasant memory from this brief encounter.

Deliberate in his movements, reasoning he had no wish to frighten her with any expectation other than treating her with gentlemanly reverence, he brushed an unruly lock of straw-blonde hair from her flushed cheek then gently tucked it behind her ear. When he smiled into her eyes he saw her swallow. Whether deliberate or from nervousness, she ran the pink tip of her tongue along the rim of her upper lip, eyes on his mouth, and it was all the signal he needed he had her permission to press his mouth to hers.

Finally, he cupped her face between his large hands and kissed her.

RORY'S HANDS slid up the soft velvet front of his frock coat, around his neck to hold on tight, fingers in his shoulder length hair, head tilting in his hands to accommodate his nose as he pressed his mouth to hers. She was determined to savor every second of their kiss, and was delightfully surprised his piratical beard was not rough and spiky but silky and velvety soft, like the soft material of his frock coat. The black bristles of his beard brushed against her skin as they kissed, and in such a caressing way that it heightened her senses. She tingled all over. She liked his beard very much. But what surprised her even more was how gentle he was, and how tentative was his kiss.

This kiss was so unlike the one shared at Romney's studio she wondered if he'd had second thoughts about kissing her. The first time they had kissed, it was with all the enthusiasm of a man who found her desirable. Now the flicker of desire was barely alight. And just as she began to melt into his arms, he snuffed that flame by breaking off their kiss. Her cheeks burned with shame, that he must have come to the realization he was not the least attracted to her when sober. Yet, he did not pull away, but continued to stare down at her, as if requiring her to provide him with an explanation.

How was she supposed to respond? She had never been left alone with a man who was not a close male relative, least of all been kissed by one, until the handsomest man in London made her dreams come true. She recognized in this kiss that she was a willing participant, and yet with no experience of rejection and how to extract herself with dignity, she froze with indecision. Mortified by such weakness of character, she was on the verge of tears.

How could she be so incompetent? Why had she fallen in love with this man? The pressure in her chest and the quickening of her heartbeat whenever she was in his company told her so. Why did it have to be *this* man, whose nefarious history with women was well-known to her, and who clearly cared little for her above the ordinary? And now that he knew her for what she was, a passably pretty ingénue, who would never be able to dance and so would never be an elegant lady of fashion, he had probably kissed her out of pity; and that made her sick to her stomach.

Slowly, she withdrew her hands from his shoulders and dropped them back in her lap. But when she began to untangle her legs, to release the pressure of her knees on his hips, face hot with humiliation to realize how low she had allowed herself to stoop, he startled her by grabbing her by the upper arms and not letting go.

Her gaze flashed up to his face, and she shivered at the intensity in his black eyes and the scowl to his mouth. What thoughts were swirling about in that handsome head? Was he struggling with the right words to offer her up an apology for his behavior? She did not want to hear it! She did not want his contrition, and she most certainly did not want his pity. Determined to maintain her dignity, she pressed her lips together and regarded him with candor, gaze unblinking and locked to his scowl. She said a silent prayer, hoping the tears welling up behind her eyes did not drop to add misery to her shame.

But he surprised her yet again by loosening his grip on her arms as his brow cleared. She watched as a look, difficult to decipher, passed across his features. It was as if he had experienced some sort of dawning revelation, something so profound that he had surprised himself with this newfound knowledge. Slowly, his gaze raked over her and followed his hands as they slid down the length of her slim arms to the cascade of lace at her elbows, before continuing over her cotton mitts, to her fingers, and here he took hold of her hands. She saw his Adam's apple move, as he swallowed hard, then his jaw tightened. It was as if he had come to a decision. What that decision was she could not even speculate. She waited with shallow breath for him to speak. But when he did, he did not offer any explanation or apology, and he certainly did not provide her with a window to his thoughts.

He left her bewildered and adrift.

TWENTY-THREE

"Oh hell..." Dair muttered. "Hell and damnation..."

Furious with himself for vocalizing his frustration at an inability to articulate his thoughts in any meaningful way that would convey the earth-shattering nature of his revelation, Dair gave up the attempt. He might not be able to explain to her how he felt, but he could certainly show her. So he kissed Rory a second time.

Hands spanning her small waist, he pressed his mouth to hers, all reticence shattered.

Ardent and all-consuming, this second kiss left Rory in no doubts as to his desire. If she did breathe, she was not conscious of doing so. If she had a single thought, it was that she had dreamed of this moment, of this particular kiss, and with him, since her tenth summer, when the fourteen-year-old Alisdair Fitzstuart had called in his regimental uniform to take leave of her grandfather and brother.

Bereft of a sense of time and space, she was aware only of the wonderful way he made her feel. She wilted yet was more alive than she had ever been. She wanted him to pick her up and carry her to a shady spot under the trees and lie with her amongst the wildflowers.

She wanted him to undress before her, so that she could again admire him, but this time all of him; and she wanted to caress him, everywhere. More than anything, she wanted him to make love to her as the couple in the temple tapestries made love, bodies unashamedly entwined, and in the throes of an all-consuming passion.

But not here. Not on Banks House land. Not within walking distance of the house where lived his son and the woman he would have married had it not been deemed an unequal match. Not with him being called from afar, so insistently, like a servant scratching at the door with some urgent purpose, and who would not go away no matter how many times ordered to do so. But... Old Bert was not one of her grandfather's servants... Why would he be calling out to her, and to His Lordship...?

That broke the spell.

With a hand hard-pressed to Dair's chest, she scrambled to untangled her legs from their anchorage, pulled her mouth from his, and sat up. She flashed him a warning then bowed her head, hands back in her lap, fingers clenched tightly together. She did not know why she dropped her chin in such a cowardly fashion, because she was not ashamed of kissing him. It was an instinctive reaction, as if she had been caught out being terribly wicked, though this was not how she felt in the least. Yet she realized her actions must have signaled this to him because his hands loosened from her waist, and he stepped away from the wall and from her. He gave an inarticulate apology she did not quite catch, such was her preoccupation with her own cowardice, though his sincerity was clear enough in his tone.

Had she been attentive, not only to the essence of his apology but the actual words spoken, she would have realized there and then that something momentous had happened, far beyond the kiss they had shared. He had called her *Delight*, as he had at Romney's Studio. It was only later, when Mr. William Watkins and her brother arrived on the scene, that she recalled Dair's apology and his use of the moniker *Delight*, and it changed everything.

For now, sitting on the half-wall of stone between the Physic Garden and Banks House, Rory was too caught up in salvaging what dignity was left to her. She slowly lifted her hands and proceeded to the mundane task of smoothing and repinning her mussed hair, not a second look at the Major. Nonetheless, she was acutely aware of his proximity, that the masculine scent of him still lingered, and the salty taste of him remained on her lips, and her face flamed to a guilty hue of pomegranate.

STILL GROGGY with desire and caught in the moment, Dair was slow to react to rejection. Breathing ragged, he stared at her, confused, not understanding why she had broken off such a perfectly wonderful kiss. Had he been too insistent? Should he have been gentler? She was young and inexperienced... That had to be it. He needed to take matters one step at a time. His ardency had frightened her. God, he was an inconsiderate loggerhead! Musing on this, he put a hand to his cheek and felt the hair under his fingertips. He pulled a face, but it gave him an idea. What if it was his beard that had made her baulk? She had not recoiled at Romney's Studio, far from it, so why now? It had to be the facial hair. Damn it! He should have shaved at Portsmouth before heading out. But he had been too eager to get home to spend the day with his son on his birthday. And he'd not even managed to do that right! Great blunderhead that he was!

He stepped away from the wall with a respectful bow, hand in his frock coat pocket clenching his silver cheroot case and muttering an apology that was out of his mouth before he thought much about it. And that's when he, too, heard his name and swiveled about on a booted heel to discover Old Bert tramping across the open field, and holding aloft a wide-brimmed straw hat with blue silk ribbons trailing in the breeze. The old retainer was red in the face and puffing. He must have run most of the way.

When he reached Dair, Old Bert gave him the hat with a nod and then dropped his gaze to the grass, not a look at Rory. His furtiveness was evidence enough he had witnessed their intimacy. That he remained where he stood after being dismissed had Dair move a step closer, realizing the old man wanted to tell him something. He just hoped that with permission to speak, Old Bert had the wherewithal to remain as one blind, as all good servants were wont, and wasn't about to mention the obvious.

"Beggin' Your Lordship's pardon. There be a gentleman in yonder garden watching. I seen him from the trees, when his head popped out of the hedgerow. Reason for callin' out in the way I did. I meant no disrespect or offence."

"None taken. What's he look like?"

"Hatchet-faced. Small eyes. Fancy hair."

"Tall or short?"

"Shorter than y'lordship."

"Seen him before?"

Old Bert shook his bald head.

Then it wasn't Grasby. Not that his best friend was given to skulking in the shrubbery. Had it been Grasby, he'd have marched straight up to him, pulled his sister off, and rightly punched his nose. Grasby wasn't a coward, and he wasn't short. But he knew one of the party on Shrewsbury's barge who was both. He hoped his intuition proved him right. He itched to rearrange the officious weasel's neckcloth.

"This sneakup got any muscle to speak of? Do I need to brace myself?"

Old Bert gave a snort of derision and smiled a toothless grin. "Not on y'life, m'lord! He's a milksop as ever I seen one. Not that I seen one. But I'd know one if I did, and he's it! You'd only have to poke him with y'finger and he'd be to the ground in an instant, with his two hands over his head and whimpering like a girl!"

"That about sums up the Weasel. Good. I'll save the new skin on my knuckles. Is he still in the shrubbery?"

"No, m'lord. As soon as y'turned your back he showed h'self—"

"Did he indeed."

"—and went direct to your sweetling, where he be now in conversation."

Dair resisted the urge to turn around. He put up a black eyebrow at Old Bert's moniker for Miss Talbot but made no comment. Fiddling with the blue silk ribbons of Rory's straw hat, he said flatly,

"Tell Jamie I'll be back up at the house within the hour. And

Mrs. Banks has permission to go through my satchels. There are a couple of bottles of port, a string bag full of oranges for the boys, and a mountain of laundry. And I need my razors sharpened."

"I'll do the razors for y'lordship!"

Dair didn't have the heart to refuse the old retainer. What Farrier would think of letting anyone else near his master's personal grooming implements he would deal with when the time came. For now he just had to get this beard off his face so Miss Aurora Talbot had no excuse not to kiss him again. And he would kiss her again, of that he was as certain as day followed night. And the next time there would be no excuses, no interruptions, and no weasel-like Peeping Tom in the shrubbery.

He watched Old Bert trudge back up to Banks House the way he came, the old retainer whistling as he went, thinking about the best way to deal with Mr. William Watkins and his perfidious propensities.

He might refer to Watkins by his Harrow schoolboy nickname Weasel, but the man was not a weasel, he was a snake. He was a back-stabbing sanctimonious coward who had slithered his way through school and had done the same to become the smug know-it-all-secretary to England's Spymaster General, and by virtue of his sister's marriage to Grasby.

The man didn't deserve to put his knobby knees under the desk of secretary to Lord Shrewsbury, where he had access to all manner of state and personal secrets; particularly the personal. There was no higher moral ground with Watkins. He was no selfless functionary doing his bit for his country. Dair had wondered how a man of Shrewsbury's masterful cunning and superior insight could employ such a self-server, only to be enlightened by the Spymaster that he knew exactly what type of creature he had employed, and that it was best to keep a snake close than to allow it to slither off into the tall grass not knowing its movements, and thus be unaware when it would strike.

Now, squaring his shoulders, Dair braced himself to play the arrogant blusterer. It never failed to put Watkins on edge, that at any moment he might be met with physical violence. But when he turned to saunter back to the wall, dangling the wide brimmed straw bergère by its blue silk ribbons, he was confronted with a most astonishing sight.

Mr. William Watkins was doing his best to keep hold of Miss Talbot's hand, while she was equally determined to have her fingers released. And when the man rose up off one bended knee to lunge at Miss Talbot, she thrusting out her arms to keep him at a distance, Dair's intended pretense evaporated like a popped soap bubble.

He broke into a stride, gripped by the primal urge to protect, regardless of the personal consequences to himself. It was an instinct first experienced upon the birth of his son, and most recently at Brooklyn Heights, when he had rescued a loyalist widow and her two small children caught in the crossfire of battle. But there was something new in the emotional mix this time, something he had never experienced before, and one that surprised and vexed him further. He was covetous—irately so.

No one touched what was now his—*no one*.

TWENTY-FOUR

"MR. WATKINS! Release my hand and stand up this instant!" Rory looked about for her walking stick, but it was not against the wall where she had left it. It must have fallen into the grass while she and the Major were preoccupied. With Mr. Watkins determined to keep hold of her hand, gripping the wall with her free hand to remain upright was all she was capable of to stop herself toppling off to join her stick in the grass.

"Miss Talbot—*Aurora*—Please listen—"

"You do not have permission to use my name, sir. Again, I say, stand up! No good will come of this."

Balancing on the balls of his feet, and calf muscles aching from such an unnatural posture, William Watkins felt the sweat of uncertainty beginning to bead at his temples. Miss Talbot's reaction was not what he had expected. She was no shaking maiden, no terrified spinster, grateful for his interference, relieved to be rescued from the brutish arms of her seducer.

Yet, he convinced himself she was not herself. That fiend Fitzstuart had drugged her. It was the alcohol talking. And it was his own alcohol intake that fueled his natural conceit, urging him to declare himself immediately or lose the opportunity. If he persisted and she was to hear him with a clear mind, she would jump at the chance to be Mrs. William Watkins. And so, he persevered with his declaration, however unorthodox the delivery. This, despite the growing loss of sensation in his right leg.

"Miss Talbot, my greatest desire on this earth is to have you as my wi—"

"No! No, do not say it, Mr. Watkins," Rory demanded. "This is neither the time, nor is it the place, for such a declaration. If you ask me, I shall be truthful, and I have no wish to embarrass you."

"Miss Talbot, when you are sober, you will see the merit in my proposal and give me the answer I want from—"

"When I am—when I am *sober*?" Rory gasped, affronted. "Mr. Watkins, clearly it is *you* who have been drinking or you would not dare suggest such an improbability! You have insulted me, and if you apologize, let go of my hand, and remove yourself from my presence, then perhaps I will forgive you."

"Forgive *me*?" His fingers tightened about her slender wrist as he rose up, unaware his right leg had gone to sleep. "Miss Talbot, I stand before you with an honest proposal of marriage. I will not remove myself until I have secured my present and future happiness, and that requires you to say yes, you will be my wife."

"Your…? *Your* present and future happiness…?"

Rory decided Mr. William Watkins was drunk, *very* drunk, and her anxiousness increased tenfold. Not so much for herself. She did not feel in any personal danger. If need be, she would slap his cheek, certain that would bring him to a sense of his surroundings, if not the impropriety of his behavior. What she feared for was the secretary's safety, should Major Lord Fitzstuart turn his shoulder from his conversation with Old Bert and catch the scene that presented itself. She was certain the nobleman would react first and deal with the consequences later.

Had Mr. William Watkins been any gentleman accosting her, she would not have hesitated to alert the Major to her situation and allow him to deal with him accordingly. But Mr. Watkins was her grandfather's trusted secretary. He was also Silla's brother, and that made him her brother's brother-in-law, thus he was part of the family. She did not want this episode to come between them and make life uncomfortable. It would be awkward from now on since he had made known his intentions toward her. Having the Major involved would vastly complicate matters, and if she were honest with herself, not knowing his feelings for her, she felt inadequate to the task of answering her grandfather's questions.

She tried one last time to reason with Mr. William Watkins.

"Mr. Watkins, please, I beg of you, release me and stand up." Adding with a bright smile she hoped looked genuine, "If you do as I ask, I will listen to what you have to say, but not today. Tomorrow. When you have had time to reflect upon your intentions. Agreed?"

"Miss Talbot, tomorrow, or the day after that, or the day after that one, will not change my determination. I must and will marry you."

She did not doubt he was sincere, and for the barest of moments curiosity got the better of her. She put aside her anxiety, stopped struggling to tug her hand free, and allowed herself to engage with him.

"Why?"

"I beg your pardon?"

"Why do you wish to marry me?"

William Watkins blinked, sodden brain scrambling to remember and put into coherent sentences all the reasons he had formulated and written up in his diary as to why Miss Aurora Talbot, granddaughter of an earl, sister of a future earl, goddaughter of a duchess, would make him the perfect wife. But while his brain floated in alcohol and his bottom lip quivered, the only substance that came forth was a drool of spittle.

"Three little words, Mr. Watkins. No more. No less. Just three."

When he looked at her queerly, with no idea that those three words were *I love you*, Rory smiled crookedly. And when he thrust a hand into his frock coat pocket in search of his handkerchief to wipe his wet mouth, Rory saw her chance.

She gripped the edge of the stone wall so as not to topple backwards, then tugged hard. Her hand came free, but she was not free of William Watkins. Her sudden movement caught him unawares. He loosened his grip, but his alcohol consumption made him slow to react and take appropriate counteraction.

Instead of staggering backwards, away from the wall, his unresponsive right leg stayed where it was. This meant his left leg overcompensated for this uncooperativeness by overcorrecting, and after taking a step away, he stumbled forward.

This sudden change in direction made the secretary dizzy. With no control over his limbs, Mr. William Watkins pitched forward, right leg collapsing under him so that he landed heavily on his knee, arms flapping, and in search of anchorage. His chin came down hard against the corner of Rory's knee, and such was the force with which he landed that he bounced up and he came down again, face first, into the lap of Rory's disheveled petticoats. Here he remained in a state of paralyzed disbelief.

Rory's knee was struck so hard she gave an involuntary yelp of pain, almost lost her balance, and cried out again, this time with fright, as she toppled backwards into thin air before quickly lurching forwards to remain seated on the wall.

She gasped her relief. But startled and in pain, she was shocked beyond words when Mr. William Watkins landed face down in her lap and there remained. She was torn between a desire to push him off and scramble along the wall to put space between them and wondering if he were seriously hurt.

Rory had no opportunity to do either.

As if by sorcery, William Watkins rose up, head and limbs hanging limp, and there he momentarily floated in front of her, before flying through the air to land, crumpled, amongst the wildflowers.

DAIR HAD WILLIAM Watkins by the scruff of the neck. With a strength fed by unmitigated wrath, he hauled the secretary out of Rory's lap and so high his buckled shoes left the ground.

For a matter of moments William Watkins levitated.

Dair wanted to throw the weasel into oblivion. Failing that, he would get him as far away from Miss Aurora Talbot as he was physically capable. He wanted to punish him, badly. Never again would William Watkins so much as put a fingernail on Aurora Talbot without fear of serious harm befalling him.

In the past he had resisted the urge to rearrange the secretary's supercilious smile, now he would permanently remove it. But as he made a fist and spun William Watkins to face him, he chanced to glance at Rory. He saw the distress writ large in her eyes, and he knew he could not do it, not here, not now, not in front of her. The last thing he wanted was to add to her anxiety. So he forced the violence back down within him and slowly unclenched his hand, flexing his fingers wide and straight.

He turned the secretary away from him, put a boot hard into the middle of his back, and shoved him into open ground, where William Watkins stumbled about, arms flapping wildly as he tried unsuccessfully to stay upright before falling, face first, into the grass.

Dair retrieved Rory's straw hat, dusted it off and came over to her. Whereupon he gently settled it over her blonde coiffure and straightened out the blue silk ribbons, leaving them trailing either side of her flushed face for her to tie. He then lifted her chin to look at her under the straw brim, gaze full of concern.

"Are you all right?"

"Yes. Yes, I am fine," she said brightly. Adding, to put him at his ease, yet realizing after the fact she had probably made him uncomfortable when his response was brisk, "It must be the novelty of being accosted that has me flustered, unaccustomed as I am to such attention." She gave a little nervous laugh, a hand to her mouth. "There must be something in the fermentation of wine this Spring to make normally sober gentlemen drunk beyond reason. Hopefully Mr. Watkins will wake with a sore head and with no recollection of events."

"Did he hurt you?"

"I may have a large bruise to my knee, that is all. Though I wish he had hit my left knee rather than my right. That poor leg has enough to contend with without being knocked about! But it's nothing to worry about, truly, and-and—thank you," she added with an even brighter smile, because his frown of concern had dropped into a scowl. "Thank you for not hitting him. I know his drunkenness isn't an excuse for his behavior. He must have thought alcohol would give him courage. Though I have no idea where he got the notion I would ever—that he and I could ever—It's utterly absurd! And if I weren't so shocked—no gentleman has ever looked at me sideways—that to receive the unwanted attentions from such a man as Mr. Watkins, my grandfather's secretary... Well, I dare say if my knee wasn't throbbing and he hadn't drooled all over my petticoats, I could find some humor in his behavior—"

She cut herself off, knowing she was babbling, but she hadn't been able to help it. The Major's scowl cleared as she babbled, and he was now looking at her in an odd sort of way, and with an odd sort of smile that she could not interpret, and which made her uncomfortably hot.

"Miss Talbot—"

"Rory. It's Aurora, but nobody calls me that. I think we've gone beyond the formalities, don't you?"

He chuckled and was bashful. "Yes, I suppose we have—Rory. *Rory*. I like it. *Aurora* is quite lovely, but Rory suits you. *Rory...*"

She felt a rush of heat to her face. The way he said her name in an almost caressing lilt, sent a shiver across her shoulder blades. Yet, she surprised herself by managing to keep her tone steady and light.

"And you? I'd like to address you as something other than Major. Too stuffy."

"My friends and family call me Dair."

"Yes, but I would like to call you Alisdair."

He frowned at that, far from pleased.

"No one but my cousin—Her Grace of Roxton and Kinross— calls me that. I don't like her using it, but you know who she is, she is not to be denied. And as she is my closest cousin; I would not refuse her." He smiled and tugged playfully at a silk ribbon of her hat. "Everyone calls me Dair."

But Rory did not want to be everyone. She wanted to be the only one to have permission to call him by his first name. She realized only mothers and wives, and beloved sisters, addressed their male relatives by their Christian names, and even then the practice was not universal, particularly if the husband had a title. Major Lord Fitzstuart might be the eldest son of a nobleman and inherit an earldom one day, but he permitted Lily Banks to call him Al.

If the mother of his son could be on such intimate first name terms with him, then she, who had now kissed him twice, could call him Alisdair. And if he refused her, then he was not as attracted to her as his kisses suggested. Her fingers tingled in anticipation of his response, but she was determined to find out one way or the other.

"Everyone may call you Dair. I prefer Alisdair. It suits you. So does—so does the beard..."

He let go of the ribbon and glanced over his shoulder, momentarily diverted by the sound of groaning. It was the secretary, attempting to pick himself up out of the grass. He turned back to Rory, and said more sharply than he intended, "My father was the only one who called me Alisdair. I detest the man. I hate the name— have hated it since I was ten."

"Oh?" Rory was unperturbed, but her heart started to beat hard that he had confided this in her. "Then perhaps it's about time someone you like, other than the Duchess of Roxton and Kinross, called you Alisdair? If you give me permission to call you by your name, then you give permission to lay those bad memories, or whatever it is you dislike about your father, to rest. So instead of thinking of your detestable father when you are addressed as Alisdair, you can instead think of—think about—"

"Kissing you?" He took the two silk ribbons dangling from her hat and slowly tied them in a bow under her chin, taking his time, as if thinking over her proposal. "I wish it were that simple... I will never change my opinion of my father." He shrugged. "Perhaps, in time, I may be able to lay those bad memories to rest, as you suggest." His mouth twitched with the hint of a smile. "Though... Hearing you address me as such, I cannot promise I won't grimace to begin with. It is an instinctive response after all."

"Thank you. No doubt, after a little while, you will stop frowning and learn to like your name as much as I do."

"I hope you are right. I know how you can help guarantee I won't frown when you say my name."

Rory blinked.

He could tell she had no idea to what he was referring and it broadened his smile into a grin.

"If you were to kiss me each time you said it."

Rory gasped, then laughed. Impulsively, she touched the embroidered front of his frock coat.

"Do you wish me to kiss you before or after I say your name? If it is before, I doubt I will get to say it, and that, I fear, is your intent, is it not? To stop me saying your name by kissing me? But I won't be tricked!"

"You, Rory, are too clever for your own good. I would like to kiss you again, now..." He looked into her eyes. "And I am not drunk..."

Rory swallowed and lost her smile. "That's different... *You're* different... I want—I want you to kiss me."

"Then say it. Say my name."

"Alisdair."

"Again."

"Alisdair."

He leaned in to kiss her.

"Again," he murmured, mouth almost on hers. "Say it, Delight."

"Alisdair... *Alisdair!*"

Her lips had barely brushed his when she jerked back, and repeated his name, this second time cried out in warning.

Dair's eyes opened wide. Seeing her safe, but with one hand at full stretch past his shoulder, as if to stave off evil, he knew there was danger at his back. Instantly, he swiveled on a boot heel.

William Watkins loomed an arm's length away. His left arm was raised diagonally across his body over his right shoulder, both hands hard about the end of Rory's Malacca walking stick, its carved ivory pineapple-shaped handle high in the air. The secretary was wielding the stick like an axe, and in an act of sheer drunken stupidity, he was about to use this metaphorical axe to fell his nemesis across the back of the head.

Dair gave the man no quarter. He delivered one swift punch to the face.

TWENTY-FIVE

"My nose! My nose, it's-it's broken! Dear God, you've *broken* my nose! You bloody fiend, Fitzstuart. You bloody brainless lout! You've broken it! Do you know what—"

"Button the language, Weasel, or I'll break your jaw as well."

William Watkins gave a snort that saw blood spurt from his nostrils and splatter the front of his exquisitely embroidered silk waistcoat. Despite the stabbing pain between his eyes, he found the mental energy to snigger a reply.

"Language? What would you know about that? You can't cobble two sentences together that make sense. I doubt a fatwitted numbskull like you can write more than your name—Dear God in Heaven, my *n-nose*!" He wiped his eyes free of tears, though they continued to water, and then ran a finger tentatively across his nostrils, saw the blood, then the blood on his clothes and collapsed cross-legged into the grass. "I'm bleeding to death! The pain! I'm *dying*!"

"No, you're not. Your nose is broken, and broken noses bleed—a lot. If you want to know pain, ask my batman. Having your mangled hand amputated, that's pain. Four sentences and one conjunction, not counting this one."

The word *conjunction* had William Watkins turning his head to stare at the Major. As if seeing him for the first time, he had to

wonder if, after all these years, he had read him wrong. But he quickly decided the quantity of wine drunk at lunch combined with the hell between his eyes had made him delirious. And when Dair winked at him with a twitch of a knowing smile, he knew it must be so.

"ZOUNDS! What a splendid facer! And brilliantly executed, my friend! Quick. Precise. Perfect. Never in all my days did I expect to witness such a sight! By Jove, Dair, you could teach Jack Broughton a thing or two!"

It was the over-exuberant Lord Grasby. Such was his excitement at bearing witness to his best friend planting his fist into Weasel Watkins' face he hardly noticed his sister, mute and as still as a piece of ornamental statuary atop the stone wall. And he certainly did not gauge the mood of his best friend, who did not react to his presence, or turn his head to look at him, but kept his focus on William Watkins while flexing his fingers, knuckles smarting from the blow.

"Grasby!? Give me your flask. The one full of cognac you always carry in your frock coat poc—"

"Hold on a dashed minute!" Grasby interrupted, a finger pointing at Dair. "You've grown a beard!"

Dair rubbed his cheek.

"There wasn't much else I could do. Those detained at His Majesty's pleasure aren't permitted shaving implements. They might use them for other purposes."

"Hold on to the reins! You've been let out of the Tower!"

Dair grinned. "Yes."

"Good God, it becomes clear to me why the two of you are best friends!" William Watkins burst out between groans.

"Should I keep the whiskers?" Dair asked Grasby, ignoring William Watkins.

He glanced at Rory, but as she had her chin down, he wondered if she was doing her best to suppress a fit of the giggles at her brother's remarkable lack of awareness. To goad her into lifting her head,

he added, "I've heard ladybirds like a piratical beard. What do you think, Grasby?"

When Grasby looked to give the notion serious consideration, William Watkins shuddered with uncontrolled exasperation, the blood gurgling in his throat.

"*Think*? With a walnut-sized brain, and it located between your legs, I can't imagine you think of anything else!"

"Walnut-sized?" Dair lifted an eyebrow.

"There's nothing walnut-sized about him!" Grasby confirmed. "Brain or-or—Egad!! Is he supposed to do that?"

Grasby had saved himself from embarrassment when William Watkins started coughing uncontrollably. The secretary dropped his head between his knees, and blood started pouring from his nose into the grass.

"Give me your handkerchief. Mine won't be enough," Dair ordered, and was about to turn away to attend to the injured William Watkins when his gaze locked on Rory. She had been watching him, and she did not look away. "Are you all right, Miss Talbot?"

"Y-yes. I will be fine directly, once you help Mr. Watkins."

A moment, not ten seconds had passed between them, but Grasby caught it, and while he was not usually quick on the uptake, he was this time. He had a foreboding that his first summation upon coming round the bend in the path was the right one. Dair had been kissing his sister, and perhaps Watkins had caught them, attacked Dair and been punched for his efforts.

"Here," Dair said to Watkins, going down on his haunches beside him and holding out one of the handkerchiefs. "The blood will stop soon, and then you can take a swig of Grasby's cognac. The sooner you get back to the barge, and apply a cold compress to the swelling, the quicker it will subside. The bruising will take much longer."

Watkins snatched the handkerchief and tentatively dabbed at his nose, eyeing the Major with loathing. The man was a gorilla-sized buffoon but he had to concede he could see why females went weak at the knees at the sight of him. Well, there was one woman's knees he was determined to keep strong at any cost.

"I give you fair warning, Fitzstuart. Keep away from Miss Talbot. She is mine and I mean to marry her."

Dair threw his head back and laughed. He gave William Watkins a shove, half playful, half forceful.

"You? Warning *me*? You and whose army? And to think I dared hope I'd knocked some sense into you!"

"Don't think I didn't not know your game!"

"Dear me, Weasel, a triple negative, and you call *me* the language fatwit." He unscrewed the cap and held out the flask. "Take a swig. You'll feel better for it. Though why I should concern myself with you..."

The secretary took a mouthful of the cognac, swilled it then spat. He then took a sip, swallowed, and thrust the flask back at Dair.

"Molest Miss Talbot again and I'll go straight to Shrewsbury with what I know about y—"

"You never fail to be predictable! You were a talebearer at school, too."

"—you and your-your *perverse pleasures.*"

"Perverse pleasures? Kissing a pretty girl a perverse pleasure?" Dair gave a huff of dismissal. "Fat lot you know about perversity! In fact, fat lot of nothing you know about pretty girls!"

A hammer banged behind his eyes, and he could feel his face swelling, but for all that William Watkins was determined to wrest the upper hand from this bearded baboon. With an over-inflated sense of his own cleverness, and an under-appreciation of the Major's intelligence, he took it upon himself to inform His Lordship, without spelling it out word-for-word, that he was well aware of the long-standing wager written up in White's betting book that dared the Major to tup a cripple. If such a repugnant wager was to become generally known, it would be the end of the Major's social acceptabil-ity. For while absurd wagers were the order of the day, there were some areas that were off-limits, even to the most base, hard-hearted gambler; the insane, the deformed, and the very young being top of the list.

"I know why you've taken a sudden interest in Miss Talbot," William Watkins said, looking past Dair's shoulder, to the wall, where Lord Grasby had retreated to speak to his sister, the siblings in quiet conversation. He brought his gaze back to the Major. "It must have taken all your powers of deduction to finally realize there was one of *them* on your doorstep. And there's none finer than Miss Talbot, that when she is seated, one can almost forget her—*disadvantage*."

"One of *them*?" Dair interrupted, at a loss to know what the secretary was babbling on about. He concluded the man must be concussed. "One of *what*?"

"Oh, come now, Fitzstuart!" William Watkins scoffed. "You're stupid, not blind! Miss Talbot is a *cripple*."

Dair's jaw set hard, and his fingers flexed. His voice was taut, his tone icy.

"And you have brown hair. Neither requires further discussion."

William Watkins blinked. His eyelids felt heavy and huge. He enunciated as if talking to an imbecile. "She has a deformed right foot and is lame in one leg, which makes her a prime victim for your perverse wager, wouldn't you say?"

Dair grabbed the secretary about the throat, high enough to close his jaw. He gritted his teeth and hissed in the man's ear. "I'd say you're about to add broken teeth to your list of injuries, if you don't keep your bread hole shut!"

He then threw Watkins off, rose to his full height and strode away, leaving the secretary spluttering for breath, mouth opened wide to take in air because his fractured nose was clogged with dried blood.

"He's all yours!" Dair barked at Grasby. "Get him to his feet. His legs can't be as useless as the rest of him."

"But what about my—"

"I'll take Miss Talbot as far as the jetty."

"No. I don't think that's a good idea," Grasby stated, coming away from the wall. "I'll take Rory—"

"Your sister has blistered feet and cannot walk, and you cannot carry her the distance." He pulled Grasby aside, saying in his ear, "If you leave me with him, I'm likely to beat the maggot to a watery pulp. Want that on your conscience?"

"Certainly not!

"Good! Then my way it is!"

Anger was one emotion his best friend rarely, if ever, exhibited, so Grasby made no further objection. He watched Dair stride over to where his sister sat, silent and observant, hands in her lap, an unsettling feeling making his stomach tighten. But William Watkins' persistent coughing made him reluctantly turn away to offer his brother-in-law his assistance. Which was just as well, because there was no mistaking the emotion writ large on Rory's face when the Major handed over her walking stick he found discarded in the grass.

TWENTY-SIX

DAIR HAD SCOOPED up the walking stick and was about to offer it to her, when Rory lifted her head so he could see her face under the brim of her hat, and all his anger instantly vanished. He was so taken aback by her expression that he stopped dead in front of her, speechless. He had meant to apologize, for his violent reaction to Watkins' behavior, for her having to bear witness to such an unseemly sight, and for leaving her sitting in the sun. But all those apologies, already formed but yet to be said, were swallowed back down his throat and forgotten.

She was smiling at him, but it was not just any smile, it was a joyful, loving smile, and it was the last thing he was expecting from her, given present circumstances. It was the most beautiful smile he had ever seen. It made him smile in return without even knowing he was doing so.

"You *do* remember me," she said so only he could hear her. She took her stick from him and laid it across her lap, then held out her hand. He took it without a second thought, and she drew him closer. "When you apologized earlier for kissing me, I heard what you said, but I wasn't listening. If that makes sense. But then you said it again just before Mr. Watkins interrupted us and tried to strike you with my walking stick. And thinking about that kiss—which was a nicer way to pass the time than watching poor Mr. Watkins' bleed into the grass—"

"I regret hitting him in front of you, but not that I hit him."

"You said: *Say it, Delight*. And that's proof, is it not, that you do remember me from Romney's Studio! You weren't drunk at all, were you?"

He picked her up without a word and carried her through the gate and along the path.

"You've had a touch too much sun, Miss Talbot."

"And you, my lord, cannot tell a fib after you've kissed me! Admit it!"

He strode on.

"Miss Talbot, would you be so kind as to look over my shoulder and tell me if you can see your brother and the Weasel."

"Call me Rory or call me Delight, but I am done with you calling me Miss Talbot! You are being stubborn because I found you out!"

"Can you see your brother or not?"

She lifted her chin, looked over his shoulder and shook her head.

"No. There are trees and they must be out of our line of—Oh! *Alisdair*! What-what are you doing?"

He had ducked into the shrubbery. Behind a hedgerow, he slid her to her feet, pulled her tight to his torso, and before she could straighten her hat or her petticoats, or knew what to do with her walking stick, stooped under the brim of her hat and kissed her on the mouth. It was only one kiss, but it was enough to bring the smile back into his dark eyes and lift the corners of his mouth.

"Now I feel much better. Thank you—*Rory*."

She dropped her stick and put both hands about his neck and went up on tiptoe to kiss him. "Was it Grasby who told you not to remember me from Romney's Studio?" She smiled shyly and looked through her lashes. "I remember you—all of you..."

"You, my Delight, are a baggage! No. Not Grasby. Your grandfather."

"Oh! That makes sense. Grand must have wanted to spare me the shame of such a predicament." She giggled. "Or wanted to spare you and Grasby the shame of yours! Will you kiss me again?"

"Not here. Not now. Not with your brother breathing down my neck."

Rory pouted and pretended disappointment. "But you will kiss me again, won't you?"

"Yes."

"And with those whiskers?"

"Ha! So you truly do like my piratical beard?"

"I am not a ladybird, but I do have a sense of discrimination. And all I can tell you is that I am yet to determine which incarnation of you I prefer: American Indian or pirate... But I will let you know after due consideration."

He laughed out loud and then quickly smothered his mirth by clapping a hand to his mouth, though the laughter still danced in his eyes. When he could speak, he said huskily, "You are incorrigible!"

"And you must be sorely missed at Banks House," she said and scooped up her stick. "I feel dreadful for taking up so much of your time when you should be spending it with your son, and on this of all days."

"Knowing Jamie, he is preoccupied with his new microscope, and when I walk into the book room and make my presence known, he will look up and smile and think I have been there all along. He has his mother's sweet nature, for which I am profoundly grateful." He went to pick her up again, then hesitated, and said with a frown, "Do you mind—about Jamie—and about—the Banks family?"

"Mind? I don't know what you mean."

He scooped her up again and rejoined the path.

"No. No, I suppose you don't. I will have to rectify that before I —I think it is important I tell you, about them and about me, before we take this any further."

Rory held her breath, wondering what he wanted to confide in her, and equally interesting, what he meant by further... Take *what* further?

"If that is your wish," she said calmly.

He nodded. "Good."

And that was the last word he spoke on that subject, as they had come to the jetty. Here he put her to firm ground just as Lady Grasby came out onto the deck of the barge. She gave such a start that Rory thought her sister-in-law about to faint and breathed a sigh of relief when a quick-thinking footman pushed a chair under her before she collapsed. Her personal maid produced a fan to cool her mistress's heaving bosom. But a glance over her shoulder, and Rory realized it was not her return which had caused her sister-in-law such distress, but the sight of William Watkins with an arm across Grasby's shoulder and a bloodied handkerchief up to his nose.

"I fear your journey home is not going to be as uneventful as the one here," Dair said at Rory's ear as he bowed over her hand in farewell. "I just hope you can ignore the high drama and find a quiet corner to discuss pineapple cultivation with Mr. Humphrey, uninterrupted."

"Oh! Is he here? On the barge?"

"Yes. He should be aboard awaiting you. I thought it only fair you have the opportunity of Humphrey's undivided expertise for a few hours, given Jamie monopolized him while you were at Banks House."

"That was thoughtful of you, my lord. Thank you." She dimpled. "I will have to think of a suitable way to repay you."

Dair raised an eyebrow and said blandly, "No need to think too hard. I am but a simple soldier, thus my needs are equally simple." He bowed again and said just as Grasby and William Watkins arrived at the jetty, "I look forward to dining with you and Lord Shrewsbury at the Gatehouse Lodge in the coming weeks, and having the mysteries of pineapple cultivation explained to me." He nodded to Grasby and said to the secretary with tongue firmly in cheek, "I do believe I've added character to your face, Weasel. Don't thank me now. Later, when the swelling has gone, will be soon enough." He then turned on a boot heel and wandered off, back up the path, hands shoved deep in his frock coat pockets.

Rory watched him go, gaze lingering on his back longer than was polite. To her shame, pineapple cultivation was the last thing on her mind.

TWENTY-SEVEN

TREAT, HAMPSHIRE
THE DUKE OF ROXTON'S ESTATE

DAIR CAME OVER the rise of manicured lawn and strolled down to the jetty that jutted out into the lake, where bobbed several moored skiffs. The sun was high in a bright blue sky, with no clouds and no breeze. It was the perfect weather for a swim. Not for the first time did he gaze enviously out across the sparkling water of a lake stocked with fish and dotted with islands. How he wished to strip, dive in and cool off. But such longing was quickly overtaken by dread. He squared his shoulders, drew back on his cheroot, and ignored the heat under his stock. He also ignored the woman at his back, who had followed him from the Duchess's summer pavilion.

He had found her there, alone with her needlework. She was waiting for her young mistress to return from her swim. A basket by a squat table had been emptied of its afternoon tea contents and was laid out on a linen tablecloth. The silver teapot on its pedestal and the necessary attendant tea things he knew had come courtesy of the Elizabethan dower house up on the hill. The Duchess of Roxton and

Kinross was due home any day; the housekeeper had told him when he had arrived unannounced on the doorstep the night before, with his valet and his portmanteaux.

His cousin Antonia, Duchess of Roxton and Kinross was one of three people who had brought him to visit the Roxton ducal seat, Treat. Lord Shrewsbury was another. He needed to debrief him about his mission to Portugal. But it was the third person he most wanted to see, and it was she who was presently enjoying the refreshing waters of the lake.

When he had offered to fetch her mistress, so the maid could remain in the coolness of the pavilion, the woman had vigorously shook her head and declared that she, and all the servants, had been given strict instructions Miss Talbot was not to be left alone. That had raised one of Dair's black eyebrows, for surely Miss Talbot was alone now, in the lake. The maid had blushed and corrected her pronouncement: Miss Talbot was not to be left alone with any gentleman other than her grandfather or her brother. Dair made no comment, turned on a boot heel and off he went to find Miss Talbot, her maid on the skirts of his cream linen frock coat.

He was almost at the jetty when he caught sight of Rory. Well, part of her. He heard a splash, was quick to look to the right of the skiffs and glimpsed bare flesh. Her round derriere bobbed up in the water then disappeared with a kick of her legs below the water line with the rest of her. He glanced over his shoulder, saw the maid huffing, a hand to her brow to shield her eyes from glare.

"Go sit in the shade," he said, pointing over to a clump of willows on the embankment. "You'll still be in line of sight of the jetty and can say with confidence you did not leave Miss Talbot alone —with me."

The sun's summer heat decided the maid, and she was gone to the shade, leaving Dair to approach the jetty, something he did with cloaked trepidation, and without looking down between the wooden boards to the water below. He had all the outward appearance of calm confidence, but the long fingers which brought the cheroot up to his mouth twitched. He cursed his Achilles' heel, cursing his father more for inflicting it upon him. But most of all, he cursed himself for not being able to overcome such a weakness, for he knew it was all in his mind.

Such bitter thoughts evaporated on spying Rory's walking stick and a pile of clothes at the end of the jetty. Using the carved amber handle of the walking stick, he prodded the clothes and picked up each article for inspection. He was well-versed in female attire and its underpinnings, and the diaphanous garments told him Miss Talbot was, quite sensibly, wearing as few layers as possible during this unusual hot spell. She had given up wearing stays under her light muslin gown, went barefoot, though there was a pair of white stockings scuffed with grass stains on the foot, and perhaps worn for modesty's sake. And unless he was much mistaken, she had eschewed a linen bathing costume as well. He set the walking stick against a fat bollard, and with the cheroot between his teeth and his right hand shielding his eyes, he searched out across the water for any tell-tale breaks in its glassy surface.

"Hello! What are you doing here?"

The voice was behind him. It was cheerful and held no anxiety—that he had come upon her swimming naked in the lake. He turned but did not look down at the water but out over the skiffs to the embankment. It had nothing to do with propriety, and everything to do with calm water. Still, he managed to sound offhand, removing the cheroot from between his teeth.

"I've come to kiss you."

When she gurgled with laughter, he grinned. But still he did not look down at her.

"You kept your beard."

"Yes."

"Did you keep it for me?"

"Yes. Much to my mother's chagrin. She says I present as a swarthy vagrant."

"You can look, y'know. Most of me is hidden behind a boat."

He smoked his cheroot, doing his best to remain calm and in control, and to forget that just a few feet under his boot heels was reed-filled still lake water. It never ceased to puzzle him that he did not have the same reaction when boarding a ship to set sail on open ocean. He would have thought vast stretches of sea water, with the constant rolling motion of the waves, the salt air, and the lack of land in any direction, would have held more fear for him. But no. It was the glassy stillness of a lake, the black pit nothingness, and the inevitable entanglement in the grasping tendrils of reeds, that set his heart racing. It also sent his mind hurtling back to his tenth birthday, when he was held under water until almost drowned, lungs flooding as he flailed about, desperate for air, his brother's screams and his father's fury ringing in his ears, as he was brought to the surface and dunked time and again. His father meant to teach him a life lesson. All it did was make Dair hate him all the more.

"Down here, at your feet," Rory called, waving an arm above her head to get his attention.

The movement broke Dair's distraction with the past and he shook himself free of such melancholy, dark eyes finally locking on her.

Rory had anchored her elbows over the side of the skiff and rested her chin on her hands, so that only her bare arms, shoulders and face were visible. She smiled up at him, hair plastered to her scalp and falling about her shoulders in long, dripping coiled tendrils. In turn, he rested a buttock on the bollard and returned her smile.

"Farrier warned me the lake was inhabited by mermaids, but I did not believe him. For one thing, mermaids are sea creatures."

"Farrier...?"

"My batman since before the war in the Americas. You may have seen him about recently, fishing from a skiff, or casting a line from the weir. He is on a fortnight's angling holiday, with the Duke's permission to catch as much trout and game as he can eat, to sleep under the stars wherever he pleases, and to observe mermaids at his leisure."

"Is he a bald gentleman with a scar to his cheek and a silver hook for a hand?"

"That's Farrier."

Rory shook her head. "I've not seen him, but Grand described him to me, and warned me the Duke had a guest using the lake."

"And still you swim naked...?"

Rory pouted and was suddenly uncomfortable.

"It's obvious you've never had to swim in what amounts to a bed gown. Hideous article! More a hindrance than some help, and likely to drown its wearer." She dimpled. "Without it, I am an exceptionally good swimmer, practically a fish. Not surprising your batman thought he had seen a mermaid."

He let his dark eyes flicker over her slim arms and shoulders, and down the tangle of long wet hair that framed her heart-shaped face and disappeared to dip in the water. She did indeed present as a beautiful mermaid. He wondered how much of her from behind was visible above the waterline, and for the first- and only-time begrudged Farrier his well-earned holiday. His batman was in his skiff, halfway between the jetty and the island, with a line in the water. But if he was angling, Dair would eat his boot. The man was directly behind Rory, with the best seat in the house. Dair made a mental note to order Farrier to remove himself as far as possible from the dower house jetty and its resident mermaid for the rest of his little angling adventure.

He pointed the end of her walking stick over her fair head in the direction of Farrier's skiff.

"If you do not wish to be caught on the end of his hook, I suggest you come up to the pavilion for nuncheon."

A glance over her shoulder, and Rory took in the small boat and its occupant. When the angler dared to doff his hat, she gave a squeal of revelation and disappeared below the water line to Dair's laughter. She resurfaced on the other side of the jetty, hidden from Farrier's line of sight but now in full view of her shocked maid and, had Dair peered over the side of the wooden planks, in full view of him, too. He swiveled to face her but remained where he was.

"I'll head back to the pavilion so your maid can help you dress. I suspect being a mermaid makes you ravenous."

Rory remained silent a moment, then said quietly, so quietly he had to strain to hear her, "Perhaps you'd like to take a swim first? It is so warm... You must be hot in that frock coat..."

"Thank you for the offer, but I—"

"Oh! Oh, I won't stay. I didn't mean you take a swim *with me*," she quickly corrected, embarrassed at being rejected. "You can have the lake all to yourself. And men don't need to strip to nothing. They can swim in their breeches. I wore Grasby's cast-offs to learn to swim, so I know how easy it is for men to—Or not," she added quickly, because of the way he was looking out across the water, but not down at her. "You don't have to swim in your breeches, if you don't want to. You can—"

"Rory. There is nothing I would like more in this world than to swim naked with you."

It was the truth. There was nothing he desired more. Correction. There was one thing, but that could wait. And if there was ever a moment to overcome his dread of lake water, this was it, and with her. But instead of seizing the moment, because the moment would have to wait until he knew how matters stood between them, he politely declined.

"I will keep your offer for another day," he said gently. "I'm going to send Farrier away now, so you can dress. I'll be up at the pavilion waiting. I have something important to discuss with you."

TWENTY-EIGHT

"**W**HAT IS SO important?" Rory asked Dair half an hour later, coming up the steps to join him in the shade of the Duchess's pretty pavilion.

She had dressed in haste. Her bodice was damp in patches where she had improperly dried her skin, most notably at her bust line, and her hair, though scraped back off her face and tied up with a satin ribbon at her nape, still dripped. But that was not a bad thing. With no breeze, even the shade of the pavilion afforded only minimal relief from the summer heat.

Dair had stripped out of his frock coat and was in his sleeveless silk waistcoat and shirtsleeves, booted legs sprawled out across a line of tapestry cushions, a hand under his head. He was staring up at the painted ceiling. He had almost dozed off when Rory's question brought him to life. He sat up and offered her the cushions opposite him at the squat table laden with a modest nuncheon: A wheel of Cheshire cheese, a jar of chutney, a loaf of fresh bread, slices of cold beef, pickled onions, and a salad of greens. As well as the silver teapot on its stand and tea things on a tray, there was a jug of pear cider, once sitting on ice, now melted to cold water, in a porcelain bucket. It was at the jug Rory looked at in puzzlement as she set aside her stick.

"Courtesy of Cousin Duchess's kitchen, just like the teapot," Dair said, pouring her out a tumbler of cider. "Tea is well and good, but in this heat, it is best to start with a cool drink. Are those really necessary?" he added sternly when Rory's maid Edith came forward with a pair of ankle boots.

Rory shook her head and Edith retreated to resume her seat between two fat columns by the pavilion steps. She picked up her needlework, one ear to the conversation.

Rory took her place at the table, tucking her stockinged feet under her petticoats, and gratefully drank the cider.

"Are you lodging at the dower house?"

"Yes."

"Why not up at the big house with Their Graces?"

Dair went about filling a plate with a variety of what was on offer on the table.

"Roxton is an excellent host, and he still owns me as family, despite my despicable behavior at the Easter regatta. But we are barely on speaking terms." He passed her the laden plate, holding her gaze. "Most importantly, the dower house is but a short stroll from here to the Gatehouse Lodge, and you..."

Rory felt her face grow hot and she smiled unconsciously. His admission of staying at her godmother's house to be close to her made her tingle all over, and she could not have been happier. Yet, she remained pensive at his mention of the Easter regatta. That had been held on the estate two months ago. Rory remembered the boat race well indeed. How could she, or any other guest forget that day?

During the boat race, one of the Duke's five-year-old twin sons fell out of a skiff into the lake and almost drowned. The race had all but been abandoned. Yet, the Major had rowed on and won the race, to great fanfare and bravado on his part. The family remained tight-lipped about the entire incident. And as no one could believe a war hero capable of ignoring a plea for help, there had to be a perfectly reasonable explanation as to why the Major had rowed on to win the race and not stopped alongside other family members to help fish the boy out of the lake.

Rory might not know the reason behind Dair's behavior but she believed she had more insight than most into the episode. She had watched the Major cross the finish line, and before the shocking incident became general knowledge, the Major and his party of followers —including a clutch of young beauties hanging on every word the dashing Major uttered—had burst into her tent in search of refreshments to celebrate his victory.

The Major was in fine voice and form. Recounting the finer points of the race with his boon companions. Rory was certain the adoring females in his party heard only one word in ten, too preoccupied, as Rory was herself, in admiring the Major's handsome and powerful physique. She had resorted to fluttering her fan, suddenly giddy to be in close quarters with such masculinity, and because the space within the marquee was suddenly hot and heavy, crammed as it now was with an audience eager to be part of the Major's victory celebrations. Finally, the Major was swallowed up by the crowd of admirers, leaving Rory looking up from her chair at the backs of frock coats, and the intricate rumpled creations of the ladies' polonaise petticoats.

Ignored and invisible, Rory snatched up her stick, eager to seek fresh air and solace on the lawn. But it was no easy task for her to rise from her chair. She was hemmed in by a crowd too caught up in the moment. But not five minutes later the crowd parted, to allow the Major, a footman at his shoulder, to move to the back of the marquee. He stopped short of Rory's chair, gaze fixed at some point over her head, unaware she was there. Here, the footman shrugged him into his embroidered silk waistcoat.

Rory's gaze never wavered from his face. She, who always sat in her quiet corner, the observer but never the observed, saw what others could not, and what he did not want others to see. The moment he turned his back on everyone else, the devil-may-care mask he wore in public fell away. Gone was the twinkle in his eye, and the self-assured grin. His face dropped with sheer relief—from what, she had no idea, but it was as if he had been given a task he was sure he would fail, only to miraculously do well. He took a deep breath and briefly closed his eyes, perhaps in thanks for having come through what surely must have been quite an ordeal, gauging by the extent of the reprieve writ large on his handsome features.

Rory instinctively knew it had everything to do with the boat race, just as she knew now, as she sat across from him in the shade of the pavilion, he wished to confide in her. So she took her time to formulate her words, pulling at the soft center of the chunk of bread on her plate. She ate it before saying, as conversationally as she could muster, a flicker of a glance across the squat table where he sat cross-legged on the cushions, piling a slab of bread with slices of beef,

"You gave quite a performance at the regatta..."

TWENTY-NINE

"**P**ERFORMANCE?**"** Dair gave a huff of laughter. "Ha! It was one of my best. It had to be or I was destined for failure. But the word failure is not in my lexicon. So from the moment I stepped onto that jetty and into the skiff, until I stepped out of it over the finish line, I put in the performance of my life. I don't remember most of it—the rowing; what happened during the race; the shouts of encouragement from the shoreline. I looked neither left nor right, and I did not stop, for anything or anyone. I cannot..."

"So you rowed on when others may have needed your help?"

"Yes. But I was assured my help was not needed."

"Surely you would have stopped had they shouted for your assistance?"

"Truthfully?" He held her gaze, despite feeling the heat suddenly burning his throat. He wondered if it was possible to see a man's blush under a full beard. "I cannot answer that. I just rowed like bloody hell, determined to cross the finish line and get to dry land in the shortest time possible."

"You could have declined to enter the race," she said, then immediately answered her own question. "No. Of course you wouldn't. Dair Fitzstuart does not refuse a wager. If he did, that would be strange indeed, and your friends would ask questions..."

"Yes... I have small consolation in knowing I was too far ahead in the race to be of any use had I been called back. Little Gus was overboard and sinking fast and Kinross dived in and had him rescued before his father had time to react."

Rory continued to tug at the bread without eating it, leaving a hollowed crusty shell and a pile of crumbs on her plate.

"I believe that had you been wanted you would've instinctively gone to his aid, all other considerations secondary."

"Thank you for your belief. It means the world to me..."

She smiled shyly at such praise, but did not drop her gaze from his.

"You gave no thought to your own safety when you rescued that family from the battlefield at Brooklyn Heights, did you?"

"Battle is different. I know how to handle myself and my men on a battlefield. And that was on terra firma."

"But surely in battle your primary goal is to secure victory at all costs?"

Dair gave a lopsided grin. "We may not have secured victory recently, but victory was ours in the Long Island campaign. Washington and his rebels would have been captured, too, had they not slunk away in the middle of the night."

"But near the Jamaica Pass you rescued a woman and her two children from a burning house; a house deliberately lit by colonial militia believing the woman was harboring the King's general. The rebels gave no thought to sacrificing those lives if it meant they could flush out and secure the bigger prize of General Clinton. And yet you went into that burning building, with musket fire all around you, and the enemy at close quarters, and saved not only those three lives, but the General's life, too."

"I see you keep abreast of the war in the Colonies, and read the newssheet reports on that little skirmish," he replied with a self-effacing smile. "But no mention was made in those reports of General Sir Henry Clinton's capture. To do so would not have been good for public morale."

Rory lost the furrow between her brows as her blue eyes widened and she mouthed the word "Oh". When Dair mimicked her actions, she dimpled and confessed.

"As the Spymaster General's granddaughter I am privy to some tid-bits not generally known to the public. Of course, I would never reveal my sources, but you are in my grandfather's confidence, too, so I do not feel I have betrayed anyone."

"Rory, you do realize there are those on both sides of any conflict who would not think twice in using innocent lives as a means to an end?"

He was thinking specifically of Lord Shrewsbury. But he would never mention him by name to her and shatter her loving view of her grandfather. Lord Shrewsbury was a cunning and ruthless Spymaster General, with no conscience when it came to winning at all costs. For him, any price was worth it. Not for Dair. Children were innocent regardless of the actions of their parents, and sometimes in spite of them. Enough of a reason why he could never take Shrewsbury's place and would decline the offer if it were made to him. But that conversation was for another day, and with his mentor. He pushed aside his plate, saying flatly, "You may find this hard to believe, but not all women are innocent bystanders of war."

"Oh, I do not find that hard to believe at all," Rory contradicted earnestly. "Our sex does not preclude us from taking sides in a conflict and acting upon our convictions."

"The husband of the woman I saved was a rebel, but she was not. She was a loyalist and a spy for us. I had to save her. I could not let her fall into enemy hands. She knew too much. But that is not why I saved her. I could not deprive her children of their mother."

"Of course you could not," Rory replied with a smile. But then her brow furrowed. "If my husband was a rebel soldier, or one of the King's men, I could not betray him by being a spy for his enemies. I would support him, help him in any way I could. Isn't that the nature of marriage? To be supportive of one another in good times and bad?"

"But what if you did not believe in his cause?"

Rory gave a little laugh of incredulity at the very idea.

"Silly. Why would I marry a man whose cause I did not believe in? I should hope that before we married we would know each other well enough, love each other enough, esteem one another, that the ceremony is but a formality. There would be no surprises, no uncertainties. We would be in accord, if not in all things, but certainly in matters of great importance to our union. If this is not the case, well, I-I—I might as well marry a *bedpost*!"

Dair had it on the tip of his tongue to quip that marriage to a bedpost was preferable to marriage with Mr. William Watkins, but he had no wish to spoil their *tête-à-tête* by mentioning the Weasel, so he said as casually as he could manage, "So what does Miss Talbot consider of prime importance in a marriage?"

Rory shrugged and lifted a hand in a gesture that suggested the answer was self-evident.

"Love. Respect. Friendship. Honesty. Trust..."

"Physical compatibility?"

"Naturally. Surely it follows that if there is love, respect, friendship, honesty *and* trust in a marriage, there will also be physical compatibility?"

His lips twitched into a brief smile.

"There can be physical compatibility without marriage..."

Rory's face flooded with color, embarrassment, and anger. His smugness and that twitch annoyed her, and more than it ought.

"That is something different entirely. That is like-like—stealing food from another man's table!" she said in an angry rush. "It may satisfy a temporary need but at what cost to self-esteem and the guilt that follows? Such couplings are surely unsatisfactory for they lack the qualities I spoke of that make physical love between husband and wife so satisfying. While I am well aware men have mistresses and females take lovers, I could never betray my husband in that base way. For him to take a mistress..." She took a deep breath, aware she had said more than she should, and stole a look at him, up into his eyes to see if he was laughing at her, for her naïve pronouncements about a matter in which she had no experience. "If my husband were unfaithful, then it stands to reason that those qualities that first brought us together no longer existed. I could not remain married to such a man."

"But there is no way out of a marriage for a female."

Rory held his gaze.

"Hence the importance of making the right choice, or no choice at all, before marriage. Though why we are speaking of marriage, I do not know, because I am completely witless on that subject and-and of-of—anything else. Thus my opinion is worthless—"

"No, that is not true. Your opinion matters, it matters a great deal—to me. I apologize for making you uncomfortable. I merely wished to express the idea that while it is possible to have physical compatibility outside of marriage, it is impossible for a marriage to flourish if physical compatibility is not present. But I take your point. If love, respect, honesty, trust *and* friendship exist, then there is no reason why a husband and wife should not enjoy physical intimacy. And if they do not, then surely the fault lies with the husband, who is the experienced partner. Although, in some rare instances, both parties may be ignorant—"

"Surely not?" Rory found the notion absurd, particularly in present company. But when Dair did not disabuse her, she lost her incredulous smile, wondering to whom he was referring, for he must have someone or some couple in mind. "Then should not both parties work equally at finding a solution to their—to their— *conundrum*?"

"*Conundrum*?" He laughed out loud. "Oh, Delight, I do so love your choice of words! *Conundrum*. It is the perfect euphemism!"

His laughter was infectious. She giggled and was about to make an inappropriate quip when they were interrupted by what sounded like a wounded mouse. It made her lose her train of thought and look over at her maid, for that was where the noise had emanated. But there was no mouse, no small, wounded animal at all. Just Edith, sitting tall, with her hands grasped tightly in the lap of her gown, eyes wide and staring at Rory, mouth shut tight, so tight the tendons in her neck were visible.

With her ear to the conversation, every word marched the couple toward an intimacy that was inappropriate between a bachelor and a spinster. And when talk turned to the wholly inappropriate topic regarding the intimate relations between a husband and wife, and then onwards to the scandalous notion of lovemaking outside the vows of marriage, Edith was unable to hold herself in check any longer.

Her disapproval expressed itself, not in words but in a thin high-pitched squeal of alarm that sounded as if a mouse had been pounced on by a cat. It had the desired effect. The couple came to a sense of their surroundings, and the unsuitability of their conversation. Yet it also made them aware of how comfortable they were in each other's company. This was evidenced when Rory glanced at Dair from under her lashes and he winked at her. They exchanged a conspiratorial smile, as if caught out collaborating in something utterly wicked. Still, they respected the maid's unspoken edict, and dutifully turned their attention to their respective plates and the food on offer.

THIRTY

THE REST OF the meal was consumed in silence, Rory picking at her food while Dair ate ravenously, as always. She wondered if large vigorous males had bottomless pits for stomachs. Despite the swim in the lake giving her an appetite, with him, she was now curiously not hungry at all.

When he drank down a tumbler of pear cider and refilled hers, she asked in a whisper,

"Why must you row like-like—*bloody hell*?"

He gave an involuntary smile at her hesitancy to swear and had an overwhelming urge to leap across the table and kiss her lovely mouth. He curbed this desire and finished off the rest of the bread piled with slices of beef and smothered in chutney, saying when he was replete, "You won't believe me—No, that is not true. *You*, more than any other, will believe me, because you see through the performance. You see *me*, do you not, Delight?"

She nodded and extended her hand across the table between the empty plates and dishes, hoping Edith had returned to her needlework, for if her maid had considered the table conversation inappropriate, she would surely disapprove of the couple holding hands.

But Rory was beyond caring what her maid or anyone else thought. She was lightheaded with happiness, but perhaps that was because she had not eaten? No! Surely this was how people felt when they were in love? Lightheaded, unable to eat, so full of joy they wanted to run out onto the lawn and share their feelings with the world. And she knew this to be so when he entwined his fingers with hers, and a warm sensation not unlike pins and needles—she did not know how else to describe it—flooded up her arm, invaded her body and settled in her chest. It was as if she were suddenly immersed in a bathtub full of warm fragrant water. But it was when he smiled into her eyes and made his frank admission that she knew in her heart that he felt as she did.

"How is it I did not see *you* until recently?" he asked with a note of wonder. "How could I have been so blind...?" He shook his head at his own amazement and grinned sheepishly. "I am not the most perceptive of men, particularly when I am inhabiting the guise Society expects of me. You said yourself I am a fine actor. I am good at hiding my true self and intentions from others. A spy must be an expert at disguise, in feelings as well as form." He rubbed his cheek then his ear lobe between thumb and forefinger. "I grow a beard, put in a gold earring, tie a red kerchief about my neck, and I can walk amongst the natives of Portugal as a privateer, undetected and unbothered. I have worn the uniforms of my enemies, faced battle for His Majesty as a dragoon without fear... Yet, when it comes to rowing, or swimming in blackened water where reeds grow thick and strong—" He leaned into the table, smile gone, and not wanting to be overheard, "I am—I am a-a *coward*."

Rory's fingers convulsed in his on the word *coward*, realizing the courage it took him, a soldier, who had risked his life upon many an occasion for king and country, to confide his fear to her. She cleared her throat of emotion and found her voice.

"A war hero is no coward. *You* are not a coward. It is as natural to fear drowning as it is to breathe. How many of us can swim or care to learn? Our sailors are not required to know how to swim, and they spend most of their lives at sea."

"Rory, I can swim. At least, I think I still can. I have not been called upon to do so in many years. I was taught as a boy. I presume it is much the same as learning to ride a horse. Once it is learned, it cannot be unlearned. You will think me doubly foolish when I tell you I have no qualms about going to sea. Sailing on the high seas does not trouble me." He shrugged. "Mayhap it is the smell and taste of the salt in the air, or the motion of the waves, or both, that quells my dread of large bodies of water? Whatever it is, it is fortuitous, or I would've had a damned awful time of it sailing to and from the Americas with my regiment."

"So it is only still water that bothers you?"

He smiled. "Thank you for using the word bother. Yes, it *bothers* me. It bothers me greatly."

She looked at their fingers knotted together and was surprised how small and thin hers were compared to his. He was a bear of a man, and it was difficult to comprehend that with such size there could be a fear of anything, least of all the cool, calm waters of a lake where she spent so many happy hours swimming, feeling graceful and completely alive.

She truly did like him with a beard. Close-cropped and as dark as the hair on his head and chest, it suited him. Somehow it made his eyes darker and his smile brighter. What a pity the fashion was for clean-shaven faces.

She was procrastinating, wondering how best to ask him what had happened in his boyhood to make him fear swimming in a lake. It must have been something monumental, something appalling that had scarred his mind, for he was a soldier who had faced death time and again and was in every other way fearless. She heard herself ask the question.

"Why does still water bother you, Alisdair?"

"Because, Delight, on my tenth birthday my father drowned me in a lake."

THIRTY-ONE

HE DID NOT SAY *tried to drown*. He said *drowned me*. Rory was more appalled than she thought possible. So many questions crowded her thoughts that she considered it wise to say nothing at all. He would tell her in his own good time, and in his own way. She did not want to say anything that might forestall him. Yet, the presence of Edith bothered her, possibly more than it did him. It was not right her maid should hear his intimate and clearly harrowing confession, so she sent her away with a few quiet words, up to the dower house to fetch a footman to clear away the nuncheon things. It must have been her stricken look, for Edith complied without a word of protest, gone from the pavilion with a quick curtsy.

Rory wondered if Dair even noticed Edith's departure, such was the faraway look in his eyes. Yet, no sooner had her maid disappeared down the stairs and out onto the lawn than he grabbed her fingers a little more tightly than he intended and confessed.

"It was my tenth birthday. Charles and I were waiting for our father to join us by the lake. He was to watch me sail my model sailing ship, my birthday gift. Well, boys will be boys, particularly boys who are forced to wait such a long time that they forget why they are there waiting in the first place." He flashed a smile up at Rory, from where he had been focused on their fingers. "Before long, we'd stripped out of our frock coats, removed our shoes and stockings, and rolled our breeches up over our knees so we could wade into the water to launch my ship. Any other day, we would have been down to our drawers. But we'd been given the lecture that we had to stay clean because our suits were new."

Dair shrugged.

"To be honest, the details still elude me. All I know is that Charles and I started splashing each other, the ship's mast snapped in our tomfoolery, and I blamed him. We got into a tussle. It was nothing serious. I was big for my age even then, and Charles was a good head shorter. I'd not have harmed a copper hair on his head... But as younger brothers are wont to do, they scream twice as loud and as long. I dunked him for his whining. He breathed in water and started coughing. Instead of being sympathetic, I laughed. And the louder his wails, the louder I laughed. Father had joined us by this time, but we hardly noticed. Charles accused me of trying to drown him.

"I don't blame him for saying so. He was only eight years old, and we both feared our father more than we feared monsters under our beds! He was a rigid, cold man who had no time for children, particularly no time for me. He couldn't fathom why I preferred the outdoors and doing things, *anything*, rather than sitting still over a pile of dusty old books. I spent my lessons gazing out the window at sheep and got the birch more times than I care to remember! My lack of aptitude and application frustrated him far beyond his limited patience. He had one view of what his heir should be, and I was not it."

He smirked and shook his head.

"Ironically, Jamie is exactly the sort of son of whom he would have been proud: Scholarly, reserved of temperament, and can spend hours with his nose buried between parchment."

"And you are proud of him just the way he is."

"Yes. But I have a sense of self-worth. I appreciate the value of difference; the value of *him*. My father was an insecure, bitter man who harbored long-held resentments. He wanted to fashion me into what he should have become and did not—But back to my tenth birthday...

"Father said I needed a lesson. He said I needed to know what it was to drown, so that I never again set upon my younger brother. He took me by the back of the head... He held me under water... My face... I remember the tangle of reeds... I didn't feel the cuts to my flesh... My last conscious moment was black water rushing up my nose...

"When I woke from the blackness, I was on the bank... I was coughing up a lungful of water, and with the water was blood. My face was lacerated from forehead to chin... There were people and shouting. By the time my mother had reached the lakeside, I was out of the water and breathing, saved by Banks, the head gardener.

"That's right," he said with a smile when Rory's fingers moved in his, "the same Father Banks you met at Banks House. At great personal cost to him and his family, Banks intervened. He pulled my father off and got me to dry land where he slapped the water out of my lungs. Later, I found out my father was too stunned to do anything about Banks' intervention. But once I was breathing, he struck Banks hard across the face for interfering. Banks did not retaliate. How could he? For striking a nobleman he'd have been strung up, or at the very least be transported. As it was, he lost his position, so did his wife, my old nurse, and their family were all cast out with no references and nowhere to go..."

"How did the family come to be at Banks House?" Rory prompted. "Did they have relatives at the house who took them in?"

Dair shook his head.

"No. They spent a year living off charity. With no place to go, and with no character references, they drifted, unable to find steady work. And then Monseigneur—the old Duke of Roxton—he found them, housed them, and found Father Banks employment at the Physic Garden."

Surprised the old Duke had involved himself in this traumatic episode in Dair's life, Rory could not help but interrupt. "My *godfather* found the Banks family a home? He found Mr. Banks employment?"

Dair looked at her as if there was nothing unusual in this circumstance.

"He not only helped the Banks Family, but when he discovered what Father had done to me, Monseigneur called him to account, to explain himself. I do not know what was said in that interview but, not long after, Father went off to the West Indies to inspect the family's sugar plantations, and he's never come back. Rumor is, he was ordered to go by the Duke. I believe it. I was sent off to Harrow, which was the best thing that ever happened to me at that time, and I got to spend a couple of my school breaks with the Banks Family."

He suddenly looked sheepish, and again Rory was rewarded for her silence when he said bluntly, "No doubt had he been able to foretell what would happen during one of those breaks, the Duke would have thought twice about allowing such visits."

"You fell in love with Lily Banks and she fell pregnant with your son."

"Rory, that is the second time you've stated confidently I was in love with Lil. I was only a boy. I was fourteen; she fifteen. What happened between us should not have happened, but it did. I cannot say I wished it had not, because I now have Jamie. We have a great affection for each other, but we were never *in love*. We were just curious children. For my *curiosity* I—I had to grow up fast. There was no Grand Tour for me. The Duke gave me no alternative. He bought me a commission in the army and a month after Jamie was born, Lil married her cousin Daniel Banks, and I went off to join my regiment. But I have no regrets, about Lil, about Jamie, about my time as an officer."

"I do not doubt that at all," she answered with a smile. "You have a wonderful boy, and he is being brought up in a loving home; Mrs. Banks is a good mother to him, and to all her sons. But," she added with a frown of puzzlement, "I do not understand why the Duke of Roxton involved himself in the affairs of your family... How he managed to have your father, who it seems was not at all a pliant and biddable man, banished. Indeed, he seems to have had a fierce temper and a limited understanding of children, of people in general. Such men are best left alone to their books, and possibly should remain life-long bachelors! I hope I have not offended—"

"Not in the least. Your summation is to the life. But surely you realize why the Duke of Roxton intervened on my behalf, why he got himself involved?"

When Rory blinked at him, still mystified, he explained.

"My father brought dishonor not only to his immediate family, but to the wider family connection, and most importantly, to the head of *his* family. By casting out the Banks Family to fend for themselves, retainers of good character and service, a family whose ancestors had served mine since the time of James the First, Father irreparably tarnished his good name. He might be an earl, but even *he* is required to answer to a higher family authority, to the head of his family."

When Rory's brows remained drawn together with incomprehension, Dair smiled and sought to patiently explain a matter he had long considered self-evident.

"We all belong to an extended set of family connections. That's how it works for people like us; that's how the nobility remains powerful and in control of the kingdom. Unlike the French nobles, who bow and scrape to their sovereign, we have the Magna Carta. Even your grandfather must, when required, bow to the wishes of his head of the family."

"I understand we are all connected in some way or other, but surely Grand, as Earl of Shrewsbury, answers to no one but himself?"

Dair so far forgot himself that he caught up Rory's fingers and kissed the back of her hand.

"He would love to hear you say so! And have you, and everyone else, believe it. As Spymaster General he certainly has more power than most. But in family matters, when it comes to personal and family allegiance and alliances, His Lordship is as compliant as the rest of us. Not that the head of our family regularly intervenes or interferes, only when there are disputes, or, in the case of my father's treatment of the Banks family, when the family's honor and reputation are at stake."

"To what extended family does my grandfather owe his allegiance?"

But as soon as she said this she had an epiphany. The look of dawning wonderment on her face widened Dair's smile into a grin; he found her adorable. He let her say it.

"The present Duke of Roxton! He is the head of Grand's family, and yours. We—you and I—we belong to the same extended family but different branches?" When he nodded, she smiled. "Oh, that is satisfying! It explains why the old Duke agreed to be my godfather. How could he refuse Grand, even when he probably wanted to, *then*. Though perhaps it was the Duchess who persuaded him...? She has such a kind and loving heart, and I know how much they loved one another. He would not refuse *her*."

Dair frowned. "Why would he refuse? Why would Cousin Duchess need to persuade the old Duke to act as your godfather?"

Rory blushed in spite of herself. She did not want to say it out loud but did.

"Because I was born—Because of what I am," she said quietly. "Because—because I am a cripple."

THIRTY-TWO

DAIR'S BROW CREASED with anger and his mouth thinned to a line. He looked as angry as Rory had ever seen him—like black thunder rolling in over distant hills. She tried to remove her hand from his, but he would not let go. She wondered what angered him more—that she had accused her godparents of being petty-minded, or that she had called herself a cripple out loud and thus made him feel awkward in her presence.

"Balderdash! That is not what you are, you little idiot! You are so much more than that, and if you think Their Graces hesitated to become your godparents over such a trifle of a thing, then you do not know them at all!"

"I did not say they regretted being my godparents," Rory replied quietly, though she blushed at his spirited defense, wondering what to make of it. "But when I was born, the physicians told my grandfather I was crippled in mind as well as body. Before I was able to walk, and before I could speak and show I had a functioning mind, it must have been difficult for Grand to ask the Duke and Duchess to be my sponsor. But I see now why my grandfather wanted the head of the family to sponsor me. By becoming my godparents, the Duke and Duchess were not only giving me their blessing, but they were also silently telling others that I was under their care, too. It had always been a wonder to me why I was readily accepted at Roxton gather-ings; why others in the wider Roxton circle invited me to balls and parties, when surely, had I not been the Duke's goddaughter, the invitation would not have been extended at all."

"You undervalue yourself, Delight," Dair told her gently, all anger evaporated. "A few minutes in your company is enough to cement a person's good opinion. Besides which, you are quite the prettiest bloom in any ballroom bouquet, all other considerations aside."

"A shame then that I've been consigned to the ballroom vase since my first season. If only I had been on the ballroom floor with the other pretty petals," she quipped with a sigh of disappointment, though the dimple in her cheek told him she was pleased with his assessment. "You may then have noticed me sooner."

"I'm grateful you remained in your vase while I was away fighting wars," he said and kissed her hand again, this time looking up into her eyes as he did so. "Otherwise, you'd be married to another and have a couple of brats by now."

"Married to another? That implies there is someone else out there for me..."

He cocked his head. "So you believe each person has only one true love?"

She did but she could not bring herself to say so, not when he had asked her with a note of skepticism. It was just as well, because his next confidence made her swallow down those words and banish the idea he could believe in the notion, too.

"My parents thought so, in the beginning. That was before they married; before they spent their first night together as man and wife."

"Your parents did not find a solution to their—to their *conundrum*?"

Dair tapped the side of his nose, signal she had hit the proverbial nail on its head.

"Precisely. I suspect his inexperience, and hers, meant a solution was unlikely."

"If they were truly in love, if they were meant to be together forever, they would have worked harder at finding one."

"What a romantic you are!"

Rory pouted. "You say it as if it is a bad thing."

"Not at all. But there is something to be said for being practical, particularly as marriage does mean forever. My parents had never even shared a passionate kiss before the exchange of wedding vows. Remarkable."

"You cannot hold that against them. It is not unusual for a well-bred girl and a gentleman intent on upholding her virtue not to kiss until married. Grasby and Drusilla did not share a kiss until they were man and wife."

"Just because they hadn't kissed each other, doesn't mean they hadn't kissed others, does it?"

Rory's blue eyes widened with shock. "Oh! You are *wicked*. Grasby, yes, of course. But Silla? No! She was a maid when she married, of that I am convinced."

Dair made no further comment, and Rory had the suspicion that he knew just who Silla had kissed, where and when. She did not care to know. Though she was inclined to think it was Dair her sister-in-law had kissed, and perhaps he had then rejected her. That would explain why her sister-in-law loathed him.

Rory had a sudden devilish thought and decided to test her supposition.

"I'm so pleased we had this discussion. I can now make it my business to kiss as many gentlemen as possible before I settle on the one I marry. It seems experience is required—"

"No you don't!" he interrupted, and finally decided the table was a barrier between them that could no longer be tolerated.

But instead of joining her on her side of the squat table by means of walking, as any sedate gentleman would do, he leapt across it. He vaulted over the clutter of their shared meal, across the array of glasses, porcelain dishes, plates and cutlery, and managed to miss scattering it, all but for a tumbler which he knocked with his knee. The silver tumbler spun on its side and shot into midair to land on the marble flooring with a loud clatter.

Rory let out an involuntary shriek at the sudden noise, startled because her whole concentration was on Dair's wild leap, hoping he would not hurt himself, or her, or break something by his impetuousness. She squealed with laughter when he landed beside her, only for the momentum to cause his feet to skid out from under him, and he landed on his side, on a cushion, legs sprawled out sideways.

She half rose up on her knees, and her hand shot out and grabbed the billowy sleeve of his white linen shirt, as if this would bring about inertia. It did not. It sent her after him, and she landed against his chest, in amongst the pile of cushions now scattered around them. He threw an arm about her waist to hold her close, and there they lay sprawled on the cushions on the marble floor, both of them laughing without restraint.

And when he held up a gold and pink silk tassel, come free from one of the many cushions, and dangled it before her eyes with a big silly grin, as if it were some prize he had captured on his mad venture across the table, they both laughed harder.

Finally still and quiet, Rory found herself nestled against his chest. Dair had one hand under his head that lay on a cushion and was staring up at the painted ceiling of the pavilion, while his right hand played with her damp hair.

"Not as elegant or as dramatic as my entrance at Romney's studio," he commented, "but I have achieved the desired result. You are back in my arms, where you belong."

Rory smiled contentedly and rested her chin on his chest.

"But where are the dancing girls to offer Your Lordship applause and praise?"

He lifted his head slightly to look down his long nose at her upturned face. Her blue eyes sparkled with mirth, her lovely mouth had curved into a cheeky smile, and there was a delicate flush to her cheeks that heightened the flawlessness of her porcelain skin. She looked radiant. At that moment and forever more she was the most beautiful creature he had ever set eyes on.

"I don't want their applause, just yours..."

She sat up on an elbow.

"You have that, Alisdair. Always..."

He shifted onto his side.

"Then why are we wasting precious time? We are alone and I

came all this way into Hampshire just to kiss you. But first you must promise me—"

She put a finger to his lips to stop him talking. Then caressed his bearded cheek.

"I know, and I will," she said gravely, but the sparkle was still there.

"You have no idea what I was going to ask you, minx!"

She nodded and pressed her lips together to stifle a smile before saying flatly, "You were going to ask me to refrain from kissing any gentleman but you."

"Well, yes, that was what I was going to ask you, but—"

"Such a request, you will agree, is grossly unfair."

He scowled. "It is?"

"Of course. Particularly after you just argued that inexperience before marriage is not an ideal state for husband and wife."

"I said no such thing. What I meant is that you and I—"

"—should kiss as many persons of the opposite sex as possible so that when we kiss each other, we know exactly what we are doing. And as you are vastly more experienced, I have a lot of catching up to do if you expect—"

She got no further.

"What rot!" he growled and crushed her mouth under his, the rest of her ridiculous argument forgotten as her mouth melted into his in one long luxurious kiss. "Catching up to do, indeed," he murmured as they came up for air. "Your kisses are perfectly wonderful without the need for experience..."

"Oh, but I shall be a much better kisser it I were to kiss as many—"

"No! No, you don't. You don't need to kiss another man, ever. Just me, you wicked creature. And don't pretend you thought I meant otherwise! And don't twist my words," he sulked, gently running a large hand down the middle of her narrow back. "You're much better with words than I, but I've always thought it best to show rather than tell," he added, leaning in to kiss and nuzzle her neck, hand coming to rest on the gathered petticoats at her waist.

"What is that scent you are wearing? It could send a man—me—mad..."

She giggled, and shuddered, tickled by the soft bristles of his beard brushing against her throat. She turned in his arms so that she was now the one lying on the cushions, he above her. "Silly! Soap. But more likely pond water since I've just been for a swim."

"No soap on God's earth smells that good," he murmured, continuing to drink in the scent of her. "And if the lake water smells this intoxicating, then I am willing to sacrifice myself to whatever perils await me out there in the deep..."

Caught in the moment, he allowed his hand to stray. Slowly, he gathered up the many light layers of her cotton skirts, exposing her feet and then her ankles... That's when she baulked. His delightful exploration was over within a blink of an eye, leaving him alone, propped on his elbows, bewildered and wondering.

THIRTY-THREE

RORY SCRAMBLED away from him to the table, hastily brushing down her petticoats. She needed to cover her feet. She felt foolish for her behavior, and more so when tears of frustration pricked her lids. She was overwhelmed with conflicting emotions: Of wanting him to continue caressing her, yet not ready for him to touch her foot. Not that he had, and that made her wonder if he had deliberately shied away from doing so. His caresses were so gentle, his kisses so passionate, that she craved more and yet, having shunned him, she was left with an aching loss, and wholly dissatisfied.

DAIR STAYED where he was, on the marble floor, one long booted leg drawn up, and watched until he could no longer bear her failed attempts to tie a loosened tab of her petticoat. He silently joined her at the table and took matters in hand.

At first she did not want him and pushed his hands away. When he persisted, when he caught up her fingers before she could slap his away again and pressed his lips to the back of her hand, her shoulders slumped with acceptance. She offered no further resistance.

He then set about tidying the cushions, picked up the errant tumbler and put it back on the table, then returned to sit opposite her. All the while he was moving about the pavilion, he was aware she was lifeless, head bowed with her hands in her lap, and no doubt with her pretty head full of all sorts of emotional castigation. He reminded himself that her experience of the world was limited to her grandfather's house and a handful of society functions amongst relatives, however distant. She was always chaperoned, always surrounded by others when not in the familiar surroundings of her home. And even when in her own home he was sure she was never left alone with a man save her grandfather or her brother.

And here he was lifting her petticoats the moment her maid's back was turned! What must she think of him? He knew precisely what her grandfather would think, and that's why he was determined to speak with him that same night. And yet there remained a kernel of doubt to his determination, a small, niggling worry he should dismiss as nerves usual for a man about to embark on a life altering path. The worry persisted because it had been with him since he could remember; at least since he had discovered the root of the problem with his parents' marriage. He had resisted marriage, particularly a marriage of convenience for the sole purpose of producing an heir. The notion made him recoil. He wanted no loveless match, and yet for a man in his position marrying for love was surely a foolhardy venture.

Looking across at Rory, he did not now think so. He had known almost from their first meeting, though he had tried to ignore the notion of fate and falling in love at first kiss. Oh, but that second kiss at the stone wall at Banks House, that had undone him! He knew then there was no turning back, that what he felt for her was much more than just lust. But what surprised him most of all, what sealed his determination, was that she saw beneath the façade and yet was comfortable with him in whatever role he cared to present to the world. She doubted him less than he doubted himself. With her there was no artifice, no second-guessing, no wondering if she were interested more in his earldom than in him. And when all was said and done, her values, what she wanted from a life's companion, matched his own.

Yet, that kernel of doubt lingered, brought to the fore by her reaction to his caresses just now. He realized he had taken matters too quickly. But if she was as ardent, if she had been in the moment just as much as he, surely, she would not have pulled away? He dreaded the thought they might not be well-suited. What if the physical expression of love repulsed her? His mother had been young and innocent and thought herself in love, and yet she had so abhorred the marriage bed it was only duty to produce an heir that had made her endure it.

And so his father had told him, not to his face, man-to-man, but in a letter, sent some years ago, while Dair was fighting for his country and his life on the other side of the Atlantic. What a revelation! It would have provided some light relief from the bloody business of war had it been any other couple but his parents' marriage laid bare in black ink. He did not reply to his father's letter. He set it alight with the burning tip of his cheroot and watched it until it had turned in on itself and into ash in the campfire.

He shook his thoughts free of his contemptible father and his last letter, poured out the final drops of pear cider and put the tumbler before Rory, saying as conversationally as he could manage, "Should we have tea, too? It would be a shame not to use Cousin Duchess's teapot..."

Rory looked across at him then, and such was her despair it took all Dair's willpower to remain inert and not rush to her side to take her in his arms.

"I-I APOLOGIZE," she said glumly, a catch to her voice. "You must think me woefully childish."

"What I think is that you have never before been in a situation such as this, and you were momentarily frightened by the unexpected. That is perfectly natural."

"Is it? How many other whey-brained maidens have you had to reassure—No! I should not have asked—"

"Only one. Lil. And she, like you, is not whey-brained. Though I possibly was, and am. We were both innocents when we embarked on our springtime romance. Since? None." When she frowned, he smiled to himself, adding gently, "You did say it was important to be truthful."

"Yes. I did. Thank you for telling me."

"But being truthful doesn't make it less hurtful..."

"I am not hurt by that knowledge. I would have been surprised had you confessed to bedding maidens. And, to be perfectly frank, disgusted. I never took you for a man who preyed on the innocent for sport. I had always assumed you conducted your affairs with females who knew what they wanted and could give you the same pleasure in return."

He inclined his head with a smile but volunteered nothing further.

Rory clasped her hands tightly in her lap and forced herself to look into his brown eyes.

"I apologize, but none of that is reassuring to me—here."

"Rory, we are in this together. You have nothing to apologize for. I am the one at fault. I should have realized—"

"No! Don't! Don't *you* apologize for my behavior. I wanted you to kiss me. I wanted to kiss *you*. I want us to make love. It's just that I-I don't want—I don't think I am ready for you to-to—"

"Rory, if you are not ready for me to touch you *everywhere*, then you are not ready to make love."

The calm even tone of his mellow voice should have reassured her. All it did was to make her feel even more awkward and unsure of herself. He was right. Perhaps she wasn't ready... Oh, but the way he made her *feel*. The way her body reacted to his touch... When he kissed her, when his hands were on her skin... Her face flamed with embarrassment, and she drank down the pear cider in one gulp, unaware of its taste or that she had drained the tumbler and set it down without thinking.

Perhaps he was right. She needed a cup of tea. It would settle her nerves. It would be best to talk about something—*anything*—else until she could find the words to explain herself...

And then she sat up tall, as if struck forcefully by an idea, and she looked at him with narrowed eyes and a mutinous puckering of her mouth. How had it come to this? They had been discussing *his* fear of still water, and now, by some trickery, he had managed to turn the subject, and before she had satisfactorily concluded their discussion on how best to help him overcome his vexatious childhood memory.

She was confident she could help him, even if it was merely to enable him to row a boat without being anxious by such an innocuous activity. She smiled to herself. She was certain she knew the place where she wished him to row. It was only a short distance from the jetty. A man of his strength could row there in minutes. It was the most magical place, a place where she could forget her own shortcomings, and where she always imagined she would make love for the very first time: The temple grotto on Swan Island.

Her mutinous expression was replaced with a dazzling smile as she formulated her plan.

"I can help you overcome your dread of still water, if you will let me."

Dair smiled doubtfully. His embarrassment at having confided his weakness to her—after all, soldiers did not admit to having any fears—made him sound supercilious.

"Let me hazard a guess," he drawled. "You intend to lure me to the jetty and when I'm not looking, push me in, hoping I'll be instantly cured?"

She ignored his flippancy.

"If it were that simple, I would do it. No. Promise to meet me at the jetty tomorrow morning, and I will tell you then what I propose."

"Perhaps we can help each other?" he suggested, extending his hand across the table. When she smiled shyly and took hold of his fingers, he added with a smile, "I'll be there, but you have to leave your shadow behind."

"Edith?" Rory let out a small sigh of sympathy. "Poor Edith. She is under orders never to leave me alone for a minute. Grand has turned positively medieval since you punched Mr. Watkins in the nose. He is recovering, by the by, but his nose will never be straight again. Thank you for asking after him."

She dimpled when he laughed out loud at his own lack of interest in the fate of Weasel Watkins' fine nose.

"Grasby told Grand everything, of course, and now Grand is furious with Mr. Watkins. Yes. I thought that would please you. But you can stop looking smug that no one caught you kissing me! I am certain Grasby suspects, but it is not the sort of conversation one has with one's sister."

"Thank you for the warning."

"Oh, I wasn't warning you. You can look after yourself, and Grasby will forgive you anything. Indeed, he took your side and not Silla's regarding the whole Romney Studio imbroglio, which has sent her into a farouche. Nothing and nobody can lighten her mood."

"I am not surprised. Grasby should not have taken sides. And he should be loyal to his wife, always."

"I thought you had no time for Silla...?"

"I don't. But I'm not married to her. Grasby is. That means he must do his duty by *her*, not me."

Rory regarded him for a moment, blue eyes keen, and said what was on her mind.

"Interesting you say that now. I'd wager fifty pounds that at the moment you and my brother dropped through that window into Mr. Romney's studio, you didn't give a tuppence for Grasby's marriage, or any other gentleman's marriage, truth told—" She paused when he shook his head and laughed, then continued in the same blunt tone. "All you cared about was your performance, and causing an almighty hullabaloo amongst a clutch of shrieking, barely-dressed dancers, worthy of newssheet ink."

He smiled thinly with a raise of an eyebrow, as if punctuating her assessment with an exclamation mark. She was dead on the mark, and he wondered if she had any idea that if he and Grasby had not dropped through that window, they would not now be having this conversation. Did he believe in fate? Before that night he would have rejected the notion as fanciful. Now, he was not so dismissive, particularly since Miss Aurora Talbot was the catalyst that had made him question his world view. He now saw it through a whole new lens. It was as if his life had been smeared across one of Jamie's small glass plates, just like a drop of blood, and slid under the lens of a microscope for intense scrutiny. And just as he had peered through the eyepiece of his son's birthday present and adjusted the lens, a whole other world appeared before his eyes, one he never knew existed or thought possible. It thrilled and alarmed him.

Rory had the same effect on him. With her, his life came into sharp relief. She made his heart beat a little too hard and his chest to ache. He was not one for deep thought or rumination, but he was confident he could think of no one else with whom he wished to share his life's journey.

"Wager?" he managed to calmly enquire. "Be careful, Rory. Have you forgotten my moniker?"

Rory grinned. "Not at all. And I advise you not to take up the offer because you'd lose!"

"Yes. Yes I would."

"I have no idea why Grand thinks my virtue needs guarding *now*," she prattled on because he was looking at her intently, the look in his eye new and unsettling. "Two months ago he gave no thought to leaving me with Mr. Pleasant unattended in the Pinery for a whole afternoon. Admittedly Cedric was helping me prepare pineapple pots ready for embedding in troughs of tanner's bark. Not even Crawford was there..." She cocked her head and grinned, wrinkling her little nose. "I suppose Grand thought having our elbows deep in horse manure was not conducive to a romantic interlude."

"It wouldn't have stopped me kissing you."

"Now who is being the romantic!" she teased.

"Did the manure stop Cedric?"

The serious tone of his question surprised her. She was incredulous.

"Don't be a silly head, Alisdair! Mr. Pleasant kiss *me*? Me kiss *him*?" She gave a little shudder. "Cedric is a dear heart but I consider him a second brother."

"I am sure a sister is not what he considers you; besides, he already has eight of those."

Mr. Cedric Pleasant's feelings for her was news to Rory, and it sounded in her voice as she shifted along the cushions to the end of the table where the teapot rested on its pedestal, a lighted candle under the base to keep the water in the pot at the correct drinking temperature.

"Truly? How odd that I never thought so..." She dimpled. "Then again, I never thought of *you* as a brother... Please stay seated and allow me," she ordered when he rose up off the cushion to assist her.

He had been determined to lift the teapot from its stand for her, a job normally performed by a butler or footman because of the heaviness of the silver, particularly when filled with hot tea. But he did as requested and resettled on the cushion.

"I may not have the same strength in both my legs, but I do have strong wrists and arms, and that is from the swimming I do at home, in the Thames, and here, on the lake," Rory told him as she arranged three Sèvres porcelain cups on their saucers. "Grand insisted I learn from a young age, determined I strengthen my body and prove the physicians wrong. I cannot take exercise in long walks or dancing, and though I use a sidesaddle, I find that long rides do not agree with my ankle. But swimming—" She lifted the silver teapot and expertly poured tea in each cup without spilling a drop and set the teapot back on its stand. "—I love to swim! I wish I could do so all year round."

She next used the silver sugar tongs to select a small sugar lump from the porcelain sugar bowl that was in the same pattern and color as the tea service and dropped this into one of the teacups. Placing a silver spoon on the saucer she stood there for a moment holding the teacup and smiled down at him.

"When I was a little girl I desperately wanted to be a bird, so I could fly free. I observed that birds with a broken foot, or with only one foot, were still able to soar high into the air. But swimming is an excellent substitute for flying. When I am in water, I feel free and-and *graceful*..." She gave a tinkle of laughter, shrugged and said teasingly, "Perhaps I am a mermaid after all? Perhaps when I am in water my legs transform into one long fish tail. You'll just have to wait until tomorrow morning to discover that for yourself. No, Edith. Please stay where you are. I will bring the tea to you. You look to have run all the way back from the house, and in this heat need something to revive you."

Dair's head snapped round, just as surprised at seeing Rory's maid, as Edith was of being noticed by her young mistress.

EDITH HAD COME up the pavilion steps panting, and adjusting the pins in her disheveled hair, from running most of the way down the winding path that led up to the dower house. She was late but full of news. She had a message for the Major, entrusted to her by a footman as she left the house, but this was forgotten in her surprise at being proffered a cup of tea. Her state of confused preoccupation was compounded watching Rory move about the pavilion in her stockinged feet and without her walking stick. In the absence of her special shoes and a stick to lean on, her awkward gait was at its most pronounced. This circumstance in itself was of no surprise to Edith, who had cared for her mistress since she was in her teens. It was that Rory chose to allow the Major to see her at her most vulnerable, a situation that was avoided at all costs, even with family members.

Obediently, Edith took the cup of tea and went to the spot on the marble bench between two fat columns where her needlework lay. She stirred the sugar lump and once dissolved, sipped at the sweet black brew, grateful for the hot drink, a wary eye on her mistress.

Rory returned to the table and fussed with the tea things. She placed a cup of tea, the milk jug and the sugar bowl before the Major, and then set the remaining cup of tea at her place, but did not immediately sit.

She was well aware of what she was doing. She knew Dair's gaze remained fixed on her the whole time she was chatting away about sidesaddles, flying like a bird and swimming like a mermaid. She could hardly believe she was prattling on like a shatter-brain. But it was nerves, pure and simple. She knew also that his eyes never left her while she poured out the tea and took a cup across the pavilion to her maid.

That was a last-minute stroke of evil genius. Out of the corner of her eye she had seen Edith come up the stairs and stop to catch her breath on the top step. Taking her a cup of tea would give her a reason to walk the length of the pavilion, without her shoes and no stick. It was not that she was worried about spilling the tea, or tripping, or making a fool of herself in that sense. She readily went about in her stockinged feet in her own apartments or out in the garden on a summer's day, if no one was about.

What filled her with trepidation, what made her nervous, was that she had put the Rory no one saw on show, for him. The lame Rory with a turned right foot and an ungainly gait. The Rory who loved silk and satin embroidered gowns and robes, and all the feminine fripperies that went with an outfit and could convince herself when standing before a long looking glass that men would find her attractive. That is, until she took a step away from her reflection. Her right foot would not obey her left foot and point forwards, nor would it lie flat. It turned inwards and the weight was on the ball of the foot, compressing her toes; it gave her a limp. She tried to blame the underpinnings or her gowns and the spangled silk embroidery for exaggerating her impediment when she walked.

But the truth was, nothing changed when she was stripped to her chemise, or in her nightgown. She would always walk in this manner. There was no escaping the raw physical facts that when she moved about on land, she would never be graceful, elegant, or pleasing to the eye.

She took small comfort in the knowledge that at least today she was dressed in a simple cream muslin gown, without stays, and with her hair an untidy damp mess down her back. Perhaps his eye would stray from her gait to find fault with her plain gown and bird's-nest hair...

If ever there was a moment for him to change his mind, to extinguish his desire for her, this was it.

Taking a deep breath, heart thumping in her ears so loudly she thought she might go deaf, she finally turned to look across at him.

And what she saw, or more to the point, what she did not, was of no comfort. She could not fathom his reaction. Reflected in his eyes was something altogether unknown to her. She held his gaze, and with each passing second the heat intensified in her throat and cheeks. She would not speak. She waited for him to do so. And she waited for him to move time on, and in the direction of his choosing.

When he did, he did so in a wholly unexpected manner. It was so unexpected that Edith's teacup slid from her hand. The hot black tea splashed and stained the hem of her skirts, as the teacup smashed on hard marble, splintering into a hundred tiny shards across the floor of the pavilion.

THIRTY-FOUR

DAIR KNEW what she was trying to do and he was having none of it.

Just because he wasn't bookish didn't mean he couldn't read a person's emotions and motives. If by this display she was trying to turn him away, break his resolve, make him realize how thoroughly unworthy she was of him, then she did not know him at all. But he suspected it was her lack of confidence that made her flaunt her physical weakness so openly. It must have cost her dearly to do so. In the eight weeks (had it only been eight weeks?) since he had scooped her up into his arms off the platform in Romney's studio, she had only ever walked in his presence with the assistance of her walking stick.

He was a little hurt she needed to test his sincerity in this way; that she possessed a scintilla of doubt he might be shallow of character; that he would not desire her, esteem her, love her, all because of a tiny flaw of God's making. Again, he reasoned her doubt came from her youth and inexperience. Her grandfather had kept her sheltered, and that was not such a bad thing. Only time would see her lose the self-doubt and strengthen her self-belief about how truly lovely she was in character and form. And he had every intention of spending that time by her side, kernel of doubt be damned. He knew in his heart they were compatible in every sense. If this walk across the pavilion had shown him anything, it was to take a good hard look at himself, and how he had allowed his parents' loveless marriage and his father's vile bitterness to determine his own outlook on life for far too long.

Here was a young woman who, through no fault of hers, lived with an impediment every day. It was a circumstance out of her control, and yet she had not allowed it to rule how she viewed the world. She was not bitter. She did not blame others. She was joyful and full of optimism. He needed that in his life. He needed *her* in his life.

He joined her by the teapot stand.

He wasn't entirely sure how to conduct himself at such a momentous crossroads in their lives. He was as nervous as she was hesitant. In fact, he was so nervous the skin on the back of his neck prickled. He thought for a moment he might lose consciousness. Why did time slow upon such life-altering occasions? It was the same the moment before the infantry drummer set his sticks to the skin of his kettle and started to beat, or the trumpeter sounded his bugle, signal to charge into battle. Terror mixed with the relief of getting on with it, and getting through it, to live another day, sent him at full gallop. But as many times as he had made the charge astride his mount, he had never done this before and knew he never would again.

It was only later that night, lying in the big four-poster bed with the windows thrown open to allow for a cool breeze, both hands under his head, and smiling up into the darkness, that he recalled what he had said, and her response.

He took hold of Rory's hands, smiled into her eyes, and gently kissed her forehead. He then let go of her right hand and, still holding the left, went down on bended knee. He looked up into her face and for an instant he smiled. He could see by her expression she had no idea of his intent. That settled his nerves enough for him to say in a steady voice,

"Rory, I love you. Will you—Will you—Miss Aurora Talbot—consent to marry me?"

When she merely blinked down at him, as if he had spoken to her in some foreign tongue only known to himself, and touched his bearded cheek, he smiled nervously and turned his head in her hand to kiss her palm. For the second time he was glad he had grown a beard; he knew he was blushing. He rose up off his knee but kept hold of her hand.

"Rory, I want you to marry me... I have never wanted anything in my life as much as I want you to be my wife, but—but only if you want to..."

Rory's blue eyes widened. She clapped a hand to her smile, as if in disbelief and shock at his offer. And then she began to laugh and cry at the same time. Her series of small nods were acceptance enough for him. She threw her arms around his neck and he gathered her into a tight embrace and laughed along with her. She clung to him, murmured that she loved him too and nothing would make her happier than to be his wife. They stayed that way, joyous and reassured, tremors of relief coursing through their bodies, until involuntarily parted when Edith dropped her teacup, and it smashed into pieces on the marble tiles.

After that, time raced forward, and too fast for him to remember all the words spoken and the promises made. It seemed within a blink of an eye of his proposal and her acceptance, he was watching his newly betrothed go off with her maid in the pony trap back to the Gatehouse Lodge.

Two things he did remember: They agreed to keep their betrothal to themselves until Dair formally spoke with Lord Shrewsbury; and secondly, he would meet her at the jetty in the morning to row her across to Swan Island. As he drifted off to sleep, he couldn't decide which of these held more dread for him.

THIRTY-FIVE

D AIR ARRIVED AT the jetty in his shirtsleeves, light linen frock coat slung over a shoulder, to find Rory waiting for him.

He was late.

He had risen early, as was his usual practice since his time in the army and taken breakfast in his rooms to write three letters: One to his father; one to his father's bankers; and one to his brother Charles. All three letters informed their respective recipients of his betrothal.

The first two letters he knew would be delivered without being diverted to Shrewsbury's secret post office, where all suspect letters were opened, read and expertly resealed, usually with the recipient none the wiser to the trespass. But his letter to Charles, a supporter of the American rebels, and who lived in France, would land in the secret post office. The wax seal with the impression of the Fitzstuart coat of arms left by his gold signet ring would be expertly removed, and the contents of the letter pored over in every detail.

There was nothing traitorous or of interest to the Secret Service in the letter. It simply informed his brother of his betrothal, but not the name of his betrothed, and expressed the wish that under different circumstances he would have greatly desired Charles to bear witness to his nuptials. He hoped his brother and his new wife had settled into their life in Paris, and to expect a wedding present from him soon. He signed off with the firm belief that one day in the not-too-distant future they would be reunited.

Although the letter's contents were innocuous and far from traitorous, he knew the double agent within Shrewsbury's secret service could not take the chance the letter didn't hide some important piece of information vital to the American war effort. Why else would the Major write to his brother, and in code? Dair hoped mention of a wedding present would be construed as code about the English army's movements in North America. It was a ruse, and he would wager his future inheritance on the traitor ensuring the letter made its destination without anyone in the secret post office, and most importantly, Shrewsbury, knowing of its existence. Now it remained for him to set the trap and wait for the traitor to walk into it, trip more belike.

He was certain the traitor was William Watkins. But proving it would not be easy, and convincing Shrewsbury his trusted secretary was selling secrets to the French an even more difficult task. He hoped his contact in Portugal would, when given safe passage to England, confirm his suspicion about the Weasel.

Shrewsbury, William Watkins, and the gentleman waiting in a Lisbon tavern, were forgotten as he caught sight of Rory on the jetty, and he lengthened his stride.

She was in her stockinged feet, the hem of her light cotton glazed petticoats just skimming her ankles. She wore a matching low-cut short jacket that laced in front, and a light gauze shawl draped across her shoulders. Her fair hair was in undress, falling forward over her shoulder in one long thick plait that reached to her waist and was tied off with a pink satin ribbon. Both hands gripped the curved handle of a wicker basket that contained a large loaf of bread peeking out from under a linen cloth. There was another larger and heavier basket by a ladder that dropped over the side of the jetty into the water, where a skiff was moored.

Seeing Dair striding across the lawn, she put the basket at her feet, where her walking stick lay beside her discarded shoes, and waved excitedly. He waved back, face splitting into a grin at her enthusiasm. He was so looking forward to spending the day with her that any nerves he felt at boarding a rowboat on a still lake were pushed back down out of the way. He was determined to row across the lake to Swan Island for her, terrifying childhood memories be damned. And being in charity with the world since she had accepted his proposal of marriage, he was even prepared to accept with equanimity Rory's maid as chaperone on their adventure. He was surprised then, taking a tentative peek over the side of the jetty, to find the skiff unoccupied.

"Edith is bedridden with a megrim, so cannot join us," Rory told him matter-of-factly, and without a hint of a smile, so that he almost believed her. "And I did not have to tell Grand an untruth because he left the house well before I did. He has business with the Duke. But I did tell Ernest, Grand's majordomo, I was taking the trap to see my godmother... Which was a half-truth because I visited the dower house before coming here to pick up these supplies." When Dair raised a questioning eyebrow, she suppressed a smile and could not look at him. "The main thing is, I didn't lie..."

Dair peered beneath the cloth covering the wicker basket at her feet, and then under the one by the bollard. Both were filled with enough provisions to feed a party of four. He draped his frock coat atop the bollard.

"Are we going away for some time? Should I have left a note?"

"Silly! I just thought—after all that rowing—you—*men* need sustenance after physical exertion..."

Dair ignored her muddled explanation and blush of embarrassment, saying matter-of-factly, as he rolled his shirtsleeves to the elbow, "How thoughtful and clever of you to obtain such a feast by half-truths."

She was smug. "Pierre thought nothing of it, truly, because the food for the Gatehouse Lodge comes from the dower house gardens. So do our bread and pastries. He was obliging, and happy to see the dinner he had prepared for the Duchess not go to waste. And he offered two of the kitchen hands to load the baskets and the *nécessaire de voyage* onto the skiff." She frowned suddenly. "You dined alone, not with my godmother, last evening?"

"She did not come downstairs but kept to her apartments. I sup with her tonight, if she is well enough. And then I have an appointment with Lord Shrewsbury."

"Strange that she is ill... I hope it is nothing serious." She looked up at him with a hesitant smile. "You are—you are going to speak to Grand today? He should be returned after dinner."

He smiled to himself at the hesitancy in her voice and chucked her under the chin.

"What a doubting beauty! I suppose you woke this morning and instantly thought you had dreamed my proposal of marriage?"

Rory gasped.

"Oh! How did you know?"

He burst out laughing and shook his head.

"Oh, Delight, your lack of guile fills me with joy." He affected a frown. "Or perhaps I should be offended you think me a fickle fiend?"

She was suddenly shy and shook her head. When she went to pick up the lighter of the two baskets, he was quick to do this for her. He followed her across to the ladder.

"No. But I am certain there will be many a young lady and her match-making mamma who will wish it was a dream when they discover the swoon-worthy Major Lord Fitzstuart is betrothed, and to me, of all the young ladies paraded before you each Season."

"Paraded before me? I hardly noticed. You don't give yourself enough credit, Rory." He put the basket down and cocked his head. "Am I swoon-worthy?"

"Do you doubt it? Did you not believe me when I said every time you walk into a room female hearts—Oh! You *are* a fiend!" she gasped when he grinned and winked at her. "You are funning with me again!"

But he lost his grin peering over the side of the jetty, down into the skiff.

"I presume you want these baskets, and me, in that boat?"

"I do. I will pass them down to you... Or do you want me to get in first, and you can pass them to me?"

He put the basket at his feet and took his frock coat off the bollard to rummage in a deep pocket. Finding what he was looking for, he removed the contents from a small velvet-covered box, then put the empty box back in his pocket and laid the frock coat across the top of the larger of the two baskets. Rory wondered if he was delaying the inevitable and was about to put her plan into effect when he asked her to hold out her right hand. He cleared his throat, and said after taking a deep breath then breathing easy,

"Before I make a complete ass of myself, faint and fall off this wretched jetty and drown, I want you to have this."

On to her ring finger he slipped a thin gold band set with an octagonal-cut pale lavender sapphire. He turned the ring to check the fit and was relieved that though her fingers were slim and her knuckle small, the ring fit snugly and could not slip from her finger.

"This was given to my mother by my father upon my birth, in celebration for giving him an heir. She never wore it and gave it to me on my twenty-first birthday on the understanding I present it to my betrothed. Now," he added with a crooked smile, "when you wake, you will have tangible evidence our betrothal is not a dream. And proof," he added, looking into her eyes, "of my love—and devotion."

She stared at the ring, almost disbelieving, unconsciously moving her fingers so the sunlight glinted in one of the eight octagonal facets. The pale lavender sapphire changed color in the light. It was the most wondrous ring she had ever seen. Tears misted her view.

"Silly. You are not going to drown," she said in a small voice, overcome. "It is—It is *very* beautiful. Thank you, Alisdair... I want to kiss you but—"

"I understand. We are standing out in the open and there are eyes *everywhere*. Quickly! Let's get to that island so we can kiss there!"

They both laughed. He was only half joking. Before he could pick up the baskets, she threw her arms about his neck and kissed his bearded cheek.

"Damn and blast those eyes!" she declared hotly, casting caution to the breeze. She tilted her chin up to him and received a gentle kiss on the mouth. "Yes. Let's get to the island," she added quietly. "I can thank you properly there. And I have a surprise waiting for you. Something you will enjoy..."

It was then, with her caught up in his arms, he realized not only was she without her stays but the tabs that kept her petticoats about her waist were tied loosely indeed. He let her go before he gave in to desire and unraveled every bow and tugged a finger in the lacings to open her jacket. He picked up the basket.

"Did you dress yourself this morning?" he asked, desire making him sound gruff.

"How else was I to dress? Poor Edith has the headache. Oh, did you think I made that up? No. Events of yesterday, and the secrecy of our betrothal, was too much for her. Of course, knowing we were off to Swan Island today only made the pain in her head pound all the more. So of course I had to dress myself, just as I am now undressing myself, and to good purpose."

While she was talking, she was doing precisely what he wanted her to do, but never dreamed of her doing it here, out in the openness of a jetty. She slid her cotton petticoat down off her hips and stepped out of it. Next, she unwound the gauze shawl from around her shoulders. Lastly, she unlaced the jacket, pulling the lacings away from the final eyelet so the two sides of the jacket fell open to reveal a thin chemise. Having pulled her arms from the elbow-length sleeves, she scooped up the petticoat and shawl and pressed all three feminine articles to his chest.

He mechanically held her clothing, gaze riveted to her standing before him in nothing but a thin chemise and white stockings. If there were eyes out there watching them, all were on her, and no wonder! Rory's chemise skimmed her embroidered garters secured just above her knees. She might as well have been naked. He had not blinked from the moment she started undressing. His eyes were void of moisture, just like his throat, which was parched. He swallowed hard and tried to clear his voice of yearning.

"Rory—Are you—are you *mad*? What—what are you about?"

He tried to return her clothes, but she pushed them back on him, a sly smile curving her lips. If she'd thought about it for a moment, she would have found his reaction to her nakedness amusing. After all, here was the Dair Devil himself, shocked by *her* behavior. But she knew what she was doing, and she had faith in her ability to take him by surprise, leaving him disconcerted and baffled, and hopefully so preoccupied he would forget what lay ahead. By these means she was confident of getting him in the skiff and rowing across to the island before he knew what he was about, and where he was.

"Put my clothes in the skiff, with everything else," she ordered mildly. "I'll have need of them later. *Au revoir*."

He had no idea what she was talking about. He turned to look down at the skiff, one arm holding a basket, the other full of her clothes, and at a loss to know what to do with either, despite her directive. Then he heard a neat splash and realized what had just happened. His head snapped round to where she had been standing. Sure enough, she was no longer there. She had dived over the side of the jetty into the lake.

He called out to her, and without a second thought scrambled down the rusted steps of the iron ladder, her petticoat, jacket and shawl bunched up under his arm and the basket in one hand. He was halfway down the ladder before he glanced over his shoulder, at the water, and in time to see Rory surface from the depths of the lake near the bow of the bobbing skiff.

"Don't forget the other basket!" she yelled, pulling herself up out of the lake, chemise heavy with water and adhering to her curves like a second skin. "And remove the rope from the bollard, too!"

Dair almost lost his grip.

Rory hung there, half out of the water, leaning her frame against the outer shell of the boat, arms extended and gripping its side to keep herself upright. Here she balanced, waiting for the water to drain off her so most of it wouldn't end up in the skiff with them. She then scrambled up over the side and into the boat, onto the curved polished burden boards.

Dair didn't take his gaze off her for a moment. But once she was safely aboard, he turned and scurried back up the ladder to do as she had directed, descending the ladder again in what would have been record time, had records ever been kept of such feats.

Rory scampered up into the stern, to haul in the rope, and to take the baskets from him, one by one. She stowed them with various other items the kitchen assistants had brought on board earlier and stacked in the bow: A small shagreen-covered *nécessaire de voyage* containing all they needed in the way of porcelain plates, bowls, cups and saucers, as well as cutlery, glasses, serving implements and a small silver teapot. A waterproof leather satchel held a bundle of candles and a tinderbox. There were also a couple of towels, and a quilted blanket to sit upon and spread out their feast.

Dair was numb to it all as he dropped onto the thwart where the oars were secured in their oarlocks. He could have been carved from stone, such was the tightness in every muscle, now that he was aware of being on water. He was conscious only of the rocking of the unmoored skiff as Rory scampered about, and that all there was between him and the murky black water full of reeds was a thin wooden hull. He just wanted to scramble out of the skiff, up the ladder, and make a dash for firm land. There wasn't even a wager in place to force him to remain or lose—not only face, but his moniker of Dair Devil, and the admiration of his fellows. But such intangibles all seemed rather trivial to him now.

He heard Rory suggest he remove his striped silk waistcoat; it was such a warm day. He did so without realizing he had, and it disappeared as if by magic, Rory folding it and putting it aside. He even removed his stock and undid the two small horn buttons of his shirt at his throat, though he had no recollection of either, or why his neck and chest suddenly felt cooler.

It was only when Rory settled herself in the stern opposite him that he forgot about the thin wooden hull, the tangle of reeds and the murky water. His whole concentration fixed on her, as if his life depended on his gaze not faltering for a second. And in a way that was true. Watching her calmed him considerably. He was able to take hold of each oar, though he gripped the shaft so hard he lost sensation in his fingertips and prepared himself to break the water's surface with the blades.

Rory had one of the towels and was using it, not to put around her shoulders or to cover her bare legs, but to dry her face and squeeze the moisture out of the thickness of her hair. She froze momentarily, shot a glance at her right hand, then breathed easy. The pale lavender sapphire was still on her finger.

Finally, she laid the damp towel across her lap, as if she had just remembered her modesty, but did nothing to cover herself. If she was aware the wet chemise clung to her like a second skin, she gave no indication.

"What a wondrously sunny day for our adventure!" she enthused. With a sigh of contentment, she closed her eyes and tilted her face up to the warmth of the sun, and settled in. "Alisdair, I think we should make a start, don't you?"

He did. With his gaze locked on to her wet and clinging chemise, he began to row. He rowed, not in the frenzied way he was used to doing, but in long, even and powerful strokes that had the skiff gliding through the water like a hot knife through butter. He rowed effortlessly, and as he continued to row in such an easy manner he began to relax, and enough to wonder about their destination, the mysterious Swan Island.

THIRTY-SIX

S WAN ISLAND was the largest island within the lake system on the Treat ducal estate, and had been off-limits since Dair could remember. It was said to be inhabited by a mad old hermit, or was it a pack of wild dogs? Whatever was living on the island, it was nasty and dangerous. It certainly wasn't swans! Swans, waterfowl and ducks glided past, but he had never heard of, or noticed, flocks of birdlife gathering on or near the island's foreshores. He was told as a boy, and it was often repeated, watercraft were to stay well clear. As for setting foot on the island, that was strictly forbidden. By ducal decree, no one but a handful of servants went there. Who knew what they did, but a gamekeeper went with them. This seemed to suggest there was something worth shooting. None of the servants who went there ever spoke of it; all were sworn to secrecy. As far as Dair was aware, this arrangement had been in place since the fifth Duke had ascended to the title over fifty years ago, and his son, the sixth and present Duke had yet to rescind his father's decree.

Not that Dair had taken much interest in trespassing. After all, it was an island, surrounded by lake water. He hadn't wanted to go near it for love or money. The only occasions he remotely got close was when participating in the regatta, which required he row past the island as part of the course. That is, until today...

As they neared the island, Rory directed Dair to row towards what appeared to be an impenetrable wall of forest that went down to the water's edge. It was, in fact, a dark narrow channel, hidden under an arch of tangled elms. Within a dozen row strokes it magically opened out into daylight and a small, secluded cove. Here was a pebbled beach, and beyond the strip of beach, a wall of dense forest. The water was deep enough to anchor the skiff close to the beach, so that with only a few swimming strokes, Rory and Dair would be in water shallow enough to wade ashore. With his height, Rory expected Dair could walk the entire distance from skiff to shore. And the water here was invitingly clear.

Dair only became aware he had rowed into a clear water cove when Rory quietly told him it was time to put up oars and weigh anchor. He realized then that while he had kept his gaze on her as he rowed, her gaze was similarly locked on him. And by the small secret smile hovering about her mouth and the twinkle in her eye, she had not been admiring his rowing technique as much as his rowing physique. Well, he would give her more of him to admire.

His shirt was damp with sweat, so he pulled it up over his head and dropped it on the thwart beside him. He then stretched his arms to loosen his muscles and expanded his wide chest with a deep breath of fresh air, not the least tired or spent. He did as she asked, and with the sandbag secured to the mooring rope, he dropped it over the side, surprised and delighted to see the water so clear. He turned about, ready to take next orders and winked down at Rory. When her gaze immediately shot to the boards beneath his booted feet, he chuckled.

"Don't be shy, Delight. It pleases me more than I can tell you to find you desire me as much as I do you."

"Forgive me. That was foolish," she said with a sigh of annoyance. "I looked away out of habit, not because I wanted to. Well-bred young ladies, maidens in particular, are forever counseled by their governesses and married female relatives that to openly admire a beautiful male body is the height of wickedness. Which is utterly absurd, when we can admire paintings and statues of men as art without a word of reproof." She dimpled. "I did not look away when you were an American Indian. Though, thinking back on it, I was in such free and easy company that night I did not feel constrained to do what was expected of me, rather I did what I wanted to do, even if it felt utterly wicked at the time."

"Oh, I have high hopes of us being utterly wicked together... When the time is right."

She hunched her shoulders and smiled as if she was keeping something from him. When he put up an eyebrow she giggled and was cryptic.

"Then we are in the right place!"

He had no idea what she meant and wasn't given the opportunity to ask. Just as she had done on the jetty, she surprised him. She scrambled over the side of the boat and disappeared under the water. This time he did not panic, nor did he hesitate to look overboard. The water being clear as the ripples disappeared, he was rewarded for his calmness when Rory came into focus just below the surface. Her chemise was tangled up around her waist and she was kicking her legs out as a frog does to propel her forward, arms making wide circles to help pull her through the water. He marveled how effortlessly she swam and definitely agreed that a bathing gown would have hampered such fluid movements.

He was just wondering how far she could swim before needing to surface to take a breath when she appeared close to shore and stood up, the water now just above her knees. She turned to face him, hands running up her face to clear her eyes, then over her hair and down her long plait, the water pouring off her, single droplets caught in the twinkling sunlight. He had never seen anything so utterly bewitching. If mermaids did exist, they looked like her.

He suddenly had an urgent need to tug off his jockey boots, strip out of his uncomfortably tight breeches and throw himself overboard; he hoped the water was as cold as ice.

THIRTY-SEVEN

"**H**OW OLD DID you say you were when you discovered this cove?"

"Thirteen."

"And you've been coming here every year since then?"

"Yes."

"And it never troubled you the Duke made this island off limits to all?"

"No. And it doesn't bother you either, or you wouldn't have rowed me over here."

"I rowed you over here regardless of my cousin's decree. That doesn't mean I am not bothered."

She stopped on the narrow path that wound through the thick forest to the clearing and turned to look at him; Dair following up behind, laden with the supplies from the skiff.

"Why?" she asked, curious.

"I can look after myself. Tackle a wild dog, a bloodthirsty ogre, or a mad old hermit brandishing a rusty knife, if it came to it. But you, you are made of much finer porcelain and should never come here alone—again."

"But I've been coming here for seven years now and never once felt in any danger."

"I wasn't only thinking of danger... But what if an accident befell you. What if you twisted your good ankle? What then? How would you summon aid? Who would know you were here?"

A mutinous light came into Rory's eyes. "I won't be put on a mantelshelf!"

He blinked. "Shelf?" Where had that sprung from? "What shelf? I just want to look after you—"

"I won't be treated like one of those fragile females who are forever languishing on fainting couches and requiring burnt feathers thrust under their noses. They never exert themselves, and yet expect their husbands or their brothers to run after them for every little thing just because they are female!"

"Of course not. I wasn't suggesting—"

"I've seen it happen often enough and it's shameful. Silla uses it to great effect on Grasby—"

"I don't doubt it," he muttered.

"—and it's not right!"

"No, it isn't."

His quiet agreement made her pause. She glanced up at him and was suddenly annoyed with herself. She pouted.

"Forgive me. You were only being protective in a nice way, and I was being overly sensitive."

"Yes."

"I never thought about getting into real difficulty and not being able to call for help. I've always been self-sufficient. Grand says that was the best way to learn to live with my-my shortcomings."

"It is. But you must also be practical. So you will promise me not to come here, or any place, alone..."

He stared down at her as if his promise was non-negotiable.

She sighed, as if in defeat, and said with feigned annoyance, "I suppose when we marry, as my husband, you can order me to do as you please, so I might as well promise."

"That is not the sort of promise I want," he stated, rising to her bait. "And if that is the type of husband you think I'll be then you had best give me back that ring!"

Rory whipped her hand behind her back, as if he truly meant to take it from her, but then stuck out her tongue like a spoiled brat. He gawped, then laughed heartily.

"You-you—actress!"

"Brute!"

They both laughed and she leaned into him, a hand to his bare chest, and lifted her chin to receive a kiss. He did his best to oblige her, though he had to squat to do so because his right hand was balancing the heavier of the two baskets on his shoulder, while under his left arm was tucked the *nécessaire*, and his left hand held the second basket.

"Thank you for wanting to protect me," she said quietly. She kissed him again. "I've never had a champion before."

"You'll not need another."

She caressed his bearded cheek. "I have never wanted another, ever. Just you..."

He rose up to his full height and they continued on their way, he saying conversationally, "So no wild dogs, beasts, or threats of any kind for me to vanquish while I'm here?"

"None. It is a peaceful place full of birdsong and the occasional duck."

"Not even a mad old hermit?"

She laughed at his disappointment. She was confident he would have enjoyed taking on any threat that came his way.

"Sadly, not even the old hermit. But I can show you his cottage, and where he is buried."

"Ah! So there *was* a mad old hermit!"

"Geoffrey was not mad; he just preferred a solitary life. Here we are!" she announced with excitement. "So what do you make of my secret paradise?"

The forest had opened out into a broad, flat clearing, tall trees on all sides, and looming large in the background the steep slope of a bluff. But what dominated the immediate landscape was man-made, a circular Greek temple, a *tholos*. It sat proudly in the center of the clearing, elevated on a series of graduated plinths, giving it eight shallow steps. Its fluted colonnades soared twenty feet into the air, each Ionic column made from sectioned marble. There was no roof, and it was open to the elements, but hanging off one end of the *tholos* was a smaller and more intimate rectangular temple, with an internal room surrounded by columns. It had a domed roof that allowed light to penetrate through a glass oculus and was accessible through the main round temple.

Rory was sure that when Dair was given the time to fully appreciate this smaller temple he would see, too, what she only came to realize a couple of years ago: That it was a scaled replica of the Roxton family mausoleum atop Treat Hill. But the temple here on the island did not honor past illustrious family members, nor was it a place to mourn. It was something else entirely. It was this temple and what it symbolized that she wished to share with Dair.

For now, though, she was content to join in his excitement at seeing the clearing and its temples for the first time. He looked as awestruck as she imagined she must have been when she made the discovery on her island wanderings, and Geoffrey the hermit caught her trespassing.

The clearing might only be a short walk through the forest from the cove, but Dair's immediate thought was they had somehow stumbled back in time to the age of mythology. It had a daydream, castles-in-the-sky feel about it, and he wondered if they had walked onto the canvas of a grand mural displaying Mount Olympus, the home of the Gods. He was so excited and intrigued, he dumped his cargo at the base of the steps in the shade of a spreading elm and ran up them and inside the circular temple.

Rory did not follow but stayed in the shade, to take the pressure off her foot. For although she had managed to walk the distance without her special shoes, and completely ruined a pair of white stockings, there was pain in her ankle and in her toes. But it was of little consequence. She was just so happy to join in Dair's wonderment of a new-found place of discovery. And when he called out that there were statues inside the temple, as if she would not know this, she did not deflate his enthusiasm but called back asking if all eight were present and correct. There was a delay of seconds and then he shouted the affirmative, which made her stifle a laugh, lest he think she was mocking him.

When nothing further was forthcoming from him, she set to shaking out one of the cloths and opened up the *nécessaire*. She took out one of the etched glass tumblers to fill with water. She was parched. But that was not surprising, and she only had herself to blame, traveling in a skiff without her parasol, and in only her chemise and stockings. She would quite possibly wake tomorrow to find her skin the color of ripe strawberries.

She had unpacked most of the crockery and cutlery before Dair reappeared from the temple. He had been gone a good five minutes or more, and there was a look on his face, hard to read, that made Rory wonder what there was here to unsettle him.

"I'm an unthinking ass," he said quietly. "I should have been here to help you. And you're thirsty. Where can I fetch water?"

She pointed beyond the steps at the front of the temple.

"See the bathing pool? It fills with water from a spring. But the freshest water is to be had from the water fountains—from the lions' mouths. It is also the coolest. You can't see them from here. See those large vases atop two pedestals either side of the steps? The fountains face into the bathing pool, so the water gushes from their mouths and into the pool. The pool isn't deep, and has a tiled floor, so you could—What—What is the matter?" she asked suddenly.

She had been looking towards the bathing pool as she spoke, but when she turned, she found him not looking at the bathing pool but staring down at her intently.

"You look to have seen a specter." She blinked and gave a little gasp. "Not—not the ghost of Geoffrey the Hermit?"

"No. No ghosts. I went into the second temple... At what age did you say you first started coming here? Thirteen? Did you go into that second temple when you were thirteen?"

She did not immediately answer the question, saying instead with a smile, "Isn't it lovely? Such gorgeous tapestries, and the carpet so thick under foot, and the gilding on the wood paneling is exquisite. It is so cozy with a fire in the grate and sun shining through the stained-glass oculus." She frowned in thought. "It must be a trick of the furnishings, as it appears much smaller on the inside than one would expect for an intimate salon. No doubt it's the tapestries that run floor to ceiling on three of the walls, which draws the room in... How do you suppose they got them across to the island? By barge?"

"The same way, I expect, they shifted marble, stone and wood across to construct the temples and the bathing pool. Though I suspect the temples were built before the land around here was flooded to make the lake."

"Oh, yes! That makes sense. I forgot the lake isn't a natural feature, though it looks as if it has been here since forever. Bullock teams could have been used to drag the marble across... But the tapestries are not as old as the island. They—"

"Rory, it matters little how they got here. It's those tapestries— that room—"

"Wait until you see it with the wall sconces lit and a fire. There's something more intimate and beautiful about it in candlelight."

"Intimate? Beautiful? Ha!"

"Alisdair, what is it?"

He wiped a hand over his mouth and took a deep breath. He wasn't sure how to put into words what he wanted to say, so he just blurted it out. Of course, his declaration made him sound angry, angry with her, which he was not. He was embarrassed by what he had seen on the walls of the small temple and his reaction had shocked him more than he thought possible.

"Rory—those tapestries—that room—they are not fit for a young girl's eyes."

"I thought—I don't understand... That was to be my surprise for you."

"Surprise?" he blustered, folding his hands across his bare chest but not meeting her eye. "It was that, and more!"

"You don't like them?" she asked, disappointed, and got to her feet. "Why? What's wrong with them?"

He looked at her then and saw only studious enquiry. It increased his discomfort. He dug a larger metaphorical hole for himself.

"Wrong with them? You want me to say it aloud?"

"Yes. Yes, I do, because it is now obvious to me that the temple, the tapestries, the room itself, has greatly upset you and I do not understand at all why it should. Particularly to a man of your worldly experience."

He walked away from her, hands through his dark hair, and then returned.

"And in your unworldly opinion, what did you think the naked couples in those tapestries were up to? No! Don't answer that. The question was asinine, like me!"

"There is only one couple," she said quietly. "One couple in many different—*situations*."

"*Situations*?" he said doubtfully. Rory thought he looked smug. "I was in that room less than five minutes and believe me, I know an-an *orgy* when I see one."

"I'm sure you do. But you're wrong."

"Rory, that's not what I—"

She cut him off.

"You think because I am a maid I should not look upon those tapestries. You possibly believe all females must be shielded from such expressions of love?"

His black brows contracted over his beak of a nose. "Love?"

"Yes. Love. Just because I have never *made* love does not mean I do not appreciate the joy physical love must bring to a couple who are *in* love. So please do not address me as if you are speaking to an ignorant fool—"

"I was not—"

"I am well aware, despite my lack of tangible experience, that there are those who indulge in venery for its own sake—"

"Aurora!"

"—which is altogether a different experience from making love. And it is the latter which is represented in those tapestries. You cannot persuade me otherwise." She looked up into his flushed face and stated bluntly, "Making love frightens you."

When he stared at her, horrified, she knew she had prodded the raw nerve of truth.

"Oh, I know you are wonderfully considerate. You would be surprised what women gossip about behind their fans, particularly when they think they cannot be overheard. But those exploits are not what I am talking about, nor do I care to know more about them than I do already. What is of importance to me is this situation we now find ourselves in. It is unique to both of us."

"It is?"

"You have never made love to the one you love, and neither have I. In that way, we are both inexperienced and—" she smiled shyly, "—more than a little bit *apprehensive*."

"I suppose when you put it like that..." His shy smile mirrored hers. "But even you cannot deny my experience puts the onus squarely on my shoulders to make you happy."

"Oh please do not negate my responsibility, just because I am a maid," she responded earnestly. "I want to give you just as much pleasure as you give me, I assure you."

He gave a deep chuckle and shook his head.

"As God is my witness, Delight, if someone had told me three months ago I would be having such a brutally frank discussion about the marriage bed, with a pretty blonde maiden whom I love and adore, I would have condemned him as a Bedlamite!"

She was momentarily concerned. "I hope I am not being too brutal?"

"With me? No. Not at all. I like it."

"Then you won't mind me saying, if all that is required for you— *for us*—to be completely comfortable with each other is to make love, then what are we waiting for?"

He could not hide his astonishment or stifle his laughter. But he was not shocked; there was truth in her words. When he had mastery over himself, he said, "I don't deserve you, but I refuse to give you up. You know just what to say to make me realize I have a head full of unfounded fears and doubts, and only you are capable of banishing them." He stroked her cheek. "I will never be able to thank you enough for rescuing me from myself."

She dimpled. "You can but try, by letting me show you those tapestries."

He pretended offence. "You want me to go back in there, into that den of iniquity, with you? And here was I thinking love was unconditional."

"Alisdair James Fitzstuart, you are a prude! For a man who can parade about a painter's studio in a loin cloth, putting on a show for a gaggle of giggling dancers—"

"It was a *show*. I was acting. I am good at *acting*."

"Not an excuse I accept!" She pouted. "Five minutes' cursory inspection of that room, you will agree, is as nothing to the hours I have spent—"

"Hours?"

"—studying and admiring those tapestries. They tell a story—"

"A story?"

"—about a marriage, a loving marriage. And because it is a loving marriage, it is quite natural for the couple to make love, many times, and on all three tapestries. Each tapestry represents a different stage in their mar—Oh! You have outwitted me!" she declared when he started to chuckle. "You are being prudish to annoy me! Admit to it."

"I admit to nothing, only that I adore you all the more, if that is possible, when you talk so ardently on a topic that is of interest to you. I can't wait to hear all about pineapple cultivation."

She pouted. "Now you are mocking me."

"Never! I am sincerely interested in pineapple cultivation."

"I do not believe for one movement of the second hand of your pocket watch that you have the slightest interest in pineapples! Alisdair!"

She squealed with fright when he suddenly scooped her up into his arms.

"What—what are you doing?"

"What am I doing?" he repeated, carrying her lightly down the temple steps to the edge of the bathing pool. "It's time we gave ourselves up to this paradise and went for a dip. *And*, I promised to fetch you a glass of water half an hour ago."

The surface of the bathing pool shimmered and rippled like a length of white satin caught up by a breeze, water pouring forth from the open mouths of two large lion heads set in enormous pediments either side of a set of broad stairs that descended to the tiled floor. Dair went down these steps without hesitation, the water refreshingly cool on such a warm sunny day, he and Rory taking a shallow intake of breath as the cold water snapped at their warm skin.

"Let me tell you just how serious I am about pineapple cultivation, wife-to-be. I have engaged Bill Chambers to design a pinery for Fitzstuart Hall."

"Chambers? *Sir William* Chambers? The Swedish architect? To build a—a *pinery*? At your family home? For-for *me*?"

He waded into the middle of the pool with Rory still in his arms, the water level at its deepest rising to just above his navel.

"Soon to be *our* home," he corrected. He frowned. "You do want a pinery, don't you? I thought it would make an excellent wedding present. It may take a year or two to build, but a wedding present it shall be."

When she clung to him, when she muffled unintelligibly into his neck, he took it as a sign she was pleased with his wedding gift. He tried to unhook her arm so that he could see her face, to reassure her and to kiss her, but she remained fastened to him. So he did the most natural thing in the world, something every good swimmer would do, but something he had not done in a large body of fresh water in many years. He slipped out from her hold on him by ducking under the water. And once underwater, and seeing how clear it was, he swam away to resurface by the steps.

Rory waved to him from the middle of the bathing pool, and he waved back before diving once again under the water and disappearing. She followed his lead and dived, too, knowing they were now engaged in a watery game of cat and mouse.

She couldn't have been happier.

Her happiness had nothing to do with his wedding gift of a pinery.

THIRTY-EIGHT

Two PEOPLE deeply in love in a secluded paradise would have required the combined willpower of all the mythical Gods to resist giving in to the overwhelming need to physically communicate such love. All other considerations were unimportant. Custom, family expectations, and societal norms, dictated they wait until they were legally and spiritually one before consummating their union. And their betrothal remained a secret, yet to receive the blessing of either family, in particular Dair's mother, the Countess of Strathsay, and most importantly, the sanction of Lord Shrewsbury, Rory's grandfather.

These considerations were mere formalities. Blessings and sanctions were a foregone conclusion for two young people from within the same social circle, who were distantly related, as all the nobility were in some form or other, dating back to the Conquest. Their union would surely be seen by all as the epitome of social, political and economic acceptability.

But to the happy couple, and in this place, none of that was important.

There was something about the forest clearing, its isolation, even from the rest of the island, with its tall deep curtain of trees, its fanciful temples and its enchanted bathing pool, that rendered the lovers—at that moment in time—invulnerable.

The handful of hours leading up to the couple falling asleep in each other's arms under a coverlet in the small temple was burned into their collective memory. They made love in the very room Dair had railed against, but it wasn't the first time or the only setting. The consummation of their union occurred under the shade of an ancient elm, and on the picnic rug by the bathing pool.

Dair had been prepared to wait, whatever his private misgivings, given his parents' disastrous wedding night, for her sake, because he loved her. Rory had other ideas, though she'd had her heart set on the temple as the perfect setting to give herself to him. But when in the throes of an all-consuming passion, reticence and the best-laid plans are irrelevant. Nothing else mattered except their love for one another, and in this paradise, the shared experience of mutual physical pleasure.

Much later, Dair carried Rory into the small temple, built a fire in the grate and boiled water for tea. While he lit a cheroot she made tea, both silent, words unnecessary to express the joy and relief both felt that the bridal night now held no fears for either of them. They could go forward into their new life together, confident and full of optimism. And while they drank tea on the coverlet spread out over the thick rug in front of the fire, Rory told Dair the story of the couple woven into the three enormous tapestries covering the walls.

She confessed that the tapestries held more meaning for her having listened to Geoffrey the Hermit's fairytale. No, not here in this room, she quickly reassured Dair. It was on her first visit to the island, when the hermit had found her trespassing in the round temple. In exchange for allowing her to come and go on the island whenever she pleased, he made her promise not to set foot in the small temple until her seventeenth summer. Despite her overwhelming curiosity she promised, and he took her at her word, though he warned her he would be watching to make sure she kept true.

And because he could see she was a good girl with a kind heart, he offered to tell her a fairytale connected with this island, about a dark-haired sprite and his golden-haired fairy nymph, and three magic carpets. How could she resist? It was only years later, when she finally viewed the tapestries (what he called magic carpets) that she realized the fairytale was true, woven in silken thread into the three large tapestries. It made the hermit's simplistic telling of the couple's life story that much more poignant...

GEOFFREY THE HERMIT had been living on the island for more than ten years when one day a couple appeared at the round temple, as if by magic. They stayed two nights, and then disappeared. He had watched them from the safety of the forest, fearing they might be evil sprites, come to do him mischief. But as he watched them splashing in the bathing pool, chasing each other through the round temple, and all the while laughing and being playful with each other, he knew they would never do him harm. Every year for the next twenty-three years they returned to the island, for two nights, to splash in the bathing pool and to chase each other through the temple.

He could tell that they loved each other beyond reason.

A week before the couple's second visit, workmen came to prune the trees and bushes about the temples, to clean the pool of leaves and the oculus of grim, and to dust and rid the small temple of cobwebs. And so it was that the hermit knew precisely when the sprites would return to the island each year.

Just before their seventh visit, the workmen brought with them a magic carpet. This they hung on a wall of the small temple. When the men left, Geoffrey went to gaze at it, and it was truly magical, woven with brightly colored silks and gold thread and as dazzling as a sunny spring day. Woven into the carpet were his two friendly sprites, and he saw that there was a small sprite, a son. He also recognized the palace across the lake from the island, and now knew where his sprites lived for most of the year, and who they were. They were in truth the king and queen of this domain—Renard, fifth Duke of Roxton and Antonia, his duchess—and when they set foot on this island, magic turned them into sprites. He knew this because they wore no gold coronets, brought no servants to serve them, and cooked their own food. Their clothes, however, were of silk and velvet, when they chose to wear clothes, which, being sprites, was not often at all.

From that day forward, every year he gathered flowers and vines and wove them into crowns for the sprites to wear on this their fairy island kingdom. He left them as offerings in the small temple just before they arrived. He knew his flower crowns pleased the sprites because he saw them frolicking about in them.

The second magic carpet arrived just before the couple's fifteenth visit to the island. This carpet was as brightly colored as the first and was all about families. There were four panels to the carpet. The first showed the sprites being as friendly as ever with each other. In the second they were with their son who had grown tall. The third panel showed the sprite family with another couple, who also had a son, and finally, in the fourth panel a third family with a mother but no father and three children, two boys and a girl had joined the sprites and their friends with the one son. Everyone was happy and holding hands.

And on this fifteenth visit, Geoffrey was surprised to see that the female sprite was heavy with child. The couple went swimming as they always did, but they did not run about the colonnades of the round temple but spent most of their time shut away in the little temple. He could see the smoke from the temple chimney from his cottage. And when there was no more smoke, he knew they had left the island to return to their palace.

Two days before the couple's twenty-third visit to the island, a third magic carpet appeared on the wall of the temple. The male sprite no longer had dark hair, but a mane of pure white, and he walked with the aid of a stick. But the female sprite was just as beautiful and as full of life as the first day he had fallen under the spell of her beauty. This visit was to be different from all the others, and the most memorable for Geoffrey. At dusk of the second night, there was a knock on the door of his tiny cottage. There standing before him, much shorter than his estimation but more beautiful than he thought possible, was the fairy queen. She had the most mesmerizing green eyes and was wearing his crown of flowers on her long golden hair that flowed past her waist.

She asked if she might enter his cottage, and he gave her his only wooden chair to sit upon near the warmth of the fireplace. He set a mug of dandelion tea before her, which she drank in tiny sips. She thanked him for the flower crowns, which were always so welcoming upon their arrival. She thanked him, too, for being the guardian of their island paradise. She was smiling, but he could see she was inconsolable. Her damp green eyes told him so. He asked her what he could do to stop her sadness. She said there was nothing to be done; it was in God's hands. She told him in a brave but halting voice that this would be the last visit to the island by her and her one true love. She told him not to concern himself, that he would always have a home on the island. And when his time came, he could be buried on the island, and she would see to it he had a headstone and his name would be carved over the mantel of his fireplace, so that he, the guardian of Swan Island, would never be forgotten.

With no smoke from the temple chimney, Geoffrey knew the sprites had returned to their kingdom and he would never see them again.

Rory had asked him to describe what was on the third and last magic carpet. It was a map of the island, and it was filled with all the wondrous things to be found there, and the wonderful times enjoyed by the two sprites. They were there, the king with his white hair, the fairy queen with her flowing golden hair, both wearing his crowns made of flowers, and they were being as friendly as ever with each other. But what pleased Geoffrey the Hermit, what brought tears to his eyes in the telling of it to Rory, was that woven into the island map was his little cottage, and looking out of the only window, there he was, smiling with his long beard and whiskers and a flower behind his ear.

Dair had then gone over to stand before the third tapestry, to study it and to find the cottage. There it was, on the other side of the clearing from the temples, in a bed of wildflowers, and woven into the flowers was the hermit's name: Geoffrey Swan. Still gazing at the tapestry, he then quietly asked about the fate of the hermit. She told him. Two years ago, she visited the island as usual but could not find Geoffrey anywhere. He often found her. She went to his cottage. It was empty, and by the cobwebs and dust it had not been lived in for some time. She found his grave not far from the cottage, in a sunny, open spot. It was marked by a fine headstone and was covered with wildflowers. By the headstone was a large urn filled with beautiful, exquisitely wrought porcelain flowers of every color and variety. Rory imagined it had been placed there by the Duchess of Roxton and Kinross so that Geoffrey Swan the Hermit, guardian of Swan Island, would have flowers on his grave, whatever the weather.

THIRTY-NINE

T HE COUPLE were discovered asleep in each other's arms, under the coverlet before the fireplace in the temple; the irony not lost on Dair. If figures woven in tapestry had the ability to mock him for being a hypocritical prig, they were doing just that as he pulled on his drawers and followed Farrier through to the cool of the circular temple and into the afternoon light.

"Beggin' Your Lordship's pardon for wakin'—

"Why are you here, Mr. Farrier?"

"There's a cottage over yonder. Neat and tidy and with a comfortable bed. I reckon it belonged to the guardian of Swan Island, Geoffrey the Hermit, cause that's what's carved into the mantel over the fire."

Dair raked the unruly hair out of his eyes and accepted the cheroot his batman offered him.

"I don't mean here, here on the island. Here, bothering me. Don't you have a few days left to your angling holiday?"

Farrier gazed out through the temple columns to the forest that ringed the clearing, the leaves against the sky now tipped with the orange glow of an afternoon sun. A curl of smoke rose into the clouds and seemed to touch a flock of ducks as they flew past in formation. The batman kept his profile to his master and puffed on his cheroot. He didn't answer the question, and he couldn't hide his smirk.

"This little glade is a paradise, ain't it? Private and out of the way... No one would know y'here... Thing is, today of all days, a gamekeeper and his two thumpin' great lads came ashore. They heard what they thought was a wild beast, but instead of headin' straight here, as luck would have it, they saw smoke and came to reconnoiter the cottage first. Got me to state m'business. And then we got to smokin' and havin' a nice mug o' tea, and I kept 'em occupied until—well, until it went quiet again. Don't reckon Your Lordship would be interested in knowin' that every bird song, every snapped twig, echoes out into the forest—"

"I'm not," Dair retorted. "What do you want?"

Farrier came straight to the point.

"There's a flotilla out lookin' for your golden-haired mermaid. Seems she left her shoes and somethin' else on a jetty that she can't do without, and that's made 'em think there's been a misadventure—"

"Damn!"

"—and so the gamekeeper and the lads were sent to see if she was here."

"What did you tell them?"

Farrier glanced at his master and said smugly, "Told 'em squat, like I always do. Not my business, is it, if yesterday's dish was breast of opera singer and today's is rump of mermaid. Your tastes are anythin' but pedestrian. But y'beard has me flummoxed. Though, in this woodland setting, and making love with—"

"Stow it, Mr. Farrier!" Dair growled, the ferocity of the order making the batman recoil, stunned. "This isn't one of my brainless pranks, and I'm not here on some idiotic wager, or lust-driven whim! Got it? She's—Frankly, she's none of your God-damn business!"

"Very good, Major," Farrier stated, saluting his superior officer. "Consider m'self cautioned, m'lord."

Dair flicked the cheroot to the ground and the batman instantly extinguished it underfoot. Dair sighed heavily and lifted a hand in resignation.

"Look, Mr. Farrier, I don't want—"

"My stick," Rory interrupted, coming forward. "I left my shoes and my walking stick on the jetty. Silly of me to forget them. That's what they must have discovered. I don't remember putting either in the boat..."

Rory had been standing a little way off, the coverlet wrapped around her as best she could manage it, the excess material gathered up over an arm, so she did not trip. Her fair hair fell around her face and about her shoulders down to her waist like a curtain. She had heard most of the conversation between master and trusted servant, waking just after Farrier had gingerly poked Dair out of a light sleep.

To Farrier, she appeared less the mermaid and more the ethereal medieval maiden he'd seen in stained glass church windows. She was prettier than he had expected of a fair-haired beauty, but she was not as beautiful as the Major's usual preference in females, which made the batman wonder at the arrangement between his bearded master and this girl. He did not have to wonder long because he had his answer when Dair turned at the sound of Rory's voice. A light came into his dark eyes, his features softened, all anger and annoyance extinguished. Farrier knew then her significance in his master's life and he mentally gave a low whistle and dropped his gaze to the dusty toes of his boots, where they remained.

The couple smiled shyly at each other and when Dair went over to Rory and gave her his hand, she took it and he drew her to him. He kissed her forehead, saying gently,

"I had best get you back before your grandfather works himself into an apoplexy, and your maid is compelled to divulge her fear something far more distressing has happened to you."

"Than drowning? Surely not." She smiled and leaned against his bare chest with chin tilted up. "He may think my loss of virtue a fate worse than drowning," she continued in a whisper. "But I do not. I was never happier of such a circumstance in my life."

He brushed the hair from her cheek. "Let's get married here, at Treat, this week. I'll have Roxton get us a special license."

"Oh? Will it take a week?"

He laughed and pinched her chin. "If I had my way we'd marry tomorrow. But archbishops require some notice, to ponder and to be important... But Cornwallis is a congenial fellow. Roxton won't have any problem there."

"A week will be time enough to have a gown fetched from home... And Grasby must be in attendance—"

"Yes. I'd like Grasby there, too. Then it's settled." He gently kissed her mouth. "I can't wait."

"Nor I... Now I must dress so you can return me to the dower house... But first I need to-to bathe—"

"Of course," he interrupted quickly, to save her any embarrassment. "I took the liberty of setting out your stockings and clothes down by the steps of the pool, in readiness."

"Oh! How-how thoughtful. Thank you," she replied, heat intensifying in her cheeks. "I-I don't know when you-you found the time..."

"I've packed up most of the nuncheon things, too, but left out the strawberries and there is a peach..."

Her awkwardness, rather than abating, grew more acute with his tactical interruptions. For some ridiculous reason only known to her heart, she felt suddenly awkward and stupidly gauche in his presence, which was far from how she had been when they were wrapped in each other's arms. She was still in awe of what had just occurred between them. And having shared the most intimate experience in the world with the man she loved above all others, she had crossed a bridge from which there was no turning back. She was now spiritually bound to him forevermore, and she couldn't be happier. All that remained was to celebrate the legal union for their happiness to be complete.

So why did she feel apprehensive? That there was a shadow cast over their happiness. He had given her a ring pledging his commitment before they had made love... And he said they would be married by special license by the end of the week... That was all the reassurance she needed—wasn't it...?

Dair sensed Rory's uneasiness and noticed how her fingers unconsciously fiddled with the unfamiliar pale lavender sapphire ring, turning it back and forth on her ring finger. But he had no idea what was troubling her or the extent of her inner turmoil. He thought perhaps the presence of Farrier was making her uncomfortable, so he put an arm about her shoulders and led her to the bathing pool and away from his batman, who stood staring at the ground as if it had all his attention.

When he returned, leaving Rory to bathe in private, Farrier had moved inside the little temple and was making himself useful by dousing the fire, and tidying the room. Dair tugged on his breeches and threw on his shirt and waistcoat but had yet to do up the buttons. He held his jockey boots and stockings.

"Mr. Farrier! A hand, if you please."

"As it so happens, I do have one of those I can offer Your Lordship."

Dair smiled. "One is all I require."

Comfortable again with each other, Farrier felt free to ask, "May I cut short m'anglin' holiday and return to your service, m'lord?"

Dair looked up from securing a breeches buckle.

"Are you sure? It's not necessary... On second thought, yes! Please do. I need to shave, and this afternoon. Reynolds is a fine valet in most respects, but he can't shave me, or take proper care of my razors, and he hasn't the foggiest notion of how to prepare a whetstone."

Farrier shook his head with grave concern.

"'Tis no wonder you're wearing a woolly face then, m'lord. I'd not want Reynolds slittin' me throat! And he has two good hands with which to do it, too. Leave it to me... There!" he added with satisfaction, now his Major was booted and dressed. "If you don't have need of me, I'll head back to the cottage to collect m'kit. My skiff is moored in the cove, too."

"Mr. Farrier—Bill..."

The batman stopped in the doorway of the temple and turned back into the room.

"Yes, m'lord?"

Dair looked him in the eye.

"My life has taken an unexpected but welcome turn since that little skirmish at Romney's Studio."

Farrier couldn't have agreed more. To his mind, the Major's confession was a colossal understatement. When Dair did not elaborate, Farrier nodded and left. He was confident they were headed into interesting times... By nightfall, even he could not have predicted just how interesting.

FORTY

Antonia, Duchess of Roxton and Kinross rose up off the tapestry cushions on the chaise longue and put her stockinged feet to the carpet. She did this without opening her eyes. And with her eyes still closed, her toes searched out her embroidered turquoise silk mules, which she had kicked off earlier. Given the way her morning sickness was making her feel, she had no inclination to dress for dinner, and this despite having her cousin to dine. How she would get through the meal, she knew not. Food was of no interest to her.

An hour earlier she had been standing at the window as two boats glided in to moor at the jetty. They were met by half a dozen men, some of whom had been out on the lake earlier as part of a search party. Her first reaction was one of relief, that her goddaughter was safe and well. The second was one of extreme interest in the company Rory was keeping. Her interest intensified to discover the young woman had been out boating on the lake with her cousin the Major.

She watched the men offload the cargo from both boats and go about their business, one handing Rory her walking stick. The Major and Rory then slowly made their way up the sloping lawn towards a pony trap waiting to return Rory to the Gatehouse Lodge. It was at the trap, more precisely, what happened behind it, that made Antonia sway and grip the windowsill with two hands, her maid thinking her about to faint.

Did the couple seriously think no one would see them kissing with an Elizabethan manor house looming large over them? But by the manner of their kiss, Antonia recognized that the couple were not thinking at all. They were so wrapped up in each other they were oblivious to all else, particularly their surroundings. There was only one conclusion to reach about her goddaughter and her cousin the Major, one that was met with mixed emotion. For while their kiss curved her mouth into a smile, it also filled her with a disquiet she could not shake.

She was reminded of that kiss while sipping from her cup of black tea as Dair was admitted into her cluttered pretty sitting room with its view of the lake. He was dressed formally, which was a surprise. And even more so when he was usually seen in a frock coat made for comfort, the habitual jockey boots, and with his thick black hair indifferently tied back off his face. This evening, he wore an elegant midnight blue linen frock coat, embroidered on short skirts, tight upturned cuffs and pocket flaps with silver sprays of flowers and spangles, and a pair of matching thigh-tight knitted breeches. Both were adorned with shiny silver buttons that matched those of a cream silk waistcoat. And for the first time in many years, his large feet were encased in plain black, low-heeled leather shoes with unadorned silver buckles. His shoulder length hair was neatly dressed and combed off his face, tied at the nape with a cream silk ribbon.

Most surprising of all, he no longer wore the close-cropped black beard Antonia had seen him with just that afternoon. In fact, his heavy chin and jaw was the smoothest it had been in many years. He had always carried some stubble, even to the most formal of occasions, as if he couldn't be bothered or didn't have the time for an exacting shave. Antonia always assumed this an affectation, like the untidy hair and the jockey boots. Props taken from his performer's bag for the benefit of his admiring female audience and, she suspected, to annoy his mother; the Countess was a stickler for convention in form and correct dress.

It was not the calculated devil-may-care cousin with the arrogant swagger who bowed over her outstretched hand in greeting but an affable young gentleman with a smile that bordered on shyness. It had Antonia sitting up and peering at him keenly.

In her heavily accented English, to tease him, she quipped, "A month in custody and you are a changed man, Alisdair."

He put up an eyebrow.

"You and I both know, Your Grace, I spent that month in Portugal."

"Ah, so not incarceration but sunstroke sees you forsake your boots?" She put aside her teacup. "This cousin you present to me looks a good deal more serious than the other one. But you should go without jockey boots more often. White stockings show off your large calves to better advantage. And the beard, it had a certain appeal, but you are far more handsome without it."

"Thank you, Your Grace—"

"Your Grace? I compliment you and you go all formal on me? And now I have you blushing! Who would have thought it possible. But I am not telling you anything you do not already know."

Dair grinned. "No, your—No, Cousin. But I will take the stockings and shoes on advisement."

"Julian knows you are here and has invited you to a concert this evening perhaps?"

Dair shook his head. "No. After I sup with you, I have an appointment with Lord Shrewsbury." When Antonia's eyebrows lifted imperceptibly, he added, "To debrief him about my trip to Lisbon. But before I can do that, I need to discuss an important matter with you—"

"With me?" she interrupted, recalling the passionate kiss she had seen him share with her goddaughter. "Naturally, I will help you in any way I can. You know that, *mon cher*."

He nodded and, suddenly overcome, easily slipped into her native French tongue. "Yes. Yes, I do know that, *ma chère cousine*... Jamie loves his microscope, and your visit to Banks House has provided the family and their servants with enough to talk about for weeks, as well as a certain notoriety in their little corner of the world.

I suspect you knew the outcome before you drove out to Chelsea in state...?"

She gave a little tinkle of laughter, and then was serious.

"People in our position have a responsibility to live up to the expectations of others, particularly those whose circumstances or position do not allow them the opportunity to come close to our social circle, least of all mingle within it. How could I not drive out in the big black traveling coach, with outriders, and me in one of my best gowns, looking every inch a duchess? What a disappointment had I turned up looking like this!"

Dair laughed and shook his head. "Never a disappointment, Mme la Duchesse. Whatever you say to the contrary, you are *always* every inch a duchess; the attire an inconsequential detail."

"I hope that remains true in the months to come..." Antonia murmured, and braced herself to stand without feeling nauseous, prompted by the appearance of a footman in the doorway of the anteroom that connected the sitting room with the private dining room. "You do not mind if first we dine before we discuss this important matter? Pierre he will tear out what hair is remaining to him if I do not at least taste the dishes he tempts me with. I am only too pleased you are here staying with me," she added with a smile, when Dair offered her his arm, and they walked through to the dining room and a table set with silver, fine crystal and Sèvres plates. "Your appetite at least makes my chef feel he is valued..."

While the cousins dined on lamb loin with a breaded mushroom crust, salmagundi, carrot puffs, stuffed cucumber and potato pudding, the conversation remained topical but not personal. They discussed the infirm Lord Chatham's surprise visit to the Lords in his sedan chair, and the defeat of his motion to end hostilities in the Americas. They both agreed that the publication of Macpherson's General History, condemning the first Duke of Marlborough's avarice, was needless abuse, Macpherson having no right to cast a stone at Queen Anne's great general. Both were intensely interested in the recent raids by American privateers on the Scottish and Irish coasts, Antonia expressing the hope the crates of her personal belongings from her old Parisian home made it to the safety of an English port without being confiscated by traitorous pirates. Dair was quick to bite his tongue and not comment that those traitorous pirates were being aided and abetted by her kinsmen, the French, who continued to hide their treacherous two-faced cowardly dealings with the colonists behind a cloak of cordiality with the English. He knew open war with the French had to be just around the corner, months at most.

Antonia was not so distracted by her nausea or the present conversation that she did not notice the sudden tightness in her cousin's strong jaw at mention of the French, so she skillfully steered the conversation away from the war with a mundane observation Horace Walpole had made to her in one of his letters. It had to do with the present folly of Society to keep later and later hours in London. She told Dair how Lord Derby's cook had given His Lordship warning he would be killed if he had to dress suppers at three in the morning, to which His Lordship had asked him coolly how much he would have to pay to kill him!

They both laughed and cordiality was restored, so much so that by the time pudding arrived, Antonia, who had managed to keep her nausea under control by eating very little, was able to indulge in a scoop of pistachio ice accompanied by a thin barberry-flavored wafer.

They returned to the sitting room for tea and macarons, where Dair finally poured forth his feelings for Miss Aurora Talbot.

Antonia listened without comment and believed in his sincerity utterly. Now the change in him made perfect sense. It was not so much that he had changed as that he had become the man he was always destined to be. If she was privately astounded her goddaughter was the woman who had brought this about, and in whom Dair had invested all his hopes and dreams for the future, that was not because she did not see the potential in Rory to be the love of a good man's life. It was that it was her cousin, who had been within Rory's orbit for many years, had finally noticed, and fallen irrevocably in love with her. She could not have been happier.

Dair pressed her hand and made her a bow. "Thank you for a most enjoyable dinner, Cousin. I must leave you now. I'm already late for my interview with Lord Shrewsbury—"

Antonia's eyes lit up. "To seek permission to marry my goddaughter, yes?"

Dair nodded, strangely overcome with emotion at her enthusiasm. He couldn't help blushing, which Antonia thought delightful.

"To ask for Rory's hand in marriage. I admit I am more than a little nervous at the prospect."

"*Eh bien*! But, *mon cher*, it is surely a mere formality?"

"Formality, it may be, but it makes the task no less difficult. Rory loves her grandfather dearly, and thus his approval is necessary."

"He will not refuse you! How could he? *Why* would he?"

She put her arm through his and halfway across the carpet she turned and stuck out her hand in farewell, and when he bowed over it, she pulled him down to kiss his forehead and to touch his cheek.

"You will come and see me later, after your return, and tell me all about it, yes? I will be awake, I assure you."

How could Dair say no to such enthusiasm? Nor could he wait to share with Rory how happy her godmother was with the news of their betrothal.

FORTY-ONE

R ORY WAS SITTING on the next-to-last step of the stairs
waiting for him.

The presence of the butler prevented the couple from being
anything but politely civil. Dair nodded and Rory, who had a hand
to the polished banister, bobbed a curtsy. Yet, the look and smile
which passed between them said it all. They were ecstatic, and tense
with excitement and heightened anticipation. Both had dressed carefully, wanting the moment to be accorded its proper due. After all, it
was not every day a couple got engaged, and in the wider Society in
which they mixed, it was rare for that couple to be deeply in love.

When the butler disappeared into the study to see if His Lordship was ready to receive his guest, they had a few moments alone.
Both seized the opportunity. In two strides, Dair was at the foot of
the stairs. He caught Rory to him and she threw her arms about his
neck.

Dair could not remember a day when he had been as happy as he
was on this day. All his past fears about marriage, about ever finding
the right woman to share his future, had evaporated, and all because
of this divine creature in his arms. He had no doubts whatsoever. He
hoped the same was true for her. So he was alarmed when, after they

had shared a kiss, the smile on Rory's flushed upturned face dropped into a pout.

"Is—Are you—Is everything all right?" he asked with heart thudding.

"I am not sure...You need to kiss me again. I am not convinced I like you without whiskers."

He stifled a laugh and instantly relaxed, whispering near her ear, "And here was I affording you the opportunity to kiss a different gentleman... You could then tell me which one you'd prefer to take on your honeymoon."

She gasped and then giggled.

He held both her hands and took a step backwards to look her up and down. He liked the outfit she was wearing very much. Over a chemise of the finest cream linen, with a wide flounce at the hem and a similar flounce to both sleeves, was a pink-lavender open-robed gown of shimmering silk. Her waist-length straw-blonde hair, too, had been carefully dressed, swept up off her face and loosely piled atop her head, pinned, beribboned, and the weight allowed to fall down her back. And her shoes, of course, matched her gown. All in all, she was beautiful and radiant, and just how he imagined a bride looked on her wedding day. He wished they were about to go up before the vicar.

He swiftly kissed the back of one hand, and then the other, as he heard the door behind him open, and let her go, saying softly, "You look so beautiful. Don't send for another gown. Wear this one to our bridal. The color perfectly matches the sapphire I gave you."

Rory beamed with happiness, so much so, her blue eyes filled with tears. All she could do to answer him was smile and nod when he asked,

"Wait for me here...?"

As Dair followed the butler into her grandfather's study, she sank back onto the step, to wait, unaware she was toying with the unfamiliar, but reassuringly present, pale lavender sapphire betrothal ring.

The meeting took much longer than Rory anticipated. More than once the butler enquired if she wanted him to fetch her a glass of wine or a cup of tea and a biscuit. But Rory was too nervous to eat or drink. She tried not to listen for sounds, and it was impossible to hear voices or conversation, but once or twice a loud burst of laughter penetrated the oak-paneled door. Then there was nothing for the longest time that Rory began to drift off to sleep. It was now very late, and she had had such a big day, a momentous one, spent on Swan Island, that with the darkness of a late night, it was almost as if she had dreamed it.

She was asleep, slumped against the banister rail, when in her dreamlike state, the door to grandfather's study was suddenly yanked wide and the man she loved strode out into the hall. On his frock coat skirts followed her grandfather. Why couldn't she wake up? Her head was so heavy. Her grandfather spoke to her, and although she heard his words and instinctively did what he asked, she could not remember exactly what he said. She rose up and he offered her his arm. But when he moved away from the stair, there was her husband-to-be. He was standing in the middle of the hall, and the front door was wide. She wanted to cross the small space that separated them, but her grandfather kept her at his side, his hold on her arm vise-like. It was then she realized she wasn't dreaming at all. She was wide-awake, and nothing and nobody was making any sense.

AN HOUR EARLIER, when the butler had announced Major Lord Fitzstuart to His Lordship, Lord Shrewsbury had greeted his best agent as he always did, with affable good humor. He was always genuinely pleased to see the young man and relieved he had survived his latest assignment unscathed. He knew most of what had occurred in Lisbon from Dair's coded report, sent as soon as he had disembarked at Portsmouth. He also knew that the most crucial pieces of information would not be in ink but reported verbally. What he most wanted was the name of the double agent within his own Secret Service; a name the Major had gone all the way to Portugal to retrieve.

So he was bitterly disappointed when Dair told him bluntly that he could not supply the name, but that he could supply the person who could give him the name, but that there were conditions attached. When wasn't there? Shrewsbury conceded.

The two men sipped fine port from crystal glasses; port brought back from Lisbon in crates by the Major, as Dair related all that he knew and been told by the spy in Portugal. Shrewsbury was surprised to discover the spy was English and intrigued he had once worked for Catherine of Russia. He readily agreed to the spy's terms for his return to England, and told Dair he would have Watkins arrange for the man's immediate safe passage home.

Mention of William Watkins steered the conversation away from Lisbon and back to England. Out of politeness, Dair asked after the Weasel's broken nose, to which Shrewsbury laughed heartily and said it was about time his secretary got knocked off his high horse and returned to where he belonged—the back room amongst a mountain of papers where he could do the least harm. For a second Dair felt sorry for the secretary, but that evaporated remembering why he had punched him in the face in the first place. Shrewsbury was having the same thought, and surprised Dair into thinking he could read minds when he said bluntly,

"I'll have you forget why you broke Mr. Watkins' nose. Best if people believe it was two men falling out over a wager of some description—I don't care what—as long as my granddaughter's name is never mentioned."

"It never will, sir."

The old man continued to stare at Dair, as if he expected him to be more forthcoming about the incident, but Dair remained silent, and Shrewsbury said in a low voice,

"Grasby told me all about what happened at the Physic Garden. He also told me he must have been mistaken in thinking he saw you in close contact with my granddaughter. Of course we both agreed this was nonsense. Grasby said it must have been a trick of the sunshine in his eyes..." Shrewsbury looked Dair up and down and visibly huffed. "You might be a womanizing lothario with dancers and actresses and the like—and the best of luck to you—but one thing we both agreed you are not is a seducer of young—"

"Sir, I—"

"—innocent females of good birth—"

"Sir, I—"

"—particularly the sisters of your closest friends, whatever Watkins might try and convince us to the contrary. My secretary has always had you pegged for a brainless libidinous muckworm, and I would hate to think his estimation had any basis in fact. But you've never let me down in the past and I know you won't now. You quite rightly forgot all about that incident at Romney's studio and I know you'll do the same now, about Watkins' idiotic attempt to ask my granddaughter to marry him." Shrewsbury shook his head. "The sheer idiocy of the man defies my intelligence. What did he think would happen? What did he think my granddaughter's response would be? How did he ever convince himself he was worthy of her?"

These were obviously rhetorical questions not requiring a response, so Dair remained silent. When Lord Shrewsbury held up the decanter, Dair shook his head and watched him refill his glass and put the decanter back on the tray at his elbow. He reasoned it was best to let him have his say, in the hopes that once he had let off steam about Weasel's pathetic behavior, he would be more receptive to Dair's proposal of marriage. And after all, he and Weasel were chalk and cheese in every way, shape and form!

"It's a damned shame I need his expertise in constructing and deconstructing ciphers, or I'd have got rid of him as soon as I learned of his reprehensible behavior," Shrewsbury confided, still warm to his topic. "Grasby's brother-in-law he may be, but that doesn't give him the right to even *think* of my granddaughter in any way whatsoever! And even if I wanted a husband for her, the last place I'd look is Billingsgate! His grandfather was a fishmonger, for God's sake! Whereas hers—*me*—is an earl! If his sister hadn't come with a fifty-thousand-pound dowry she'd still stink of fish, too! Speaking of my dear granddaughter-in-law, my grandson and his dear wife are due here tomorrow. I told them not to give Watkins a seat in their carriage; he deserves to be left out in the cold. Justifiable punishment for his gross presumption. Besides, if there is to be a celebration, it will be for *family only*."

The old man's eyes lit up and he gleefully rubbed his hands together. He couldn't keep the excitement from his voice.

"Grasby has some news... News! He wouldn't put it in ink. He says he must announce it to me in person. I can tell you, my boy, I pray to God it's that his wife is breeding—*finally*! I'm not getting younger, and neither is my grandson's wife! Three years married and nothing to show for it. Now, if you were to marry, my guess is you'd have your wife with child within the month, if not the week! You've already proven you can breed. But I don't blame Grasby. I blame her. Flighty, nervy creature... If you'll take my advice, marry a widow with children. A pretty little widow, but one with children, so you know she can breed. If I'd given it more thought, and not let that fishmonger's ransom addle my brain, I'd have found a nice fertile widow for my grandson..."

When the Spymaster General paused to sip at his port, Dair gauged it was the right moment, and Shrewsbury in the right frame of mind, for him to broach the subject of his own marriage.

"As it so happens, sir, I have rather important news of my own to share with you."

The old man sat up, all attention, and Dair found himself clearing his throat. Still, he managed to keep his deep voice steady and impassive.

"I've decided it is time to follow in Grasby's footsteps and marry."

Shrewsbury's face split into a grin and he smacked his silken knee in delight.

"By Jove, but this is excellent news indeed, my boy! *Excellent* news!"

"Thank you, sir. Your support means the world to me—*to us*. I've written to Lord Strathsay, and to his man of business, giving them my news, and requesting the necessary arrangements be made for me to assume management of the family estates. And my mother has been advised of my intentions and the need for her to quit Fitzstuart Hall and take up residence in the dower house. Of course, not at once, but arrangements need to be made so my wife can take up her position as lady of the house."

"So marriage is more than a new thought? You've been contemplating the notion for some time?"

"That is difficult to answer. Had you wagered me upon my return from the war that I'd marry within a twelvemonth, I'd not have risked coin on the possibility." Dair shrugged and smiled self-consciously. "But life, thankfully, is not ruled by the betting book, is it, sir? Which leads me to request that I be released from my obligations to the Service. I am sure you agree I cannot, when I have a wife and family, and estates to manage, continue to act as a free agent."

"No. That is entirely understandable. Marriage comes with a set of obligations and responsibilities, particularly for a man in your position, who will one day inherit his father's earldom. It pleases me no end you are taking the institution seriously. There are some within our ranks who treat marriage with less than the dignity it deserves. Not that I'm advocating you take your vows literally. You don't have to become a plaguey priest upon marriage; far from it. But I do advise you not to waste time on your mistress until your bride is breeding. Once you've accomplished the deed, you can return to your mistress, or what filly takes your fancy, with a clear conscience in having done your duty. If your bride is a sensible, compliant creature—and I do not doubt you've chosen one who is—she'll be relieved to be left alone. Who is the—"

"I beg your pardon, sir, but I want to assure you I have every intention of taking my marriage vows seriously, for what is the p—"

The old man waved a hand in dismissal at Dair's assiduousness.

"Young men mean well, but let me tell you from experience, it rarely, if ever, happens that we remain faithful. It's not in our natures to do so. Frankly put, why should we? Females bear the burden of having our children and so it is they who need to be damn well faithful to us! It's the way God made Adam and Eve, and there's an end to the argument."

"Sir, that is not the sort of marriage I intend to have. The Duke of Roxton is a faithful husband, like his father before him. They are my yardstick for what constitutes a good husband, a good father, and a marriage worth having."

Shrewsbury was dismissive.

"Aberrations, both! And let me tell you, before he fell under the spell of that divine creature he married, old Roxton was a libidinous goat! There was a reason he was called the noble satyr, my boy, and I should know." He leaned forward in his wingchair, as if not wishing to be overheard, and chuckled knowingly. "From what I've heard of your escapades, you easily fill old Roxton's breeches. So unless you've found yourself a rare and magnificent beauty such as your Cousin Antonia to marry, which I very much doubt, I'd not lose sleep over a trifle of a thing as fidelity. Trust me, neither will your bride." He sat up. "So who is the lucky creature? An heiress, I don't doubt. One of the Spencer girls, or a Cavendish relative of Deborah Roxton? Or have you preempted my advice and gone and got yourself a fertile young widow. No need to prove yourself, is there? How many brats has that mistress of yours given you now? Four or is it five? All healthy sons, too. Knowing your luck, you'll have the new wife pregnant before the sun rises on the night before!"

"I have one natural son, sir," Dair said in a measured tone, gripping the upholstered arm of the wingchair to maintain calm. He was furious. "His mother has been faithfully married for almost nine years. Her four younger sons belong to her husband."

"Yes. Yes. If you say so, my boy. I'm not one to quibble over bastard offspring. If it gives her husband comfort to think the brats are—"

"Sir! My lord! Mrs. Banks is no adulteress, and I am no liar!"

Dair had shot to his feet. It was only the esteem in which he held the Spymaster General that had kept his anger in check for this long. He had not wanted to offend him. Now, he could not care less.

"I did not come here to be lectured on the institution of marriage, or how I should conduct myself as a husband. I don't need your advice, nor do I care greatly for your good opinion, because it seems you have no good opinion of my character as it is!

"I was an eyewitness to my parent's hell on earth, so I am well versed in how *not* to conduct myself as a husband and a father. But I also know a loving union when I see it, and with the help of the woman I love, I intend to have the sort of marriage, be the sort of husband and father, that will make my wife and children proud. I love your granddaughter with my whole heart and I would never do or say anything to ruin her happiness, or our marriage. There is your assurance. I give it honestly. It is for Rory's sake I seek your blessing to our union. I hope you will give it freely and make her happy. She is waiting outside in the hallway... Shall I fetch her in so you can tell her so yourself...?"

FORTY-TWO

ORD SHREWSBURY slowly rose out of his wingchair by the
fire while Dair was in the midst of his earnest discourse,
surprised by the young nobleman's uncharacteristic fit of temper,
but prepared to forgive him for the same reason; the boy had never
before been so discourteous. But what he was not prepared for was to
hear Rory's name trip so familiarly off the Major's tongue, and he fell
back into his wingchair, in shock.

Not in a thousand years would he have suspected his granddaughter to be romantically linked to *any* man, least of all this man.
Why had he not seen this coming? Why had he not been wary of the
warning signs of a clandestine attachment? Why had none of his
servants, his agents, her own brother, seen it too, and warned him?
The only person who had hinted at Major Lord Fitzstuart's interest
in Rory was William Watkins, and stupidly he had dismissed the
man's insinuations as ridiculous, fueled by an incomprehensible
jealousy.

Dair's declaration left him incredulous and disbelieving.

Why would a healthy young man of action, a decorated soldier
and a spy, a young man who risked his life as if it meant nothing to
him—whose masculinity had the effect of causing some females to
faint at the sight of him—why would such a man be interested in his

granddaughter? His beloved Rory was a naïve cripple who had rarely strayed beyond her family's garden gate. She was pretty in her own way, with her mother's Norwegian fair hair and his deep blue eyes, but she was not so beautiful as to catch the roving eye of the hot-blooded Major Lord Fitzstuart. She was no Antonia Kinross, no voluptuous beauty who could heat a man's blood with one look.

It just didn't make any sense to him, and so he told Dair in as many words, though his speech was halting and garbled at times. Nonetheless his incredulity was blatant, as was his opposition to the couple's betrothal.

He forbade it.

He would not give it his blessing.

In his opinion, Rory was not mentally or physically capable of marrying anyone.

The idea of this lusty lothario bedding his innocent grand-daughter made him physically ill. As far as he was concerned, Rory would spend the rest of her days as his companion and die an old maid.

DAIR WAS JUST as incredulous by Shrewsbury's violent opposition, not only to Rory marrying him, but to the very idea of her wedded at all. It soon became apparent the old man had suffered such a severe shock that it was pointless arguing any further with him that night. But he expected Shrewsbury to put on a brave face and not disappoint his granddaughter. Regardless of what he thought of the betrothal, Dair was going to marry Rory, with or without his blessing.

"After all, when she turns one-and-twenty we won't need your consent," Dair stated flatly. "Or your blessing. But for the sake of her happiness, I would rather have it as not. And we want to get married without delay."

Shrewsbury was not to be appeased. Shock gave way to anger and resentment. He thumped the arms of his wingchair and shot back up to his feet and stayed there this time.

"I'll not give it! Now or-or *ever*. You can't seriously expect me to believe you want to marry her? Ha! This is some sort of joke! A damned awful one, but a joke nonetheless! How much money have you got riding on the outcome of seeing me bamboozled? Eh?" When Dair pulled a face of revulsion at the idea, Shrewsbury let out a harsh laugh. "That's your best piece of acting yet, Fitzstuart! But I'm not fooled! I know all about your revolting wager to tup a cripple. Watkins told me—"

"I beg your pardon? I never—"

Dair swallowed back the rest of the sentence. He was suddenly speechless. A blinding recollection, one that meant he could not refute Shrewsbury's outlandish claim, flashed into his mind at the Spy Master General's mention of the crude expression *to tup a cripple*. Dair was hurtled back to a place and time in his past.

It was before he had gone off to fight in the American Colonies. He had just turned fifteen and with a group of fellow officers at a Covent Garden Turkish Bath. Wishing to be accepted as one of them, he had boasted there wasn't a wager too daunting, too unlikely, or too outlandish that he wasn't prepared to accept. Somehow this particular wager found itself written up into White's betting book. He suspected William Watkins had something to do with that, but like the wager itself, he had not thought much about it since then. That was nine years ago, and he had risked his life again and again for his country that such a wager seemed infantile in the extreme to him now... Yet he could not refute it because it was true.

"But, sir! That has nothing to do with the here and now," he blustered. "I deeply regret having agreed to such a preposterous wager, and if you knew the circumstances—"

"Don't make a fig of difference," Shrewsbury interrupted dismissively. "You bragged about it before witnesses, and it's inked up for everyone to see, and that's all that matters. Whether you meant to carry it out is neither here nor there to me. I couldn't care less, but it will mean a great deal to my granddaughter."

Dair was too horrified to speak.

Shrewsbury looked supremely smug at his response.

"But if you call off this ridiculous betrothal, she'll not hear about the wager from me."

Dair made one last attempt to make Shrewsbury see reason.

"Sir, I love Rory with every fiber of my being. I want to marry her, take care of her, cherish her for the rest of my days…"

The old man was unconvinced. He did not understand couples marrying for love. His wife had been chosen for him by his father, and he had chosen who his grandson would marry. Parents knew what was best in a mate for their children. His son had foolishly married for love and that had been a disaster for everyone concerned. Rory was the most precious thing in the world to him and he would never subject her to the pain and heartache of a love match, nor would he give her up. And so he told Dair, unmoved by the young man's open and honest declaration of his feelings.

Dair sighed his incomprehension and threw up a hand impatiently.

"One day I will be Earl of Strathsay, and she my countess. Surely, that must count for something with you, even if nothing else I've said does?"

"It does. That, too, works against you. She is not equipped to take the stage in Society as the wife of a nobleman. Enough heads turn as it is when she limps into a room, and not in a good way. Imagine her on *your* arm. What a spectacle! What a-a *farce*. She can't even dance, for God's sake! You'll make her a laughingstock and I won't have it. It would break my heart, and hers."

Dair shook his head in disbelief.

"You have so little regard of what she is truly capable, that you fail to see beyond the obvious. She is not some flawed diamond to be kept in a velvet box for fear a tiny imperfection is all that will be noticed. She is a magnificent unique jewel whose true worth should be allowed to shine. Let her take her place at my side and watch her sparkle. She deserves nothing less of life. And that life is with me."

Shrewsbury was incredulous at this young man's presumption. To be lectured to about the person he loved most in the world turned his face purple with rage.

"Shine? Poppycock!" the old man spat out. "She won't shine,

she'll wilt and die as sure as you'll return to your devil-may-care ways once you've had your fill of her! God knows what perverted lust demon drives you to want to marry a creature who can no more climb the stairs on the other side of that door, as fly! I know about men like you. No one suspects but deep down you have unnatural desires, inclinations and urges that if allowed to bubble to the surface wreak untold damage that can never be repaired! I won't let that happen again, and not to her. Find yourself a lame female elsewhere. There's a cathouse in Covent Garden that caters to such perversions—"

"Enough!" Dair growled, spinning away from the fireplace, where he had his head lowered, gripping the mantel to stop himself from grabbing Shrewsbury by the throat. "I've heard enough of your salacious drivel! If you weren't her grandfather, I'd shut your foul mouth with my fist!"

He took a deep breath, shoulders hunched, and reminded himself Shrewsbury was seventy years of age, and it was the love he had for his granddaughter making him lash out with irrational and absurd statements. In such an emotionally charged state, it was fruitless to continue arguing with him. He decided the old man needed time to come to terms with his proposal. He hoped that with the dawn, Shrewsbury would see that what was best for Rory's future happiness was to give his blessing to the match. If the old man proved immoveable, then the marriage would take place without him, and the sooner the better.

There was nothing left for him to do here tonight. Yet, the thought of walking out of the study and seeing Rory on the stair, smiling with happiness, blue eyes full of expectation, was almost too much for him to contemplate, and he wished he could scramble out of a window and make off across the park, like a thief in the night. Still, he was no coward. But how was he to allay her natural distress when she learned her grandfather had rejected his proposal? He must give her a word, or a look, before being shown the door, so she knew he was determined to marry her, and would brook no opposition.

"I'll say goodnight," he said calmly. "But I will return tomorrow morning—"

"That would not be wise or welcome."

"I will come anyway."

"No. You won't."

"You cannot stop me."

Shrewsbury sneered his superiority. His tone was full of quiet menace.

"No? Some time ago I requisitioned that particular betting book from White's in the national interest. I will show Rory the offending wager if necessary. But I hope it does not come to that. You must understand I will do whatever it takes to preserve her innocence and her happiness. If that means locking her up, I'll do it. Regard me, Fitzstuart: I am deadly serious."

Dair believed him. But two could play his game, and he fully intended to return at sunup and kidnap Rory if need be. With nothing left to say, he bowed civilly to the old man and followed him out of the study and into the hall, where the butler waited by the front door.

And there was Rory, curled up asleep on the stair, head resting on her arm, blonde hair falling across her flushed cheek.

Dair took a step forward, to go to her, but Shrewsbury put a hand on his linen sleeve to forestall him. He then brushed past him and, like a sentinel, stood between the couple, blocking Dair's view. The old man jerked his powdered head at the butler and the front door was opened on the night air.

Dair hesitated, hands clenching and unclenching in frustration. As much as he wanted to go to Rory, take her in his arms and leave this place with her, he could not do so, knowing the old man was fully capable of creating a distressing scene. So he turned on a heel and left.

He calculated there were less than eight hours until dawn.

FORTY-THREE

Antonia waited up for Dair to return from the Gatehouse Lodge. When he did not seek her out, and because she could not sleep and it was a warm night, she went for a moonlit walk down to her pavilion by the shores of the lake. A footman with a flambeau lit the way for her. Her lady's maid followed, a woolen wrap over her arm, refusing to let the Duchess go alone.

The footman and Michelle were ordered to wait at the base of the stairs, and Antonia ascended the steps into the pavilion alone. There was enough moonlight to see the way. On the top step the pleasing aroma of a lit cheroot made her pause. It reminded her of her duke who was presently far away in Scotland. Wishing he was returned, and lost in thought, she hesitated, and long enough for a familiar male voice, deep in the shadows, to offer to stub the cheroot. She shook her head.

"No. This scent, thankfully, it still pleases me. It reminds me of my husband..."

When Dair did not reply, she went towards the sudden red glow as the tip of the cheroot came alive, and found her cousin in his shirtsleeves, a shoulder leaning against a marble column. His face was turned away from her, she assumed so that he could exhale smoke. But when he did not face her but continued to gaze out on the silvery light across the still surface of the lake, she drew closer.

"You did not come and see me, Alisdair..."

Finally, slowly, he turned. As he did so, the moonlight sliced his face, illuminating his dark eyes. They were bright and glassy, the light striking them in such a way that she saw they were brimful of tears. He looked away, swallowing hard, and puffed on his cheroot. Shocked at the change in him since dinner, Antonia kept her composure and waited for him to speak, wondering what had gone wrong with his visit to the Gatehouse Lodge.

"You told me once that I hide behind a façade; that I have inhabited the role of blustering care-for-nobody for so many years now, that I cannot tell the difference between the real and the imagined me. But you are wrong, Cousin," he said, looking down at her again. "It is because I know exactly who I am, where I have come from and what I must become, that I chose to hide myself away. It was the only means I knew how to bear my father's—*your uncle's*—bitter disappointment I was not the bookish heir he wanted. It was how I endured my parents' hate-filled marriage. This façade—this mask— you derided helped me survive many bloody years in the army, and it got me through more than one perilous scrape as an agent of the Crown. But never did I lose sight of who I was or what I wanted from life..." He quickly turned away and put his face in his shirt sleeve to wipe dry his eyes, then turned back to Antonia with a crooked smile. "You'll be surprised to learn that what I have always wanted from life is what you had with M'sieur le Duc, and what you also have with your new duke. It is what Roxton has with his duchess, and what I never thought I would ever have—a happy marriage, wed to the love of one's life, and with children of my own to nurture. Is that too much to ask?"

"No. No, it is not."

"Do you remember telling me once that being in love can be terrifying?" When she nodded, he continued. "You said that being in love can be more terrifying than anything else, if doubt exists that love is not reciprocated, or if there is an impediment to a happy outcome... Do you remember saying that, Cousin?"

"Yes, *mon chou*. Of course. I stand by what I said."

Dair nodded and took a great shuddering breath. He glanced down at the smoldering cheroot between his fingers then at Antonia's face, partly concealed in shadow, and fixed on her green eyes. Antonia did not look away. When he finally spoke, he was barely audible, but Antonia heard his torment as if he had shouted it from the rooftop.

"Cousin... I am—I am—*terrified*."

DAIR WAS SEATED on a woolen shawl on the top step of the entrance to the pavilion, with a cheroot—or was it his second—between his fingers, and pouring forth his heart to Antonia, before he realized where he was or what he was doing. His anguish was all-consuming, and he saw no clear way out of his predicament. Antonia did not interrupt his revelatory self-castigation, and her servants were acute enough that one look and a sign from their mistress and they went off and returned with hot tea for her and a bottle of something much stronger for the Major.

His hands were shaking and his throat dry. Spying a tumbler of spirits on the step below the toe of his shoe, he snatched it up and drank it down, the fiery liquid barely registering on his tongue. He set aside the crystal tumbler, and out of the shadows stepped a footman who refilled it before disappearing back into the night.

Antonia listened without comment, criticism or question until Dair drew breath and reached again for the tumbler. It was only when he declared he had no other option but to kidnap Rory and make for Gretna, that she decided it was time to intervene.

She could see his distress was such that he was incapable of thinking rationally. His only thought was to get Rory away from her grandfather long enough to vindicate himself. He needed time to explain to her he was no libidinous monster, no seducer; that his intentions were honorable and sincere.

To anyone other than Antonia, his desperation to allay Rory's fears about his intentions would have been mystifying. After all, he had proposed and she had accepted, and there was the pale lavender sapphire ring as tangible proof he meant to marry her. But Antonia knew the couple had spent the day on Swan Island. It was an island for lovers, a mystical yet sensual place where she and Monseigneur had been free to enjoy each other in every way without interruption. Now, for her, the island was a sad place, full of happy bygone memories and another life. To row over there now her beloved was no longer with her would surely unravel her peace of mind. But to a young couple deeply in love, the secluded island with its fanciful temple grotto, bathing pool and small tapestry-lined temple, was a magical place to make love and be loved.

Of course, Dair and Rory had made love on Swan Island, of that Antonia was convinced. This was why her cousin was distraught beyond reason. Justifiably so. If Shrewsbury told Rory about the ridiculous wager, doubt would surely be cast in Rory's mind as to Dair's true intentions, and more importantly, as to his true character. What sort of man was capable of accepting such a loathsome wager?

An unthinking, arrogant and foolish boy was Antonia's firm belief. The despicable wager was in no way a reflection of the young man who sat next to her with head bent. The wager was not worth the paper it was inked on. But as easy as it was for her to dismiss such a wager, it would be difficult for Rory to do so.

That Rory had given herself to Dair before marriage, must surely be pressing on her conscience. It would be natural for her to then ask herself what sort of man seduces his bride before the wedding night, if he truly intended to marry her? With her grandfather adding gravitas to the wager, and his opposition to a match with the notorious handsome and roguish Major, Rory's view of the loving man she thought she was marrying would inevitably start to crumble.

Antonia could hear the old man now, filling Rory's little ear with all sorts of distressing tid-bits about the man she loved, to cast doubt, to engender distrust and misery, and all to make certain Rory remained unmarried and by Shrewsbury's side for the rest of his days. Well, Antonia was having none of it! Her cousin and her goddaughter were in love and deserved their happily ever after. She would make it happen, even though it would mean invoking a secret

Monseigneur had entrusted to her, only to be used in the direst of circumstances. She knew he would understand and forgive her. When she visited the mausoleum on the morrow, she would explain everything to him and tell him the all-important and startling news she was to have a baby in the new year. But that visit would be after she called on England's Spymaster General.

Dair was convinced the only solution to his predicament called for action: Kidnapping Rory out from under Shrewsbury's nose.

But when Antonia argued that kidnapping was unnecessary and not to worry, all would be set to rights by tomorrow afternoon, Dair was incredulous, that stamping her pretty foot at Shrewsbury would be an interference he could do without.

She ignored his rude dismissal. After all, she was not going to make plain her thoughts or her methods, and he was under considerable emotional duress. Instead, her reply was cryptic, as she got to her silk-slippered feet and shook out the folds of her satin embroidered banyan.

"All men have secrets, Alisdair. Even spymasters. And this spymaster, he has more to hide than most. But that is all I will ever tell you. Now you must go to bed and try to sleep. Tomorrow, after breakfast, I intend to call on Shrewsbury unannounced. You will come too but wait in the carriage until called."

She smiled up at him as he rose slowly to his feet after stubbing the cheroot on the heel of his shoe.

"Tell your man to pack up your belongings and take them over to the big house first thing in the morning. That is where you must stay until the wedding—"

"Wedding?" Dair frowned." Whose wedding?"

"Yours, silly! Under no circumstances must the bride and groom stay under the same roof until they are married, and as Rory will be here with me you must go and stay with Roxton and Deborah."

"Rory is coming here? To-to stay with *you*?"

"Yes. Until you are both married in the chapel over at the big house. Tonight, I will write and invite your mother and your sister—"

"Write to Mary? And to my mother?"

Antonia let out a sigh. "What is it about the hearing of young men these days? Do you all need hearing-trumpets? No! Do not answer that, and do not interrupt me again. Just listen—"

Dair grinned and made her a little bow, suitably chastened.

"Yes, Mme la Duchesse—Forgive me—I am more than a little dull—Ah! And I have interrupted you again."

"You have, but it is of no matter," she responded gently, watching the cloud lift from his brow, and liking to see him finally smile. "To tell you again: Your wedding it will take place in the Roxton chapel. Until that is arranged—and believe me, arrangements are already underway—you will stay in the big house, as will your mother and your sister. Charlotte she will expect nothing less of her son. And I am sorry, Alisdair, but me I cannot abide Charlotte to stay with me. Even more so with Rory staying here." She dimpled. "It is for the best if your bride she spends as little time as possible in the company of her future mother-in-law, yes? It is to my son and his wife you must give your thanks for-for—"

"—everything," he interrupted softly, dark eyes bright and wet. "But mostly to you..." He grabbed her hand and kissed it, before looking into her eyes and saying with a catch to his voice, "If you are able to bring about this miracle, I will be forever in your debt. I can never thank you enough—"

"Attend me, Alisdair!" Antonia interrupted brusquely, because her green eyes were also filling with tears. "*Naturellement* I would do anything for you. Does not the same blood run in our veins? Are we not first cousins, descendants of the great Stuart king Charles the Second? Do we not have a duty to give our royal ancestor the legitimate heirs he did not have himself, so that he may live on through us?" She laughed then and touched his flushed cheek. "How full of self-importance I am! But your grandfather, whom you never met, but whom I lived with in the last years of his life, he was proud to be the son of Charles the Second, of having royal blood in his veins. His one regret was that he was not made a duke as his royal father had made his other natural sons. But that was the fault of his mother, and a story for another day.

"Now I have letters to write, and you must go to bed," she added with forced cheerfulness. "Tomorrow morning after breakfast, you and I we will call at the Gatehouse Lodge and everything it will arrange itself."

They retired for the night, neither saying what was on both their minds: The hope Shrewsbury had allowed Rory an uneventful night, and they would arrive at the Gatehouse Lodge before the Spymaster had the chance to shatter his granddaughter's hopes and dreams.

FORTY-FOUR

THE NEXT MORNING, Antonia entered the Gatehouse Lodge, announced by the butler, into a drawing room where the tension crackled louder than the fire in the grate. Why there was a fire on such a warm day, she could only wonder at, as she stripped off her silk half-gloves and shrugged bare shoulders out of a pretty India shawl. Both articles were mechanically handed into thin air, and swiftly taken by her lady-in-waiting, who had accompanied the Duchess with her own task to perform. At the first opportunity, she was to slip away and seek out Rory's maid, to have Miss Talbot's personal belongings packed up and ready to be transported up the hill to the dower house.

Antonia then swept across the threshold in a rustle of petticoats —the Duchess of Roxton and Kinross, noble host come to see the occupants of her Gatehouse Lodge. Everyone was instantly on their feet, to bow or curtsy, and then politely remained silent waiting for the Duchess to speak. After an exchange of pleasantries and a few inane comments about the weather, Antonia asked lightly, looking about the cozy room for added effect,

"I do not see my goddaughter. I trust Rory she is well?"

"Very well, Your Grace," Lord Shrewsbury replied quickly.

"Would you care for a dish of coffee? We have just had a pot and it would be no trouble to have another fetched…"

Antonia closed her eyes at the thought and waved a hand in refusal.

"Apparently my little sister has taken to sleeping late in the country," Lord Grasby offered, his tone suggesting he did not believe it for a moment. Antonia saw his gaze dart to his grandfather as he added, "I thought she would be up and awaiting our arrival, particularly when my letter hinted we have an exciting announcement we wished to share with her—"

"Lady Grasby has made us all the happiest of men," Lord Shrewsbury announced proudly with a wide smile. "I am to be a great-grandfather in the new year, Grasby a father, and Mr. Watkins a proud uncle."

Drusilla, Lady Grasby gave a light laugh behind her fluttering fan and needlessly confided in Antonia.

"I thought it was the intolerably hot weather making me peevish. But then I realized I have not been myself for some months now. And a visit by the physician confirmed what I had hoped for, but did not dare to dream could be the real reason for my indifferent health." She put a hand to her shoulder, and her husband, who was standing behind her chair, took it in a firm clasp. She looked up at him before returning her gaze to Antonia with a smile that resembled the cat who had found the cream. "Even though it must be many years since your last pregnancy, no doubt Your Grace can recall that feeling of utter elation that comes with knowing one is fulfilling the hopes and dreams of an entire family."

"*Grands dieux*, another baby on the way. There must be something in the water," Antonia muttered, then smiled at the happy couple, offering up her congratulations and adding cryptically, "Believe me, Lady Grasby, that feeling of elation of which you speak was only yesterday for me. You have made your family happy, particularly your husband's grandpapa. I pray you have a son, but a healthy child is what is most wished for. But where is Rory?" she continued in a practiced tone of enquiry, head slightly cocked. "You did not wait to share your most exciting announcement until all the family it could be together?"

"That's what I wanted, but—"

"Under the circumstances, Lord Shrewsbury gauged it best not to wait," William Watkins stated, cutting off Lord Grasby, and with a swift glance exchanged with Lord Shrewsbury, which alerted Antonia that both men knew more than the Grasbys why Rory was absent.

Antonia's green eyes widened. "Circumstances, M'sieur Watkins? What circumstances are these that preclude a loved family member from such a momentous occasion as knowing a baby it is on the way? I was told Rory she was not unwell...?"

"That's what I said, Your Grace," Grasby agreed with a pout at William Watkins. "After all, Rory will be an aunt, and no one would be more excited than she at the prospect! I don't see why we couldn't wait until—"

"She is well, Your Grace," Lord Shrewsbury stated, cutting off his grandson not only with words, but with a look. He quickly refocused his attention on his visitor, saying with a forced smile, "But you understand why my grandson's wife could not wait to tell me. Particularly as it is such badly wanted news. We were about to toast the health of Her Ladyship and the baby and would be honored if you would join us."

"Of course," Antonia said, gaze now firmly on the old man. "When Rory she joins us. Please to have her fetched, Edward."

"That is not possible, Your Grace."

"I have a great desire to see my goddaughter. That is why I am here."

"If you returned on the morrow perhaps then—"

"No. That would not suit me at all. It would be most inconvenient. I am here now. I wish to see her, *immédiatement.*"

Lord Shrewsbury took a step towards her.

"Your Grace, as I said, I regret that it is not possible."

Antonia looked past the old man's velvet sleeve at Lord and Lady Grasby who were exchanging a puzzled glance, while Mr. William Watkins was uncannily composed.

"I am certain her brother he would like Rory to join in the toast. Perhaps, Harvel, you would be so good as to fetch your sister?"

Mention of him by his birth name gave her Lord Grasby's undivided attention and he said without a second thought, "I do want Rory here when we make the toast, Your Grace. She should be here with us. I'll go and fetch her, and we can—"

"No! I said no," Lord Shrewsbury snarled through gritted teeth. He took a deep breath and was again his urbane self. "I forbid you or anyone to go near her room! Is that understood? Grasby?"

Grasby looked from his wife to his brother-in-law, to the Duchess, and then to his grandfather. "Why, Grand? Why can't I see my sister? What's-what's going on?"

"Edward, a word. Alone," Antonia commanded.

She was not required to explain herself. Lord and Lady Grasby bowed to rank and silently shuffled from the room. Antonia gave a jerk of her upswept coiffure to the door, and her lady's maid curtsied and went off to do her bidding. Mr. William Watkins hesitated in the doorway, as if he was somehow excluded from the imperious command because he was also Lord Shrewsbury's secretary. A haughty lift of Antonia's arched brows and he bowed and was gone, leaving the Spymaster and the Duchess alone in the heated drawing room.

THE DUCHESS HAD been inside the Gatehouse Lodge for less than fifteen minutes, leaving Dair outside in her carriage, when he decided it was ten minutes too long. He hated being confined, but he hated being sedentary more. He needed to be doing something, anything, than sit idly until fetched. One booted leg was unable to keep still, while the other was stuck out along the length of the silken cushion, toe tapping against the door's silken padding. He took another look at the pearl face of his silver pocket watch for something to do, noted the minute hand had moved all of three minutes, and slid it back in a pocket of his waistcoat. He then shoved a hand in a pocket of his light linen frock coat, found his silver cheroot case and small engraved tinder box, which he could not remember placing there, and decided he had had enough of staring at the opulent dark blue watered silk walls of his carriage prison.

He scrambled out into the fresh air, using the carriage door on the far side of the Gatehouse Lodge, and walked a little way off, towards a stand of tall white rose bushes, keeping the carriage between him and the house, so that he would not be seen from the windows. On his haunches he went about using the contents of the tinderbox to light a cheroot. And once lit, he stayed low, and smoked, dark eyes squinting in the bright sunlight at the serene view of a well-ordered landscape familiar to him since boyhood: The gravel path leading to a winding road just beyond the gate that skirted the lake, then spliced through a long luxuriant avenue of majestic elms, crossed a three-span wide stone bridge, and curled on up to the palatial mansion of the Dukes of Roxton that dominated the second highest point on the estate. Only the family mausoleum commanded a higher vantage point. Yet, on this day the view barely registered. Major Lord Fitzstuart's mind was crammed full of possibilities and scenarios of what must be occurring within the walls of the Gatehouse Lodge.

He was used to taking charge of a situation, thinking through the problem and its logistical challenges, and putting a suitable plan into action. But he had promised his cousin he would wait until called; that he would not do anything rash. She had actually ordered him to "not play the hero", by which he was certain she meant not kicking in doors, climbing a rope or scrambling a drainpipe, and smashing in a window to enter Rory's rooms by force, if not stealth. All these possibilities were given serious consideration until Antonia made him promise otherwise.

So he was reduced to pacing back and forth the length of the blind side of the carriage, from driver's step to footman's rail, cheroot between his fingers. It wasn't long before his mind wandered back to storming Rory's bedchamber. After all, he needed to be prepared in case his cousin's visit did not go as she planned. He decided Rory's room would not be upstairs after all, but on the ground floor. He'd noticed the narrow stairwell the night before, and how the steps turned sharply out of sight. She may have been sitting on the lower step waiting for him, but he was sure she did not use the staircase day-in and day-out.

That got him ruminating about his ancestral home, Fitzstuart Hall, the grand staircase in particular, and the private apartments on the first floor he was going to have remodeled and enlarged for his bride. There were other modifications to the house he intended to have commissioned to make the house as comfortable as possible for her, the first being the installation of a flying chair like the one Shrewsbury had at his Chiswick house. Perhaps he would have two installed, one in each wing so that Her Ladyship would not need to retrace her steps if she wished to go downstairs, and it would give her even easier access to all rooms of the mansion. And of course there was the Pinery to be built to cultivate pineapples, oranges, lemons and limes, and perhaps exotic flowers, if such things took his wife's fancy.

These considerations kept him occupied as he paced, stopping occasionally to smoke and drop ash and grind this into the crushed stone of the drive with a toe of his jockey boot.

This visit he was dressed for comfort, in knitted breeches and jockey boots, white shirt and a plain linen frock coat of Prussian blue. And though he had let Farrier shave him yesterday, today he would not be shaved. It was partly a superstitious act. The one time he put in an effort to have his suit of clothes as neat as a pin, and his face as smooth as a nymph's lovely behind, Shrewsbury had rejected him out-of-hand as suitable husband material for his granddaughter. But mostly his slapdash grooming was how he was most comfortable, now he no longer needed to make an impression. This time he expected Shrewsbury to accept him. But he couldn't care less one way or the other. All he cared about was Rory's happiness and marrying her without delay. And that day couldn't come soon enough!

The longer he paced and smoked, the more worried he became that his cousin was having about as much success as he'd had the night before. That is, until a footman fetched him to come indoors.

Dair was so nervous with anticipation his every muscle was as tight as an over-wound watch. He strode past the footman and into the small house, ready to do battle with anyone and everyone, with a lift of his heavy chin, both hands fisted. His dark eyes quickly scanned the entrance foyer in search of the only beautiful face that mattered. She was not there. Why was she not there? But before he could ask the question, a crystal champagne glass was thrust between his fingers, and in amongst the chattering and laughing he heard the sound of corks popping.

It was only then he realized he was being greeted with a warm welcome by a clutch of smiling faces, while two footmen scurried about pouring champagne into glasses.

FORTY-FIVE

Meanwhile, the Duchess of Roxton and Kinross was still ensconced in the drawing room with the Spymaster General.

"I am too unwell to expend energy on your stretches of the truth, so I will come to the point," Antonia said in her native tongue. "You, Edward, will then do what is best for Rory. *Vous me comprenez?*"

"What I understand, Mme la Duchesse," Shrewsbury replied politely, "is that you are interfering in a family matter that is none of your concern."

"Is it not my concern? You vastly underestimate me if you think I have no interest in the happiness of those two children left in your care since the tragic deaths of both their parents."

At that, the Spymaster lost patience and threw up an arm.

"For God's sake, Antonia, why bring up such tragic history on this of all days, when I have just been told I am to be a great-grandfather? Leave my son and his wife to rest in peace and allow me to enjoy the moment. This is a day for celebration."

The Duchess had not given him permission to use her Christian name, but she ignored this social lapse as Edward Shrewsbury had been her first husband's boyhood friend since their days at Eton. Instead, she took a turn about the small, cluttered room, to distance herself from the smell of stale coffee coming from the tray of used coffee things. She unlatched a mullioned window and pushed it open, hoping for fresh air, before turning to face back into the room.

"I am happy Drusilla is to give your earldom a future beyond Harvel. And I certainly would like nothing better than to leave Harvel and Rory's parents to lie peacefully in their graves. But you, Edward, do not deserve your happiness when you are trying to deny Rory hers."

"Happiness?" he spat out. "I have saved Rory from a lifetime of heartache. I will tell you what I told Fitzstuart: Rory is not equipped to be the center of Society's attention as the wife of a nobleman, and he would not make her a fit husband. I will not give my blessing to such a union, and I will use every recourse available to me to keep them apart. Rory belongs with me. There is nothing you can say or do that will make me change my mind. It is fixed. So, please, Mme la Duchesse, I appreciate you came here with the best of intentions, and no doubt at Fitzstuart's behest, but it is to no purpose. You can tell him from me: If he persists, I will have no hesitation in showing Rory the wager inked in White's betting book as tangible proof his intentions were nothing more than lascivious."

"You do know he loves her with his whole heart and soul?"

Shrewsbury blustered his disbelief. "So he tried to convince me!"

Antonia's green eyes narrowed. "You have never been in love, Edward, so how would you know?"

At that he laughed, as if she had told him something highly amusing. And then his blue eyes went cold, and he dared to look her over as a man does a woman he desires but cannot have, gaze finally fixing on her décolletage. "Perhaps not. But I know lust and how to scratch an itch."

"That is a pathetic attempt at intimidation, even for you. Lift your eyes to my face, Edward, and attend me! You do not frighten me in the least. This is what you will do: Put to the flame that page of White's betting book with that ridiculous wager scribbled down by a group of silly boys and accepted by an even sillier boy. No doubt in their drunken state they thought it a great lark! You will also give your blessing to Rory marrying the man she loves. If you do not do both these things at once, I will go to my son and tell him what I know about you."

"Go to—go to your-your *son*? Tell *Roxton* something about-about *me* that *you* know?" Shrewsbury's shoulders shook with silent laughter. "Oh! I do love to admire you when you are fervent! God, you must have exhausted my dearly departed old friend between the sheets!" He lost his smile. "I won't give in to either of those foolish demands. Now, please, Mme la Duchesse, won't you stamp your pretty foot for me, and have done with this melodramatic nonsense."

"I do not think I am being melodramatic when I say you greatly respect my son, because he is a man of the highest morals, and it helps he is also the most powerful duke in England. Roxton regards you with great affection. You would not want to lose his respect and worse, have him force you to retire from your post as Spymaster General in disgrace."

Again, Shrewsbury laughed, but this time in disbelief.

"Dear God, Antonia, are you threatening *me*? I am more aroused than ever!"

Antonia pulled a face of disgust and put up her little nose. "I do not threaten. It is what will happen if you do not do as I say."

The old man shook his head and put his chin in his hand, done with the playful banter.

"By all means go to Roxton with your tales. I think you will find your son's moral sensibilities will be far more disturbed by Fitzstuart's behavior and his wager to tup a cripple, than anything you can possibly tell him about me."

Antonia took a deep breath and made one last attempt to make Shrewsbury see reason.

"Edward, you would truly break Rory's heart than see her happily married to the man she loves, and who loves her?"

"Yes. It is for her own good."

Antonia's shoulders slumped. But then, resolved, she straightened her back and clasped her hands in front of her.

"Then you leave me no choice... I did not become Rory's godmother because you asked it of me, but because her mother, she asked it of me before her baby was born. Yes. That surprises you. You forget perhaps that your daughter-in-law she and I are the same age or would have been had she lived. Our sons, too, were near in age. We met in Green Park and then began having afternoon tea and would watch our babies play together."

It was obvious this was news to the old man. He pulled a face of disbelief.

"What could you, a duchess, possibly have in common with a Norwegian seamstress of indeterminate lineage? She could barely write her name, least of all speak English."

"I told you. We were the same age and had baby sons around the same age. What more than that was needed? And we spoke in French. English it was unimportant. *J'ai compris*! You think as a duchess I should have spurned her because of her low origins? She was married to your son and heir, and as such was Lady Grasby. What's more, she had the sweetest temperament and was the kindest person, just like her daughter Rory. They have a great look of each other, although Christina she was prettier. When we strolled up the Mall we would often be mistaken for twins, such was our likeness. We would sometimes wear similar clothes to make it so, and giggle behind our fans as people looked at us and looked a second time..." Antonia made a motion of dismissal with her hand and brought her emotions under control before such bittersweet memories got the better of her. "None of that is important now. What is, is Rory's happiness, and that I know the truth: Christina took her own life not because her baby had a deformity, but because she could no longer live with the shame of what she had permitted you to do to her."

There was an imperceptible pause, and Antonia thought she saw Shrewsbury's arrogant façade crack, but he quickly regained mastery of himself and gave a bluff response.

"*Me*? She threw herself off a balcony just hours after giving birth to her baby daughter. What mother leaves a newborn to fend for itself? And she made her five-year-old son motherless into the bargain!"

"That is fact, but it is not why she killed herself. Your son, he too, took his own life, out of grief, because he loved his wife, and from shame, because he knew you, his father, was a depraved monster."

"Depraved? Monster?" Shrewsbury blustered. His smile was supercilious. "Fanciful moonshine! Any amount of unsubstantiated stuff and nonsense comes out of the mouth of the insane. None of my daughter-in-law's pronouncements bear close scrutiny."

"But my husband, your best friend, he was not insane, and he never spoke nonsense of any kind, thus what M'sieur le Duc told me, I believe. He thought you a monster, too. But he wanted to spare Christina's children, and he could not let social ruin befall you because it would befall them, if the ugly reality of what you had done ever became public. So M'sieur le Duc he agreed to take your loathsome secret to his grave." Antonia dared to smile slightly. "But before he did, he told me."

"I don't believe you!"

"M'sieur le Duc he never promised you he would not tell me. Which he did, because he did not trust you, and he knew such knowledge would be useful should England's Spymaster General decide to become an enemy of my family."

"My old school friend would never betray a friend's trust, not for anyone."

Antonia gave a little sigh.

"Again I say it is obvious, Edward, that you have never been in love. If you had you would know that when you love someone, you will do everything and anything in your power to ensure their happiness and well-being. That is what M'sieur le Duc did for me..." She frowned. "He did not like telling me. It pained him to have to recount your unconscionable behavior, but he knew I would rather know as not. He also knew it would not change my feelings for my goddaughter. Although, it did forever change how I view *you*." She came away from the window. "So now, I will fetch my cousin, and you, you will fetch your family and Rory, and we will all join in a toast to Lady Grasby's breeding, and to the forthcoming marriage between your granddaughter and my cousin."

Before she could go to the door, Shrewsbury caught her by the upper arm and spun her to face him.

He, the keeper of other people's vile little secrets, who had no conscience in using those secrets to further his ends as Spymaster

General, had been bested at his own game. In a moment of supreme weakness, he had confided in the old Duke of Roxton. He had felt better for having purged his conscience, little realizing that his own vile little secret would be tucked away, but always at the ready should it ever be needed. Yet he had enough arrogant self-belief that he tried one last time to intimidate her.

"Perhaps I will snap your pretty neck, here and now," he breathed down at her. "Then all those petty little secrets locked away in that beautiful head will be gone forever, and you can join your precious M'sieur le Duc sooner rather than later."

"To do so would not save you, M'sieur," Antonia replied, his proximity and hot breath making her instantly nauseous.

She pulled her arm free and stepped away, to put distance between them, brushing down the delicate tiered lace flounce of her sleeve, as if cleaning off the stench of him. It also served to give her a moment to compose herself. After all, he had just threatened to kill her. But a wave of nausea brought everything back into clear focus. She knew she must get through this interview for the sake of her cousin and her goddaughter. Forcing down her morning sickness, she spoke in a clear, strong voice.

"I know you too well, and of what you are capable. A sealed letter sits propped on my dressing table. It is directed to my son. I have instructed it be sent to him in the event something untoward befalls his maman. My servants—"

"Clever!"

"—they will not fail in their duty. Kill me and you will be ruined. So, too, your grandson and his family, and to the everlasting sorrow of your daughter—"

"You mean granddaughter."

"Do not play me for a fool, M'sieur! I meant what I said. You seduced your son's wife. Rory is your granddaughter, but she is also your daughter! *N'est-ce pas?*"

Shocked to hear it openly stated, Shrewsbury held up a hand, as if to shield himself from the truth. After two decades, he had almost convinced himself that all Rory was to him was his granddaughter;

that she was also his daughter, the product of his forced seduction of his daughter-in-law, he had carefully suppressed.

"You must understand. Christina—Christina—Rory's mother bewitched me. There was nothing—*nothing*—I could do to stop myself! Men are but weak creatures against divine beauty. It is a-a sickness—"

"*Ne parlez pas*! I will hear no more! It is no wonder the poor creature she jumped to her death. *Mon Dieu*, I do not know how Monseigneur he did not run you through with his rapier upon hearing your pathetic confession!"

She took a deep breath and forced herself to regain her calm, to remember why she was putting herself through this distasteful ordeal. If she had a grain of sympathy for this abhorrently loathsome man, it was because he had been a doting grandparent to both Harvel and Rory.

The supreme irony was that because he had raised Rory to regard her frailty as just another characteristic of her being, and not a hindrance to her existence, Shrewsbury unwittingly gifted her with self-belief and confidence. But he had wrongly assumed no man would want to marry her, and thus she would never leave him. She would be the ideal companion of his old age. It had clearly never crossed his mind that Rory would fall in love, and he certainly never imagined that the man who would steal her heart would be Major Lord Fitzstuart, an heir to an earldom, and ruggedly handsome to boot.

"I will allow you a few moments to compose yourself," the Duchess continued flatly, "and to find a way to rid White's betting book of the offending page. Then you will give the performance of your life and be happy for the engaged couple. After the toasts, Rory she will stay with me until the wedding day, which is a week from tomorrow. It will be in M'sieur le Duc's private chapel, with family present. If you value her happiness, and her new husband's goodwill, you will attend."

Shrewsbury stared at her with seething resentment but he knew when he was defeated. When he spoke, his tone was meek and pleading.

"Promise me, for Rory's sake, and the sake of my family, you will burn that letter to your son."

Antonia pretended to contemplate his request. In truth, there was no letter. Not in a hundred years would she commit to ink Rory's true parentage and the sad story behind her parents' deaths. It had been a bluff. One that had thankfully worked, for she had not formulated an alternative plan had Shrewsbury not swallowed her story and her threat.

"For the sake of my goddaughter and my cousin, and your family, yes. I will do as you ask. But only after they have been up before the vicar and are pronounced husband and wife."

Shrewsbury nodded, satisfied. He shuffled across to the fireplace and retrieved an innocuous, leather-bound volume that had been propped beside the leg of his wingchair. He opened it out to a dog-eared page, folded it into the margin then carefully tore the offending page from the book. He crumpled it up and tossed the paper ball onto the grate atop the smoldering logs.

Antonia's green eyes widened as the fire came to new life as the paper ball was consumed by flame. He did not need to tell her the page was from White's betting book, and that the aberrant wager was now no more. Her hand was on the doorknob when Shrewsbury called her back. She looked over her shoulder, but did not move.

"You are wrong, Mme la Duchesse. I do know how to love. I love my daughter. I love her beyond words."

"*Bon*. Then as a loving father you will be overjoyed she is to marry well and for love. Oh, and Edward, if you dare to look at me in that offending way again, I will have my husband put out your sight."

FORTY-SIX

"Y OU'RE JUST IN time!" Grasby announced, stepping forward to greet his best friend as Dair entered the foyer. "What luck you happened to arrive just now, as we're about to toast our news. Apologies I didn't write and tell you, but Silla wanted to wait until we'd told Grand. Which is the right way to go about things. Still," he added confidentially, sidling up to the Major to say at his ear, "if I'd known your whereabouts this past fortnight, I'd have told you anyway. What luck you're staying with the Duke."

"What's going on, Grasby?" Dair asked curtly and drank down the champagne without tasting it. He hadn't realized just how parched he was. "Where's your sister?"

"Steady on! We've not had the toast yet! Here, take my glass," Grasby insisted and put out his hand for another from a footman. "You're bleached white as falling snow, as if you've come bang up against a specter. Are you all right, dear fellow?"

"Perfectly. Where did you say your sister was?"

"She was feeling poorly. Had a bad night of it, but she'll be down directly."

Dair's brows contracted with worry and then he set his jaw, anger just simmering away under the surface of his congenial façade. If

Shrewsbury had caused Rory any distress, there would be hell to pay. His left hand clenched again.

"We can't have a toast to a new Talbot without his aunt present, now can we?" Grasby rattled on. "Oh, drat! There I go and spoil the surprise. You won't tell Silla I told you, will you?"

"What's that you say, Grasby? A new Talbot?" Dair came out of his angry abstraction enough to smile and slap his friend's back. "Not a word, dear fellow! Congratulations. Good for you! About time, too. Rory will be thrilled to pieces to be an aunt."

"Between you and me, I was despairing of ever becoming a father after that whole Romney studio debacle," Grasby confided with a roll of his eyes and a sigh of relief. "At least now Silla's with child she's willing to forget that ghastly night ever happened—"

"Surely not ghastly? Well, not ghastly for you...?"

Grasby snorted his embarrassment. "Steady on! Not so loud!" When Dair lifted an eyebrow, he rolled his eyes again and conceded, "Oh, all right, not ghastly for me! They were lovely, weren't they, those girls—"

"Very."

"—but a chap has to remember what's important in life and being allowed to sleep in the matrimonial bed is important."

Dair threw back his head and laughed, which caused a pause in conversations as heads turned in his direction. "Egad, Grasby! You always put matters into perspective!"

Grasby grinned like an idiot. "Do I? I do! Yes, of course I do! Oh, and you'll be pleased to know the wife has forgiven you, too."

"I hardly deserve such munificence. When did you say Rory would be here?" Dair asked, glancing about the foyer as a door clicked open.

A footman stood aside to allow the Duchess to leave the drawing room. But she did not cross to him but went to an open window where she stood fanning herself, face turned to the fresh air. Next to appear was Lord Shrewsbury. He did not look Dair's way either, but slid behind two footmen holding trays, and went lightly up the staircase. Dair would have crossed to the Duchess but then Lady Grasby, with William Watkins a step behind, imposed on her solitude and offered her a glass of champagne, so Dair remained where he was, for now.

"Don't get too comfortable," Grasby warned near Dair's ear. "Silla being Silla, she immediately withdrew her forgiveness upon learning you'd socked her brother in the face and broken his nose!" This time Grasby snorted laughter. "My God, you planted him a beautiful facer! None better, and so I told Cedric and the fellows, who instantly laid down a hefty sum that you'd do it again to him before the year's out."

"No more dares, Harvel," Dair stated and clapped his best friend's shoulder when Grasby's mouth dropped open. "Sorry to disappoint, but that's how it's going to be from now on. No exchange of serious blunt and none of it written up in White's betting book. I'm done being an unthinking ass. I guess that's not a bad thing, for you, too, what with impending fatherhood. Do you think Rory will be much longer?"

"Listen, Dair. That's the third time you've called my sister by her name," Grasby grumbled. "If you've a mind to lead her astray I'll be the one socking you—"

"Not at all, dear fellow. Quite the opposite."

"Eh?" Grasby was baffled, but the smile on Dair's face carried no lewd insinuation. In fact, he looked pleased with himself, and in a nice, happy sort of way that Grasby's fears were alleviated. "Well then. That's all right. I just thought I should mention it because the Weasel has been making some pretty rough insinuations to Silla about your intentions toward Rory. And I can tell you, if he wasn't my plaguey brother-in-law, and you hadn't already broken his nose, I'd be the one socking him in the face!"

"Be my guest. But do me the favor of waiting until he's properly healed before you put a hand to him. And you'll have to forgive me for not being so forthcoming with *you* with *our* news, but it will all become apparent—"

"Forgive you? Forthcoming? Apparent? What will? *Our news*? Whose news? Dair? Dair!"

"Excuse me, Grasby," Dair muttered, distracted, and stepped past his friend.

Suddenly he was deaf to his friend's questions, and lost all peripheral vision, so was blind to Lady Grasby and her brother crossing the room to make themselves known to him; Lady Grasby's smug smile shrinking to an undignified pursing of her lips when Dair ignored her. All he saw was the staircase and all he heard was the pumping of his heart hammering in his head. He realized he was still wound as tightly as a pocket watch and might pass out with the anticipation of seeing Rory, and of what was to come after that.

Lord Shrewsbury walked out onto the landing first, and then, there she was, his Delight. She took her grandfather's arm and leaned lightly on her walking stick as she carefully came down the stairs. He unconsciously broke into a grin. She was tired about the eyes, but in every other respect she was his beautiful darling girl. And just as he had done when he entered the house, once she was at the base of the stairs, she looked about her, as if she, too, had lost something or someone.

And then she saw him.

FORTY-SEVEN

JUST BEFORE coming downstairs, Rory had marveled at the rolling high seas of emotion she had experienced in the past twenty-four hours, from the heavenly heights of unbridled happiness to then be plunged into the depths of black despair, with seemingly no way to claw herself out, only to be lifted up again into the heart-fluttering bliss of loving contentment.

From the heightened anticipation of her grandfather's welcome response when Dair came to call to formally ask for her hand in marriage, she was left bewildered at finding herself alone in the hall, Dair gone without a word. And then came the numbing desolation of being told, in a matter-of-fact way, how much her grandfather admired Major Lord Fitzstuart's bravery in accepting an assignment to return to the Colonies on the first available ship, to infiltrate a rebel spy ring on the outskirts of New York, a loyalist stronghold.

Rory instantly disbelieved her grandfather. She had wanted a servant sent after the Major, to have him called back. She had to speak with him. It was a matter of the utmost importance and could not wait. She would have the news of his departure from the Major's lips and no other.

Her grandfather had been completely at a loss to understand her distress. He had patiently sat with her on the stair and asked her to explain why she was so upset by such news. But as she had fallen all to pieces to think the Major had not told her grandfather he was engaged to her, and had accepted a mission to spy on the other side of the Atlantic—as if there was nothing holding him to England— she could barely form a coherent word, least of all form a sentence explaining herself.

Her grandfather had offered her his handkerchief and held her in his arms while she sobbed until her ribs hurt. He suggested she had exhausted herself swimming in the sun that day, was even suffering from sunstroke. He had noticed at dinner there was more color in her face and to her arms than usual. A good night's sleep would set everything to rights. They could talk again in the morning.

But Rory knew everything would not be all right in the morning. She had to see the Major *that night*. Her grandfather had to understand. Tomorrow was too far away. She had to see him now, tonight, that instant.

Such was her distress that she refused to go to her rooms, and again demanded her grandfather send a servant out into the night to call the Major back. He was staying with his cousin the Duchess, just a ten-minute stroll down the lane.

When he again patiently refused, saying he would not disturb the Duchess's household at such an hour, and that she was being uncharacteristically unreasonable to make such demands, she declared her intention of calling on the Major herself, and at once.

It was only then that her grandfather became angry. He called her selfish. She was to desist with her unbecoming behavior at once. Did she not remember who she was, the granddaughter of the Earl of Shrewsbury? Displaying the manners of a fishwife, and before servants, was unacceptable. He would not stand for such behavior from his own blood. He had ended his scolding with the heartfelt hope that she had not lost her head to the likes of the Major.

He had raised her to have a discerning mind, to know her own worth, and to behave accordingly. She was not a hair-brained, penny-pinched nobody prepared to offer herself to any nobleman, body and soul, in the hope of entrapping him into marriage. Did she not have a sense of discrimination?

Certainly the Major would one day inherit a noble title. But he, Shrewsbury, knew him better than anyone. The Major was the last man on God's green earth he would allow any female of his acquaintance to marry. He was a known seducer, a reckless risk-taker, with his own life, and anyone else's if it suited his purpose. He had bastard children practically littering the countryside. Did she not understand there was good reason his moniker was *Dair Devil*?

But what had stopped her sobbing and caught the breath in her throat was his quiet, almost pitiful, prediction that she would break her grandfather's heart and his health never recover if he discovered she had so much as permitted the Major to kiss her hand. As for having her pretty head filled with ridiculous notions that such a man could love her and would offer her marriage, she could banish such thoughts. If the truth be told, he was just the sort of conscienceless libertine to make up to her, all to satisfy some ludicrous wager made between young men of the Major's ilk. But he was confident she had the sense and sensibility to see through such schemes.

Unable to breathe, Rory collapsed.

She awoke in the arms of a footman, who was carrying her, not to her bedchamber on the ground floor, but upstairs, where she was set down on the bed in the small guest bedchamber over the front entrance. Edith came, and her grandfather, too. She lay there, listless and cold. She honestly wondered if she could be bothered breathing at all, such was the pounding in her head and the ache in her heart.

In her fog of despair, she heard her grandfather tell Edith he was locking the door. He did not want his granddaughter doing anything foolish in the night, such as run off to the dower house. He would unlock the door at a reasonable hour in the morning, when he hoped a good night's sleep would see Rory recover her wits.

Rory's gaze must have wandered to the window, for he added that it was impossible, for whatever reason, to open the window. And as there was a considerable drop, and nothing between the window and the gravel drive to break her fall, should she smash the glass and climb out, she would surely break every bone in her body, if not kill herself.

He then kissed her forehead and told her she meant the world to him and that he loved her so very much. With the turn of the key in the lock, she burst into tears and cried herself to exhaustion and fitful sleep.

She woke with the dawn and found Edith asleep in a chair at the foot of the bed, most uncomfortable and shivering with cold, the wrap pulled up over her having slipped to the floor. The fire in the grate had gone out, the maid unable to access the room to provide more wood for the night. Rory was so sick in her heart she felt nothing except the ring on her finger...

The ring! The pale lavender sapphire ring Alisdair had slipped on her finger after asking her to marry him. Why had she not thought to feel it on her finger before now?! With dawning wonder she stared at the beautiful stone in the gray morning light until her eyes went dry, fearing that if she blinked it would not be there, that she was dreaming. But it was still on her finger, exquisitely cut, beautiful in its soft lavender hues, and *hers*. The ring became her talisman of hope and belief.

She realized then that Alisdair had gone away without a word to her, but not for any reason that would suggest he had forsaken her. He did love her. He did want to marry her. The proof of his words was in this ring. But perhaps her grandfather had rejected him as a suitable husband—he had said as much the night before—and, dejected, Alisdair had not the heart to face her with such news. But she was confident he had left the house only to come up with a plan, and that he would not leave England for America without her. If she had to elope with him to the war-torn Colonies, then so be it. Nothing and nobody would stop her!

Feeling so much better, and confident the day would bring Alisdair to her with some plan for their future, Rory drew the wrap back up across Edith, adding one of the two coverlets from the bed for good measure, to ensure her maid was kept warm. She then snuggled in and fell asleep almost instantly, she was so achingly tired. Waking to a late breakfast brought up on a tray, she surprised Edith by eating well and then declaring she would bathe, and wear the soft green silk gown à *l'anglaise*, with the embroidered under-petticoats. Then Edith could bring her a cold compress for her eyes to take away the puffiness, and dress her hair in a coil of braids and curls.

When Lord Shrewsbury enquired of Edith how her mistress was holding up after the night before, Edith was able to tell him that when she left Rory in her bath, she was singing to herself; it was as if the previous night's melodrama had never occurred. Far from looking pleased, the old man's frown deepened.

He wondered what scheme his granddaughter was hatching to see herself reunited with the Major. He ordered the footman to keep his granddaughter locked in the upstairs bedchamber, with only her maid to be given access; a footman to stand guard at the door at all times.

Rory was bathing when Edith brought her the news that Lord and Lady Grasby and Mr. William Watkins had arrived from Chiswick. She was then again locked into the bedchamber, and this time without warning or explanation, which worried her as to her grandfather's motives for keeping her locked up, even from her own family members.

And then Major Lord Fitzstuart did return! She was dressed and ready to go downstairs when a second carriage turned into the drive. Edith was at the window and called her over in time to see the carriage door furthest from the house fling wide and the love of her life appear. Rory could have fainted with happiness at seeing him. She pressed her nose to the glass to better see him when he went down on his haunches to light a cheroot, and wondered if she shouted he would hear her.

But then she reasoned, so would the rest of the house, so best to keep quiet and be ready to flee when he kicked in the door. Perhaps she should think of a plan to help him in his rescue of her. To this end she had Edith help her remove the candles from their brass holders. She played with the weight of them, judging the best way to hold a candlestick to use it with force. Edith swayed with worry at the passion for violence her young mistress displayed when demonstrating the use of a candlestick as a weapon.

But neither candlestick was required to be misused. Nor was the door kicked in.

It was unlocked by a footman to admit a short, upright lady who introduced herself in French as lady-in-waiting to Mme la Duchesse d'Roxton et Kinross. She came with orders for Edith to have Mlle Talbot's belongings packed up and sent out to the Duchesse's waiting carriage. Mlle Talbot would be spending the week at the house of her godmother in preparation for her marriage to Major Lord Fitzstuart.

Not understanding French, Edith looked to Rory for translation. But upon hearing the phrase... *in preparation for her marriage to Major Lord Fitzstuart*, Rory again went into shock and forgot to breathe, crumpling to the floor in a heap of billowing petticoats.

Revived, Rory existed in a heightened state of awareness, the mixed emotions of relief and disbelief causing not only her heart but her mind to race. And while Edith went off with the Duchess's lady-in-waiting to supervise the packing of portmanteaux, the footman locked Rory into the bedchamber again with the apology he could not free her until word came from His Lordship.

Finally, her grandfather did fetch her, and with the news everyone was awaiting her presence in the drawing room. He did not speak of the events of the night before, and while there remained so many unanswered questions, Rory could not bring herself to ask him. He looked to have aged overnight. His shoulders stooped and his hands had acquired a slight tremor. Worst of all was the haunted expression in his blue eyes. He could not meet her gaze, and when he spoke he sounded frail.

How could she stay angry with him? She kissed his cheek, put her arms about him and said she forgave him and would always love him. He broke down, asked her forgiveness for being over-protective, and in an about-face, he said the Major was indeed a good man who was worthy of her. They then both shed a tear. When sufficiently composed, they went downstairs, arm-in–arm, Shrewsbury resigned to being a bystander, Rory to greet the first day of the rest of her life.

FORTY-EIGHT

IN TWO STRIDES Dair was before her.

Rory smiled up at him.

He grinned down at her.

They were so happy to see each other they giggled. Rory let go of her grandfather's arm and handed him her walking stick. But when she turned to look at Dair again, when she saw that he was indeed still there before her, she was so overcome with relief she crumpled. A shaking hand to her mouth and tears in her eyes, she sobbed.

Dair instantly scooped her up and held her against him, face nuzzled in her hair, silent, feeling the strong tremors of release coursing through her lithe frame. But then he realized the tremors were not only hers. He did not speak, just held her, and let her cry until she stopped of her own volition. When she moved in his arms, he let her go. He gave her his handkerchief. And when she had dried her eyes, he quickly wiped his own and thrust the handkerchief away.

Neither was certain who moved time on after that. But she was in his arms again, on tiptoe, chin tilted up to kiss him. He stooped and crushed her mouth under his, all social constraint abandoned. They were too relieved, too overjoyed, too in love to be bothered with convention and propriety. All that mattered was they were together, they were to marry, and as soon as possible. Everything and everyone around them disappeared in a fog of unimportant movement and noise.

WITH THE DUCHESS of Roxton and her mother-in-law the Duchess of Roxton and Kinross putting their heads together to organize every aspect of Rory and Dair's wedding, from the guest list to the dishes to be served at the wedding breakfast, there was little for Rory to do but enjoy each day closer to the ceremony with a heightened sense of anticipation, and as if she were living a dream.

She did not even have the drama of indecision regarding what gown would be most suitable. Her sister-in-law tried to convince her an ivory or lemon silk would be best for a bride, but neither suited Rory's pale complexion. And she had promised Dair to wear the pink-lavender open-robed gown of silk and matching shoes he had seen her in on the stair of the Gatehouse Lodge. Edith knew just how to arrange her hair; despite Silla's insistence she was more expert in such matters. And as for jewelry, Rory was perfectly content with her lilac sapphire betrothal ring; the color perfectly matched her choice of gown. Again, Silla said this would never do. She would find something suitable for Rory's décolletage and wrists. Secretly, Rory hoped her search was in vain.

The next day Lord and Lady Grasby strolled up to the Dower House from the Gatehouse Lodge to have morning tea with Rory on the terrace. Enjoying their second cup of tea, they presented Rory with a flat square jewelry case. Inside, nestled on a bed of velvet, was a four-strand choker of luminous pearls and a matching bracelet. The set had belonged to Rory's mother and worn on her wedding day in Oslo, and now it was Rory's, a wedding gift from her brother and his wife. Rory was brought to tears, surprised Silla could part with such pearls.

Silla ruined the moment with the revelation she had a much more expensive five-strand choker with a long length of pearls fitted off with a gold and diamond clasp, and that it came with two matching bracelets and a pair of earrings. The set was a gift from her parents on her marriage into the Talbot family. Rory made no comment other than she was certain Silla's pearls were beautiful indeed, to which Silla replied Rory would see them for herself when she wore them to the wedding ceremony the day after tomorrow.

Rory exchanged a look with her brother, who merely rolled his eyes, bit down on a retort, and silently drank his tea. Yet not five minutes later, Silla outdid herself with an insensitive reply to Grasby's innocent enquiry as to which of her walking sticks Rory had chosen to use for the big occasion. The Malacca cane with the ivory handle carved in the shape of a pineapple, was Rory's preference. In fact, he had given it to her on her nineteenth birthday, did he not remember? It was also the one she had with her that fateful night at Romney's Studio. Grasby laughed at that and said it was the perfect choice. He wondered aloud if his best friend remembered the offending instrument.

Silla found nothing to laugh at. In fact, she was alarmed to think Rory was going to be married with a walking stick at all. Setting her teacup in its saucer, she was blunt, oblivious her words were in the least offensive.

"Rory cannot possibly be married with her stick, Grasby. Have you ever seen a bride with a walking stick? No. It simply won't do. You must lean on the Major's arm. That is more fitting and thoroughly acceptable for a new bride. People will then think you are emotionally overcome by the ceremony and will be none the wiser—"

"Silla! How can you say—"

Grasby was cut off.

"As it is a family wedding, Silla, everyone is wise to the fact I use a walking stick," Rory replied without heat. "And I am not such a poor creature that I am likely to faint at my own wedding." She dimpled. "I am more likely to be wearing a silly grin of happiness, which I must temper, or I shall appear a fool." She touched her brother's upturned cuff. "You will tell me by some signal or other, if I start grinning like a Bedlam inmate, won't you?"

"But, dearest, you've never been the center of attention before," Silla argued. "And you've never danced. You've always sat in out-of-the way places at functions. There are quite possibly those who have no idea who you are! Believe me, having everyone stare at you is more nerve-wracking than you can possibly imagine."

Rory suppressed a smile at her sister-in-law's conceit, and said levelly, but with tongue firmly planted in cheek, "Even more reason to use my stick upon this occasion. After all, one day I will be Countess of Strathsay, so the sooner I become accustomed to being the center of attention the better. Don't you agree, Harvel?"

"Most certainly. In my book, you can't become the center of attention soon enough, sister dear."

Brother and sister laughed but Silla saw nothing to be amused about. After thoughtful consideration she said, "I suppose that is true, Rory. And with so many titled relatives in attendance, we can't have the bride falling flat on her face."

"No. No, we cannot," Rory agreed. When her brother pulled a funny face at her, out of his wife's line of sight, she giggled into her teacup. Regaining her composure, she added, "What an inauspicious start to our marriage if I were to trip, twist my good ankle, and land on my face! Poor Alisdair!"

Silla gave a prim little cough into her gloved fist.

"Dearest, it is only ever Alisdair when you are private, and once he is your husband," she enunciated in a patronizing tone. "*Always* Fitzstuart in company, and *my lord* before the servants and other menials."

Stunned by such an unwarranted rebuke, Rory could think of nothing to say, so went about organizing the tea things, undecided if she should be angry or embarrassed.

Grasby stepped in, patience worn thin. His wife might be with child, and he warned not to upset her delicate nerves at such an early stage in the pregnancy, but he was not going to sit idly by and let his sister be told how to conduct herself, which was none of his wife's business. Irritated to anger, he said what was on the tip of Rory's tongue but which good manners dictated she not voice aloud.

"Where do you get your singular notions to lecture *us*? My sister is a Talbot, and we Talbots know how to conduct ourselves in any company. Besides, she can say what she jolly well likes; call her husband Rover or-or Spot if it pleases *him,* for all I care! By the by, where is Rover—er—the lucky groom?" he asked, taking his temper down a notch, and shifting in his chair to look left and then right, as if he expected his best friend to leap out from behind a statue to frighten the life out of him. It had happened before. "Shouldn't he be here, with you?"

"Not until nuncheon today," Rory told them. "He has business to discuss with the Duke."

"I thought we'd done all the settlements and such yesterday," Grasby remarked. And when Rory frowned, explained. "Grand and me, Roxton and Dair, worked out the settlements, your dowry and pin money." He smiled as if he was well-pleased with himself. "I don't mind telling you, sister dear, that you are being well looked after, with all eventualities covered."

"Eventualities?" Rory had no idea what he was talking about.

"You know... If anything were to happen to Dair—not that it's likely to!" he assured her quickly when her frowned deepened. "He's given up playing at spy—Now there's something I didn't know about him, and he my best friend! A spy all these years! But, Rory, please. Don't look at me like that! I hadn't the foggiest notion. But he's given all that shadow and stab stuff up. And so he should, now he's to be married. He has other responsibilities—you being the most important one; and so I told him! But I haven't any worries, have I, when he's practically stitched himself to your skirts!" He teased his sister. "And if he's not sewn to you, he's looming large like a shadow, just one step away. And the poor fellow can't keep his eyes off of you. I'd say he's got it bad—"

"What? What's he got?" Silla asked swiftly, a hand to her bodice. "It's not contagious, is it? The baby—"

Lord Grasby put up a shoulder and stuck out his bottom lip. "That's difficult to say..."

"Oh, stop your teasing, Harvel!" Rory admonished him lovingly, cheeks flushing with embarrassment. She smiled at her sister-in-law. "Your baby is perfectly safe, Silla."

Lady Grasby heaved a huge sigh of relief and fanned herself, as if she truly believed Major Lord Fitzstuart was infected with the plague.

"Thank Goodness! The Duchess of Roxton has put such an effort into your wedding, and she heavy with child, too," Silla said dramatically. "What a disappointment for her and Her Grace of Kinross, if after all their planning and hard work it was to be called off because the Major is struck down with the flu!"

"Oh yes! Let's not disappoint the Duchess—*two* Duchesses, in fact," Lord Grasby scoffed and put aside his teacup and saucer. "Never mind disappointing his bride!"

When Rory opened wide her eyes at him, he knew he had gone too far with his chastisement of his wife and did his best to temper his annoyance.

It was not only his wife who had put Grasby out of charity. If he was honest with himself, he had been out of sorts with the world since learning of his sister's engagement to his best friend. Selfishly, he did not want her leaving the family fold. He did not entirely understand why she was staying with the Duchess of Roxton and Kinross before her marriage, and not at the Gatehouse Lodge with her immediate family. His grandfather's explanation was that the Lodge was small, and with William Watkins in the house, it was best for Rory to be elsewhere.

But then William Watkins had departed for London under a cloud only the day before. He was not given the full explanation, only that the Weasel was needed in the city on Crown business. Grasby knew that was only part of the story. The other part he had heard loud and clear through the thin walls of the Lodge, because he just happened to be sitting just outside the study, on the first step of the staircase, reading the Gazette.

The Weasel accused Dair of being a traitor (nothing new there; he was always trying to discredit the Major that it had become a long-standing joke between Grasby and his grandfather). But this time the Weasel said he had proof, a letter in the Major's fist written to his brother Charles. It had come into the Weasel's possession by mysterious means he was not prepared to divulge. There was then a lot of back and forth arguing between the Weasel and the Spymaster General that Grasby could only catch the odd word. The upshot was the Weasel screaming for Shrewsbury not to toss the offending letter into the flames.

Mr. William Watkins had then exited the study, took one look at Grasby, and blurted out that the House of Lords was filled with blackguards, and the sooner it was abolished, the better for the country! To which Grasby replied mildly that such words were treasonous, and if he really wanted to make a difference somewhere there was a revolution going on in the American Colonies. He was confident the patriots would welcome a man of the Weasel's abilities and philosophical leanings with open arms. He then returned to reading the Gazette as the Weasel stomped past him up the steps to have his bags packed.

Memory of the exchange brought a smile back to Grasby's face and he was more in charity with the world thinking the Weasel may yet decide to throw in his lot with a bunch of revolutionaries and run off to America, and so leave him and his wife in peace.

"There's nothing at all wrong with Dair," Grasby told his wife gently. "To point out fact, all's right with our Major. He's just in love with my sister, and hooray for that." He smiled at Rory. "I couldn't be happier for you both. I should have known it when I saw you at the Banks House wall." He sat back with a wink at Rory. "If Dair's not needed here, Cedric and I will claim him tomorrow morning. We're off hawking with Roxton and a few of the local gentry, all come to celebrate the poor fellow's last hours of freedom; before he's leg-shackled for life and can never move again without the wife demanding to know his whereabouts."

Silla, not seeing Grasby's wink, sat up very tall. But before she could launch into another lecture, the object of their discussion came into view, crossing from the stables to the house.

FORTY-NINE

DRESSED IN A riding frock and jockey boots, his shoulder-length hair wind-tussled, Dair had just ridden over from the big house. He was, as always, slightly disheveled, and had not bothered to shave, all the more handsome for the stubble to his face. This was Rory's assessment as her blue eyes lit up as he came lightly up the stone steps to join them. Her brother was of the same opinion, watching his sister's skin glow pink at the sight of his best friend, and his wife sit forward and gaze up at him with limpid longing, she, too, wishing to be noticed by the Major. But Grasby held no malice, and just shook his head, not only on the effect the Major's untidy masculinity had on the fairer sex, but also that the man himself seemed oblivious to his effect on females.

"I should warn you; two carriages are on their way from the big house," Dair told them as he came to stand by Rory's chair. He placed an ungloved hand gently on her shoulder and her fingers immediately found his and held on. "One full of children, the other full of their attendants. The Duchess has invited them for a picnic lunch. I was able to ride over here, but Cedric had no such luck. Roxton's twins have taken a shine to Ced, so he was bundled into their carriage before I could save him."

"Ha! I'll wager you made no such effort! Poor Ced," Grasby

replied without sympathy, as he scraped back his chair. "Serves him to rights for being about as tall as a shrub. Possibly mistaken for a brat himself. Come, wife! Best take you home. You need to rest, and we can't have the baby exposed to mites with coughs and snotty noses, even if they are ducal mites."

Lady Grasby showed no objection. In fact, she could not move fast enough to put distance between her and the Dower House. She was off down the terrace steps ahead of her husband, who stopped to have a last word with the couple.

"Not abandoning you. I'll return as soon as I have Silla settled," he confided. He held Rory's gaze. "Perhaps we'll get to have a proper chat about that matter I spoke to you yesterday..."

When Rory nodded, Grasby took his leave. But even with her brother out of earshot, and she alone with Dair, she did not elaborate on the cryptic sentence. Dair did not need to be told the subject matter to know something grave was weighing on Rory's mind. Her thoughts should not have been clouded by anything more serious than her wedding gown and last-minute preparations for their impending nuptials.

He did not like to see her so solemn. And although he could not help her if he did not know what was the matter, he knew he could fix the immediate problem. Without warning, he scooped her up and ran with her across the lawn to the pirate treehouse. Before she could stop gasping and squealing with laughter at the same time, he had hauled her over his shoulder as if she were nothing heavier than his frock coat. He then climbed the ladder up a three-hundred-year-old oak and into the magical world of a two-level treehouse fashioned like the bow of a pirate ship.

Dair lifted Rory onto the floorboards, and she crawled away from the ladder and the long drop to the ground, and to allow him space to hoist himself up to the safety of the wooden floor. Once secure, she sat up on her knees and took a peek over the side of the painted railing at the view.

"Oh! How delightful! You can see everything from the terrace to the pavilion and across to the jetty. I wish I'd come up here sooner. Though this ship seems to have appeared from nowhere. It wasn't here last summer. Perhaps it sailed in on a cloud by a band of fairy pirates and got stuck? What do you think?"

"This is only my second time aboard. Kinross had it built for the Roxton brood, just after Easter. But I like your explanation better." He joined her, crossed arms leaning lightly on the railing. "The boys will be here soon enough and will head straight for the gangway to clamber aboard. This pirate ship is all they can talk about!"

He turned from the view and sat with his back up against the side of the ship, long booted legs sprawled out before him. When she joined him, sitting to face him, he took hold of her fingers and gently pressed his lips to the back of her hand. He smiled wistfully.

"We've not had a moment alone since your grandfather toasted to our future happiness, have we? We're forever surrounded by a hive of activity, and I suspect it won't let up until we can run away together after we're married. I know I've been kept occupied going over settlements, estate documents, and discovering precisely what mess my father left for the old Duke and then Roxton to clean up after he ran off to Barbados! But what about you? Lady Grasby looks to have recovered from her dead faint at our announcement..."

"Oh, but we must feel for her position," Rory said with a smile that mirrored his own. "She is finally breeding, which is such badly wanted news by the family. And what do we do but spoil her moment in the sunshine by announcing our engagement to be married. She should still be basking in all the attention. As it is, her baby has become secondary to our wedding. So I do have sympathy for her. Though, I could do without her good advice on being a bride, of which I've had a milk-pail full." Her smile was impish. "The only topic she has *not* broached is the wedding night, and I am certain her restraint is only due to my brother's presence. Poor Harvel would faint from mortification if he ever suspected she would dare try to give me advice about *that*."

"I can't imagine what she could possibly confide in you," he commented with a chuckle.

She misconstrued his meaning and blushed.

"I'm certain I still have much to learn—"

"I meant her advice, Delight."

"Oh! I see...."

He moved closer to lift her chin, so she had to look in his eyes.

"What is it? You have not been yourself since yesterday. Have you had second thoughts about—"

"—marrying you? *Never!*"

"—giving yourself to me on the island. Perhaps you would have preferred to wait until our wedding night?"

"Oh no!" She was emphatic. "How could you think that? It is a day I will never forget." Her smile was bashful. "I'm sure every girl dreams her first time will be just as glorious as mine. And you made it so for me."

"Thank you. That means the world to me. *You* mean the world to me."

"As you do to me..."

She shifted to lean in to kiss him gently. First the stubbled underside of his chin, then his throat, on up over his square jaw, across to his cheek, then the bridge of his strong nose, and finally his wide brow. Teasingly, she avoided his mouth. She punctuated these light butterfly kisses with conversation that was just as playful.

"If Silla does try and give me advice, I shall tell her politely that I do not need her wifely wisdom, because I cannot wait to make love, *again*. But this time, with my *husband*. She will fall into another dead faint, but that can't be helped, because I will not lie. In fact, it is most distressing you are staying at the big house and I am here. From my bedroom window I can see Swan Island and it is a constant reminder of our time together alone. And then I have the most wicked remembrances of us making love. If you were staying here, you could row me over there at night, no one in the house the wiser, and we could—"

He caught her face between his hands and kissed her passionately, no longer able to withstand the torture of her barely-there kisses, her banter, and the sweet delicious vanilla scent of her skin. But as much as Rory returned his kisses, she was not so lost in the moment that she was unaware of their surroundings and the potential for a scandalous predicament. So she was the one who broke their fervent kissing. The instant she did, he stopped.

He stared at her, short of breath and wondering what he had done, but it only took a few seconds before he came to a sense of his surroundings.

"That was my fault," Rory apologized, feeling awkward. "I should not have enticed you with my silly wishful thinking—"

"It was not silly," he interrupted. "But you were right to stop me. This is not the place. Now, won't you tell me what it is that has been bothering you? Perhaps that will be enough to pour cold water on my ardor?" He chuckled. "Unless, that is, you do have some cold water to hand!?"

Rory frowned. "Cold water...?" When he looked away, a ready flush to his face, dawning wonder opened wide Rory's blue eyes. She sighed her understanding. "It is so different for men, is it not? We females can more easily hide our frustrations so no one need know, but for men—Is it painful if you do not find release?"

Acute embarrassment mixed with the studiousness of her enquiry made him burst out laughing.

"Oh, Delight. I do love you so! Yes. In a way. But more uncomfortable than anything else, and quite embarrassing if not dealt with. But won't you tell me what is bothering you, that we should discuss before our wedding?" He chucked her under the chin. "We must share our worries as well as our blessings. It's the only way a marriage will work."

She nodded. "Yes. Yes, you are right. I am in a bit of a quandary." She again scrambled to sit before him, layers of her petticoats tucked up under her knees, closing the gap he had put between them. "Grasby was to help me find a solution so that I need not bother you with it. You have been so caught up in business affairs, and I know how much you hate being indoors, that you do not need any more aggravation—"

"Rory, let me stop you there. Firstly, I will never be caught up in anything, be it business, or anything else, that you should ever feel you cannot interrupt me. Secondly, you will never aggravate me. Thirdly, I understand you have been used to going to Grasby for assistance and guidance, he is your brother after all. But I hope now we are engaged and soon will be married; you would be comfortable enough to come to me first." He smiled crookedly. "That sounded as if I am envious of Grasby. To own a truth, I am, a little. Mary—my sister—would never think to come to me for advice. I guess because she is two years older than me, and was married off while I was still at Harrow... Let me guess your quandary... You are worried about your grandfather and how we shall all go on from here, now your allegiance is to me—"

Rory interrupted him. "How did—"

"Because I know you. And because I don't want you to be troubled, Shrewsbury and I have called a truce. I respect the fact he loves you very much and only wants what is best for you. He has come to the realization that he and I share that common goal. I also know you are concerned about the Royal visit to your grandfather's pinery taking place four days after we are married, when we should be enjoying the start of our honeymoon month. I assume you have been wondering how best to tell me?"

Rory's blue eyes grew round

"How did—"

It was his turn to interrupt, and with a smug smile. But he couldn't keep up the pretense of oracle for long and shook his head at her look of wonderment.

"Also your grandfather. We were discussing settlements and the like with Roxton and two dreary men of business, and I must have been fidgeting in my chair. Believe me, Delight, three hours stuck in a library surrounded by wall-to-wall books almost undid me! I was ready to throw myself through a closed window, climb the bookcases, anything to get myself into fresh air! Shrewsbury knows me well. So he called me away for a stroll on the terrace, to have a cheroot, while the Duke dealt with an interruption from his surveyor. Your grandfather graciously asked my permission for you to attend the presentation of the Talbot pineapple to their Majesties. After all, it was you who cultivated it..."

He let the sentence hang, waiting for her reaction, and to add something to the discussion, but when Rory remained mute, waiting for him to continue, he threw up a hand and then pulled her to him.

"Good God, Rory. What did you think I would say? No? After

all your months and months of hard work growing the jolly thing! Other than Portland's gardener Speechly, who else is the foremost cultivator in the kingdom of such a majestic fruit? No one but you. I know how much this pineapple means to you, and to your grandfather who watched you put your heart and soul into his pinery. The second time I met you, you dropped a gardening treatise at my feet—"

"You remember that?"

"Remember it? It is burned into here," he said, jabbing his temple. "I'd given your grandfather my word I would not let on I remembered anything about our fortuitous meeting at Romney's studio. So here was I wanting to scoop you up in my arms with the joy of having found you again and forcing myself to pretend I had no idea who you were. I can even remember the name of the book. A first for me. *A General Treatise of Husbandry and Gardening* by Richard Gradey—"

"*Bradley*. Richard Bradley."

"Yes, well, him. So of course I know how much it means to you to present the Talbot Pineapple to their Majesties. You will be there; we both will." He chuckled. "Besides, who better to make the presentation than Lady Fitzstuart, wife of a descendant of Charles the Second, who was the first monarch to be presented with a pineapple—"

"—by John Rose. I've seen the painting by Danckerts."

"Yes. I suggested to your grandfather that he have the auspicious occasion painted, too, and by Romney, and that a second copy of the painting be presented to His Majesty. Shrewsbury thought it a splendid idea. I've requested a copy also, to be hung in the Great Room at Fitzstuart Hall. My mother will be impressed."

When she threw her arms about his neck, he kissed her swiftly, but did not allow himself to be distracted by the feel of her in his arms. Reluctantly, he disentangled himself, as he had more that needed to be said before their big day, and before Roxton's brood arrived with Cedric and came aboard.

"We need to be in accord on an important aspect of our marriage, Rory. When we marry, legally and spiritually husband and wife become one and the husband is that one. But that is not how we are going to conduct ourselves as husband and wife. Do you understand me? I have been witness to that sort of marriage; it is degrading and destructive. You are to always be you, and me, well you are going to have to suffer me as I am! And we will both make important decisions together. You were the one who told me what you consider important in a marriage: Love. Respect. Friendship. Honesty. Trust. And I believe that sincerely. Do you understand, Rory?"

Rory snuggled into his embrace and nodded her agreement, adding cheekily in a meek voice, "Of course, my lord. Whatever you say, my lord."

"Desist, wicked creature!" He kissed the top of her hair, adding, "I will tell you here and now, so you can be comfortable and enjoy the ceremony and wedding breakfast without the worry of wondering about our postponed honeymoon month. We are spending the first two nights as husband and wife on Swan Island."

Rory gasped. "Truly? How are we to manage rowing over there after the wedding breakfast without our family knowing? Without the Duke knowing? You must have a plan!"

He shook his head, grinning. "No. No. No, dear heart. Nothing so underhanded. Though, I grant the prospect of whisking you off to a forbidden island is a more romantic notion. No, Delight. It is a gift from my cousin; your godmother." Suddenly emotion got the better of him and he swallowed hard and took a moment to collect himself. "She—She has gifted us the leasehold for one week a year for our lifetime. She was delighted when I said we would be honored to continue the tradition begun by her and the fifth Duke. And she has granted my request to hang our story in thread, when we feel the time is right, above the fireplace on the fourth and final wall of the temple."

Rory was too overcome to speak. But there was no need for words. Both were awed by such a gift. And then Dair heard the distant sounds of activity, and the distinct high-pitched crescendo of unbridled excitement that only children can manage. He made movements to leave and helped Rory to stand.

"Time we jumped ship, Delight, before we are boarded and taken captive. Louis and Gus are fierce pirates; so they keep telling me. Louis has even threatened to make me walk the plank should he catch me!"

"You should let him. Nothing would make that little boy happier."

"Yes. Yes, you're right, of course. I will." Dair winked at her. "But I won't make it easy for him." He drew her into his arms. "That which is hard won is all the more precious for the struggle..."

There was the scuffle and scramble of many feet competing on the ladder. Whispers and giggles followed. Then a young voice blurted out,

"*Pauh*! Kissing. Gus! *Gus*. Look! It's disgu—disgu—it's *awful*!"

"Louis! Move!" Frederick ordered his younger brother and squeezed past him on the ladder.

The eldest son and heir to the Duke of Roxton then poked his head up into the treehouse, took a look around, saw the two people his grandmother was looking for, and then squeezed past Louis again to go halfway down the ladder. Meanwhile, Gus passed him and joined his twin, Louis, who had moved up a rung and was determined to enter the treehouse regardless of the disgusting sight before his eyes. The twins scrambled up into the bow and whipped out their painted wooden cutlasses that had been secured in a colored silk sash around their waists. Gus even wore an eye patch. Both pointed their weapons at the two prisoners.

"We've found them, Mema!" Frederick shouted down to his grandmother the Duchess of Roxton and Kinross, who was standing with half a dozen upper servants at the base of the ladder, his sister Juliana in her arms. All were looking skywards, up into the boughs of the old oak. "They're here, Mema! They're kissing! And Louis says he's going to throw up!"

FIFTY

THE WEDDING ceremony of Major Lord Fitzstuart, heir to the Strathsay earldom, to Miss Aurora Talbot, granddaughter of the Earl of Shrewsbury, was due to commence in just under two hours, and Dair was staring critically at his reflection. His valet was to one side of the long looking glass, his two best friends, mute, on the other. All three were staring at him. Dressing for his wedding had taken some time and was conducted in solemn silence. Lord Grasby and Mr. Cedric Pleasant were dressed and ready, and upon admittance to their friend's closet, found him as he was, dressing almost complete and before the long looking glass.

The groom had chosen a silk suit of dark burnished gold, almost chocolate brown, depending on the light, with matching breeches, waistcoat, and frock coat. The front of the waistcoat and its pocket flaps, the lapels and collar of the frock coat, the knee bands of the tight-fitting breeches, and the fabric buttons to all three garments were heavily embroidered with delicate arrangements of lavender, rosemary, dianthus blooms and arum leaves. It was a stunning ensemble, completed with white clocked stockings over muscular calves, highly polished black leather shoes with a low heel, diamond buckles to shoes and breeches, and frothy layers of lace at firm wrists, with matching lace in the white cravat about the strong neck.

As well as being uncharacteristically clean-shaven, the groom's hair was pomaded and scraped back out of his eyes. A wide ribbon of white silk was chosen by his valet to tie off his hair, but Dair had his own ideas. He gave Reynolds a much narrower ribbon of lavender silk. This was obediently tied up in a neat bow, without Reynolds batting an eyelid; he rightly assuming the ribbon had once belonged to his master's bride. And while it might not look as elegant as the white silk ribbon he had chosen, the romantic sentiment brought a tear to Reynolds' eye.

It only remained for Dair to be shrugged into his frock coat, slip on his gold signet ring, which he rarely wore except on the most formal of occasions, and collect up the various gentleman's accoutrements that belonged in his pockets: Silver pocket watch, white linen monogrammed handkerchief and silver tinderbox.

Yet he lingered before his reflection and tweaked at the lace under his shaved chin as if all was not satisfactory.

"It's all a bit too much, isn't it?"

The valet looked worried. Lord Grasby and Mr. Cedric Pleasant grinned and shook their heads.

"Not a bit of it, dear fellow. You're getting married. You're supposed to look like a prize fighting cock!"

"Fighting cock? Ha! More like a peacock. And I feel as weak as a blancmange!"

"All perfectly natural," Grasby replied, still grinning.

He hadn't stopped grinning since breakfast. He grinned through a quick game of billiards with the Duke, Dair and Cedric, all to calm the groom and make him forget what was to come. He grinned through the impromptu toasts, and even grinned while smoking a cheroot, his first. He just couldn't help himself. If his face didn't ache, his throat did from imbibing too much cognac mixed with tobacco smoke, and all this before midday. He was just so happy that his best friend and his sister were to be husband and wife.

"And while my limbs feel as wobbly as a pudding, my head pounds," Dair grumbled. "It's as if I've just been told I'm destined for the gallows, not the chapel. And I don't want to feel like this at all."

"Yes. Yes. All quite normal," Grasby assured him and gave Mr. Cedric Pleasant a nudge in the ribs so he would add his assurances.

"What? Oh! Er, yes, all perfectly normal," Cedric Pleasant added. "Not that I've ever been in your dire—I mean euphoric—condition, Dair. But I'm told by reliable sources that feeling God-awful is perfectly natural for a groom on his wedding day."

Dair's head snapped round at his two best friends, and he glared at them and growled, "You're both enjoying this, aren't you?"

Cedric Pleasant started to shake his head when Grasby laughed out loud.

"Yes! Yes we are! Why not? The tables are quite turned, dear fellow. I've been there and done that. And who better than my best friend, and soon to be brother-in-law, to experience the unmitigated terror as the bell tolls the last hour of a groom's freedom. I was unequivocally petrified; I don't mind telling you!"

"Don't worry, Dair," Cedric assured him. "Grasby and I will be right beside you the entire ceremony, to prop you up, should you falter."

"I won't falter, and I won't need propping up. And I am not terrified! I want to marry Aurora. I love her. You both know that don't you?"

His two best friends lost their smiles and nodded.

"Yes. Of course."

"Yes. We know that. Wouldn't let you marry my sister otherwise. Come on, let's get you into your frock coat and downstairs," Grasby added, a nod to the valet, who stepped forward with the frock coat opened wide. "The Duke must be wondering where we are by now..."

Dair nodded. He allowed himself to be shrugged into his silk frock coat without argument and remained docile while Reynolds fussed with the fit at the shoulders and tugged gently on the skirts so that the silk folded nicely. He even allowed the man to take one last look at him from hair ribbon to shoe buckle, before turning away from the looking glass.

"Thank you, John, I'll take it from here," he said quietly to his valet, who nodded and with a bow retired to stand on the other side of the dressing table.

"I have it," Grasby said when Dair started to pat the pockets of his frock coat as if he had misplaced something. He patted the inner pocket of his silver spangled embroidered waistcoat. Contained within it was a small velvet box and nestled inside was Rory's gold wedding band.

"And I have your cheroot case," Cedric offered. He smiled kindly. "For after the service, at the breakfast. If you need to slip outside..."

A sharp single knock to the outer door had all three gentlemen looking that way. Farrier poked his head into the room.

"Just your vedette, m'lord. Come to tell you that this is definitely the last call-to-arms. His Grace is waitin' downstairs to take you on through to the chapel."

The gentlemen silently filed out of Dair's rooms. On the landing, Dair sent Grasby and Cedric on ahead so he could have a quiet word with Farrier. His best friends weren't going anywhere. They continued down the sweeping staircase but only far enough so their friend remained within eyesight, if not within earshot.

"Very smart, Mr. Farrier."

The batman, dressed in a new suit of fine blue linen, courtesy of his master, made him a bow, then held up his silver hook with a smile. "All spit and polished and gleaming, m'lord."

Dair smiled, and in a move that had the batman swallowing the emotion back down his throat, he gave Farrier's upper arm a squeeze as he said, "You've always been there for me, Mr. Farrier. Whether it be running through a hail of enemy fire, helping me escape a painter's studio, or watching me go up before parson. Thank you."

"Always, m'lord."

"I wanted to reassure you. I may be getting married and rusticating on the family farm, but it doesn't mean I won't have need of you. I'll have an estate to run, and I need someone who knows me, whom I can trust implicitly. A home steward of sorts, to run my private household. Her ladyship and I are in accord on this, and we both want you to take on the job. That's if you're up for it." Dair smiled. "That's if you don't think you'll be bored in such employment."

"It would be an honor and a privilege, m'lord. Always saw m'self retirin' to the country someday."

Dair laughed and nodded and became serious. Something else was weighing on his mind. "Keep an eye on the boy and his grand-parents for me. While they'll be accorded every welcome, there are those who won't be pleased to see them here." He was thinking specifically of his mother and the straight-backed sticklers of her ilk.

Farrier knew His Lordship was talking about his natural son Jamie and the boy's grandparents, Mr. and Mrs. Banks.

"Don't you worry about a thing, m'lord. I looked in on 'em yesterday evenin'. They'd settled in nice and snug at the Swan inn on the High Street. And then this morning, Her Grace sent a carriage to bring 'em here, and I went with it."

"Did she? That was kind of her. And of you. Thank you."

"And Her Grace and me, we put our heads together about the seating arrangements—"

"Her Grace and-and you—*put your heads together…?*"

"Her Grace didn't want to trouble you. Said you had enough on your mind. So it was decided I would sit with Master Jamie and his grandparents in the chapel, and later, at the wedding breakfast Master Jamie is to sit with the Duke's younger lads so he'll be comfortable."

Dair was surprised but also relieved. "Well then, there's nothing for me to concern myself about…"

"Nothin' whatsoever, m'lord. You just ease up and enjoy the moment with Her Ladyship. That's all you've got to do." Farrier grinned. "It ain't like you are ever goin' to do this again!"

"Too bloody right, Bill! Never."

Farrier came to attention and saluted his Major. He then stuck out his only hand. "I wish you both all the happiness in the world, m'lord."

Dair returned the salute and then took his batman's hand in a firm grasp. "Thank you, Mr. Farrier."

"Dair! Dair? Oi! Fitzstuart!"

The shouts came from the first landing. It was Grasby and Mr. Cedric Pleasant.

"For God's sake, Fitzstuart! Get a move on or the bride will be there before us!"

This last exclamation came from the Duke, and it had Dair, with his batman following, down the stairs in an instant, to the applause of his wedding troop.

RORY HAD NEVER looked more delicately beautiful in her lavender silk petticoats, straw-blonde hair upswept and arranged, pinned and beribboned, and with a cascade of curls falling over one bare shoulder. She wore a black choker ribbon from which dangled a small gold pineapple, and her only other jewelry was the pale lavender sapphire betrothal ring. If there was a change in her wardrobe from the night Dair had seen her sitting on the stair of the Gatehouse Lodge, it was her shoes. From her grandfather's home in Chiswick, she sent for her pair of specially made silk shoes with pineapple motifs embroidered across the bridge and heels. They matched the choker, and her walking stick, and the little pineapple purse, crocheted by Edith for her twenty-first birthday, and which now dangled from her wrist.

When her grandfather brought her to stand beside Dair, she wondered if he was as anxious as she. But she could not bring herself to look at him. The importance of the occasion weighed heavily with her. And being married before their peers, with all eyes upon them, particularly her, made her feel faint. She kept her gaze straight and could barely feel her fingers about the ivory handle of her walking stick, she was gripping it so tightly. And while she heard the Duke's chaplain speaking, such was the ringing in her ears, she had no idea what he was saying. She doubted then if she would make it through the ceremony without mishap.

And then, within a few seconds, everything changed. She was no longer nervous or worried.

Dair felt for her hand and gave her fingers a little squeeze.

Rory finally found the courage to steal a nervous glance up at him.

He smiled down at her and winked.

She saw then that he was just as nervous, and yet he had made the effort to put her at ease. And while she continued to appear solemn, as the situation demanded of a bride, she was flooded with such happiness she could not stop smiling on the inside.

A little while later, she dared to glance up at him again. This time she noticed his bronzed silk frock coat with its beautifully embroidered collar, the froth of lace under his clean-shaven chin, and how his hair was dressed formally, and so unlike the Dair she knew. But it was at the ribbon tied in his hair that she stared, and for a good few seconds. Then she quickly glanced away, a hand to her mouth to stop a sob, but she could not stop her tears.

He was wearing the lavender satin ribbon he had taken from her as a spoil of war, the night he had collided with her at Romney's studio. She had quite forgotten about that ribbon, but he had not. It was such a heartfelt gesture she could hardly breathe.

Before she knew what was happening, she had a handkerchief pressed into her hand. But such was her emotional state, she was left bewildered by it. She had no idea what she was supposed to do with it. And then, as if by magic, her chin was lifted and her cheeks gently patted dry. Dair disposed of his handkerchief in a frock coat pocket. He then squared his shoulders and nodded to the chaplain to continue. All of this done with a minimum of fuss, and to the collective sighs of every female in attendance.

The bride and groom survived the rest of the ceremony without mishap. Neither faulted on the declarations. They exchanged vows in a clear voice. And the groom managed to keep hold of the wedding ring when Lord Grasby offered it to him. The slim gold band slipped on to Rory's finger with ease. It was only then that there was a deviation from the service. Dair could not help himself. With the ring secured, he lifted Rory's hand and kissed the gold band, another smile and a wink at her before releasing her fingers and turning back to the vicar. Not only was there another collective sigh from the females in attendance, but one of their number burst into tears and continued to sob throughout the blessing.

With the register signed by both parties, and witnessed, the newly married couple faced their family and relations with blushing smiles. They acknowledged the Duke and Duchess of Roxton with a bow and a curtsy, and then with the same to the Duchess of Roxton and Kinross, who blew them a kiss. And then they turned and bowed and curtsied to the Countess of Strathsay, who was sniffing back tears, her face half-buried in her lace-bordered handkerchief. Dair took a step forward, kissed his mother's cheek and then his sister's, too, before rejoining his bride to accept the smiles of congratulation from one and all as they made their way along the aisle towards the open doors and the crowd waiting patiently to see them.

Outside the family chapel, they would receive more congratulations from family, friends, the ducal household, and most of the village, who had walked up to catch a glimpse of the bride and groom in all their splendid glory.

But the couple had not taken many steps along the aisle towards the doors when the new Lady Fitzstuart stopped and smiled up at her husband. Those who were following the bride and groom wondered why. Dair did not wonder. He swiftly kissed his new wife's hand and then stepped forward to embrace his son. Jamie held on so tightly to his father, Dair knew the boy was overwrought and so he gave him a moment. He then kissed the top of his dark red curls, had a word in his ear, and when Jamie nodded, let him go. He then put out his hand to Mr. Banks, and the old gentleman, overcome to be so acknowledged, gripped Dair's hand tightly. All the while, Mrs. Banks cried her happiness into her damp handkerchief, and when Dair leaned over to kiss her cheek, and to say something in her ear no one but she could hear, she wailed all the more and fell into her husband's arms.

There were those sticklers for propriety amongst the congregation who thought this behavior extraordinary. They swiftly looked to see what the Duke of Roxton made of this social lapse—the heir to an earldom acknowledging his bastard son, and the old couple who were socially one rung below that of servant, and before his bride no less! But the Duke, like everyone involved in this emotional scene, did not care what others thought. He cared only that those in attendance were full of joy upon this auspicious of occasions. And happiest of all were the bride and groom.

Dair and Rory left the chapel to rousing cheers of congratulations and walked arm-in-arm into the sunshine of a bright and loving future, two souls now as one.

~ THE END ~

AUTHOR NOTE

Petrus Camper, circa 1780

WHILE RESEARCHING disability in the eighteenth century, in particular soldiers returned from battle with one or more limbs incapacitated or amputated, I found a remarkable little treatise entitled *On the Best Form of Shoe*, by an equally remarkable man Professor Petrus Camper (1722-1789) who was Professor of Medicine, Surgery, and Anatomy, at Amsterdam and Groningen.

What is self-evident today (but is still widely ignored by many consumers) was a revelation to most in the 18th Century. Camper concluded that shoes were made in ignorance of the anatomy and growth of the foot, and constructed to the absurdities and dictates of the fashion of the day. Camper used the term "victims of fashion" to describe persons wearing a particular shoe form, not for comfort, but because it was the fashionable thing to do. He voiced the hope that enlightened parents would avoid inflicting "torture" (his word not mine), on their children by allowing them to wear shoes that fit their foot for comfort, and praised enlightened parents who allowed their children to go barefoot in the house, and thus allowing the growing foot to form naturally.

Camper's book includes a chapter on club feet and through his scientific observations and findings concluded (wrongly but enlightened for the time) that such a deformity occurred in the developing fetus while in the womb, and that it was unlikely to be corrected by the use of the wooden and steel contraptions of correction available then; footwear, like those for the normal foot, should be made specific to the shape of the foot itself.

Camper's findings were so remarkable for the time that *On the Best Form of Shoe* was translated almost at once into several European languages and considered worthy of reprinting for the next 100 years.

Explore real places, objects, and history in *Falling IN* on Pinterest:
www.pinterest.com/lucindabrant/falling-series

Lucinda Brant Author

lucindabrant

22.6k followers   596 following

Falling Trilogy

Falling IN: Book 2

Miss Rory Talbot

Giovanna Baccelli (dancer)

Henry Clinton (British Officer)

Porcelain flowers

George Romney (painter)

In the Chelsea Physic Garden

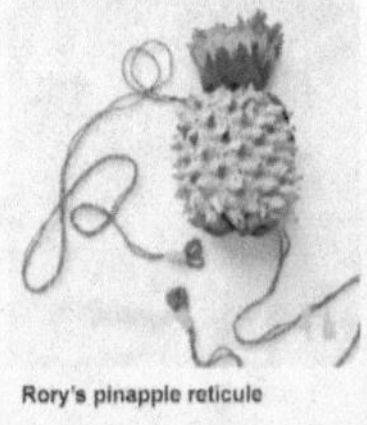

Rory's pinapple reticule

Indienne print dress

Flying chair (first elevator)

Original 1700's Club foot shoes

Nécessaire de Voyage (picnic set)

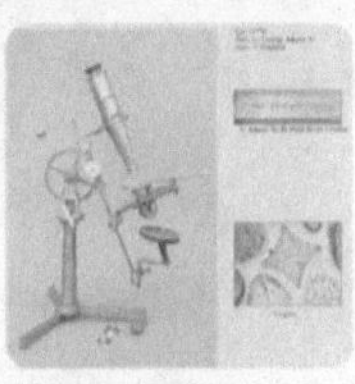

Microscope by George Adams

1700's Pineapple cultivation

Dair Devil cover reveal

My blog post on Dr Camper

FALLING
OUT
Lucinda Brant
NEW YORK TIMES & USA TODAY BESTSELLING AUTHOR